"An exciting, heartfelt paranormal world I adored spending time in. Queer disaster teens, magical mystery, scary spirits and a slow-burn enemies-to-lovers romance that will have you screaming 'just kiss you fools!' I loved every moment!"

ROSIE TALBOT, author of *Sixteen Souls*

"A winning combination of sweet, hilarious, and intense . . . Miles is not only funny but also relatable. His dynamic with the spiky recluse Gabriel is perfectly set up, and their rivals to lovers arc is beautifully done."

FRANCES WHITE, *Sunday Times* bestselling author of *Voyage of the Damned*

"Full to the brim with creepy atmosphere, vivid characters, and whip-smart prose . . . the perfect spooky fall-flavored fantasy!"

KESHE CHOW, *Sunday Times* bestselling author of *The Girl With No Reflection*

"A magical, genre-bending read . . . I can't wait for the sequel!"

LILLIE LAINOFF, author of *One for All*

"Propulsive, perilous, endearing, and full of heart—Raines has written your new favourite comfort read."

COURTNEY SMYTH, author of *The Undetectables*

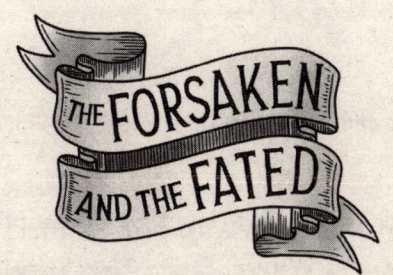

THE FORSAKEN
AND THE FATED

*Also by Camilla Raines
and available from Titan Books*

THE HOLLOW AND THE HAUNTED

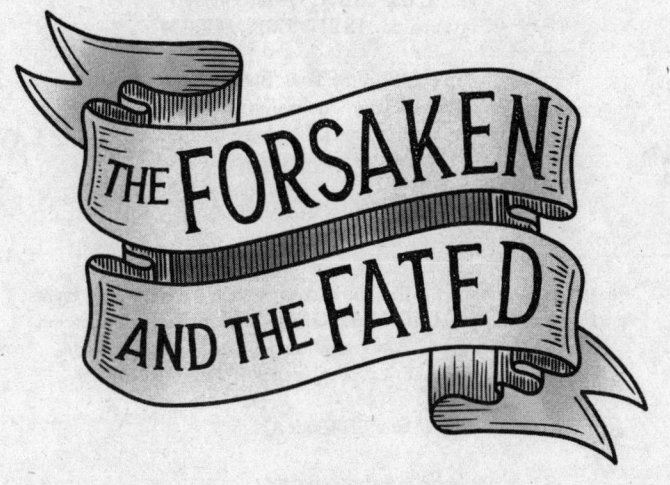

CAMILLA RAINES

TITAN BOOKS

The Forsaken and the Fated
Print edition ISBN: 9781803369990
E-book edition ISBN: 9781835410004

Published by Titan Books
A division of Titan Publishing Group Ltd
144 Southwark Street, London SE1 0UP
www.titanbooks.com

First edition: October 2025
10 9 8 7 6 5 4 3 2 1

A CIP catalogue record for this title is available from the British Library.

EU RP (for authorities only)
eucomply OÜ, Pärnu mnt. 139b-14, 11317 Tallinn, Estonia
hello@eucompliancepartner.com, +3375690241

Printed and bound by CPI Group (UK) Ltd, Croydon CR0 4YY.

*To anyone who has ever been brave
enough to make their own fate.*

1

Getting cursed out by a teenage ghost in a curly mullet and a sweater that looked like the eighties threw up on it was, unbelievably, not the worst thing to happen to Miles today.

That honor was reserved for the throbbing ghost bite on his arm, which had a solid fifty-fifty chance of giving him supernatural rabies.

"Will you just tell me if you've seen him?" Miles asked tiredly, holding up the charcoal drawing of Gabriel he'd done earlier. "That's all I want to know. He went missing Tuesday morning—"

"*I don't care what you want,*" the ghost cut him off, crossing his arms like a petulant child. The neon colors he was wearing were making Miles nauseous. "*You drag me here without warning and start bossing me around? What's your damage?*"

He'd been pissed since the moment he appeared, taking one look at Miles and Charlee before launching into a rant about never being summoned by anyone interesting or hot. He seemed most upset about the hot part, calling Charlee a freckled freak and yanking one of her curls.

"I mean..." Miles glanced at Charlee for help, but she

shrugged. "That's how this works. We summoned you. If you'd answer our questions—"

"*That's how this works*," the ghost mocked in a high-pitched voice. "*Bite me, asshole.*"

He gave them the finger and disappeared with a pop that reverberated in Miles's ears and through his teeth. A whirl of ghostly wind whipped around his room, sending his tacked-up pictures flapping like crow's wings against the wall and his homework flying off his desk. His dresser drawers crashed open with a *bang*, and several books fell off shelves.

Well. That was rude.

"Another dud," Charlee grumbled, blowing out the candles and wafting the smoke towards the open window with a pillow. "We're three-for-three. These ghost douches would rather die again than help you."

"I know, I just—" Miles raked a hand through his tangled hair. He hadn't gotten any sleep last night, the sickly-sweet smell of the vanilla candles was giving him a headache, and Gabriel had been missing for over three days now. He might be losing his mind. "I don't know what else we can do."

No news. No sign of him. No overnight reappearance. Not even a call or text to reassure Miles he was still alive.

Silence. Suffocating, unbearable, maddening silence.

Charlee hadn't picked up anything helpful from Gabriel's scarf, so they couldn't even get a hint of where to start. These séances were her idea, set up in his bedroom when he got home from school. They couldn't exactly go around putting up missing posters of Gabriel, knocking on doors and asking strangers if they'd seen him. But they could manage something close with the spirit world.

Most séances were used to contact a specific ghost, summoned by name or with one of their personal items. But they could also be used to seek information. If you were lucky and had a powerful enough medium, an ask could summon a ghost with an answer.

Miles had seen it done a few times, mostly to contact long-dead witnesses who could answer questions about what injustice had created a vengeful spirit or where a body was buried. Desperate attempts to piece together enough of a breadcrumb trail to get that name, that personal item, that gravesite.

According to his dad, these attempts were usually more trouble than they were worth. It was never going to be a sure bet. When you were aimlessly calling into the void for answers, everything had to be left open for the ghosts to come through, the path as clear and accessible as possible. They couldn't put down a salt ring, Four Thieves Vinegar, or even protective crystals. It was the strategy of the truly desperate, and it was dangerous.

Miles was starting to get that.

He was using the world's sloppiest séance setup—a circle of blue candles and clear quartz around Gabriel's scarf and the drawing of him—risking their safety and his mom's wrath for something he didn't even know would work. He'd been cussed out, told that Gabriel had been spotted burning in hell, and chomped on by a feral, potentially rabies-ridden ghost hard enough to draw blood before Charlee chucked a handful of salt at it from their *oh shit* bowl. And they'd only been at this for a little over an hour.

A scream had been inching its way up Miles's throat for half of it. His arm was throbbing nearly as hard as his head, and his knees were sore from kneeling on the bedroom floor.

He had no idea what they were doing.

"Let's take a break," he told Charlee, hearing the exhaustion in his own voice. He tried not to feel guilty. He wasn't giving up, just catching his breath. Recuperating. "I'll text Edmund, see if he's heard anything."

After leaving the Hawthorne estate on Tuesday, he'd received a message from an unknown number—Edmund, asking if he'd found anything in Gabriel's room. Miles had managed to get him to agree to wait longer before telling Felicity, but that clock was steadily ticking down.

The sympathetic look Charlee gave him made that inevitable scream inch up his throat a little farther. "Yeah, sure. We need to let it clear out in here anyway. The last thing we need is the smoke detector going off and your mom breaking down the door."

Thankfully, Miles and his mom had made a silent agreement to avoid each other. She hadn't been up in his room in days, not since she found out he'd been secretly seeing Gabriel.

"She'd probably let me burn," Miles muttered. Sarah still hadn't apologized or even tried to get his side of the story. She was barely talking to him beyond telling him it was his turn to do the dishes or that he needed to help his sisters with their homework.

Charlee stretched before falling back onto his bed, mattress springs groaning. She had her own mom drama to deal with now that Aunt Robin was up and about.

Miles grabbed Gabriel's scarf and clumsily got up from the floor, his legs stiff and one foot asleep, and joined her, crawling around her fan of red curls. Charlee shifted closer, pressing their arms together.

"I wish I knew he was okay," Miles whispered. He wrapped Gabriel's scarf around his hand tightly enough to ache, sinking his fingers into the plush knit.

Knowledge had been such a terrible burden these last weeks that Miles hadn't realized how awful *not* knowing would feel. Having someone vanish without a single clue, without any idea of where they were. Not knowing why they'd left. If you'd ever see them again.

He knew what Charlee thought: Gabriel had gotten spooked and run away. She didn't understand that he wouldn't do that. He hadn't fled when his death was looming over him. Why would he now that he thought he was safe? When they had the grimoire, when they'd kissed, and Miles had pledged to help him break the curse?

Charlee had suggested that Jocelyn had appeared to Gabriel with her warning too, and he'd panicked. But Miles knew he'd never leave Bram.

Something *made* him leave. Someone had taken him or forced him to go, to vanish without a trace and leave his phone behind. He was either being held against his will, or dead.

No. He couldn't be dead. Miles would feel it if he was.

And Jocelyn had told him the future was unchanged. Gabriel was still destined to die in that tomb, Miles watching him go.

But their whole quest hinged on the belief that that future could be changed. If they could do it, why couldn't someone else? It wasn't like they'd know if someone else already called dibs on murdering Gabriel.

Nothing felt guaranteed when he was gone.

Miles's focus drifted across the room to the mirror atop his dresser. After spending too much of the last few days staring into Gabriel's eyes in it, asking him where he was—knowing he wouldn't get an answer—he'd put himself on mirror restriction. Looking at Gabriel only made him feel like a failure and sparked an awful fear that he wasn't ever going to see him in person again.

It was still tempting. Miles had to fight the urge to look for a quick glimpse of pale skin and ebony hair.

He held out the scarf for Charlee. "Will you try one more time?"

"It's not going to change."

"I know, just—just one more time, okay? Please?"

She sighed but took it from him. A heartbeat passed, then two.

"I can barely feel him anymore," she apologized. "Your emotions are too strong. They've latched on. But what I can feel is the same as before. He's hurting and cold, a darkness pulling him in. There's a pain, here"—she gestured to either side of her collarbone—"and he's thinking of you. Scared for you, but thankful you're with him." Her hazel eyes opened, glassy before she blinked the fog away.

Miles had heard this already, decided it was from the last time he'd seen Gabriel wearing the gray scarf down in the tunnels of the old Hawthorne house, when the shadows had tried to consume him.

He must not have touched it before he'd left. Or his emotions from the tunnels were too strong, drowning out anything else.

Either way, it was useless.

Miles took it back, struggling to swallow around the lump in his throat. "Do you think we should tell Felicity? If he's in real trouble and we're wasting time—"

"What's Felicity going to do? We both know she won't be any help. We'll find him, okay? If not with these séances, then something else."

She pointedly didn't mention that they had nothing else.

"I don't think the séances are working," he admitted, fidgeting with his necklace—he'd had to get a new chain after his broke in the cemetery, and it didn't lie the same now.

"Yeah, this idea might be a bust."

"It's not a bust, we're just… not very good at it." His bitten arm throbbed.

Charlee snorted. "We suck."

It would help if one of them was a medium. They struggled to get the ghosts here in the first place, and once they were, couldn't hold them. The summoning was slippery in Miles's mouth, like trying to find his footing on an icy sidewalk. He'd never had a knack for it, which was one of the reasons he'd been so thorough and cautious with the ritual to summon Florence.

He didn't even know if the ghosts who'd appeared knew anything about Gabriel, or if they'd been random catches.

Charlee stared up at the ceiling, freckled hands folded over her lavender sweater. "We could peek through your parents' contacts, see if there are any mediums we can recruit."

Miles shook his head. Too much could go wrong. There were too many secrets he couldn't share, too big of a chance they'd go to Felicity—or worse—his parents.

It did make him think… There was one other person he knew who might be able to help, but it would be tricky.

"Wanna do something risky?" he asked Charlee.

"Riskier than this?" She pointed her toes at the shoddy séance spread across Miles's tan shag rug. "Why the hell not?"

2

When Emily knocked on the front door, Miles had been waiting there nervously for several minutes. "Hey. Thanks for getting over here so quickly."

"No problem. It was raining at practice, so I'd have taken any excuse to leave early." She scanned him curiously. Her backpack was slung over one shoulder, and she was wearing a puffy marshmallow jacket, her green soccer jersey visible around the collar. "I was surprised to hear from you, to be honest. And you were… concerningly vague."

"I know, sorry. I'll explain everything in a minute." Miles could hear footsteps in the kitchen coming their way. "If we make it past my mom."

On cue, Sarah stuck her head through the open kitchen doorway, brushing blonde hair out of her face. "Who are you—?" Her gaze found them and widened. "Oh! Emily, hi. I didn't know you were coming over."

Miles could've paraded a herd of elephants through the house and she would've been less surprised.

Emily gave her a sheepish smile and a wave. "Hi, sorry, I should've called first to make sure it was okay, but I was headed home from soccer practice and remembered Miles mentioned he had Mr. Wilson last year. I've got this huge test tomorrow that I'm totally freaking out about. I was hoping he might have leftover notes I could borrow."

She sold it perfectly, not even blinking beneath his mom's scrutiny. Clearly, Emily either had more experience lying than he did, or she was a natural.

He nodded. "Yeah, I think I've got my old math tests and stuff in my desk. If not, I can help you go over the study guide, see if I remember anything."

Sarah frowned, clearly conflicted.

"Oh. Sorry. I forgot." Miles gave Emily what he hoped was a believably apologetic look. "I'm not supposed to have people over right now."

She took his cue flawlessly. "Oh no, sorry, I knew I should've called first. Sorry, Mrs. Warren, I didn't mean to—"

"No, no, it's fine!" Sarah rushed to reassure her. "It's just that I was about to head to the store…" Miles didn't know if her hesitation was because she was taking his grounding seriously, or she didn't want to miss the opportunity to snoop. "But this is a special circumstance, your grades are important. Stay as long as you need."

Emily's face lit up, so bright Miles had to blink. "You're a lifesaver, thanks so much. I'll leave as soon as I'm done, I promise."

"Don't worry about it. And if you're going to stay through dinner, let me know and I'll set an extra plate." Miles could practically see the gears spinning in his mom's head, the matchmaking ideas forming with terrifying speed. Even her righteous anger at Miles couldn't outweigh her desire to set him up.

He gestured for Emily to head through the living room

to the stairs. As he passed his mom, she mouthed, *"Door open."*

It was so absurd, he didn't know if he wanted to laugh or cry.

Upstairs, he led Emily down the narrow hall, floorboards creaking underfoot. "That was perfect," he whispered, not bothering to hide his awe. "You killed it."

"It's the dimples. They make me look trustworthy, like a big innocent baby."

He laughed. She wasn't wrong.

Charlee was waiting for them in his room, her curls restrained in fresh twin braids and her knit quarter-zip done up to her chin. She looked like she meant business. On the floor, she'd spread a blanket over their séance setup, hiding it from view.

"Hey." She gave Emily a stiff nod. "Long time no see."

Emily grinned and crossed the room, pulling Charlee into a quick hug. "I missed you at the Bryant party the other week." She leaned back and studied her. "You look great. How've you been?"

"Fine." Charlee's cheeks were pink beneath her freckles. "Did you guys have any trouble getting past Aunt Sarah?"

"Not really. She's making a store run, but I doubt she'll be gone for long, so let's be quick."

Emily perched on the edge of Miles's bed. "So who's going to tell me what this is all about? It must be juicy if we're lying to your mom."

"Juicy is one way of putting it," Charlee muttered.

Miles sat in his desk chair, straightening a stack of papers. He didn't know where to start. "You remember Gabriel from the party?"

"Hard to forget him." She didn't say it with any real bite. "You two are friends, right?"

"We… yeah. I've been helping him with something, but he's gone missing."

Quickly, Miles explained what'd happened since his first visions of mirror-Gabriel. Running into Gabriel at the Hawthorne party, him showing up at school, the second vision and the ones that followed. He told her about Jocelyn, Florence, the grimoire, and the Hawthornes' unnatural gifts. How he and Gabriel had banished Florence and thought his death was averted—until Jocelyn's warning. And that now, Gabriel had vanished without a trace. It was harder than Miles expected to get through, a messy storm of emotions swelling behind his ribs.

"Wow." Emily blinked a few times when he'd finished. "I mean, *wow*. Okay, still processing, but I think I followed everything. You must be so freaked with Gabriel missing." She reached across the empty space between them and gave Miles's hand a comforting squeeze. Her worry was gratifying, but threatened to release the panic he'd been keeping on a carefully tight leash. "You really have no idea where he could be?"

He shook his head. "Not a clue. Which is why I asked you to come over. I'm hoping you can help find a spirit who might've seen him."

With a dramatic flourish, Charlee whipped the blanket off their séance setup. Emily's eyebrows shot from furrowed concern to surprise with lightning speed.

"I've never done this without my mom's help," she admitted, unzipping her jacket and shrugging out of it. Her jersey beneath was splattered with mud. "But I'll give it my best shot."

"That's all I'm asking."

They sat around the circle of candles and quartz. Miles placed the scarf and drawing back in the center while Charlee struck a match and lit the wicks. The sickening scent of vanilla made Miles's stomach roll. After this, he was tossing out Charlee's nasty dessert-scented candles and replacing them with some that were less repulsive.

"Hold hands," Emily told them, extending her own. Once they were all connected, she took a deep breath. The hairs on Miles's arms prickled and stood to attention as the air thickened around them, swelling like a storm on the horizon.

"Will any spirit who has recently seen Gabriel Hawthorne please come forth? If you have any information, we're willing to bargain—"

"I can help too."

Miles jumped out of his skin, knocking the candle by his knee. Hot blue wax splattered across the hardwood floor and the edge of his shaggy rug.

"Jesus!" Charlee glared at Amy, who was hovering in the doorway, Jenna peeking over her shoulder. "Learn to knock!"

"Why would I knock when the door's open?" Amy peered at Emily, then the circle. Charlee snatched up the drawing of Gabriel, hiding it from view. "You're doing a séance, right? I can help if you want."

They were so screwed. Jenna could keep her mouth shut, but once Amy knew, it was only a matter of time before she blabbed to their mom.

Emily beamed. "Oh my God, you two have grown like a foot since the last time I saw you."

Amy resented her most recent growth spurt, claiming

she'd die before becoming a giant like Miles and their dad, so she scowled like she'd been insulted.

"Don't be nice to them," Charlee told Emily. "They're being snoopy brats."

If Miles kicked them out, Amy would get their mom the second she was back. If he brought them in, he'd be testing his already precarious luck. It was a bad idea on so many levels—but at least if Amy was going to use it to blackmail him for the rest of his life, he could gain something from her first. "Both of you, come here."

They scurried over, sitting between him and Charlee. Jenna crossed her legs and picked at the frayed cuffs of her periwinkle hoodie. Amy plopped down like she belonged.

"We're not saying anything until you swear you won't tell Mom or Dad about this." Miles made sure Amy was paying attention before continuing. "I'm serious, this is life or death. Promise me you'll keep your mouths shut."

Amy and Jenna simultaneously held out their pinkies. "Promise."

Miles shook them, satisfied it was the best guarantee he was going to get. Charlee put Gabriel's picture back in the circle.

"It's Gerald!" Jenna blurted, the tips of her ears going scarlet.

"Yeah. Except... his name isn't Gerald."

"Shocker," Charlee muttered.

Miles ignored her. "Gerald's real name is Gabriel. He's a friend of mine and he's gone missing. That's why we're doing this séance—we're trying to see if any spirits in the area might've seen what happened to him or know where he's gone."

"Why can't we tell Mom or Dad? Maybe they can help."

"*No.*" Miles didn't know what his sisters had been told about the Hawthornes. "They don't like Gabriel's family. It's a long story, but he's my friend and we need to find him."

He expected more arguing, more pushback, but they both nodded.

"We can help, right?" Amy turned to Emily. "The more mediums you have in a séance, the more power and control?"

"That's right."

Amy's chest puffed so much with pride, it was a miracle she didn't pop like an over-inflated balloon.

"What about me?" Jenna stared down at her knees. "Should I leave?"

"No way, we need you too," Emily replied without hesitation. "Your energy will be a big help."

That earned her a shy smile.

"Everyone, hold hands," she instructed again, "and focus on sending your energy to me. If we all reach out at the same time, it will get muddled and twisted up. It's like… throwing a net to catch a fish. If we all throw one, they'll just get tangled together into a knot. But if you give me yours and I make them into one big net, we have a better chance."

They all went silent. Miles envisioned his energy swirling around the circle, finding Emily like a beacon.

She cleared her throat. "We call to the spirit world, seeking information. Someone lost to us. If you've seen Gabriel Hawthorne"—she nodded to the drawing—"please come forth and speak to us."

To Miles's right, Jenna's hand tightened around his. The

candle flames flickered, then flared. Outside his bedroom window, the sun went behind a cloud.

The ghost of a man appeared, hovering above Gabriel's picture. He looked around twenty, pulled straight out of a bad early 2000s rom-com with frosted tips gelled into stiff spikes, an oversized green polo, and a puka shell necklace. His face was friendly and open, a stranger you'd be comfortable asking for directions on the side of the road.

Amy sucked in a triumphant breath, then gave a little squeal of excitement.

"*Hey.*" The ghost looked down at Gabriel's picture, cocking his head. "*I've totally seen this guy.*"

"Where?" Miles blurted, earning him a warning squeeze from Emily.

"What's your name?" she asked the ghost kindly.

"*Blake.*" He wasn't very solid, but he'd been dead for a short enough time that he still sounded coherent. Ghosts who didn't start out as malicious spirits could last decades before the madness started to set in.

"It's nice to meet you, Blake. Can you tell us where you saw our friend? Was it recently?"

That was a loaded question. Most ghosts didn't understand time anymore; it didn't move in the same way for them as the living.

Blake didn't hesitate. "*He was on my bus a few days ago.*"

"Your *bus*?" Miles had seen the look Gabriel gave the buses in the school parking lot—he'd chew off his own arm before riding one. Or any kind of public transportation for that matter. "Are you sure it was him?"

Blake studied the drawing again and nodded enthusiastically. "*One thousand percent sure.*"

"How were you on a bus?" Jenna asked tentatively. "I didn't think ghosts could move around much."

His expression fell. "*I died on it. A crazy guy with a knife stabbed me when I was on the way to the movies. My girlfriend and I were going to see* House of Wax... *we wanted to see Paris Hilton get ganked, you know?*" He peered around hopefully. "*How was it? Was her death totally sick?*"

"It, uhhh…" Miles had never seen it. Neither had anyone else, based on the blank looks. "Yeah, totally sick. Really… gory."

"*Nice.*" Blake grinned. "*Anyway, yeah, the bus. I've tried to get off a million times, but I can't get past the stairs.*"

Everyone around the circle wore identical grimaces. It was hard to imagine a worse fate than that. It was a miracle Blake hadn't gone full mad, foaming-at-the-mouth raging ghost after the first month.

It made Miles wonder if everyone who died in an ambulance and came back as a ghost was doomed to haunt it. That would get seriously crowded.

"I'm sorry," Emily finally said. "That sounds terrible."

"Seriously." Charlee winced. "A public bus has to be the worst afterlife ever. Ouch."

Miles threw her a warning look—the last thing they needed was to piss him off. But Blake didn't look offended.

"*You're telling me. I guess it's going to be ugly purple seats and stinky bus smell forever. I must've really pissed God off.*"

"Sorry." If he helped them find Gabriel, Miles would personally find a way to make Blake's soul move on. "If Gabriel was on your bus, he must've gotten off. Did you see where?"

"*Not exactly. Things outside the bus, they don't quite… they're hard to focus on. Seattle for sure, but that's as specific as I can get. But the stop he got off at, I always recognize it because it hurts when we stop there.*

"It *hurts?*" Miles repeated. What did that mean?

Blake shrugged. *"I dunno, man, it's like a pressure pushing against me. If I don't move to the far side of the bus and wait it out, I'll blip."*

Emily leaned in. "Sounds like anti-ghost mojo," she murmured.

It sure did. If the bus was stopping in front of a building with protective wards or items on the property, it would have that effect on spirits. They wouldn't even be able to get close, depending on the level of protection and how fresh they were.

Not much of a lead, but Miles would take it. It couldn't be a coincidence that Gabriel had gotten off there.

"Was someone with him?"

"I don't think so. He wasn't sitting with anyone."

Miles could feel Charlee's sideways look. There were plenty of ways to make a person go somewhere without physically forcing them. Blackmail. Threats. A trick. It didn't mean anything that he'd been alone. "Thanks, Blake. I appreciate the info."

"No problem. It was worth it just to get off the bus for a few minutes. You'd think being dead would save me from motion sickness, but apparently not."

This had to be the unluckiest ghost Miles had ever encountered.

"Any chance I could hang for another minute?" Blake asked. *"Before you send me back? Let me take in the change of scenery?"*

"You're spending your afterlife trapped on a bus," Charlee

pointed out. "Changing scenery is literally all you have."

Miles pinched her. "Sure, you can stay for a minute if you'd like."

"*Cool.*" Blake's face lit up with enthusiasm. "*Tell me more about Paris's death. How gory was it? Are we talking buckets of blood? Decapitation?*"

This was about to be the longest minute of Miles's life.

3

Miles woke up to a message written in blood on his bedroom wall.

"It's too early for this shit," Charlee grumbled, squinting up at the words. She hadn't been thrilled when he sprinted to her room and yanked her out of bed. "What kind of freak does this before nine o'clock on a Saturday?"

"This isn't funny," Miles snapped. He couldn't look at the crimson smears anymore, but it didn't matter. They were burned into his brain.

I HAVE GABRIEL
COME AND GET HIM

Beneath that was an address for somewhere in Seattle. Neither of them had looked it up yet.

"You're right, it's messed up. Who would do something this unhinged?"

"I don't know."

"How did they get in here and do that without waking you up? And how do they know who you are? Or where you live?"

"I don't know!" He was already on the verge of a full

meltdown imagining some creep sneaking in here with a tub of Gabriel's blood.

She held up her hands. "Excuse me for trying to get the facts straight."

"That's blood, Charlee. *Blood*." Miles could hear the panic in his own voice. "What if it's Gabriel's? What if they've hurt him? Oh God, this is some crazy serial killer thing, isn't it? *Come and get him*? They're clearly baiting us; it's going to be a murder trap where he's strung up in a warehouse and—"

Charlee flung a hand over his mouth. "Calm down. You're freaking yourself out. We don't know anything yet." She steered him to his bed, shoving him down. "We need to figure out who this is and what they want."

Miles pushed her hand away. "I told you he was taken. You thought I was being stupid, but I knew it. He probably got a message like this telling him to take that bus."

"Yeah, yeah, you were right, congratulations." Charlee stared at the message, twisting one of her curls around her finger. "Why tell us where he is? It can't be a hostage thing, we don't have any money. Unless you have something they want."

Unbidden, Miles's attention slid to his desk, where Florence's grimoire was locked away. But that didn't make any sense. No one knew he had it. And if they wanted him to bring it to trade for Gabriel, wouldn't they have mentioned it in the message? It seemed like a crucial piece of information to forget.

"What if it's someone in Gabriel's family?" he suggested, trying to calm down enough to think. "They found out Gabriel and I are snooping around, trying to break the curse, and they're going to threaten him until we agree to stop."

"Could be." Charlee snatched his phone from his bedside table, tossing it to him. "Let's see where they want us to go."

Miles typed the address in three times to make sure it was right.

"I don't get it." He showed her the search results.

Her eyebrows scrunched together as she read. "Sage and Starlight? What is this, a tacky occult shop? It doesn't look legit."

Occasionally you came across the real deal, carrying more than herbs and crystals. Miles's mom liked to visit one a few cities over when she ran out of the rarer ingredients for her protection kits.

"It could be like, a neutral place to meet?" Miles had seen that in movies before. "Somewhere public." Fear gripped him by the throat. He didn't know what to think of this, but he knew one thing—they couldn't just leave Gabriel to fend for himself. "Charlee... we have to go."

"I know. But first, we need to get this cleaned up. If your mom or sisters see it"—she gestured to the bloody mess smeared across his wall and dripping down his art—"we're done for."

Thank God Charlee was here. "And then what? We'll head over to this place?"

"We don't have any other choice."

Miles wasn't too proud to acknowledge the jolt of terror that went through him. "We don't know what we're walking into. I've never even been in a real fight, or—"

Charlee silenced him with a look. "You're freaking yourself out again. No one's going to fight us, this is just a cheap intimidation tactic. Whoever did this is trying to rattle you, okay? Don't let them."

She was right. All that mattered was getting Gabriel back safely.

When they slipped out of the house—his mom and Aunt Robin had gone on a supply run, and his dad was snoozing away upstairs—Emily was waiting for them on the sidewalk with a purple bike.

"I was just about to text you." She sounded slightly out of breath. "Sorry for the at-home ambush, but this couldn't wait. I think I figured out where Gabriel got off the bus."

"Oh. That's—" Miles fumbled, trying to gather his thoughts. "I mean, that's great, but it doesn't really matter anymore."

Emily's face lit up, and he realized how that sounded. "He's not back," Charlee explained curtly, zipping her coat up. It had rained all night, turning the whole world soggier and grayer than usual. "But there was a message in blood on Miles's wall telling us where to find him."

The color drained from Emily's cheeks. "Holy moly. Was it… real blood?"

"I mean, we didn't test it or anything, but yeah, I'm pretty sure. It was all drippy and gross."

A car flew by, sending up a spray of water that narrowly missed splashing Miles's jeans. "It's a trap, right?" Emily said.

"Probably, yeah."

Charlee crossed her arms with a huff. "It's not a trap. Some jerk is just messing with us."

Emily didn't look convinced, but she leaned her bike against their fence and adjusted her backpack. "Are we going there now, then? What's the plan?"

Miles could have hugged her. Squeezed the air right out of her. "You want to come along?"

"Of course I'm coming." She hesitated, biting her lip. "It's not an empty parking lot behind an abandoned warehouse, is it? Where no one will be able to hear us scream?"

Jiggling her keys, Charlee led them over to her car and unlocked the doors so they could climb in. "You're both so dramatic. Miles and I looked it up, it's an occult shop in Seattle."

Emily froze as she was sliding across the backseat. "What occult shop?"

Pulling up the address, Miles passed his phone to her. "It's called Sage and Starlight. I've never heard of it before."

Emily swore. "That's what I came here to tell you. After I went home yesterday, I started thinking over where Gabriel got off the bus. Somewhere with a protective spell didn't really narrow it down since there are like, loads of psychic families in Seattle, right?"

Miles had hit the same dead end. "Right."

"But then I remembered what Blake said about the bus: it had ugly purple seats." She wiggled out her own phone and showed them the website for Whirlwind Transit, leaning over the center console. Miles recognized their buses—he'd seen a few wheezing their way downtown, electric blue with purple-and-gold swooshy wind art on the sides. "They're the only buses around here that have purple seats. And I was like, hey, these buses have routes they have to follow. So, I printed the ones that go through Seattle"—she pulled a paper from her jacket pocket, unfolding it to reveal a map with highlighted lines and bright red dots—"and cross-referenced them with all the addresses I had of psychic families in the city."

Woah. Miles traced the highlighted lines weaving around Seattle, tilting the paper so Charlee could see it too. "Where did you get the addresses?" she questioned.

"My mom. She's got them all on a spreadsheet on her computer. She says they're for holiday cards and parties, but I think she's keeping tabs on my prospective marriage options."

Ew.

"I added all the addresses to the map, and look… none of them land on any of the Whirlwind routes. None of them match." She jabbed the red dots. Most were scattered on the outskirts of Seattle, in the neighborhoods, while the buses went downtown.

But there was one stop that had been circled furiously.

"When none of the addresses matched, I figured, okay, he didn't get off at one of the families' houses, but he did get off somewhere with protective spells set up. I started looking around for anything else that could be in the area, on one of the bus lines. And I found a certain occult shop with a reputation for all sorts of bad stuff." She lowered her voice, despite them being alone in the car. "The family who runs it, they're big-time bad news. They sell all kinds of haunted and cursed stuff to normal people and let gifted families clean up the mess. My dad's been trying to get them shut down for years, because the owner doesn't care who gets hurt. She's like… the mistress of evil."

Felicity Hawthorne had someone coming for her crown.

Charlee's hazel eyes narrowed. "So, it's not just a meeting place?"

"No way. They're responsible for taking Gabriel for sure. I wouldn't put anything past this woman."

Miles's stomach sank. What would someone like that want with Gabriel? This was the worst-case scenario.

"I can't believe you did all this." He studied the map again. It must've taken Emily all night. "Thank you."

"Well, yeah… we need to find him, right? Especially now we know he's in trouble."

She made it sound so simple.

"It's amazing. You're like, a super sleuth."

She glowed pink, glancing away to look out the window where the mailman was parking across the street. "It really wasn't that hard."

But she'd bothered in the first place. For Miles, and a guy who'd been a jerk to her the first time they'd met.

It wasn't her fault they were apparently planning to enter a lair of nightmares, run by the mistress of evil herself, but good news would've been nice. When Miles had wished earlier for a better idea of what they were walking into, he should've specified something reassuring, for once.

Emily put her hand on his shoulder, giving it a gentle squeeze. "We're going to get him back, okay?"

"Damn straight," Charlee muttered, starting her car with a rumble.

Maybe it made him a naive fool, but Miles believed them.

4

Sage and Starlight wasn't hard to find. The streets were predictably clogged, so the closest parking space Charlee could wedge her car into was over a block away.

"I hate this city," she complained, slamming her door shut and giving the cars around them a filthy look. It'd taken her four tries to parallel park before she'd gotten close enough to the curb.

Miles had a bit of a love-hate relationship with Seattle. Driving here sucked—the traffic was awful, one-way streets appeared without warning like jump scares, and the drivers were a special kind of rude—but the city captivated him. The sensation of being surrounded by massive skyscrapers, of bustle and noise sweeping around him should've spiked his anxiety, but instead, it made him feel comfortingly invisible.

"I love it," Emily declared as they hurried across the street. Cars honked at them, even though the crosswalk was green. "It's at least ten times the size of Thistle."

"Bigger doesn't mean better," Charlee countered sourly. "It means more people, more noise, more garbage…"

Miles let their back-and-forth fade as they made their

way down the block, focusing on steady, grounding breaths. Apprehension twisted low in his abdomen at what might be waiting for them. Feats of daring and white-knight moments usually required more bravery than he had on hand; it was taking everything in him to put one foot in front of the other. It helped that a big part of him was pissed off that some random lady he'd never met had kidnapped his kinda-maybe boyfriend and destroyed his life for the last few days.

Charlee touched his elbow. "Stop scaring yourself. Gabriel's going to be fine."

"How can you know for sure?"

"Because I'm a rational adult." She sidestepped a pile of mysterious city-goo on the sidewalk. "We get in, find Gabriel, and get out. Easy as that."

If Miles had learned one hard lesson recently, it was that things were never that easy.

Sage and Starlight sat sandwiched between a little Vietnamese restaurant and a yoga studio, the sign bright purple and gold against black. Colorfully patterned curtains were tied back from the front windows to show off displays of propped-up books—generic titles about witchcraft, astrology, and self-care—surrounded by candles, crystals, and little brass figurines. Beyond them, Miles could make out shelves of jarred herbs and a collection of various altar bowls.

He carefully avoided his own reflection in the glass, not wanting to see Gabriel. The cherry on top of getting him back would be that Miles could stop feeling like a vampire, dodging every reflective surface he passed.

"Huh." Charlee took in the shop. "It doesn't look like an evil lair."

It looked like the kind of place where the girls from school who never stopped talking about horoscopes would hang out.

Emily nodded solemnly. "I know, it's diabolical. Think how many unsuspecting people they lure in."

They lingered for a minute—the message hadn't included any instructions for once they got here. No one was waiting for them. There were no clear signs of what to do next.

"Looks like we're going in." Miles's hands were shaking, so he fisted them at his sides. "We stick to the plan. Find Gabriel if we can, but first sign of trouble, we get out, okay?"

He'd made Charlee promise: no fighting unless they had no choice. If they walked in ready for one, he had an awful suspicion they'd manifest it. Charlee's and Emily's safety had to be the priority. This shop was dealing in dark magic and artifacts, which meant a lot of potential risks. He wouldn't be able to live with himself if either of them got hurt.

Miles opened the door, a cheerful bell jingling overhead. The second he crossed the threshold, multiple dark auras reached out, poking him, nipping at his mind. Beside him, Emily and Charlee shuddered.

"Welcome!" a friendly voice called from the front counter. The person running the register looked a year or two older than Charlee, with an oval face, warm olive-brown skin, and long, straight hair the color of espresso. Their black jean jacket was covered in pins and patches, embroidered flowers coming out of the breast pockets. They grinned brightly at the two women checking out as they scanned items.

They were really committing to this facade of friendliness. Miles might've bought it, if he couldn't feel all the foul auras polluting the air.

Emily and Charlee broke off in different directions, searching the shop. It wasn't very big, so it only took a minute to reconvene back by the tarot card display. Miles had pictured this going differently: Gabriel beaten and tied to a chair with a circle of armed goons around him; another set of instructions written in blood; that they'd be jumped the moment they walked in.

Compared to some of the places Miles had been recently, this was one of the least sinister. The incense smoking on the front counter made it smell homey and floral. Everything was neatly organized, if a little cluttered. In one corner, there was even a squashy armchair with a mosaic lantern hanging overhead, a small sign tacked on the wall that read: "Feel free to sit and read if you're unsure about a book!"

Plastic rustled as the cashier handed the two women their bags, chatting about spell jars and whether fresh or dried herbs were better. A completely normal, non-nefarious conversation. Weird.

"I don't see any sign of Gabriel. Maybe you're wrong," Miles whispered to Emily. "Maybe this is just a meeting spot."

"No way. Even if it was, where's the person we're supposed to be meeting?"

She was right—it wasn't adding up.

"Maybe they didn't expect us here already." Emily picked up a box of cat-themed tarot cards and studied the art.

There hadn't been a time in the message. What if they'd expected Miles to head here later? Or as soon as he'd woken up?

Oh God, what if they'd been waiting here and Miles hadn't shown? And Gabriel thought he'd abandoned him?

"If we have the element of surprise, we should take it," Charlee murmured, scanning the store.

"And do what? It's not like we can just walk up and ask if they're holding Gabriel hostage in the back."

Charlee flipped her red curls over her shoulder. "Watch me."

"Wait—"

She marched to the counter, footsteps muffled by the worn floral rug, leaving Miles to chase after her. The bell tinkled again as the two women left.

"Hey." The cashier gave Charlee a genuine smile, their silver septum piercing gleaming in the light. This close, Miles could read the name tag pinned on their jacket: NADIA. "You ready to check out?" Their attention shifted down to Charlee's empty hands. "Or did you have a question?"

"A question." Charlee pulled a can of pepper spray out of her purse, pointing it directly at the cashier's face. "Where's our friend?"

The cashier—Nadia—froze, their hands jumping up.

Emily's jaw dropped.

"Jesus!" If Miles weren't so shocked, he might've lingered on the fact that Charlee had referred to Gabriel as a friend. "What're you doing? We agreed, no fighting."

"I'm not fighting. I'm asking a question." Charlee shifted her finger to the trigger. Miles could only stand there. "Gabriel Hawthorne. Dark hair, stupid scowl, ugly sweater vests. Where is he?"

Their lips parted. "*Gabriel?* He's—yeah, he's in the back." They pointed at a plain wooden door behind the counter.

No way was it that simple.

Nadia turned to Miles. "You must be Miles, right? Gabriel's fine, go see for yourself."

How did they know his name? Were they the one who'd left the message? They didn't look like a potential serial killer, but then again, how could you really tell?

He wasn't stupid enough to go into a backroom by himself. "If he's fine, call him out."

Nadia didn't hesitate. "Gabriel! Can you come here for a sec? Right now?"

Behind the door, something thumped, then it creaked open. "What is it? I told you, I'm—"

Gabriel spotted Miles and stopped dead. His gaze flitted to Emily, to Charlee and her threatening pepper spray, then back. He tried to hide it, but Miles caught a flicker of surprise.

He looked fine. Tired, twin bruised circles under his eyes, his clothes wrinkled like he'd recently woken up from a nap and his white button-up crookedly rolled up to his elbows, but *fine*. Not tied up, not knocked out, not in any distress.

"We have a little situation," Nadia told Gabriel pointedly.

Gabriel ignored them, focus locked on Miles. "What are you doing here?"

"I…" Miles swallowed, his dry throat clicking. Ugly realization was starting to sink in and *ouch*, it hurt. "You've been missing for days. There was a message written in blood on my bedroom wall telling me to come here and get you. We thought someone had taken you, that they were threatening you to lure us here."

He wasn't sure why he felt defensive, like he needed to explain himself.

Gabriel shifted his glare to Nadia. "What did you do?"

They winced. "That's... my bad. I might've used the message mirror. That thing is so small, and do you know how much space an address takes up? I had limited word count, but I didn't realize they'd take my... conciseness as a threat."

"*I have Gabriel, come and get him*," Charlee quoted coldly, but she lowered her pepper spray. "Written in blood. How exactly were we supposed to interpret that?"

"In retrospect, I acknowledge it does sound a little ominous."

She snorted. "Well, as long as you acknowledge you messed up, I guess all is forgiven. It's not like we've been panicking, thinking Gabriel was being tortured while we were walking into a trap."

"You said it wasn't a trap," Emily piped up.

Charlee's eyes blazed with green fire. "Of course I did, Miles was two seconds away from a panic attack."

Awesome. Now everyone knew he was a big baby who had to be lied to.

Nadia grimaced. "I really wasn't trying to freak anyone out. I was just desperate and didn't think it through." They twisted their rings. "Sorry, Gabriel, but I've been telling you to leave, you know you're wasting your time—"

"I'll decide what's a waste of my time," Gabriel snapped, his hands fisted at his sides. "You had no right to invite them here."

"This is my shop. I can do whatever I want," Nadia fired back, nostrils flaring. "And you've overstayed your welcome. Excuse me for wanting to get you out of here. You've been moping around all week, bringing the vibe down, and I can only take so much."

Miles couldn't follow their argument. His brain was still processing the fact that Gabriel was here, totally fine, and apparently put out that they'd come to rescue him.

He hadn't wanted Gabriel to be in trouble, but he'd been so certain. So worried. He'd put Charlee and Emily at risk, been ready to do something seriously stupid to save him.

To save someone who hadn't needed saving.

"Then you should've messaged someone else," Gabriel bit out. "Not him."

Him. The way he spat it hit Miles like a slap in the face.

Charlee made an irritated noise. Miles put a hand on her arm, more to steady himself than stop her.

"Who, then?" Nadia challenged. "Your family? I'm not suicidal."

"Uhm, sorry to interrupt." Emily raised her hand like she was in class. "But can you explain what's going on? Because I'm lost."

"Yeah, I'd like that too." Miles could hear the accusation in his voice. Charlee's glare narrowed in on Gabriel with laser-like precision. "Because we've spent the last four days trying to find you. We thought this was a trap, and we came to get you anyway."

His confusion was fading away. Riding on its heels was a slow curl of outrage.

Gabriel strode forward to grab Miles's jacket sleeve. "We need to talk."

Miles didn't know what else to do, so he let Gabriel pull him into the backroom. Behind him, Emily sheepishly blurted to Nadia, "So sorry about the whole pepper spray thing. If it makes you feel better, Charlee never would've actually done it."

41

"Don't bet on it," Charlee countered.

The backroom was larger than Miles expected, but crammed full, cardboard boxes and wooden crates stacked floor to ceiling. In the limited space, there was a worn brown couch beside a small table covered in books, papers, and a lonely red mug, a teabag string hanging limply over the rim. A folded blanket sat on the couch, Gabriel's wool coat slung over an armrest.

The dark auras were stronger back here, overlapping and battering against Miles's mental walls. It made his brain rattle like a cowbell was ringing in each ear.

Gabriel closed the door behind them and shoved his hands in his pockets. He didn't say anything. The silence was unbearable, but Miles let it stretch. Let it ache in the air between them, thicken until it was suffocating.

Gabriel's shoulders curled, but he still didn't speak.

Miles caved. "Fine, I'll start. What the hell? Seriously, what the actual hell?" Anger rose in him, heat spiking in his chest like he'd taken a big gulp of boiling tea. "You're such a jerk, you know that? You have no idea how much I've been freaking out, trying to convince myself you weren't dead. And Edmund, Bram… do you know what you did to them? We thought you'd been kidnapped, or that you'd run off and abandoned us." Miles gestured around the dimly lit room. "What are you even doing here? Did you get a sudden urge to go shopping for cursed items? Because we didn't already have enough on our plate."

He hoped Gabriel was listening in on his thoughts and could hear exactly how pissed he was. How close he was to walking straight out of here without him.

Gabriel's lips pressed into a hard, unwavering line. He

was considering lying, pushing him away, Miles could tell. The edges of that cold, cruel mask were sliding up and he knew something awful was perched on the tip of Gabriel's tongue.

"*Don't*. Don't you dare lie to me right now. The least you owe me after the last four days is the truth, and you know it. If you're an asshole right now, I swear, we're done. For good."

It wasn't a threat. Just the truth, scraped raw off his heart, and it hurt.

Even knowing he'd sense nothing but a dark cloud, Miles still reached out to try and pick up Gabriel's emotions. He needed something, a shred of remorse or regret. All he got was that cold, empty void.

Conflict swirled in Gabriel's gaze, a storm building on the horizon. Then he pressed his palms to his face. When they fell away, his expression was tight with resignation and fear. It scared Miles badly enough that his outrage fizzled into nothing, a hot spark stomped out.

"What?" he whispered, apprehension slithering down his spine. "What happened?"

Gabriel came to a decision. "Okay," he started, sinking onto the brown couch. "The truth, then." He knit his slender fingers together, knuckle bones straining to press free of his pale flesh. "I saw your death."

Miles heard the words fine, but it took a second for them to make sense. Of all the things he'd been expecting Gabriel to say, this hadn't been one of them.

"I..." He shook his head, trying to clear away the white noise droning in his ears. "What are you talking about?"

"I saw it in a dream the night we banished Florence."

"You—I died? You actually saw me…?"

"Yes."

The world tilted. *I saw your death.* Such a short sentence. Only four words. They shouldn't have the power they did.

Miles didn't realize he was sliding to the floor until Gabriel was there to catch him and guide him down.

"I'm fine," Miles reassured him. And he was. It wasn't panic rushing over him, not even the tell-tale dizziness that he was going to faint. He was just… processing. And his knees had decided they didn't want to stick around.

He'd known at every step of this quest that he could die. And he almost had. The car accident, the tunnels, the graveyard—he'd been dodging death since the moment he decided to help Gabriel.

This felt different. It scared him more, an icy clamp around his ribs, squeezing so tight he thought his cowardly bones would splinter beneath the pressure.

Gabriel was still on the floor with him, holding his arm tightly enough that it throbbed.

"Maybe it's not—" Miles tried weakly.

"It is."

He didn't argue. Gabriel would never say it if he wasn't sure.

"How do I… how does it happen?"

Gabriel's words were barely a murmur in Miles's ear— as if he was afraid to say it out loud, to make it real. "It's the same place from your visions. The tomb with Jocelyn. I don't know why, but it's you now. I saw you there"—his breath hitched—"on the floor."

A painful laugh bubbled up. What a hideously ironic twist of fate.

"Was it... the same as when it was you?" Miles touched his head.

"No." Gabriel's grip tightened, the bones of Miles's wrist grinding together. "I saw... blood on the front of your shirt and the ground beneath you. I don't know if you were shot, or stabbed, or..." He sucked in a sharp inhale. "I don't know."

A bloody death. Apparently, that was all that was waiting for anyone who dared to go up against the Hawthornes. Miles shouldn't have thought he'd be an exception.

"Okay." His voice only trembled slightly. "So, I—I mean, it's me now. Okay, I—" Something plinked onto his sleeve. He blinked down at the droplet, confused and uncomprehending.

"Don't," Gabriel pleaded, his voice aching. The last time they'd been this close, he was kissing Miles breathless in the graveyard. How could that feel so long ago? "Please, Miles, don't cry."

"I—" He lifted a hand to his face and sure enough, it was wet. He didn't know why he was crying. "I'm sorry, I don't know where they're coming from." He wiped his eyes hastily, mortified.

"I'm sorry," he repeated. Gabriel hadn't cried when Miles told him about his death premonition. "Really, it's not—it's just been a stressful few days. I think it's all catching up with me." He took a deep, quaking breath, letting his lungs swell to the point of bursting.

Gabriel's jaw was steel, tight enough to crack teeth. "This is why I didn't want to tell you. I didn't want you to know how this felt."

"I'm not a child, I can handle it." Miles was aware of

how ridiculous that sounded considering he was currently sobbing on a dusty backroom floor. There was nothing to do but accept it. If wishing things were different worked, Gabriel would've been saved weeks ago.

Wait.

"Your vision doesn't make any sense."

"I don't understand what changed either, but denial won't—"

"No, I mean, it *can't* make sense." Miles's head was stuffy, the dust in the room making his nose itch. "Jocelyn came to me the day you left with another warning—the future remains unchanged. Florence deserved to go, but she wasn't the one who was going to kill you. You're still going to die."

Gabriel frowned. "But how? My premonitions are never wrong. I assumed banishing Florence somehow saved me, but damned you. It's the only thing that made sense."

"Could we both die?" Miles dismissed the idea as soon as it left his mouth. "No, wait, that wouldn't make sense. In my vision, I see you die, and in yours, you see me. They can't both be true. One of us would die first and make the other vision impossible."

Focusing on this latest puzzle helped rein in his fear, quiet his mind.

"When Jocelyn came to me in my dream, she mentioned other paths. What you saw could be a possible future. The path we're on now, you die. We step off it onto another path, I die." That wasn't exactly reassuring when they had no idea what the path looked like, let alone how to know if they were already on it. But it proved what Miles had been fighting for—one could exist where they both lived.

And if it didn't… Miles would have to make it.

"Why do you sound excited?"

That was a strong word. "I'm not, I just—this feels like our first good sign from the universe, you know?"

Gabriel stared at him. "You think a premonition of your death is a good sign?"

"I mean, no, but it shows we have options. The future *can* change. We might already have changed it, so why can't we again? Last week, your death was the only path we knew, and now look. We've got it down to a fifty-fifty shot."

"We've bettered my odds at the expense of yours. How comforting." Sarcasm was a dangerous weapon when wielded by someone as scornful as Gabriel.

"The point I'm trying to make is, we know there are other paths out there now."

"I choose to stay on this one." Gabriel yanked away and to his feet, leaving behind a smear in the dust. "It's not worth the risk. We leave it be, let the future happen as it's supposed to. If trying to save me is going to get you killed, I don't want it. I won't do it."

There was a bruise in Miles's chest, one he wanted to press harder. It was a good kind of pain, the sweetest sting. He selfishly wished he could bottle this moment—Gabriel, defiant and afraid for him, willing to do something so irrational and stupid to keep Miles safe—and tuck it away to keep.

"You know I won't do that. I promised you." He'd told Gabriel, that night in the graveyard, that he wouldn't leave him to face his fate alone.

"I don't care about your promise," Gabriel said fiercely, spitting the words from between clenched teeth. "Take it back. I don't want it anymore."

47

He was ready to walk away. It played out in Miles's mind with crystal clarity: unanswered phone calls, ignored texts, a locked iron gate. Gabriel could make it happen, and there was nothing Miles could do to stop him.

Except, possibly, one thing.

"That decision might be what puts us on the path where I die. Because I'll keep going alone. We both know we're going to end up in that tomb, and if you're not there with me, watching my back…" He let his words hang long enough for Gabriel to fill in the blank. "The vision might be a warning that if you give up now, your death becomes mine."

It was manipulative of him, but not untrue. They couldn't separate now, Jocelyn never would've involved him if he couldn't stop it. He had to keep faith.

"You don't understand," Gabriel snapped. "I saw you *die*. I was on my knees beside you, your blood on my hands. I felt you take your last breath. I felt—your mind extinguished and gone dark. There was nothing inside you, just this awful emptiness. You were gone."

He sounded like he was standing on a cliff, the edge crumbling beneath his feet.

"You know I understand. I've known since day one you were going to end up in a grave if I couldn't save you. I've been living with this for weeks now." And it was supposed to be his burden to bear alone. He'd never wished it on Gabriel. "I'm willing to carry that weight and fight if it means saving you. But you want to call it quits and run away."

"That's not fair."

"It's true."

"It's different for you." Gabriel's face was bloodless, so pale he almost blended in with the white wall behind him.

"You're better than me. Braver. When you told me you would change the future and wouldn't let me die, I believed you. But I don't believe in myself. I'm not like you."

His words slid between Miles's ribs, razor-sharp. He knew Gabriel thought he was speaking the truth. That he wasn't brave, wasn't worthy, wasn't *good*.

"I know you. You're not going to let me die because you're scared. I believe in that, in you, more than anything." Had anyone ever told Gabriel they believed in him before? "That's why you're here, isn't it? Trying to find a way to save me?"

Gabriel's shoulders slumped. "I was going to tell you once I found a solution, so you didn't have to be afraid. I needed you to stay away from me and safe until I knew how to fix it."

This conversation was giving Miles serious déjà vu. "You said that's not how the future works. We can't alter it by avoiding each other."

"I changed my mind. Your optimism must finally be wearing off on me."

Miles didn't know if he should laugh or cry. "Well, I'm glad you're feeling so positive, but we agreed we were in this together. You should've talked to me, explained what was going on so we could try to—"

"Try to what? I don't know if you've noticed, but our way hasn't worked. We've only made things worse." Gabriel glanced around at the stacked boxes. "Nadia's family has a huge collection of magical items stored here. If there's something that can help us change the future and save your life, it's in here. I just need to find it."

"Emily told me what kind of items this place deals in. Interacting with dark magic is the last thing you should be doing." Miles could still picture the black stain spreading hungrily across Gabriel's skin, trying to swallow him whole.

"I'm fairly certain the last thing I should be doing is letting you die." If Gabriel was aiming for humor, he missed it by a mile.

"This isn't just about us," Miles reminded him. "Bram's counting on you to break this curse. He needs you."

"You're asking me to choose between killing you and dooming my brother."

"I'm asking you to do what we've been doing this whole time: telling fate to go fuck itself and making our own future."

That was the only way this could end—stopping the curse, the murderer, their deaths, this cycle of pain their families were caught in. All of it.

"It's you and me," he stated, repeating his promise from that night in the cemetery. "I'm with you as far as this goes, remember?"

Their gazes caught and held, the whole tumultuous sky in Gabriel's eyes. Miles felt stripped bare, all his vulnerable insides exposed with nowhere to hide. He didn't dare look away.

Gabriel let out a grim laugh. "Fine. You win. Let's see this suicide mission through to the end, whatever that may be."

5

Gabriel sank down onto the couch, as if yielding to Miles had swept his legs out from underneath him. In the other room, the shop bell tinkled, and the murmur of voices grew louder. The tension was draining out of Miles, leaving nothing but exhaustion.

Shuffling across the floor, Miles leaned against the faded leather to press against Gabriel's knee, a silent thank you for believing in him. In them.

He'd barely made contact before Gabriel jerked his leg away. A searing flash of embarrassment raced through Miles. Gabriel was pointedly avoiding Miles's gaze, expression unreadable.

Gabriel might've agreed, but he hadn't said he was happy about it. Was he being a sore loser, or had Miles overstepped?

A tap on the door interrupted his thoughts and Nadia slipped in. "I made apology tea," they declared, handing over the twin steaming mugs in their hands. "Did you two kiss and make up?" It was a miracle they could talk without choking on the awkward tension in the room.

Miles didn't know where to look. "We're fine," he mumbled, hoping it was true. The tea smelled comforting, sweet honey and gingery spice. But with the dark auras still surrounding them and Emily's warning about the shop owner swirling in his mind, he didn't trust it.

Nadia gave Miles a knowing look, head tilted like a cat about to pounce.

Gabriel set his mug on the table with a *thunk*.

"Be pissy if you want," Nadia told him. "But you didn't warn me about your little horde of murderous friends. One of them threatened me with pepper spray in my own store." A considering smirk curled at the corner of their mouth. "Though she's cute, so I can't be too mad about it."

Charlee would lose it if she heard that.

Gabriel scoffed under his breath.

It was hard to know what to make of Nadia. They claimed this was their shop, but that couldn't be right—they had a patch of Mothman on their jacket that read "Support your local lurkers," and purple glitter eyeliner. Not exactly evil incarnate. And there was an easy, confident charm in the way they spoke. It made Miles want to relax, drink their tea, and trust what they were saying. That unnerved him more than anything else in this place.

He peered through the cracked door, far enough that he could see Charlee and Emily sitting unharmed at the counter.

Nadia followed his look. "Let's move this party out front. I closed the store for lunch, so no one will bother us. We've got things to chat about."

Back in the main room, Emily graced Gabriel with a friendly, dimpled smile. "Hi again."

Charlee's reception was distinctly less warm. Her expression was one she typically reserved for scuttling bugs and garbage in the street.

"It's fine," Miles insisted wearily. He leaned against the counter, leaving room, but Gabriel moved around him and planted himself at the opposite end. "It was… a misunderstanding."

"Nadia explained what he's doing here," Charlee said cooly. "That he panicked and ran off."

Impressively, Gabriel didn't cower. "I didn't panic. Leaving was intentional."

"Intentionally idiotic. And pointless. And a waste of everyone's time."

Squirming in her seat, Emily muttered something about her parents' divorce.

"Think what you want. Your opinion wasn't asked for or noted."

Miles winced.

"We know you were trying to help," Emily jumped in. Charlee pursed her lips, but let it be. "Nadia told us about your latest death premonition." She leaned over in her stool to grip Miles's elbow, Gabriel's eyes tracking the movement. "You okay?"

"Yeah." Honestly, he didn't feel as terrible as he probably should with his death looming over his head, but he was drained.

"We'll figure it out," she assured him confidently, then turned back to Gabriel. "We're all relieved you're not dead or being held hostage."

Nadia wheezed. "If anyone was held here against their will, it was me. He's been a pain in my ass."

"That's not what you said once you realized I'd be organizing your storage room for free."

"There are worse things to be than an opportunist." They

reached under the counter and pulled out a brass-framed hand mirror, extending it to Miles with a sheepish look. "To prove I didn't have nefarious intent with that message. I didn't have your phone number or address, so I thought this stupid thing would work. I was aiming for... to the point, not threatening."

Against his better judgment, Miles believed them.

"How does it work?"

"It was for communicating, before cell phones were a thing. With a name and enough intention, you can send a message. It's supposed to appear near them, obvious enough to be noticed. Apparently, the magic decided your wall was best. Sorry about that."

"And the blood?"

Nadia held up their pointer finger, the tip wrapped in a Band-Aid with little pink stars. "You have to write with your blood, but in my defense, I had no idea it would show up like that on your side. I was picturing more of a... whimsical gold font."

Charlee snorted.

"I've never used it before! Lesson learned. Sorry."

"Hey, accidents happen," Emily soothed them with an easy shrug. It was a stark difference from her apprehension when they'd first arrived. Clearly, Miles had missed something.

"You mentioned this was your shop," he prompted.

Nadia slid the mirror back under the counter. "Yep, I own the place. Inherited it from my grandma Dima when she retired a few months ago. My parents think I'm too young to run a business, so I'm doing my best to prove them wrong." They cracked up at whatever face Miles was making. "Yeah, your friends told me all about my supposed den of devilry here. My grandma will be thrilled to hear about her reputation, and that it's passed onto me. Raining chaos and terror upon the masses and… what was it? Eating babies? Stealing souls?"

"Sending innocent people home with things that'll kill them," Charlee answered with a hint of ice. "And leaving us to clean up the mess."

Delight brightened Nadia's face. "Has anyone ever told you that your eyes turn the prettiest shade of green when you're angry?"

Oh, this wasn't going to end well.

Charlee's cheeks reddened, but she didn't look away. "You're not going to charm your way out of the fact you're putting people in danger."

"If you think this is me being charming, you're not going to survive our first date."

Miles nearly choked. Emily was watching the exchange eagerly. Gabriel tugged at the wrinkles in his shirt, looking bored.

"Anyway," Nadia drawled with the easy confidence of someone who knew they'd won, leaving Charlee spluttering for a response. "Don't believe everything you hear. The gifted families in the area have been painting my family as villains for a long time." Irritation hid in the tight set of their mouth. "When Grandma Dima opened this place, they tried to shut her down within the first week. Those elitist assholes only want to help people on their own terms… No offense."

"Uh." Miles cleared his throat. "Not to sound like an elitist asshole, but Charlee's right—regular people shouldn't have access to haunted or cursed objects. It's dangerous."

"They shouldn't?" Nadia fixed him with a steady, unwavering look. "Does your back hurt from carrying around all that self-righteousness? Your cousin gets a pass because she's cute, but you don't."

Gabriel smirked down at the counter as Miles flushed.

"Grandma Dima built this as a place people could come to if they needed help. Our methods might be a little unconventional at times, but conventional doesn't always cut it. Not every problem can be solved with herbs and sending good juju into the universe. If you believe that, you have no idea how privileged of a life you've lived."

Miles expected Charlee to jump in and argue, but she was uncharacteristically silent, letting Nadia continue.

"If a girl comes in looking to get away from her abusive boyfriend that the cops can't be bothered with, I'm sending her home with a watch she can put under his pillow and make him forget they ever met. Or if a skeezy landlord is raising rent to force a family out and they want to leave a cursed painting that makes the whole place smell like it's rotting, then that's karma." They tapped their painted nails against the counter. "We never give anything that could really hurt anyone, nothing truly dangerous or uncontrolled, and never anything that could affect another innocent person. It's not perfect, but our track record is clean. We're better than car companies who sell to drunk drivers or any place that sells guns."

It was an argument they clearly had ready, rehearsed multiple times.

Miles knew the real world wasn't always black or white, that not everything had an easy answer. He was just lucky enough to not have to make that kind of call often. If what

Nadia was saying was true and no one was getting hurt—in most cases, they were even being helped—did that make it okay? He'd never stopped to think about it before.

"What about people who come in here looking for something dangerous?" Miles pointed out. "They could lie about their intentions. Or not understand what you've given them."

Nadia shook their head. "No one leaves this place without knowing exactly what they're taking with them. I don't mess around with informed consent. And this bad boy"—they patted a squat porcelain cat sitting beside the register—"is spelled to detect any sort of dishonesty. If you want to even discuss our specialty items, you get vetted by him first."

The cat stared blankly across the store with cool, blue painted eyes.

Miles could feel Nadia's sincerity through his exhausted shields, hear it in their voice. "I'm sorry. I shouldn't have assumed." He didn't know if he agreed with it completely, but he didn't have the right to judge Nadia or their clients.

Charlee didn't apologize but there was a gleam of interest in her eyes as she studied Nadia. If no one else was here right now, he suspected she'd pick their brain for more information.

"So, what do you have that can help Miles?" Emily asked.

Gabriel beat Nadia to an answer. "Nothing so far. But there are still—"

"I'm sorry, but if you were going to find something, you would've already."

"I can't believe that in your entire collection, you don't have one thing that could help. A way to reveal the killer, or control my premonitions so I can see more, or an object to protect Miles…" He trailed off with a frustrated noise. "I refuse to accept this was a waste of time."

"Refuse all you want, it doesn't change the fact that what you're looking for isn't here. I warned you that most of what we carry isn't made to save people."

Miles felt no disappointment. The second Gabriel had explained what he was doing here, he'd known it wouldn't be that easy.

"Still"—Nadia pushed away from the counter, jostling the porcelain cat—"just because you didn't find what you were looking for, doesn't mean you have to leave empty-handed."

They vanished into the backroom, cardboard rustling and glasses clanking. When they reemerged, they held two objects: a clear jar like Miles's mom made pickles in, and a narrow shape tucked under one arm.

"I'm not gifted," they explained, "but items will reach out to me occasionally, give me a nudge if they want to go with someone. It's a sort of intuition."

"And these two…" Miles started.

"Want to go with you. Take or leave them, it's up to you, but I'd recommend listening to the forces at work. Usually there's a good reason when they speak up."

More of the universe yanking them around. He was so sick of it.

"This one's for you." Nadia handed the long item to Gabriel. "It's been reacting since you first got here."

Gabriel unsheathed it. It was a dagger with a worn wooden hilt and a pointed silver blade about half a foot long. Simple and plain in a way that only made it more sinister.

It didn't feel evil like the grimoire or Florence's ring, but it radiated a chill.

He slid it back into its sheath and set it on the counter, like touching it repulsed him. "I don't want this."

Nadia made no move to take it back. "You're going to need it."

"Why? Why this?"

"I have no idea, I'm just the messenger. All I know is that this knife never does anything by half-measure—it deals killing blows only, and it can kill anything, so make sure you mean it before you point it at someone."

A charged silence fell over the room. Everyone had to be thinking the same thing—was this the knife that would save Gabriel's life? If it came down to kill or be killed, would he be able to use it?

"I don't want it," he said faintly.

"Then don't take it. I can't make you. But know that you might regret not having it."

"Take it," Miles insisted. It didn't mean he had to use it. But having that knife when he needed to defend himself could mean the difference between living and dying.

After a long moment, Gabriel picked it up.

"This one," Nadia declared, turning to Miles, "is for you."

The jar was full of cloudy liquid, a fleshy blob floating in it. "What is it?"

"It's one of the rarest things in this shop, so be careful with it. I'm loaning it to you, not giving it. I expect it back." They twisted the metal lid, making sure it was fully sealed. "Have you ever heard that cheesy Hallmark crap about letting your heart be your compass?"

"Uh, no, sorry." But Emily and Charlee both nodded.

"Well, now you have. And take that literally. This is the heart of a pure black fox that was shot by an oak arrow under a new moon in a field of feverfew. When you're lost, it will show you the way."

It was packing serious magic. That didn't make it any less disgusting. "Should I... expect to get lost?"

Now that Blanche was gone, his driving time had been cut down significantly. And he rarely left Thistle, whose streets he knew well enough to navigate while half-asleep and nursing a concussion.

"I certainly wouldn't count it out."

Great. One more ominous warning to worry about.

Miles turned to Gabriel as Nadia snagged a notepad from under the register, scribbling. "Why'd you get the badass weapon and I get a nasty organ in a jar?"

It was a strange, uncomfortable thing to realize that in the last weeks, he'd gotten so used to Gabriel's small smiles, it hollowed out his chest when he didn't get one.

Gabriel's pensive gaze flicked between the two items. "Fitting, I suppose."

Before Miles could ask, Nadia ripped the paper they'd scribbled on and handed it to Charlee with a grin. "And this is for you."

Miles peered over—it was a phone number.

Charlee didn't react. "Is this another intuition thing?"

"I sure hope so."

She rolled her eyes, but tucked the paper into her pocket.

Leaning into Miles, Emily whispered, "Should I be offended I'm the only one going home empty-handed?"

"You want the magical GPS heart?" He shook it, the liquid sloshing.

"Please, I have an amazing sense of direction."

Charlee stood, kicking her stool under the counter. "Let's head back before Aunt Sarah sends out a search party."

Miles's gut gave a nervous lurch.

"Dare I ask what car we'll be riding in?" Gabriel inquired dryly. "And if it would be faster to simply walk home?"

Typical. He thought Gabriel had learned a thing or two after Blanche, but apparently not.

Charlee whirled around so fast, it was a miracle her head didn't fly off. "Let's get one thing clear. After the hell you put Miles through this week, the only reason I'm not throwing your ass out of my car the moment we hit full speed on the freeway is because in some idiotic way, you thought you were helping him. But give me one reason, Hawthorne, one more entitled comment, and I swear, you're going to learn what pavement tastes like."

Gabriel nodded solemnly. Miles wished they'd both stop being so damn dramatic.

"Let's just go," he urged, cradling his heart-jar carefully.

Nadia ushered them out onto the rain-splattered sidewalk. "Good luck. Hope you don't die and all that."

"Uh, thanks. I think."

He caught his reflection in the glass shopfront window, his own face staring back at him once again.

6

Dinner at the Warren house was an unusually somber affair.

It was taco night, the smell of chorizo and vinegary salsa filling the kitchen, never failing to conjure content, full-stomached feelings of home. But a cold front had settled since Miles's "betrayal." His mom was pissed about Gabriel —but for the record that no one seemed to care about, Miles was mad at her too. He was being punished when he'd done nothing wrong, and refused to apologize to appease her.

They'd hit a stalemate, and everyone in the house was suffering for it.

Sarah was resolutely silent as she ate. Aunt Robin and Jenna were talking quietly on the other side of the table, Amy failing to act like she wasn't listening in as Adam tried to talk to her about school.

Miles didn't bother joining the conversation. He couldn't discuss anything that was on his mind.

Beside him, Charlee methodically broke a tortilla chip into tiny shards. She hadn't said much on the ride home, even when they'd pulled up to drop Gabriel off outside the Hawthorne estate's massive iron gate. Whatever was waiting for him inside—if his brothers were going to be furious with him, if Edmund had told Felicity everything—Miles was too tired to worry about it. Let it be a problem for future him.

All he cared was that he'd see Gabriel at school on Monday. He'd made him promise to be there before letting him out of the car.

"Miles." Sarah caught his attention from across the dinner table. Her tone was cool but noticeably less barbed than it had been. That probably had to do with the meaningful glances from Miles's dad. "We have a job for you Monday night. There's a house over in Glenwood the owners suspect might be haunted."

Miles despised going to Glenwood. It was one of those rich-person areas where all the houses looked identical, the grass an artificial bright green, trash cans lined up perfectly on the curb. Sprinklers went off at the same time every morning, there was a minimum of one patriotic decor item for every three houses, and anyone out walking was a potential HOA spy in disguise. Every time he went, he could feel himself being judged from all sides. Even the dogs in that neighborhood tracked his movements with critical eyes.

He caught his scowl before it could grow. He'd been practicing Gabriel's expression of cool disinterest, but he wasn't very good at it yet.

"It'd be a big help if you could go check it out for me, see if it needs my attention," his dad added with a tired smile. "I'm swamped right now."

Most presumed-to-be-haunted houses could be blamed on regular old house things—groaning pipes, mice in the attic, creaky floorboards—and his dad didn't have the time to determine if every potential client had a real ghost on their hands. He'd send Miles over to check it out, see if there truly was a ghost hanging around before scheduling a visit to deal with it.

When Miles crawled into bed at night and let his anxious brain catalogue the pros and cons of leaving the family business, not having to creep around other people's dank basements in search of bloodthirsty poltergeists always landed firmly at the top of the pros.

"Okay." Short and sweet. Nonconfrontational. Miles kept his gaze on his plate, two uneaten tacos staring back up at him, cilantro wilted from the heat.

He could sense his mom's frown. Either she didn't like his tone, or she'd been expecting an argument.

What could he do? She wouldn't care that he had more important things going on. A frustrated, vindictive part of him wanted to tell her that it was *his* life at stake now, see if that got her attention, made her worry.

It was already going to be difficult enough to see Gabriel outside of school, with Blanche gone and Miles grounded. Antagonizing his mom further would be a stupid move. He stabbed his fork into his beans and tried to listen to his own logic.

Adam murmured something to Sarah, and she cleared her throat. "Thank you. We appreciate it."

She was only playing nice because she was being pushed into it. Miles didn't know if he should continue to be mad, or accept the truce she was offering. He'd never done this before, never even had his mom truly angry with him. He was treading unsteady ground with no idea where to step next.

He took the coward's way out, defaulting back to the job. "Are Amy or Jenna coming with me?" After his parents had mentioned it was time for the twins to start getting more involved, he'd been waiting for the inevitable moment they were pawned off on him.

Adam shook his head. "Not this one. We don't know what's there."

Sure. Send Miles into the jaws of a potentially evil, murderous ghost, but let the girls stay home.

"Jenna can help me," Aunt Robin suggested. Since she'd come out of her room, she'd been taking Jenna under her wing. It was kind of her, and Jenna was blooming under the attention. "I wanted to sort and refill our herb stash, and could use an extra pair of hands."

Charlee stared down at her plate, a muscle in her jaw twitching.

She found it weird her mom was showing such interest in Jenna all of a sudden, but Miles thought it was sweet. He knew his aunt could connect with feeling useless; taking Jenna under her wing was good for them both. She'd had a new sense of purpose these last few days.

"I can help Miles," Amy insisted, forgetting that she'd pitched a huge fit over the whole thing. She gave him a wide grin, wiggling her eyebrows like a dork.

Great. Between the séance yesterday and being told they'd successfully found Gabriel, Amy clearly thought she was part of the team now.

"No," his mom stated decisively, turning back to Miles. "Take Charlee with you if you don't want to go alone. But it doesn't seem like a two-person job. The clients reported only low-level haunting stuff."

"I've got better stuff to do than waste my time crawling around someone's dusty attic," Charlee declared, her tortilla chip now a pile of yellow dust. "You can take my car, though."

Miles also had better things to do, but he wasn't about to tell his mom that.

After dinner, he followed Charlee upstairs into her room. She sidestepped a stray pair of shoes and tugged off her sweater, tossing it onto a pile of clothes. Wordlessly, she crawled into her bed and under the comforter, holding it up for Miles in clear invitation.

He joined her, tucking his socked feet under her legs so they didn't hang over the edge.

Breathing in the scent of her coconut shampoo and lavender pillow spray, Miles's agitation melted away. He was warm, he was safe, and Charlee was beside him.

She shifted closer until her head rested against his shoulder. A stray red curl tickled his neck. They lay there in silence for a few minutes, listening to the rain pounding on the roof and dripping outside the window, the sky a plummy, bruised purple.

"I'm scared," she exhaled, an admission meant for only his ears. "I don't want you to die."

A painful lump formed in Miles's throat, a burning hot coal. "Don't be silly," he managed. "I'm not going to die. Not anytime soon, at least. Check back in fifty years."

She didn't laugh. "What if this is karma for judging my mom when she gave up after losing my dad? What if the universe is trying to teach me a lesson?"

"Charlee. I'm not going to roll over and let death come for me. I can't... I don't know what to do." His current plan was to try not to think about it too much. Keep it in his periphery without looking at it head on. "All I can do is keep moving forward and find a way to change things. We believed I could do it with Gabriel. It's not any different."

Now he understood Gabriel's infuriating nonchalance after finding out he was going to die. What else was there to do but compartmentalize and push forward?

"But what if you can't?"

He stared up at her fairy lights, willing himself not to cry. "C'mon, don't make me do this. I already had to give Gabriel a big speech and convince him not to give up. My brain is about to start leaking out my ears. Nothing is set in stone, okay? The future can always change."

Charlee sniffled. The shoulder of his shirt was wet from her tears, but neither of them mentioned it. "What am I supposed to do?"

"What you always do. Stick with me. Have my back."

"That's bullshit. Give me something I can actually do. A way to help."

He understood how unbearable it was to sit around doing nothing. "I don't know," he admitted. "I'm not blowing you off, I just... I'm not sure what the plan is. We're back to square one on the murderer with no leads, but we still have the grimoire. I guess we'll focus on trying to break the curse." He muffled his yawn into Charlee's hair. "I'll talk to Gabriel on Monday, okay? We need to regroup and re-plan."

"I don't like that we're supposed to work on the curse when you're the target of a killer now. They could pop up at any time and murder you," Charlee muttered. "That should be our priority."

"What a comforting thought."

She dug her knuckles into his side. "You don't get to act all nonchalant about this now because the target's on your back instead of your boyfriend's."

"Ow!" He wiggled away from her attack, one of her

fuzzy blankets slipping onto the floor. "I don't think that's how it works. There isn't a serial killer breathing down my neck, waiting to strike. Gabriel and I are both going to end up in that tomb and at some point, I guess whoever's going to kill Gabriel might change their mind and go for me. It's fifty-fifty."

"Those odds aren't remotely comforting."

Miles wasn't sure how to explain that in a way, it was. "I don't want to waste time on something with zero leads when we could be breaking the curse."

She didn't agree, he could feel it, but she didn't argue. "Then you tell Hawthorne to get his head in the game. We can't afford to waste time chasing after him again."

"You know why he did it," Miles argued, trying not to sound like he was defending Gabriel, because he wasn't. He was still *so* mad at him. But if Miles was being honest with himself, he was also touched that Gabriel had tried so hard to protect him. That he cared enough to put Miles first. That seeing Miles's death had affected him in such a visceral way.

God, he was a terrible person. A rotten, selfish person.

"That doesn't mean I have to like it," she grumbled. She fidgeted with her hoodie tassel before saying carefully, "You really don't have any suspects?"

He stared straight up at the ceiling so she wouldn't see the answer. Jocelyn had given them two vague clues: it was a woman, and she needed to be kept away from the grimoire. Only one woman came to mind who would potentially use the grimoire's magic for her own gain.

Felicity.

Florence's taunting words to Gabriel had haunted Miles since he'd been warned that the future remained unchanged:

If I'm not the one to kill you, someone else will be. I imagine someone close to you, one of your family perhaps, will do the deed. After all, murder is in our blood, isn't it?

But he didn't have anything more than an awful intuition. That wasn't proof, certainly not enough to drop the bomb on Gabriel that his own mom might be the person to kill him.

He'd keep it to himself for now. But from Charlee's pointed question, he wondered if he wasn't the only one who suspected Felicity.

"Nope," he made himself say. "I really thought Florence was the one."

"We'll have to be extra careful, then. If anyone comes at you, I'll pepper spray first, ask questions later."

A laugh escaped Miles. It was impossible not to feel safe with Charlee watching his back.

"That tactic isn't as effective as you think. Nadia sounded kinda into being threatened."

"Of course they were."

Miles waited, but she didn't continue. "So…" he prodded. "Are we going to talk about them?"

"You're trying to change the subject."

"Sorry I don't want to talk about being murdered anymore." He tugged one of her stray curls, getting swatted for it. "You kept their number. Were you just being nice, or are you going to text them?"

Charlee was silent for a second. "I haven't decided yet."

That wasn't a no. Miles had absolutely zero right to be touchy with anyone for not sharing the details of their sexuality, but it still stung a little. Did she not trust him?

Charlee knew him too well. "Don't do that. It just didn't

come up. I like who I like, and I don't think it's anyone's business. I shouldn't have to explain myself."

"Sorry... I guess it felt weird to not know that about you, that's all."

She sighed. "It honestly didn't seem worth telling. I realized I like everything. Anything. Whatever. I'm not picky, good for me. That's not newsworthy."

A snort escaped Miles and his tension slid away. Outside, a car alarm went off down the street, horn blaring.

"For the record, I think they're cool," he told her. "You should ask them out."

The look she gave him scorched the side of his face. "Are you seriously giving me relationship advice when your boyfriend ghosted you for half a week?"

Ouch. "That's different and you know it. And we haven't really talked about what we are or... what happened." Charlee made disgusting kissy noises in his ear, and he elbowed her away. "I don't want to push him."

Especially after Gabriel recoiled from him earlier. Miles was trying to not get in his own head about it or let his worries run rampant, but he kept replaying it. Gabriel had refused to even look at him.

"Talking isn't pushing."

That was easy for Charlee to say. She wasn't potentially destroying a relationship before it got a chance to really start.

"Can we go back to talking about my death?" he begged miserably.

Charlee snickered.

7

"You showed." Miles had spent the whole bus ride to school convincing himself Gabriel wouldn't be waiting at their courtyard table Monday morning, that he'd vanish without warning again. He hated the tentativeness in his voice, how uncertain he felt as he sat down to join him.

Gabriel looked like he hadn't slept much, but that wasn't uncommon. He also didn't look particularly pleased to see Miles. "And, apparently, I missed something while I was gone."

"What do you mean?"

His disdainful scan of the crowd could've curdled milk. "Have you somehow failed to notice the alarming number of costumes?"

A group in animal onesies walked by; behind them, a girl dressed as Barbie was handing textbooks to a boy in full pirate garb. It was the coldest morning of autumn so far, but that hadn't deterred anyone. A sea of colorful outfits blanketed the walkway and grass, and there was more energy in the air than a usual Monday.

"Oh, yeah. You missed the assembly on Friday—it's Spirit Week." At Gabriel's blank expression, Miles added, "It's for the homecoming dance. Every day this week has a theme you can dress up for. Friday is a big football game, and the dance is Saturday night. It's tradition."

"Are these required activities?" Dread colored Gabriel's voice.

Miles considered saying yes just to watch him panic. "Nah, it's to show your school spirit or whatever. Classes have competitions for dressing up, but it's not serious."

"I refuse to believe people are willingly dressing like that."

It was a lot, even for Miles, but it had its charm. "C'mon, costume day is a classic. It's like early Halloween, minus the free candy."

Gabriel didn't crack a smile. "Halloween is never this frightening."

If he was this grumpy over costumes, Miles could only imagine his reaction to pajama day. Knowing him, he exclusively wore matching old man button-up pajama sets in thrilling varieties of black and gray. And he probably managed to make them look great.

He shot Gabriel's dark plaid scarf an envious glance. Gabriel pulled it off better than Miles ever could, the knotted fabric making him look mysterious and brooding instead of like the president of the drama club.

"So, how'd everything go with Edmund and Bram?" Miles asked. "And your mom?"

"Fine."

Miles waited, but Gabriel didn't continue. "They weren't mad at you?"

"Bram doesn't know how to stay angry, so he forgave me immediately." Gabriel dragged the words out, like he was put out by having to share. "Edmund was as dramatic as you'd expect. Apparently, the stress of the last few days and generally being my brother has taken years off his life."

Yeah, that sounded about right. Miles could picture Edmund draping himself across the nearest piece of furniture as he bemoaned Gabriel's choices, unable to bear it a moment longer.

"Did he tell your mom?"

Sneaking around to meet with Gabriel already wasn't ideal, but having to dodge Felicity on top of that was a worst-case scenario.

"No. He won't admit it, but I think he was too scared to tell her. Apparently"—Gabriel's mouth twisted bitterly—"she didn't even realize I was gone."

Felicity was a monster, but man, Miles was a little jealous of her nonchalant approach to parenting. "Well, that's a relief."

He realized his mistake when Gabriel's shoulders stiffened, lifting towards his ears.

"I mean"—Miles stumbled over his words—"she sounds like she's been pretty busy. I'm sure that's the only reason she didn't notice."

"It's fine," Gabriel replied curtly. "Better than fine. It saves me a lot of trouble."

Yep, Miles had put his foot in his mouth. Felicity was awful, even her own kids thought so, but she was still their mom. He couldn't blame Gabriel for waiting for the day she'd start caring. Maybe that was why he was in such a mood this morning.

"She should've realized," he stated firmly. "And I'm sorry she didn't."

He reached for Gabriel's hand, intending to give him

an apologetic squeeze safely hidden beneath the table, but the moment their fingers grazed, Gabriel pulled away. "It doesn't matter. I have more important things to focus on than my mother's questionable parenting. We need to discuss our new plan."

It stung, but Miles let him change the subject. The touchy-feely talk might've been too much for him. "I don't think much has changed. Your premonition"—it was easier to call it that than 'your vision of my upcoming death'— "doesn't really affect anything. And Jocelyn didn't bother sharing any new cryptic hints. I wish I knew what her deal was so we could—" He stopped, something occurring to him. "Wait, why is she even giving me warnings? I assumed her unfinished business was stopping her sister, but Florence isn't the murderer."

"Perhaps since the curse started with her, she sees it as her duty to end it." Gabriel focused on the trees across the courtyard—their leaves were that comforting shade of golden-orange that never failed to make Miles think of warm tea, thick sweaters, and his mom's butternut squash soup.

"Or she's acting like your guardian angel, since you're family." Miles thought back to his dream as a blonde girl dressed as a fairy slipped in the dewy grass with a shriek, her friend cackling. "When I talked to her, it seemed like she was in pain. She heard me reach out but couldn't respond because her bonds were too strong. I think she hasn't moved on because she can't. Something's holding her here."

It could be some kind of binding ritual, like ghost jail. Was that even possible? He'd never heard of anything like it.

"Tragic, but it doesn't do much to help us. We can find a

way to free her spirit after we deal with the more pressing matters."

Plus, Jocelyn being present in Gabriel's death premonition was enough to make Miles apprehensive to actively seek her out.

"I guess until we get a new lead on the killer, we should focus on the grimoire, right? Tackle the curse."

"I don't agree. The killer's identity should be our priority."

"I'm not saying we ignore the fact there's a killer coming for us," Miles said placatingly, "but we shouldn't waste our time. We have the grimoire. It would be stupid to set it aside."

A loaded beat of silence passed. Leaves crunched as a group of students trudged through the grass, one girl struggling with a massive posterboard tucked under her arm as the wind picked up.

"Fine. At least until I find a new lead on the murderer."

How, exactly, did he expect to do that—was he going to conjure up a list of Thistle's most likely killers from thin air?

"Deal. The grimoire's going to be complicated, though. You're not handling that thing alone. I would offer"—the thought made Miles's skin crawl—"but I'm worried someone at home will sense it if I have it out of the containment box for too long. I guess I could take it somewhere else, but that's going to be tricky without Blanche." Poor, beautiful Blanche. It was tragic that you could never fully appreciate something until it was snatched away by a murderous ghost trying to barbecue you. "It'll have to wait, either way. My parents are sending me on a job tonight. And now that I'm under house arrest, getting away is going to be harder than normal."

"House arrest?"

Miles realized he'd never had the chance to tell Gabriel what had happened. They'd had to deal with Florence. He'd planned to break the news to Gabriel the next morning, but then Gabriel went and distracted him with his confession before disappearing.

"Yeah, I guess you missed that part." He raked a hand through his hair. "Long story short, my parents found out about you. The police report from the car accident had your name on it, and when my mom confronted me, I kinda… made things worse. It got pretty ugly."

Gabriel scoffed. "How could it not? Let me guess—my family are all evil and you shouldn't taint yourself with our presence? She must've been relieved when you told her about my upcoming death."

Shock stole Miles's voice for a few moments. It had been a while since he'd heard Gabriel speak so cuttingly about his family or the feud—he barely sounded like himself.

He swallowed, sensing he was treading around hidden mines. "I tried to tell her about the premonition, but she wouldn't listen. She's not—" He knew his mom wasn't spiteful enough to wish Gabriel dead, but this wasn't the time to defend her. "It doesn't matter. The good thing is, I didn't let it slip you're going to school here. But she's watching my every move. The only reason I'm being let out of the house tonight is because they're putting me to work."

"What's the job?"

"Checking out a potentially haunted house over in Glenwood, which always takes forever." Miles had to raise his voice to be heard as two boys with twin plastic swords walked by, arguing about skipping PE if it started raining.

"We'll have to push the grimoire back until tomorrow night. The only chance I'll get to see you, aside from at school, is more sneaky late-night meetups." He might have to upgrade from tea to coffee with a schedule like that. Hey, sleep was for the weak, right?

Gabriel pondered this for a moment. "I'll come with you."

"Tonight?"

"Yes. You're going alone, correct? Bring the grimoire and I can start reading while you do your... investigating. Text me the address. I'll have Edmund drive me over."

He didn't sound enthusiastic, but it wasn't a bad idea. It might even be a good one. And, as a petty bonus, Miles's mom would be pissed she'd unknowingly handed him an opportunity.

"Okay, but we're reading it together."

"I'm not an infant. I don't need to be kept under constant surveillance."

Miles snorted. "Of course not. It's not like the last time you read it, you got all obsessive and creepy and nearly bit my hand off for touching it. I don't trust you not to run off with it if I'm not watching you."

"I can't tell if that's a jab at me for leaving, or for being susceptible to the grimoire's influence."

"Neither. I know you can't help how that stupid book affects you. And I'm still too mad at you to make jokes about you running off."

"Yes, I can tell you're furious."

Asshole. He'd deserve it if Miles kicked him in the ankle. "I'm being the bigger person. Don't confuse that with a free pass."

He expected one of his usual scathing retorts, but Gabriel just frowned and looked away.

"Are you pissed at me or something?" Miles blurted.

"Excuse me?"

"You're acting all… weird. Like you're holding a grudge because I talked you into not giving up, or that I came to find you."

"You're imagining things."

Gabriel's tone was so dismissive that Miles's ears warmed. "Obviously I'm not. What's going on? If you're not mad, are you worried about your premonition? My death isn't—"

"Why would I be worried?" Gabriel interrupted icily. "According to you, good intentions and the power of positive thinking are going to save the day."

So that was a solid *yes* to him being pissed.

Miles felt like he'd tripped and fallen back through time, landing in a terrible place weeks ago where they could barely stand to talk to each other. There was no warmth or humor warming Gabriel's gray eyes, no softness in the line of his shoulders or clench of his jaw.

"I'm worried too," Miles told him quietly. The dark clouds gathering overhead looked ready to start pouring any moment now. "But we have to work together, and have each other's backs, or we won't—"

"I'm here and doing everything you're asking of me," Gabriel snapped. "Focusing on the curse instead of the killer, offering up my time to read the grimoire, letting you make all the decisions. What more do you want from me?"

Something twisted painfully in Miles's chest, making it impossible to answer. He wanted things to go back to normal, to how they'd been before Gabriel had his premonition and ran away. He wanted Gabriel to take his hand and tell him why he was upset instead of lashing out.

Gabriel might've shown up, resigned to accept whatever course Miles set them on, but something was wrong.

What if it wasn't about the curse, but about *them*?

Insecurity rose in Miles. He tried to shove the thought away, but it was too late—the little seed of doubt had been planted. They hadn't talked about the cemetery, the kiss, what it all meant, and that was the only thing that had changed aside from Gabriel's premonition.

Maybe he'd thought the kiss was terrible. Maybe it hadn't meant the same thing to him. Or maybe he didn't want to bother now that he thought Miles was a dead boy walking. Who would waste their time on someone like that?

Ouch.

Miles couldn't make himself meet Gabriel's eyes, knowing the hurt and embarrassment would be written all over his face. He should just ask, but the question refused to come out, settling with pricking spikes somewhere low in his throat.

Sighing, as if he was bored of the conversation, Gabriel stood and slung his bag over his shoulder. "I'm going inside before it starts raining."

He didn't invite Miles to come with him. Without a backward glance, he marched off towards the school, leaving Miles sitting alone as thunder rumbled threateningly overhead.

8

"What kind of self-respecting ghost would haunt this place?"

Miles adjusted his backpack and headed up the tidy, bush-lined driveway. "Pretty sure they don't get a choice." He was positive, actually, after talking to Blake the bus ghost.

Gabriel squinted at the blue two-story house, with its yellow trim and flower boxes in the front windows, as if he could see straight through the walls to any lurking spirits. "It doesn't look remotely haunted."

"If all haunted houses came straight out of an episode of *Scooby-Doo*, it would make my job a lot easier." Miles forced amusement into his voice. "I don't even know if there's a ghost, that's why I'm checking."

"So, you're a cadaver dog and a human EMF detector."

It was a shadow of their usual banter. There was a vacancy to Gabriel's voice that made them feel hollow. Like he was reading a script.

He'd acted this way all day. During class, he'd barely spared Miles a glance, and he'd vanished completely at lunch. Miles was shocked he'd showed up tonight.

Taking the hint, he resolved to give Gabriel the space

he wanted, but Miles was suffering for it. His brain had been spinning all day, each thought worse than the last until he was nauseous. Part of him wanted to grab Gabriel and demand he stop being so selfish and just *talk* to Miles instead of keeping him in this awful, unknowing silence.

Instead, he made himself smile, and said, "Except I work. EMF detectors are only good for dramatic moments on cheesy ghost hunting shows."

Casual. Cheerful. Unaffected. If Miles had survived that first week with Gabriel, he could do this. Hell, he could do anything.

Sure, he'd pictured their reunion going a little differently —a gratefully rescued Gabriel awestruck by Miles's bravery, one of those relieved, desperate kisses straight out of a movie, maybe even a new shiny boyfriend label—but that was his own fault for daydreaming.

"That woman across the street is staring at us," Gabriel warned him as they approached the front door.

Miles had clocked her when he'd pulled up. She'd taken one look at Charlee's battered Honda and planted herself in her driveway like a guard dog in a purple tracksuit. She was harmless—if she were going to call the cops, she would've done it already. "Ignore her and she'll go away."

Not only was this neighborhood full of nosy people, but nosy people who took one look at Miles and thought he was *trouble*. He'd had the cops called on him more than once for suspicious activity, which was just code for "there's someone who looks poor in my rich neighborhood, he must be here to rob us."

Ugh. He despised Glenwood.

A massive sunflower wreath all but obscured the door

knocker, but Miles didn't need it. He lifted the welcome mat to reveal a silver key winking up at him, right where the owners had promised it would be. The door unlocked easily, and Miles followed Gabriel through. It was surprisingly cozy inside, with more character than he'd expected. The living room housed a monstrous peacock-blue velvet couch and colorfully beaded pillows, a plush cream rug beneath a mosaic-tiled coffee table. A massive TV was wall-mounted across from it, flanked by huge potted plants. The only immediately off-putting thing was the heavy scent; Miles could taste artificial pumpkin in the back of his throat.

They crossed the living room—avoiding the immaculate rug—into the dining room, where a six-person table of polished oak squatted. The kitchen was right there, the marble island and stainless-steel appliances visible through the open doorway, but Miles didn't go in. If there was a poltergeist, the last place he wanted to be was the room with all the knives.

Being in a stranger's house while they were gone was always strange. Unsettling. Miles didn't consider himself especially snoopy, but he always felt like he should peek around to make sure there weren't any bodies in the basement.

"We'll set up here," he told Gabriel, wiggling off his backpack and placing it on the dining room table.

"How does this work, exactly?"

"I walk around the house, check things out. If there's a ghost, I can usually sense it even if I can't see them. But calls like this are usually a false alarm—creaky old houses with rattling pipes and mice in the walls. People love any excuse to tell their friends their house is haunted, until they start freaking themselves out." He shook his head. "I really don't know when living in a haunted house became a cool thing. People don't understand what a pain in the ass real ghosts are. But it keeps my parents in business, so I guess I shouldn't complain."

"Old houses have had more time for a horrific death to happen inside," Gabriel pointed out, sitting at the end of the table closest to the kitchen.

The inside of the house looked modern, but Miles had noticed the historical home plaque mounted by the front door. "Which is why I'm checking."

"And what happens if there is a ghost here?"

"I'll try to communicate with them, find out what I can. My parents prefer to learn who the ghost is so we can release its spirit, or find out if it needs something specific to move on instead of just cleansing the space or banishing it. It feels… nicer that way. More respectful. Like we're giving them a better chance of finding peace, I guess."

Miles started unloading his bag, laying out crystals and candles on the wood. He was careful not to jostle the sweater-wrapped heart in a jar he'd shoved to the bottom. It seemed like a good idea to keep it on him in case of an emergency need-direction situation.

The silence felt uncomfortably deliberate, so Miles blurted out, "You've really never had to do anything like this before?"

"Like what?"

"You know…" He waved around them. "Investigate a haunted house. Dig up a grave in the middle of the night. Banish a poltergeist as it's trying to bash your head in against the nearest wall. Dispose of a cursed mirror that makes people claw their own faces off."

"No."

"So it's true then that your mom just does séances for

rich people," Miles muttered, then winced. "Sorry, that was rude. I meant—"

"It's true. And it's very profitable work."

Something about the tone of Gabriel's voice felt like a challenge, a calculated edge of arrogance he wanted Miles to react to. Poking, to see if Miles could be goaded into a fight.

He smiled, feeling just petty enough to hope it annoyed Gabriel, and changed the subject. "You okay chilling here while I scope out the house?"

If Gabriel was disappointed, he hid it well as he slipped off his peacoat and draped it over the chair beside him. "I'll be fine." He scanned the house, lingering on the bookshelf in the living room and the photographs on the wall, much like he had in Miles's home. There was a hungry curiosity in the way he examined other people's lives.

"Don't touch the grimoire," Miles warned, pointing at his bag. It was locked up in its containment box, but he knew the second he opened it, nasty little tendrils would come out, searching for anything they could latch on to, probing against his protective charms, licking at his skin like sandpaper.

With the way Gabriel was acting right now, he wasn't sure he trusted him not to do something stupid just to frustrate Miles or make some asinine point.

Crossing the kitchen to the stairs, Miles cautiously lowered his mental shields. He could sense something, a low thrum of energy in the air. It wasn't malicious or evil, just... sad. Grief and fear—the sneaky kind that kept you in bed for days, sobs muffled into pillows and salty tracks on skin. There was something about it that suggested innocence, an undercurrent of confusion.

It was awful, but he'd rather deal with a sad ghost than an angry one. Dreary was always a safer bet than murderous.

The stairs creaked loudly as he climbed, making him feel like he was in a low-budget horror movie. Next, the lights at the top were going to flicker and go out.

He peeked in each room—four neat bedrooms and two bathrooms—but didn't see anything. The energy was an ache in the back of his teeth, not tethered to anything specific as far as he could tell. The ghost was most likely attached to the house itself—or a person in it.

Back in the dining room, Gabriel was scrolling idly through his phone. His pale fingers drummed against the tabletop.

"There's definitely a ghost here," Miles informed him, "but it doesn't feel too dangerous. It might be a kid."

"A kid? How can you tell?"

"Their energy always feels a little different. Innocent, kind of… shallow. If you focus, you can probably feel it."

"All I can feel is the grimoire."

Through the containment box? Gabriel was so attuned to it, he was being affected in ways that shouldn't be possible. Worry itched under Miles's skin that he was making a terrible mistake even letting Gabriel near it.

"Well, trust me, this ghost feels like a fluffy little kitten compared to some of the ones I've wrangled. Or Florence."

"A fluffy little kitten. Very intimidating. Should I grab the salt?"

"Shut up." Miles knocked his hip into Gabriel's chair. "You don't get to act like a macho ghost expert just because you banished one."

He pulled the containment box from his bag and Gabriel

stood to attention like a dog who'd spotted a ball. Yeah, that made Miles feel loads better about handing it over.

Cautiously, he opened the box, scowling at the grimoire's plain leather cover and the frigid chill that blasted forth. He hadn't missed it these last few days.

"If you start to feel weird—" Miles caught himself. "Weirder than normal, let me know."

"I'll be fine." Gabriel took the grimoire. His skin erupted into goosebumps where he'd rolled up his sleeves. "I know what to expect now."

"Knowing what to expect doesn't mean it's not going to sink its nasty little hooks into you. You went full Gollum last time. It was creepy as hell."

He sank into his seat, watching closely. Their feet bumped under the table. Gabriel shifted away as he cracked open the grimoire, turning to the first page.

No darkness spread across his skin. Pain didn't send him hunching over the table.

Gabriel's gaze flitted up from the page as Miles pulled a Ouija board from his backpack. "Please tell me you're not serious."

"Sometimes spirits need a little help when they're trying to talk."

He positioned the planchette in the middle of the board, then lit two blue candles and mint incense for communication. At the four corners of the board, he placed chunks of blue kyanite and clear quartz.

"Don't you need to turn the lights out?" Gabriel needled. "Set the scene?"

"This isn't an episode of *Specter Seekers*." Real ghosts couldn't care less about the lighting.

Miles finished setting everything up, leaning back in his chair to listen to the house, Gabriel's breathing, and the whisper of paper as he turned the page.

"If there's a spirit in this house, I'm here to talk," Miles said loudly. "If you're trying to reach out and I can't hear you, I have these helpful tools in front of me that you can use." He tapped the planchette. "You can move this around the board to spell what you want to say."

"How do you know the kid can spell?" Gabriel muttered.

Miles ignored him, waiting, but nothing happened. He didn't sense anything beyond the general aura.

"It's okay if you don't wanna talk. I'll hang out here for a bit in case you change your mind."

He watched Gabriel while he waited. He always looked vaguely concerned when he was reading, but he wasn't bleeding from the eyes or foaming at the mouth, so they were doing pretty well.

But he looked exhausted—dark under his eyes, and tight around his mouth like he hadn't unclenched his jaw once in the last twelve hours. It made being grumpy with him difficult, no matter how rotten Miles was feeling. He wanted to wrap Gabriel in a hug and make him take a nap.

Despite his anxieties and the insecurities whispering in his ear, he *knew* Gabriel cared about him. After the shit he'd pulled, his reaction to Miles's death premonition, Miles would have to be an idiot to pretend otherwise. It was the life raft he was clinging to while riding out Hurricane Gabriel.

Part of Miles hoped this was all about his death. That Gabriel was afraid and handling it badly. Still pissed that Miles thought it was a good sign. Because the alternative was that Gabriel was trying to not-so-gently let him down, to make it clear their kiss hadn't meant anything—or if it had, he'd changed his mind. And that made Miles feel like his heart was being stomped on.

"I can't read with you staring at me like that," Gabriel muttered without looking up. "And thinking so loudly."

Heat scorched Miles's face. "Sorry," he stammered. "I wasn't—"

"Look at this." Gabriel spared him from a messy, mortifying explanation, tilting the book so Miles could see. "I found our mystery monster from the tunnel."

The page was yellowed and stiff, filled with jagged, knife-sharp writing that was nearly impossible to read. Halfway down there was an ink drawing of the thing that had attacked them: claws and curling smoke, hollow sockets for eyes, broad-shouldered pit bull stance and massive jaw. Seeing it again made Miles's gut shrivel up with fear.

"What is it?"

"A protector. Once summoned, it's bound to the bloodline and acts as a guard. It must've been left behind at the old house to watch over the grimoire."

"That's why it attacked me instead of you. And why you could"—Miles twirled his hand—"poof it. It had to obey you."

"Interesting." Gabriel flipped to the next page, fingers skimming down it as he read. "Speaking of interesting, I found a summoning spell."

Miles leaned in, trying to read. There were a few lines and what looked like a list of ingredients. "What about it?"

When Gabriel looked up, there was an eager gleam in his eyes. "You believe something is holding Jocelyn here, and that it's preventing you from communicating with her. What if this spell—given the grimoire's unnaturally powerful magic—is strong enough to supersede the one restraining her? She could tell us who the killer is and how to stop them."

A shudder rolled through Miles. "No. No way. Who knows the cost of a spell like that?" The possibilities were endless, and horrifying. "And it might not even work—if she's bound here by a spell from the grimoire, the magic could refuse to act against itself."

"Or it could be the only magic powerful enough to stand a chance," Gabriel countered. "It has to be worth a try."

"It's not. We'd be idiots to use it without knowing anything about how it works. For all we know, once you use it, you're bound to it forever. What if that's how your family's curse started?"

Gabriel's chin lifted stubbornly. "Then I suppose it's a good thing I'm already cursed. Using it shouldn't affect me."

That was so far from reassuring, they weren't even in the same zip code. "Do you not remember what happened the last time you messed with that magic?" Miles would never forget the shadows slinking up Gabriel's skin, his gasps of agony. "The second you open that door, it'll slip in and take you over."

"That's a risk I'm willing to take." Miles didn't like the way Gabriel said that, the hungry way his gaze roved over the page. The whole direction of this conversation made Miles uneasy.

"I think it's time for a break."

Gabriel glanced up, annoyance creasing his features. "We're in the middle of a discussion."

"And we can continue to discuss it. *Later*, when I know if

you're just being reckless, or if the grimoire is pushing you to use it."

A beat of loaded silence crawled by, Gabriel's throat flexing like he was swallowing down retorts.

"Of course." He closed the book deliberately, then held it out for Miles. His hand trembled. "Here."

He let Miles take it without a fight, as if to prove he could. The second it was out of his grasp, he sagged back, color leeching from his face.

Miles reached for him—then caught himself and pulled back. "Are you okay?"

Gabriel waved him off. "Fine. It… sneaks up on me. I don't even feel it until it's gone."

"What's it like?"

"Like it's taking a piece of me with it. Like I need to do whatever it takes to get it back."

Miles tossed the wretched thing onto the table. "I wish we didn't have to use it. I want to throw it in the nearest fire."

Gabriel flinched, then looked surprised. "Oh. I think it's compelling me to feel a degree of protectiveness over it."

"And that doesn't worry you?"

"It's a necessary evil."

Understatement of the year. The second it stopped being necessary, Miles was ripping it apart with his bare hands and flushing the scraps down the nearest toilet.

A thump sounded over their heads.

"Burglar, or ghost?" Gabriel asked.

"Fifty-fifty." Miles leaped to his feet. "I'll go check it out. Don't touch the book while I'm gone."

9

If there was a burglar lurking around, Miles lost the element of surprise the moment he stepped on the creaking stairs.

"Is anyone up here?" he called, scanning the open games room at the top, with a giant TV, controllers spread across the coffee table, and a mini-fridge sitting beside the overstuffed couch. "Do you want to talk?"

The lights overhead flickered. Miles's skin prickled as the temperature took a nosedive.

He followed the chill to the bedroom at the end of the hall. It had to be one of the owners' kids', the walls painted a dusty green where they weren't covered in video game and superhero posters, a narrow bed pushed into the corner and toys littering the floor.

In the middle of the room, a ghost appeared.

Miles had been right—it was a kid, a young boy dressed in a pair of blue dinosaur pajamas. His hair was messy like he'd recently rolled out of bed, cheeks round and ears sticking out. The edges of him were faded, blurring into the wall behind him. Judging by his clothes, he hadn't been dead long.

"Hey." Miles kept his voice low, not wanting to scare the

kid off. He already looked pretty spooked, arms wrapped tightly around a ratty, stuffed brown dog. "Hey there. What's your name?"

"*Jake.*" His voice was the tail-end of an echo, fading as soon as it started.

"Nice to meet you, Jake. I'm Miles."

"*How can you talk to me?*" he demanded suspiciously. "*No one ever hears me.*"

"I've got a special gift. I'm psychic. Do you know what that means?" Miles felt intimidating looming over the poor kid, so he sat down casually, crossing his legs.

Jake shook his head and crept a step closer.

"It means I can talk to ghosts." Lots of ghost kids didn't understand the implications of that. "Do you get what that means?"

"*I know I'm dead, if that's what you're getting at,*" the kid replied sullenly. "*I'm not stupid.*"

"Sorry." Chagrined, Miles asked, "Do your parents still live here?" He doubted it—if you were worried you had a ghost, a deceased kid was a pretty big thing to forget to mention.

"*No. They left me here.*" Overhead, the bulbs dimmed to almost nothing. The yellow striped curtains fluttered. "*They forgot about me. I don't think they love me anymore because I died.*"

Miles took it back. He'd face a murderous poltergeist any day. This kid being stuck here proved that the universe was capable of incomprehensible cruelty.

"No, Jake, they just… they didn't know you were still here, or they never would've left you. I bet they moved because they love you too much. Being here and missing you so badly probably made them sad."

Jake nodded, but his chin was wobbling. He looked so small in the darkness of the room. "*I don't want to be here anymore. I miss my mom and dad and Boots.*"

"Who's Boots?"

"*My dog. He's brown with floppy ears and he snores when he sleeps.*"

"He sounds awesome. It must be hard, being here without him." This was usually the point in the night where he could call it quits and let his dad know the haunting was legit. But it seemed wrong to leave Jake like this. "You know, you're not going to be stuck here forever. You can… move on. To somewhere you might see your parents and Boots again."

"*Like their new house?*"

Miles wanted so desperately to lie, but Jake deserved better than that. "No, not their new house. I honestly don't know where you'd go. A nice place, I hope, safe and warm. That's better than being trapped here, right?" He motioned to the room that had to be a nightmare—full of toys Jake couldn't play with, a bed he couldn't lie down on, a window he couldn't open.

He wished he could provide something more comforting, but Miles didn't know what he believed was waiting for the dead. It was easier not to think about it. He was in a business he would never fully understand, dancing around an answer he wouldn't get until the day he himself died.

"*I guess,*" Jake agreed dubiously. "*But I've tried to leave before, and it doesn't work.*"

"You just need a little help."

Before he could continue, the stairs squeaked. Gabriel's voice floated up. "Miles? Were you attacked by a burglar? Do I need to perform a daring rescue?"

93

Very funny.

"I'm fine," Miles called back. "I found our ghost. Come say hi."

"Do I have to?" But footsteps climbed towards the second floor.

"*Who's that?*" Jake asked, clutching his stuffed dog and flickering in and out of sight.

"It's okay. This is my friend, Gabriel. He can see you too."

Gabriel stepped into the room, his eyes finding Miles, then Jake. The corners of his mouth turned down. "You were right about the childish energy."

"Eventually, you'll stop doubting my skills." He noticed Gabriel's empty hands. "Where's the grimoire?"

"Back in its box. It didn't like being ignored." He sat down beside Miles, copying his crossed legs. "Now that you know he's here, what's next?"

"He can hear you." Miles gave Jake an exaggerated eye roll. "We were talking about how to help him move on."

"*I don't want to scare the people who live here anymore,*" Jake added with a guilty look. "*I don't mean to. Sometimes I get upset when they can't see me, and things happen. But not on purpose.*"

"We know," Miles reassured him gently.

Gabriel was watching Jake with a puzzled expression, like a riddle he couldn't solve. Ghost kids were pretty rare, and never failed to fill Miles with a sense of wrongness. Naively, he wanted to believe children were too young to know true trauma or hatred or spite, but here was proof otherwise. It was the worst example of how rotten and unfair the world could be.

"Do you want me to try and find your parents?" Miles offered Jake. "I could tell them you've moved on—"

"*No*," he insisted.

That made Miles pause. Such a quick reaction would normally make him wonder about the circumstances of Jake's death, but he missed his parents, and spoke about them with love.

"Are you sure? They'll want to know if—"

"*I said no!*"

A wave of energy surged from Jake. The bedroom shook, plaster dust raining down as the walls rattled and toys fell from the shelves. Miles tried to get to his feet, but the floor bucked beneath him, sending him tumbling into Gabriel. They landed in a heap of flailing limbs as the bedroom door slammed closed. Overhead, the low hum of the lights became a high-pitched whine.

Miles swore, pulling Gabriel's face into his shoulder and ducking his own head a split second before all the lightbulbs exploded. Shards of glass rained down on them as the bedroom plunged into darkness.

Silence settled over the room, still and heavy. Miles waited a moment, ears ringing and mouth full of an acrid, burnt toast taste. Gabriel was a tense line against him, his hair tickling the bare skin of Miles's throat. Nothing else moved.

"You okay?" he murmured, pulling back enough to check Gabriel's face. This close, Miles could only take him in in slivers, fragments of beauty. The arc of his lashes. The dip in the bow of his upper lip. The jump of his pulse beneath the thin skin where his jaw met his throat.

"Fine." Gabriel reached up and brushed glass out of Miles's hair, fingertips slipping down to his face. His touch was an electric shock. Miles went still as he lingered, thumb brushing so lightly it was almost imperceptible.

Unable to resist, Miles leaned into his hand with a relieved exhale. Gabriel's expression shuttered, slamming a wall between them, and he jerked away.

"*I'm sorry*," Jake said, making Miles jump. His knees were tucked, stuffed dog cradled close as he watched them remorsefully. "*I didn't mean to.*"

"It's okay, that was my fault." Miles climbed to his feet, glass crunching beneath his shoes, and offered Gabriel a tentative hand. It went ignored, Gabriel looking everywhere but at him. "I won't find your parents if you don't want me to."

There was a lamp on the desk; he turned and hit the button, dim yellow filling the bedroom and revealing how Jake's chin wobbled. "*When they talk about me, all they do is fight and cry. I want them to forget about me so they can be happy again.*"

Miles's heart plummeted so fast, it made him sick. He swayed for a moment, dizzy from the uncertainty of what he could say to make it better.

Gabriel stepped forward and sank to a crouch in front of Jake. "They're never going to forget you," he said. "Even if they could, it wouldn't make them happy. That's not how missing someone works."

Jake ducked his head. "*That's not fair*," he mumbled into his stuffed dog's fur.

"It's not. Death is rarely fair for the ones who get left behind."

An unexpected lump formed in Miles's throat. "Your parents love you. But you're gone, and that means part of them will always be sad. They're always going to miss you and wish you were still here. But it might make it easier for them, make it hurt a little less, if I can tell them you're at peace."

If any part of them had suspected their son was still here,

they'd always wonder. Always worry. Never find closure.

"Not knowing is the worst," he told Jake. "Wondering and worrying when they're gone, not knowing where they are or if they're okay, it's… it eats you up." He could feel the heat of Gabriel's stare on the side of his face. "Let me tell them they don't have to worry anymore."

Jake hesitated, then nodded. "*Okay. And Boots too. He was really sad when I died. I don't think he has anyone to play ball with anymore.*"

"I'll make sure Boots knows too."

Miles's parents would be able to find them—even if the current owners of the house didn't know anything about the previous ones, you could find out anything online. And his mom was persistent.

Gabriel straightened, turning to face Miles. There was a crease pinched between his eyebrows. "Can I talk to you in the hall?"

Miles gave Jake a reassuring smile. "We'll be right back."

The lights were still on, but Jake's surge of ghostly energy hadn't been contained to the bedroom—a few framed photos hung crooked on the wall, and one was on the floor.

"Are you okay?"

"We need to release him," Gabriel commanded, his voice low. "Like we did with Florence."

Miles blinked, caught off guard. "We—I know. But this was supposed to be information gathering. I don't have any supplies for a ritual." He'd already decided he couldn't leave Jake to wait for his dad. But his backpack was full of tools for communication and—prepared for the worst-case scenario—protection. There was nothing for releasing a spirit. He might have to run all the way home.

"Then we'll get them. Or use something else." Gabriel sucked in a low hiss through his teeth. "We're not leaving him here. It's wrong."

The jagged edge to his words made Miles stop and really take him in: the tension coiled in his jaw, his balled fists, his lashes damp with unshed tears. Like a single touch could shatter him into a thousand pieces across the floor.

A rotten feeling curdled in Miles, suspiciously close to shame. He'd forgotten that Gabriel hadn't done this before. He'd called him up to see Jake without thinking about the fact he wasn't much younger than Bram.

"We won't." Instinct made him want to reach for Gabriel, but he knew it wouldn't be welcome. "I'll see what I can find here. Will you talk to him"—he nodded back at where Jake was waiting for them—"and make sure he's okay with us doing this?"

Gabriel nodded jerkily and slipped away.

When Miles returned ten minutes later with an assortment of supplies, Jake and Gabriel were talking on the edge of the bed. There was a timid smile on Jake's face as he fidgeted with his stuffed dog.

Gabriel spotted Miles hovering in the doorway and murmured something to Jake, leaving the bed to come over. He seemed more composed now.

"We good to go?"

"Yes. He was apprehensive at first, but after we spoke, he agreed to let us try."

"What did you say to him?"

Gabriel shrugged, lacking any nonchalance. "That he shouldn't have to stay here another day. That he could trust us to help him." His gaze dipped to the floor. "That if it was my brother, I wouldn't want him to wait."

"Don't ever feel bad for caring," Miles said softly.

"He should never have been left here in the first place," Gabriel snapped, bristling like an agitated cat. "Forgotten and alone."

"I know. We'll help him, don't worry." Miles mustered up a smile and lifted the bag of supplies he'd managed to gather. "This is about to be the jankiest ritual of all time, but it should work."

"It will work."

Miles wasn't sure if Gabriel's conviction was because he had faith in Miles, or because he needed it to so badly that he refused to accept any other outcome.

He gave Jake a broad grin. "You must be ready to get out of here, huh?"

The kid nodded. *"Can you really do it?"*

"I'll try my best. I have a good feeling."

"Is it going to hurt?"

"No." This ritual was different from the banishing one they'd used on Florence. Gentler. The equivalent of holding a door open for the spirit to walk through, instead of stomping on their toes, kicking them in the knees, and shoving them through headfirst. "I promise it won't hurt at all."

Jake visibly relaxed, knocking his feet against the side of the bed.

"Okay, let's do this." Miles dumped the supplies onto the mattress, not missing the critical look Gabriel gave them. "Hey, I warned you I'd have to make do with what I could find."

"I heard you, but"—he picked up a small glass bottle—"is the Italian seasoning really necessary?"

"It's the only thing I could find with sage in it."

It wasn't the only compromise he'd had to make. Instead of moon-purified water, he had water from the fridge purifier. Overly expensive essential oils that weren't even organic. Pink-handled kitchen scissors, instead of the Warren family heirloom shears.

They'd have to do. The only thing working in their favor was that this ritual mostly relied on the ghost being willing, and Jake was totally on board.

"This works better if we have something that belonged to the spirit," Miles murmured to Gabriel. "Since we don't have… you know." The body or bones. But there wasn't anything of Jake's left in the house.

Over their shoulders, Jake whispered to his toy dog about leaving.

"You're sure this won't hurt him?" Gabriel asked, leaning in close so he wouldn't be overheard.

"I'm sure. This ritual is different from Florence's… no salt, no fire, no force necessary."

"What about the scissors? Those aren't the friendliest tool."

"You wouldn't say that if you saw how dull they were. But they're just supposed to cut his ties to this world."

He poured the water into a plastic bowl and set it on the desk, carefully avoiding the expensive-looking keyboard. The Italian seasoning went in next, followed by a few drops of eucalyptus and lavender oil. He'd prefer angelica or myrrh—for releasing a spirit and healing their pain, they packed the most punch—but neither was a common find in scent-focused essential oil packs.

Dipping the wilted sprig of rosemary he'd gotten from a

bundle of herbs in the fridge—hopefully he wasn't ruining anyone's dinner plans—he swirled everything around to mix it.

Jake gasped.

"What?" Gabriel asked sharply. "Does it hurt?"

The kid shook his head. *"It feels weird. Like a tug in my tummy."*

That meant the ritual was working.

"Okay." Miles dropped the rosemary into the water and grabbed the kitchen scissors. "If this works, it's the last part."

Jake sucked in like he was about to jump in a pool, small chest swelling in his dinosaur pajamas. *"I'm ready."*

Whatever was waiting for this kid in the afterlife, Miles hoped he'd find peace.

"Goodbye, Jake," Gabriel said.

Miles held the scissors over the swirling bowl and gradually brought the blades together. There was a slight moment of resistance, like something solid hovering between them, before they closed with a *snick*.

The air prickled with electricity, the lamp flared, and when Miles looked up, Jake was gone.

Gabriel's shoulders slumped.

They cleaned in silence—Miles picked up broken glass scattered across the carpet, making a mental note to have his parents warn the owners before their kids ran back up here, while Gabriel gathered the supplies. Down in the kitchen, he rinsed lingering herb flecks from the bowl and put it on the drying rack.

By unspoken agreement, they packed up to leave—it was late, and felt wrong to linger. Miles checked the containment box before shoving it into his bag, making sure the grimoire hadn't grown legs and scurried away while they were gone.

"Sorry we didn't have much reading time," he told Gabriel as they padded out onto the front porch. The neighborhood was hushed, illuminated by porch lights as crunchy leaves blew down the pavement. One house had carved pumpkins on their steps, grinning ghoulishly across at them. "I guess this was kind of a bust."

"That seems to be a trend with us." Gabriel sounded more tired than critical. He pulled out his phone and sent a quick text. "Edmund's on his way. I'll see you tomorrow."

Miles had been expecting the dismissal. "I'll wait with you," he offered, locking the door and tucking the key back under the mat. "You might need backup if the neighborhood watchwoman shows up again."

He sat on the top step, Gabriel reluctantly joining to watch the unmoving street.

They'd done a good thing tonight. Despite all the other worries rattling around in his head and the chill radiating from Gabriel, Miles let that warm him.

"What I said to Jake was true." Miles tilted his head back to look at the night sky. It was too cloudy for the stars to shine through. "Not knowing *is* the worst. When you were gone, I was losing my mind. And even though you're back now, I still feel in the dark."

Gabriel was silent, wind rustling the bushes lining the walkway.

"All I want to know is what's going on in your head." Miles sighed, the whole day weighing on him. "If you want space, tell me instead of just pushing me away. If there's something I can do for you, ask me and I'll do it. If you've…

changed your mind about your feelings for me, be honest." A self-conscious laugh tumbled out of him. "I'm not some self-centered dick who won't take no for an answer. And you don't have to be scared I'll leave you to the curse because you turned me down. I hope you know me better than that."

The words were hard to get out, each one resisting. They felt too revealing, too confrontational, stripping him bare in the most vulnerable way. But he needed Gabriel to know he cared enough to be hurt. Enough that he wouldn't let hurt control him.

"Knowing what's in my head isn't going to change anything."

God, he was so stubborn. "Having an answer is always going to be better than worrying about every possibility."

Gabriel stared resolutely across the street at the glowing pumpkins.

Despite his determination to keep calm, a swell of frustration rose in Miles. "Is this how it's going to be between us now?"

"Maybe it's how it should be."

Surely he didn't believe that, or he never would've kissed Miles. Never would've opened himself up in the first place. "If you're going to lie to me, at least look me in the face."

When Gabriel did, it was impossible to read his eyes with his back to the dim porch light. "What an uncharacteristically self-assured response. Now that I think about it"—a razor-thin smirk curled his lips—"you've been rather presumptuous in assuming this is all about you. Did this sudden arrogance grow while I was away?"

Miles gaped, face heating with indignation. "I'm not—of course it's about me, you wouldn't be such a *jerk* if it—"

He caught himself. Gabriel was trying to pull him into an argument and fluster him. Combat was safe, familiar territory for him. When pushed, he bit back and relished any blood he drew. "Nice try, but I'm not going to fight with you."

"That's a shame," Gabriel deadpanned. "Tonight might've finally gotten interesting."

If he was trying to be exhausting, he was doing a great job. But he'd forgotten one key thing—Miles lived with two preteen sisters and *Charlee*. It was going to take more than a few jabs to break him.

A shiny silver car pulled up to the curb with a purr, and Edmund rolled down his window. Despite the late hour, he looked wide awake, face split in a cheeky grin. "Look at me, always interrupting your cutesy little moments. Did you two have a good date?"

Miles winced and Gabriel's smirk was replaced by his trusty scowl. "You're always interrupting because you're never invited. Perhaps you should ask yourself why."

Edmund put a gloved hand to his chest. "Ouch. That one almost hurt."

Miles expected Edmund to peel out as Gabriel climbed into the passenger seat, but he leaned farther out the window.

"Hey." The usual playful look was gone from his face. "Thank you. For finding him. And bringing him back."

Gabriel muttered something too low for Miles to make out. Edmund ignored him. "If you need anything, don't hesitate," he continued. A dog barked down the street, an inquisitive *woof* quickly followed by its owner calling it back inside. Miles would bet one of the neighbors had already speed-dialed the HOA to complain. "I owe you one."

Pleasant surprise bloomed in Miles. "No, you don't. But thanks anyway."

Edmund's huffed-out laugh was almost identical to Gabriel's. "You might regret that. I'm sure my brother hasn't mentioned it out of petty jealousy, but I'm a man of many talents. You never know when one might come in handy."

Miles didn't doubt it.

He waited for them to pull away, Edmund's cherry-red brake lights disappearing around the corner and into the night, before climbing into Charlee's car and starting the long drive home.

10

"Hey!" Emily settled beside Miles at the courtyard table, making him jump. Her pink coat was so bright, he didn't know how she'd managed to sneak up on him. "Where's Gabriel?"

She waved goodbye to the group of girls she'd left— probably her soccer teammates—who gave him curious looks.

Miles mustered up a passable smile. "Running late, I guess." Intentionally, he was sure.

Emily studied him. "Everything okay?"

It was a more loaded question than she realized. "Yeah, Gabriel's just… been in a mood."

"Did you guys have a fight?"

"Nah, not really. I think he's struggling with all this curse stuff, the new premonition, me not calling it quits… take your pick." He couldn't mention the romantic limbo he was currently caught in. A girl walked by with a tray of coffees, the rich smell wafting across the courtyard. "Gabriel internalizes when he's having a hard time, so he's being more distant than usual."

Emily's brown eyes softened with sympathy. "That's a lot for him to manage at once. Leaving had to be tough, and it didn't even pay off. He probably feels like a failure for not finding what he was looking for at Nadia's. He doesn't seem like the type to brush that off easily."

God, maybe she was right. Maybe Gabriel was right too—Miles *was* being presumptuous by assuming this was all about him. Lashing out because he didn't want Miles's compassion or understanding was a very Gabriel thing to do.

"He's not." Miles traced a Sharpie heart on the icy tabletop with his finger. "And he's already blaming himself for the new premonition."

"Even if he wasn't feeling guilty, it's really fresh," Emily noted. "Don't forget you had time to come to terms with Gabriel's death before you really knew him. He distracted himself with denial and his quest to find a solution at Nadia's, and now he has to face the reality you might really die. Anyone would be having a hard time."

Showing up at school this morning, Miles had admittedly been feeling grumpy. Part of him wanted to be a jerk right back to Gabriel, give him what he wanted, but he knew he wasn't cut out for it. Gabriel would probably laugh in his face the first time he tried to snap back.

Now he felt rotten for even considering it. A stupid lump ached in his throat. Seeing something in his face, Emily reached over and patted his hand.

"Am I interrupting something?" Gabriel appeared over Emily's shoulder, collar flipped up against the morning chill, making him look like a disgruntled turtle. His expression darkened further as a couple paraded by in matching plaid flannel. Pajama Day was here.

Miles swallowed down his emotions, knowing Gabriel would hate the pity if he picked up on it.

"Nope," Emily chirped. "We're just talking over the

game plan. Brainstorming curse-busting ideas."

"I didn't realize you were involved now," he said coldly as he sat down across from her.

"She helped save your ass even though you were rude to her," Miles pointed out. "She gets to be part of the dream team."

"There was no saving. I was never in any trouble. And I don't seem to recall ever agreeing to be part of a team."

Miles opened his mouth but Emily beat him to it. "It's cool," she told Gabriel with a shrug. "I don't have to be here if you don't want me. I'm just surprised. I thought you'd be happy for more help to save Miles."

A beat passed.

Gabriel scowled down at the table. "Fine. Join us if you want to so badly."

"We don't have much to do right now," Miles explained. A gust of wind sent the flag at the front of the school snapping, a kid on the stairs jumping up to chase after a runaway granola bar wrapper. "Just reading through the grimoire to see if we can find the curse."

"That's not true," Gabriel countered. "We're going to try and summon Jocelyn."

Miles nearly choked. "No, we're not! We talked about this last night—it's too dangerous."

"Actually, you said we could discuss it once I was away from the grimoire's influence. But there's nothing to discuss. Jocelyn is the key to ending all of this."

"Even if the ritual worked, she's not going to tell us anything. Did you forget how unhelpful she is?"

"The situation is different now. I can convince her to talk."

Because Miles's life was at stake? It was flattering that

Gabriel thought that was worth something, but Miles doubted Jocelyn would agree.

Gabriel kept going before he could argue. "Releasing her spirit could still unravel the entire future she foresaw. If she's not in that tomb, perhaps we won't be either."

Desperation or optimism, Miles could understand either as a motive. But that didn't make it a good idea. If Emily was right and he was feeling guilty or like a failure, it could be pushing him to set aside logic and take an unnecessary risk. "You know I'm all for finding a different path, but not if we're going to get ourselves killed in the process. That kinda defeats the purpose."

"No one is going to die using the grimoire. You're being dramatic." Gabriel crossed his arms, glaring at a girl in a fluffy pink robe crossing the grass. "When you weigh risk versus reward, the outcome is clear to me. But at the end of the day, she's my ancestor. It's my call."

"That's not a thing!"

"It is now."

"Why?" A car honked in the parking lot, the shrill punch of noise making Miles grind his teeth. He had to forcibly relax before he could speak. "You know we're going to find Jocelyn eventually, she's in the premonition. We have the grimoire, we're working on the curse—"

Emily had been letting them bicker, but now she cleared her throat to interrupt. "Hypothetically, how would we summon her? Is there a way we could make the ritual less dangerous?"

"It's in the grimoire, which means it's black magic," Miles explained. "There's no changing that."

"It's a simple spell," Gabriel answered, like Miles hadn't

spoken. He pulled a notebook from his bag, flipped to a page and showed them. "And I have the ingredients here."

It was a short list.

- Sap from the manchineel tree
- Queen of poisons (fresh)
- Baby teeth of a firstborn son
- Nails from a tainted coffin
- Bone of a black cat

Miles scanned it dubiously. In the distance, a leaf blower whined as the custodian started his daily sweep along the school sidewalks. "You did this from memory? Are you sure it's right?"

Gabriel scoffed, like he'd never heard a more ridiculous question. "Of course I'm sure. I told you, I have near eidetic memory."

Well, excuse him for asking. "I don't even know what most of these things are. And we can't do the ritual without them."

"We could ask Nadia," Emily suggested, then bit her lip when Miles shot her a betrayed look. "Sorry. Gabriel has a point—if we could end things with one spell, we should do it. Charlee and I can come. If we're all there watching each other's backs, it doesn't get much safer than that."

She hadn't been around the grimoire. She didn't know what it was like. But the thought of being able to get rid of it so soon was tempting. Life could get back on track.

He and Gabriel could get back on track.

"And what if something goes wrong? What if the magic takes one of us over, or something evil comes out of the book?"

"We'd have to all agree the moment something feels odd or doesn't go according to plan, we stop and regroup," Emily said. She made it sound simple. Easy.

"Every plan we make has a risk." Gabriel's voice was softer than it had been in days as he met Miles's eyes. "At least with this one, we won't be walking in unaware. If it keeps us away from that tomb, we should try."

It had to come down to risk versus reward, and living without the Grim Reaper breathing down their necks was an enticing prize. Miles might be able to sleep through the night without seeing Gabriel dying in his dreams again and again.

His resolve wavered. "We're only doing this if we have the right stuff—we got lucky with Jake. I'm not giving the grimoire any chance to screw us over. And if Charlee agrees," he added. She'd tell him if this was a terrible idea.

Gabriel gave him Nadia's number. Miles sent a picture of the ingredient list with a quick explanation. If Nadia couldn't help, they were out of luck—there was no way Miles's mom kept a stash of baby teeth next to the dried rose petals.

He supposed he should be relieved there wasn't anything worse on the list, like a live kitten sacrifice or fresh baby's blood.

Gabriel pulled a face when Miles sent the text. "Don't get too close to Nadia. They might stab you in the back."

"Let it go." A brave squirrel scampered by them, beady eyes fixed on the box of doughnuts a tall, red-haired guy had just opened on the table beside theirs. "They were trying to save you from yourself. How many more days would you've spent in that freezing backroom if we hadn't come?"

"That's not the point."

"If it makes you feel any better," Emily offered, waving at a pair of girls in matching polka-dot pajamas, "I'd already figured out where you were. A bus ghost ratted you out."

Gabriel blinked. "The ghost of a—"

"No, no. A ghost *haunting* a bus. The one you took to Sage and Starlight."

A disgusted noise escaped Gabriel. "And I thought I was unlucky."

"Speaking of, how was riding a public bus for the first time?" Miles teased with a grin.

"Enlightening. My chauffeur deserves a raise."

Miles laughed, the sound mingling with the bell as it rang, echoing across the campus. Around them, everyone started gathering their things to head inside.

There was nothing to do now but wait to hear from Nadia. Miles wasn't thrilled about the potential risks, but he had to admit it did feel nice to have a plan again. Even if it was a wildly dangerous, borderline suicidal one.

During the last chunk of English, the class was given free rein to partner up and study for tomorrow's test. Chairs screeched and chatter filled the air as Gabriel got up to drag his seat to Miles's desk. A cluster of girls gave him hopeful looks until he smoothly sidestepped them. Their deflation was simultaneous and immediate.

"Did you hear back from Nadia?" Gabriel questioned. He had to scoot in close to avoid blocking the aisle, twisting in his chair so their knees didn't touch. Miles was starting to feel like he had the plague.

"Uh…" Miles fumbled getting his phone out of his pocket. "Yeah. A few minutes ago."

> this is the wildest summoning spell ive seen
> its badass
> i should have most of this stuff let me check
> my stock

"They're going to see what they've got. Fair warning, if they charge us, I'm making you cover it. I'm officially out of cash."

"I'll settle it." Gabriel was unconcerned in that unfair way rich people always were.

Miles sent back a quick message.

> Thanks… you're a lifesaver

> ive got everything except fresh queen of
> poisons but that should be easy enough for
> you to get
> youll have to come to me though im running
> the shop all day

"Do you know what queen of poisons is?"

Gabriel pulled out his own phone. "It's either a murder mystery," he shared a moment later, scrolling through Google, "a lipstick, or another name for wolfsbane."

"Gotta be the lipstick," Miles joked. His mom had a small fenced-off garden in the backyard where she grew her more dangerous herbs and plants—he was pretty sure wolfsbane was one of them, a few purple blooms still lingering from summer.

113

Before answering Nadia, Miles fired a text to Charlee. He'd sent her one earlier laying out the plan and—he wasn't sure if he was relieved or disappointed—she'd agreed it was worth a shot.

> How do you feel about driving to seattle for summoning supplies... nadia has them ready to go so you'd be in and out. Unless you want to stay for a bit

He flipped absentmindedly through his textbook while he waited, mostly to keep his hands busy. Gabriel didn't bother, fixating on the posters tacked up along the back wall. Neither of them spoke.

When Charlee finally responded, Miles could feel the prickle of defensiveness in her words.

> What's that supposed to mean?

> Nothing... just saying. Can I tell them you'll stop by

She deserved a little ribbing after all the shit she'd given him—and continued to give him—about Gabriel.

"What did they say?" Gabriel asked, leaning in to see the screen.

> Fine. I'll leave in a minute. And I'm not staying

"It's Charlee." Miles sent her back an obnoxious flood of heart emojis. "Nadia has everything we need, so she's going

114

to run over to the shop. As long as I can get the wolfsbane, we're good to go."

"Tonight?"

He bit back a groan. These late nights were going to start catching up with him in an ugly way. Uglier than the dark bags under his eyes and perpetual sleepy yawns. "I guess we'll have to. Another midnight adventure at the cemetery... awesome."

"As long as no ghosts try to kill us, it'll be an improvement on the last one."

"Did you just 'look on the bright side' me? Who are you and what have you done with Gabriel?"

Gabriel wasn't amused, scoffing under his breath. "Nothing will go wrong."

"Right, because the monster in that tunnel was a figment of my imagination."

"I'm certain that was an unfortunate one-time anomaly."

"I'll remember you said that when another one shows up and tries to eat us." Miles hesitated, choosing his next words carefully. "You know... there's no pressure to do this, right? If you're second-guessing or worried about using the grimoire? We can just keep searching for the curse and go from there."

"Why would there be pressure?" Gabriel asked bluntly.

"I..." This wasn't the time or place to bring up his guilt, reassure him he's not responsible for saving Miles's life. "I just want to make sure you know we can call it quits anytime. And that we have other options."

Gabriel twisted the button of his cuff. "I'm aware, and I have no intentions of throwing away our best chance."

Miles swapped back to Nadia, letting them know Charlee would be on her way.

perfect
help me woo your cousin and ill let you keep
the compass heart

       I don't want it... I literally can't wait to give it
                back to you

fine
help me woo your cousin because youre a
romantic at heart
we might be soulmates you dont know

"Nadia's seriously got a thing for Charlee," he told Gabriel, relieved to be talking about someone else's love life. "Think I should warn them that they're playing with fire?"

Gabriel's nose wrinkled. "They already met her. They know what they're getting into. At this point, they deserve to get burned."

"You're just bitter they kicked you out."

His answering silence said it all.

       Charlee isn't really the type to get wooed

    give me something to work with
    pretty please
    with a hefty discount for your supplies on top

Damn it. Miles was a sucker for a deal and, if he was being honest, he *was* a romantic at heart. Charlee never had to know.

> She has a mega sweet tooth... the way to her
> heart is through sugar. But that's all I'm telling
> you

youre a real one
good luck with whatever nasty magic youre
working tonight

The end-of-period bell rang overhead.

"Don't forget to finish *Lord of the Flies* by tomorrow," Mr. Keller called as everyone went back to their desks and packed up. "We're starting Shakespeare next, so get ready for group reading."

The class collectively groaned. Beside Miles, Gabriel stiffened.

"Shakespeare doesn't have to mean *Romeo and Juliet*," Miles pointed out swiftly. Gabriel's words from before he'd disappeared echoed in his head—*it's been a comfort to know that my time wasn't up yet. That I still had at least one more day because you hadn't made a terrible joke about Shakespeare*—and nausea took over.

Gabriel snatched up his binder. "Of course it does."

Miles packed more slowly. "Really, it doesn't mean anything. We know the future has at least a few potential paths. We shouldn't treat any of them like solid fact. And it's not like the second after I make that joke, we'll be teleported into the tomb to die. We've still got time."

He was trying to be optimistic, but it did feel a bit like the finish line had suddenly sprung up right in front of him. And it led right off the edge of a cliff.

"Who knows," he continued, slinging his bag over his

117

shoulder. "Maybe your vision takes place after we both survive."

Gabriel gave him an incredulous look.

Yeah. Miles didn't believe it either.

"Mr. Warren!" Mr. Keller called from his desk, a wooden monstrosity tucked into the back corner of the room. "Stay behind for a minute."

Nerves clenched Miles's lungs. Had they been overheard? Or—more likely and potentially more terribly—did he want to chew Miles out for all his recent missing assignments?

"Go ahead," Miles mumbled to Gabriel. "I'll see you in Pre-Calc."

Mr. Keller settled back in his chair, fingers steepled over his thick middle. Miles liked him, liked the way he didn't talk to his students like they were stupid kids, which was going to make his disapproval that much worse. He was a cool teacher, but Miles doubted he'd accept ghosts and death premonitions as an excuse for not doing homework.

"This'll just take a minute," Mr. Keller declared once the rest of the students had left. "I'm sure I don't need to tell you that your grades have been dropping."

Miles winced. "I know, I'm sorry. I've had… family stuff going on lately. I guess I'm not managing my time very well, but I'll try to do better."

Mr. Keller considered him for a long moment. "You're a good student, and from how strong you started this year, I know you care about your grade. You show up, you pay attention, and that's more important to me than finished homework." He sighed, leather chair creaking as he leaned forward. "But I can't make an exception and let you turn in your assignments late. It's not fair to my other students.

If you want to get your grade back up, you'll have to work for it."

"I know, and I'm sorry. I'm just having a hard time keeping up. I'm hoping once everything calms down, I can get back on track."

"I get it," Mr. Keller said kindly. He lifted his glasses up to rest in his salt and pepper hair, rubbing the bridge of his nose. "I see it every day with my team—most of them struggle to keep their grades up when they're practicing after school every day of the week." He coached the football team, a choice Miles had always thought was out of character for an unflappable English teacher. "What I can offer right now, to help give your grade a boost until life simmers down, is an extra credit opportunity."

That would be great—if Miles had any free time. Or the mental energy. It was impossible to focus on analyzing the themes of class warfare in *Animal Farm* while worrying about not getting murdered.

"What's the extra credit?" he hedged, hoping he didn't sound ungrateful.

"The homecoming committee needs some serious help for Spirit Week. They've tried hitting up my team for volunteers, but we're too busy with the game. If you want to stay after school and help out, I'll count it as extra credit. It won't be a lot, but it'll keep your grade from sinking any lower for the next week or two."

It was generous of him, which made Miles feel worse that he was going to have to say no. He was too swamped already, trying to create excuses to get out of the house for grimoire reading with Gabriel that his mom would buy—

Hang on.

This might work. He needed a believable reason, one that wouldn't make his mom suspicious. What was more legit than a school assignment?

"I'd love to help." Miles aimed for enthusiastic despite cringing at the thought of glittery banners and balloon arches. "Thank you, I appreciate it. Can I give you my mom's email so you can let her know? She's a bit paranoid about me getting home right after school. Stranger danger and all that."

He must've sold it, because Mr. Keller handed him a pad of paper and pen to jot down his mom's email.

"I'll let the homecoming committee know to expect you after school tomorrow," he told Miles once he was done. "Show up and help out. I won't monitor you, we'll keep this to the honor system, okay?"

"Okay. Thanks again."

Gabriel was waiting for him out in the hall, leaning against the wall with his arms crossed. Everyone gave him a wide berth, skirting around him like he was protected by an invisible bubble.

"You didn't have to wait."

"I'm aware." Gabriel lifted his chin towards the classroom door swinging closed behind Miles. "Is there a problem?"

"Nah. A solution, actually." They fell into step together, heading towards Pre-Calc. "But I don't think you'll like it."

11

"You know, most of my family's buried here," Miles mentioned conversationally as he helped Gabriel unload supplies from the trunk of Charlee's car. They'd parked underneath a tree bordering the Thistle Cemetery gate, deep shadows cloaking the vehicle from potential passersby. "Because we're normal people who don't have a private graveyard out back."

"I must have missed the part where I had any say in that." Gabriel pulled out the bag Charlee had brought back from Nadia's shop. It was comically cheerful, covered in colorful little cartoon cats wearing absurd hats. No one would ever guess its gruesome contents.

"I just wanted to remind you how weird it is."

"At least I won't have to compete for a spot with the rest of Thistle's dead if your premonition comes true. Perhaps I should pick one out and let Edmund know, just in case."

Jesus. "Wow, that's… disturbingly morbid."

"We're breaking into a cemetery to summon a ghost because we've seen each other die in various grisly fashions. I'm simply embracing the theme."

"Someone's cheerful tonight," Charlee muttered. She nudged Miles out of the way to dig into her trunk.

"I wasn't aware you even knew what cheer was," Gabriel snipped.

Charlee pulled a battered shovel from the depths of her car. Miles was worried she was going to whack Gabriel over the head with it, but she just gave it a considering look, then slung it over her shoulder.

"We're not digging anything up," Miles told her.

She gave him an incredulous look and slammed her trunk closed. "Never go into a cemetery without a shovel."

The groundskeepers might have something to say about that.

A tinkling bell rang out, and Emily emerged from the darkness on her purple bike. "Hey! Am I late?" She hopped off and leaned it against the trunk of the tree, adjusting her backpack. She'd taken the stealth factor of tonight very seriously, dressing head to toe in dark colors.

Charlee handed her a camping lantern. "Just in time to help us haul everything over."

"Thanks again for coming," Miles said. "You didn't have to."

"I'd never miss all the excitement."

They trekked through the creaking gate into the dark cemetery, leaving the glow of the streetlights behind. It smelled like freshly mown grass, neat lines running between the graves to guide their path. Sightless eyes of looming angels and more than one Virgin Mary watched them as they passed, pale stone turning silvery in the moonlight. Miles shivered as the midnight wind picked up, rustling dried flowers and faded wreaths placed among the headstones.

They didn't have to walk far, only until they found a tombstone wide enough to set up the ritual on. Emily put her lantern down, illuminating the engraving. Miles hoped Travis Carroll didn't mind his marker being used as a table.

They unpacked, bags crinkling and glass bottles clinking as a foggy mist crawled its way through the graves. Between that and the plummeting temperature, Miles was starting to wish he'd listened when Gabriel had protested doing the summoning ritual here. It was the safest choice—they didn't know where Jocelyn's body was, so they might as well hedge their bets by picking the place with the highest dead-body-to-square-foot ratio in Thistle—but he was seriously regretting the added creep factor now.

Once all the supplies were lined up with the few stems of wolfsbane left in Miles's mom's garden, he dug the containment box out of his backpack.

When he opened it, Emily's whole face scrunched. "What *is* that?"

"The grimoire." He removed it gingerly. "Sorry, I should've given you a heads up. It's pretty nasty."

The first time he'd shown Charlee, she'd nearly thrown herself out of his room in her haste to put distance between herself and the book. It repelled everyone it came into contact with—except Gabriel.

"That's an understatement." Emily leaned in for a closer look, visibly torn between disgust and curiosity.

Miles passed the empty box to Charlee—her job was grimoire containment duty if things started to go wrong. He hated the idea of her touching it, but she'd insisted she wasn't scared of the musty old thing. She had something to prove after it'd spooked her so badly.

When Gabriel held out his hand, Miles shook his head. "I'm going to read it."

"We agreed it would be me."

Unless Miles had blacked out, they absolutely had *not* agreed that. "It affects you worse than anyone else. The last thing—"

"I'm the one who's already cursed." Gabriel grabbed for the grimoire, and Miles dodged, nearly slipping in the damn grass.

"You *for sure* getting messed up versus me *possibly* dealing with magical repercussions… I know which is less of a risk."

Gabriel glowered. "You're delusional. Hand it over, or I'll leave right now."

Please. Like Miles was gullible enough to believe that.

"Holy shit," Charlee griped, zipping her jacket to her chin with a sharp yank. "Give it to him, Miles. This was his idea. He can deal with whatever happens."

This only made Miles more certain he was right. She didn't understand what the grimoire did to Gabriel. If there was a repeat of what had happened in the tunnels, Miles wasn't sure he could save him again.

"I don't know…" Emily twisted the end of her chestnut-brown ponytail. "Miles has a point. If it's less of a risk for him, he should do it."

That earned her the ultimate dirty look from Gabriel. "No one asked you."

"She's right. Plus, I'm the experienced one," Miles pointed out. "All sorts of things can go wrong during your first ritual."

"Miles." Gabriel caught his gaze, hooking him and refusing to let go. "We both know if this goes badly, the magic is going to come for me, no matter who reads from the grimoire. I need you free of distractions if that happens."

He didn't say it, but Miles could see it in his eyes. *You promised you'd have my back. Prove it.*

"Fine," he caved. "But be careful."

"I will."

Gabriel took the grimoire, flipping a few pages in as Emily lifted the camping lantern for him. Where the light caught Gabriel's hair, it gleamed like a crow's wing.

<u>Heed My Call</u>
Spell to summon living or dead, spirit or flesh

Offerings:
- Sap from the manchineel tree
- Queen of poisons (fresh)
- Baby teeth of a firstborn son
- Nails from a tainted coffin
- Bone of a black cat

Lay the offerings before you on a piece of linen. Add parchment written with the name of the intended. Wet offerings with the blood of the summoner. Gather into a bundle and tie linen closed with twine. Burn until extinguished.
    Best performed at witching hour on nights of a waxing moon.

The things this ritual required were so far from what Miles typically used. It was grotesque.

He scanned the inky sky. The witching hour wasn't for a while still, but they had the waxing moon for a little extra oomph.

"What's the best way to approach the blood step of the

ritual?" Gabriel asked, then reached into his coat pocket and pulled out a knife.

"Jesus!" Miles's heart leaped into his throat. "What the hell are you doing carrying that around in your pocket? You could've stabbed yourself."

"I'm not an imbecile." It was a small kitchen knife, the kind chefs in Miles's mom's favorite cooking shows always used to peel apples. "The ritual needs blood and I didn't want to cut myself open on anything we'd find at a filthy cemetery."

"Because a filthy kitchen knife is better?"

"Obviously I cleaned it first." Gabriel had the gall to sound exasperated. "Tell me how to do this. Should I simply—?" He swung the knife down towards the palm of his hand.

Miles caught his wrist. "What did I tell you about not believing things you see in movies? If you slice your hand open, it's going to hurt like hell and take forever to heal."

Charlee muttered something that sounded suspiciously close to "Amateur."

Ignoring her, Miles explained, "Cut the back of your arm and keep it shallow."

"How much?" Emily interrupted.

"What?"

"How much blood does it need?"

"Uh, it doesn't say. Enough to… mix in, probably."

"Then how about we put the knife down?" She passed Miles the lantern and swung her pink canvas backpack off, crouching to dig through it. "Give me a second."

Gabriel got the rest of the ritual ready, laying out a piece of linen cloth. In the center of it, he laid the wolfsbane, three rusty coffin nails, two yellowed bones, and a couple of baby teeth shaken from a grimy jar. Nadia had assured Charlee that most of these ingredients were fairly common for darker rituals, but it still skeeved Miles out.

Gabriel held up the glass bottle of manchineel sap. "Should I pour it on?"

"I guess so."

It dripped out thick and viscous, honey slow.

In the damp grass, a stickered blue water bottle, creased soccer jersey, and a brush piled around Emily. "Found it!" she announced, holding up a zipped pouch.

"What is it?"

"My sewing kit. One of my electives is fashion design, so I've become the designated torn-jersey mender." After digging through the pouch, she triumphantly held up a slender silver needle. "Perfect. Give me your hand."

Gabriel grimaced. "Don't tell me you're going to stab me with that."

"You were about to slice yourself open with a knife, but a little needle is too much? I'll only poke you. A few drops of blood should be fine."

Gabriel reluctantly held out his hand, flinching when she jabbed the tip of his pinky. A bright red bead of blood immediately welled up.

"So nasty," Miles muttered as Gabriel applied pressure, dripping crimson onto the cluster of offerings.

"Disgusting," Charlee agreed, not sounding remotely bothered.

Blood added, Gabriel gathered the corners of the linen, bundling everything in a little sack. He clumsily tied it off with a piece of twine, then grabbed the lighter.

The linen caught easily, the fire hungry as it devoured the thin cloth. Gabriel set it down, snatching his fingers away to watch the flames burn blue, then a deep purplish red.

A charge sizzled through the air, Charlee's unbound hair frizzing with electricity. The moon shifted behind a cloud. Shadows lengthened across the misty grass, reaching for Gabriel. The air thickened, sour on Miles's tongue, coating his mouth as his protective charms grew warm.

"You guys feel that?" Emily whispered, her voice uncertain.

"Yeah," Charlee answered. "I don't like it."

But there was no darkness spreading over Gabriel's skin, no sign that he was being taken over. In the distance, an owl hooted. The surrounding trees were still.

"Did it feel like it worked?" Miles asked Gabriel.

"How would I know?" He stared down at the page, eyebrows furrowed. "I did all the steps correctly, and I—"

A noise broke through the night, a loud crack that rattled Miles's teeth. Several yards away, one of the headstones shook, dirt churning and frothing at its base before it toppled over. More started to tremble, the smell of fresh earth and decay filling the air.

Charlee clutched Miles's sleeve. "What's going on?"

Where the first headstone had fallen, a mangled hand punched through the soil, fingers clawing at the surrounding grass. Miles watched in horror as wiry arms followed, then a concave head. Long hair twisted in grimy tangles, gray-tinged skin hanging in strips from the face to reveal the rotting meat beneath. Another emerged from the ground beside it—dried flesh split over flashes of milky bone that glowed in the moonlight—and scrabbled at the dirt.

The dead were crawling out of their graves.

Panicked white noise droned in Miles's ears. He couldn't move, couldn't breathe.

"We're all seeing this, right?" Emily asked weakly.

"Yep." Charlee's fingers tightened in the denim of Miles's jacket. "What the hell do we do?"

Miles choked on a painful wheeze. "Those are zombies, Charlee. *Zombies*. Oh my God, I knew we shouldn't have used this stupid book, I knew it."

Charlee whirled to Gabriel. "What went wrong, and how do we fix it?"

He dove back into the book, flipping the pages frantically. "I don't know. The ritual was meant for Jocelyn, we named her specifically, so it should have—" He cut off.

"What?" Miles forced himself to look away from the graves, away from the undead painstakingly pulling them-selves free of the soil like butterflies wriggling out of a cocoon. Rotting, bloodthirsty, undead butterflies. "What is it?"

"The spell is to summon living or dead, spirit *or* flesh. If it wasn't able to reach Jocelyn, the magic still has to go somewhere." His gaze flitted to the zombies. "This must be the flesh."

"That doesn't make any sense!" Miles was too far gone to be embarrassed by the hysterical note in his voice. "We didn't summon zombies."

"We're in a cemetery. The closest flesh it could find would be corpses."

"Stop acting like this is okay! There are literally *zombies* coming out of the ground right now. We're five seconds away from having our brains eaten."

"I'm simply saying, I understand why the magic chose—"

"Uh, it's coming at us," Emily interjected in a panicked squeak.

The first zombie had completely broken free of the earth and was slowly lumbering towards them. Thick black ooze dribbled from its hamburger-meat lips.

"It's coming at *me*," Gabriel corrected. "I'm the one who summoned it."

"Do we run?"

"We can't run away and let zombies loose on the town," Charlee hissed. "We need to do something."

Miles flushed. She was right, of course she was, but *zombies*. Everyone had told him it was an irrational fear, that they didn't exist, but here he was, smack dab in the middle of his worst nightmare come to life. He could barely think, let alone formulate a plan.

Charlee snatched up her shovel from the grass and sprinted forward, swinging it like a baseball bat. The flat blade smashed into the side of the zombie's head with a sickening crunch, knocking it to the ground. A moment later, it moved to push itself up with unsteady limbs, but Charlee stomped it back down.

Miles had never loved his cousin more.

"You two figure out how to fix this," she barked at Miles and Gabriel. "Emily, grab a weapon and help me keep them back."

More corpses shambled forward, birthed from the darkness and swirling fog. They weren't particularly fast, more than one stumbling over their own feet and bumping into tombstones, but it was unnerving how focused they were on Gabriel.

Emily whirled helplessly, hands flapping. "What am I supposed to use?"

Two rows of headstones back, there was a flag jammed into the ground beside a grave. It wasn't very long, standing only slightly taller than the tombstone, but that didn't stop Emily from ripping it free and charging at the nearest zombie with it like a jousting pole. Miles could only watch, jaw dropping, as she skewered it with a wild shriek. It pierced through but didn't knock the zombie over, Emily and it both staring down at the protruding stick in confusion.

"Damn it," he heard her swear, before she yanked it free. The flag twisted and bunched around the pole, wet with rotten guts and more of that slick black liquid. Instead of stabbing again, she started whacking, beating the zombie to the ground with a determined grimace.

Behind her, a near-skeletal head went flying as Charlee's shovel drove it off a set of shoulders.

Holy shit.

He and Gabriel shared a look of awed disbelief before turning back to the grimoire.

"We need to stop them," Miles muttered. "Maybe a... mass banishing spell?"

"To banish what? They don't have spirits."

Miles frowned, cautiously lifting his mental shield and reaching out to the nearest zombie. Gabriel was right—there was no spark of life, no soul, only the dark taint of the grimoire's magic stuffing their limbs with power.

How did you kill something that wasn't even really alive?

"Wait, do you have the knife?"

Gabriel whipped out the kitchen knife from earlier and offered it to him.

"Not that knife—the overpowered kill-anything one!"

Gabriel frowned. "Why would I have that?"

"In case something exactly like this happens!" The same reason Miles had been lugging around that disgusting heart. It wasn't like they'd get a heads up before needing it. "Okay, I'm done coming up with plans, it's your turn."

Emily and Charlee were doing their best, but the zombies were closing in around them, lumbering back to their feet faster than they could knock them down.

Gabriel set down the grimoire. "The magic animating them feels similar to the guardian in the tunnels. I might be able to take hold and release it."

"But the darkness went into you." That was exactly what they were trying to avoid. Miles wasn't sure he'd be able to save Gabriel again. The last time had been one big rush of desperation and instinct. "We can't risk it."

"There's no time to dig through the grimoire for another spell. If we don't stop them now, they'll hurt someone."

He was right. Miles hated it. "Fine, but come into my head first so I can protect you."

"I can't do both. Hold your mind open for me, and I'll step inside if I need to."

Miles liked the idea that he was a place of safety. That Gabriel could stand with one foot over the threshold of his mind, half in the light, half in the dark.

"I will," he swore.

Gabriel's fingers dipped beneath the sleeve of Miles's jacket to encircle his wrist. A moment later, that now-familiar tap announced his presence.

Charlee bashed her shovel into the torso of a particularly decrepit corpse, then jumped back with a noise of disgust as it snapped at the waist, top half toppling to the grass in a cloud of dust. Its legs kept going, staggering around.

"When I pull the magic, close yourself off if you feel it starting to transfer to you."

"Yeah, sure." As if Miles would abandon him.

Gabriel sucked in a jagged inhale. A crackle in the air made Miles's hair stand on end as Gabriel went rigid, his nails biting crescent moons into Miles's flesh.

All the zombies, even the ones half-freed from their graves, froze mid-shamble.

Emily panted, slumped against an angel statue with her flagpole, unbelievably, still intact. Beside her, Charlee stood guard, shovel raised and ready.

A quiver raced down Gabriel's body, tendons straining in his hands and corded on his neck. He was crushing Miles's wrist to the point of pain, so Miles twisted in his grip until their palms met, weaving their fingers together.

In eerie unison, the zombies' faces tilted up, kissed by the pearly moonlight. A beat passed. Then, that black fluid streamed from their mouths, hovering in the air like threads of liquid night plucked from between the stars. It twisted, mirroring the tendrils of fog below before surging towards Gabriel.

Miles flinched, about to tackle him to the ground, but the streams collided with each other a few feet away, forming one glistening ball, darker than the shadows of the cemetery surrounding them, with a mesmerizing oil-slick shine.

The zombies toppled over, unmoving.

"You got them all," Miles told Gabriel. "You can release it now."

Gabriel's free hand lifted, curling into a fist before the orb. It bobbed closer, pulsating.

In the tunnel, the creature had dissipated immediately.

"It's not listening," Gabriel breathed, his eyes glazed. Unfocused. "It wants… inside."

No. No, no, no.

"Let it go. Step back and let it go."

"I can't. We conjured it. We owe it." Gabriel sounded far away, like the darkness was already dragging him under, taking him far enough away that Miles couldn't reach him. "It's hungry and needs to feed."

Miles tried to expand the bubble of his mind to envelop Gabriel, but slammed against an immovable wall. Backtracking, he lunged for the gentle weight of Gabriel's presence instead, for any part of him he could yank back to safety. With a sickening lurch, he fell straight through the open doorway between them into Gabriel's mind.

Gabriel's emotions hit him full force.

Fear, coating his mouth in ash, packed down his throat until he couldn't breathe.

Yearning, the taste of sweet citrus bursting across his tongue, making his head swim and his pulse race.

Self-loathing, a rancid, bitter rot creeping sluggishly through his veins.

Hope, the sweetest fizz in the pit of his stomach, flowers blooming up into his ribs to cradle his thumping heart.

Miles fell to his knees in the damp grass, the oxygen knocked straight out of him. It was too much, everything drowned out beneath the force of Gabriel. He couldn't find himself.

This was why the first thing his dad ever taught him was

to construct a shield and protect himself. It was too easy to get pulled in, lost inside someone else, sucked down and buried beneath the weight of their feelings. He needed to climb back to himself, but he couldn't remember the way.

Then, he sensed it.

Something else was here with him, something that didn't belong inside Gabriel. Like grabbing a ripe apple and sinking your thumb into a rotten spot. Lifting your face to a fresh breeze and catching a whiff of decay. A wrongness. An infection.

This must be the feeling Gabriel had told him about, the evil thing living under his skin.

It responded to the magic trying to slither inside Gabriel, calling and reaching out to it, assuring it would satiate its hunger, give it a warm body to nest in, a vessel to fill. It radiated power, temptation; it took everything in Miles not to reach for it, to see if its darkly honeyed promises were true.

Gabriel wasn't just fighting against the magic they'd summoned, but a part of himself that had been planted in a forgotten corner against his will, spread its roots and grown.

Anger roared in Miles, the sudden flare of emotion snapping him back into his own mind. He emerged with a gasp, finding Charlee and Emily crouched beside him, twin looks of alarm on their faces. Above him, the ball of darkness rested in the outstretched palm of Gabriel's hand, black ooze slicked down to his wrist.

Shrugging off Emily and Charlee, their protests a distant drone, Miles stood and grabbed the orb. He'd claw at it, tear it, anything to rip it free of Gabriel and throw it as far as he could.

The moment it met his skin, pain flayed open his flesh

and seared down his nerves. He screamed as it slid up his skin like hot oil, but he couldn't move, couldn't pull away.

Let us in, the thing breathed, the words echoing and endless. *Let us in and the pain will cease. Let us in, and you will never know hurt again.*

The fire burned hotter across his body, until Miles thought he'd hear his skin sizzle, his bones crack. He would've done anything to make it stop.

Let us in and it will stop.

Uttering a simple *yes* was the easiest thing he'd ever done.

Hot blood flooded his mouth, a blade slicing into his very being, cutting down to his core. It was ravenous, shredding him apart to feast, pleased with this new offering, opening its maw wide to—

It ripped from his mind like a barbed hook. The pain of it leaving hurt almost as much as the sudden relief once it was gone, and Miles had a terrible feeling it had taken some part of him with it. His legs gave out.

Only a second behind him, Gabriel dropped to his knees with a keening whine. He sank forward to clutch at the grass, tearing it up in fistfuls and shuddered like he was rattling free of his own skin.

A terrible cold pulsed around them, ruffling Miles's hair and sinking under his clothes. The sheepskin collar of his jacket crusted with frost, the sweat soaking his shirt turning frigid.

Gabriel's eyes rolled back, nothing but whites, and he went limp, slumping forward.

"Gabriel," Miles croaked. Cleared his throat and tried again. "*Gabriel.*"

He didn't move.

Miles was about to puke, and every inch of his body hurt, but Gabriel wasn't moving. Too weak to stand, he shuffled closer. "Hey." He shook Gabriel by the shoulder, clumsy and a touch too rough. "C'mon, talk to me."

"Miles." Charlee sounded strange. "Look at the grass."

It was withering, turning brittle and brown. Bouquets of flowers on surrounding graves decomposed into sludge, bushes collapsed in on themselves. There was a thud—Miles turned to see a bird on the ground, frozen in death. One, then another, more thumps in the darkness. It was as if a foul miasma had settled around them, killing everything it touched.

Gabriel shifted with a low groan, curling in on himself. "I had to," he whispered, scraped as raw as Miles felt. "The magic had to feed, or it would've taken you."

Jesus. It was sucking the life straight out of their surroundings, devouring anything it could reach. It'd been so close to doing the same to Miles. Would he have turned into a husk, skin melted into rot? Would he even have had a second to scream before the magic killed him?

"I'm sorry," Gabriel choked out. His arms tightened around his body, knuckles stark where he clutched his coat. "I had to."

Miles crawled over to wrap his arms around him as he shook. He held him and wished the doorway between them hadn't closed so he could share his anguish, carry part of it for him.

"It's okay," he lied, murmuring the words into Gabriel's hair. It was far from okay, but there was nothing he could say to fix it. Gabriel hadn't killed the plants and the birds, but they were dead all the same.

How did you thank someone for saving your life when the cost was so horrible?

"You were right." Gabriel shivered so violently Miles's vision blurred. "We shouldn't have used the grimoire. I should've listened to you."

"You didn't know. This isn't your fault, okay?"

It was all their faults. They'd all agreed. This cemetery was supposed to be for the deceased to rest, to find peace. Because of them, they'd been ripped from their graves and puppeted around. Now, the few living things in this place were dead.

Charlee crouched down to place a hand on Gabriel's shoulder. She waited until he looked up, eyes hollow pits, blood gathered in the corner of his mouth where he must've bitten his tongue. He dipped his chin, resigned to face whatever judgment laid upon him.

"Don't…" Miles started.

"It's done." Her voice was softer than she'd ever spoken to Gabriel before. "You said it yourself—you had to. If I had to pick between Miles and a couple of birds, I would've made the same choice. I would've left this whole cemetery in ashes before I let it take him." She stood and offered her freckled hand. "So, it's done. Now we need to clean up our mess."

Gabriel's ribs swelled beneath Miles as he took a deep breath, then gripped Charlee's hand and let her pull him to his feet.

12

Calling what they'd done a mess was an understatement.

Even without the corpses, there were toppled tombstones, gaping holes in the ground, and all the carnage from the grimoire's magic. It looked like Thistle Cemetery had been struck by a very selective earthquake, a horde of giant moles, and a plague, all in the same night.

Whenever Miles did a little gravedigging, he made a point to clean up after himself, to leave things as neat as he'd found them. That wasn't an option tonight.

"What do we do?" Emily asked, ashen but resolute. Zombie gunk and dirt were smeared down the front of her coat. "We can't leave all these bodies like this."

"We'll have to." Miles didn't want to say it, but Charlee nodded in agreement. "Even if we had more than one shovel, we'd never get them all reburied before morning."

"The workers will just think it's a messed-up prank," Charlee added. "Or graverobbers."

That wouldn't explain the dead plants, but Miles had learned that when the average person was faced with something unnatural, they looked for the easiest explanation. There'd be uncertain whispers, but the moment someone

139

suggested a bad batch of pesticides or a spreading fungal disease, they'd be forgotten.

Emily worried at her bottom lip. "I don't like it. It feels disrespectful."

The corpses were littered across the ground like a kid's broken toys, a clutter of body parts, bones, and torn clothing.

"We'll lay them in a line," Miles said. It was the most they could do. Not much, but something.

Charlee and Emily went over to a still-decomposing woman in a blue dress, glittering clips hanging from her greasy clumps of hair. Charlee took her feet and Emily her arms, carrying her over to an open stretch of withered grass.

Standing silently, Gabriel stared at the nearest dead bird. It was small, some kind of sparrow maybe, speckled white and brown. Black ooze leaked from its empty eyes like obsidian tears.

A lump formed in Miles's throat. "We're going to clean up a bit." He tentatively touched Gabriel's elbow. He'd take any reaction, even one of Gabriel's frustrating dodges right now, but he didn't move. "Then we'll get out of here."

"I should help," Gabriel remarked, but he didn't shift, didn't even blink. He sounded empty.

Miles wanted to take his hand so badly it ached in his bones.

"No, it's okay. Stay here and"—what? Rest? Recover?—"wait. We'll be quick."

It wasn't that Miles didn't think Gabriel could do it; it was that he shouldn't have to. Not just because he'd saved Miles's life. This kind of work—dirty, cold, sweaty work that left filth under your nails and the stink of decay in your nose—was Miles's normal. Gabriel was meant for nicer things.

He expected an argument, but Gabriel didn't protest. That scared Miles more than anything. But in the tunnel, it had taken him time to recover enough to even hold his own weight. He'd be okay once he had time to shake it off. Once they were out of here and he could stop looking at the wreckage.

Miles went to where Emily had a body by the shoulders— leathery stretched skin holding bones together—and stooped down to grab its feet as his own heels sank into the damp dirt. It was unnervingly light, easy to carry over to Charlee, who was straightening another corpse's pink lace dress.

They worked in silence until the dead were neatly laid out in passably dignified positions. A few were little more than dust and bones that broke apart when lifted, so were left where they'd fallen. If it hadn't been for the grimoire's magic fueling them, they never could've made their way out of the ground. The air was filled with the smell of freshly turned soil and rot.

"It'll have to do," Charlee declared grimly.

"Yeah." Miles didn't feel great about it, but his priority was getting Gabriel out of here. "Let me get all the ritual stuff"— he gestured to the fallen bottles, baby teeth, and coffin nails scattered in the damp grass—"and we can head out."

Charlee joined him, but Emily picked up the shovel and went over to Gabriel.

"Hey," she said. "I thought we could bury the birds before we go. We won't need a big hole."

Gabriel's gaze slowly focused on her. "It's irrational, but I don't want to leave them like this."

"It's not irrational." They'd just spent half an hour hauling bodies to spare them the indignity of being found scattered around like trash. All creatures deserved respect, even in death. Emily tilted her head towards a tree outside the dead zone. "Let's dig there. It's a nice spot."

She led the way, shovel over her shoulder and Gabriel trailing behind.

Charlee pulled Miles's attention back. "You okay?"

He took the teeth from her and dropped them back in their bottle one by one. "Not really."

His body hurt from what the magic had done to him, trembling with the echoes of pain. His mind was scattered and uncertain, and he kept checking that his shield was up.

And his heart ached for Gabriel. For the emotions he'd felt, and for what he'd done.

Charlee leaned into him, a steady, comforting weight. They watched together as Emily finished digging a shallow hole at the base of the tree.

"What about him?" Charlee tracked Gabriel as he made his way to the first bird, lifting it carefully with the shovel.

"You almost sound concerned."

She shrugged, tucking the bottle of manchineel sap into the bag. "As much as I'd like to, I don't hate him. Even when he makes stupidly frustrating decisions, it's because he's trying to keep you alive. Hard to hate someone with the same priorities as me." She slid Miles a sideways look. "Don't tell him I said that."

"He probably wouldn't believe me if I did."

"So really, is he okay?"

"I doubt it. Gabriel's a lot of things, but he's not a killer. And whether it was his fault or not…" Miles scrubbed a hand down his face. "I don't know how to help him with this."

He'd experienced the forlorn swirl of Gabriel's emotions, how loudly fear and self-loathing resounded through him.

Tonight could easily send him into a downward spiral.

Miles knew Gabriel struggled, had heard it in the dismissive way he talked about himself, so quick to decide he was beyond saving. The lonely chill he radiated, even in his own home. The way he spoke about Felicity and his absent dad. But this was the difference between seeing a Band-Aid and knowing there was a wound, versus peeling it back and taking in the infected gash.

"He shouldn't be alone tonight." Charlee handed over the grimoire, safely packed up in its containment box.

The last thing Miles wanted to do was drop Gabriel off at his dreary, empty house and let him dwell on what had happened, but—

"I can't exactly invite myself to the Hawthorne estate for a sleepover."

Charlee grimaced, the way she did every time he mentioned Gabriel's house. "I meant he should come home with us. Stay with *you*."

"You're joking."

"Why would I joke about that? We'll sneak him in, and I'll run him home in the morning before school. Your mom's avoiding your room like the plague, she'll never know he's over."

She was serious. She wanted to sneak Gabriel into their house, under his parents' noses, and… What? Throw a slumber party?

Miles's body went hot, then cold.

Before he could respond, Emily and Gabriel rejoined them.

"We were just saying that you should come home with us for the night, Gabriel," Charlee told them. "If you want to. Miles thought you wouldn't want to be alone tonight."

Gabriel would protest. Of course he would. And Miles wouldn't take it personally, he'd honestly be relieved because—

"I don't want to be alone," Gabriel admitted. He crossed his arms, as if the admission had cracked him down the middle.

Charlee nodded, like that was that. "Emily, do you want to—?"

"No offense, but I really need to collapse in my own bed tonight." She snagged her backpack from the ground with a groan. "And not get up for at least twelve hours."

"We've got school," Miles reminded her.

She swore. "Can we all agree to save the late-night cemetery sessions for the weekends from now on?"

"How about we just avoid cemeteries altogether for a while?" Miles suggested tiredly.

"Deal. Now let's get out of here." She glanced back at the corpses, regret heavy on her face. Knowing they'd done all they could didn't make it any easier to leave them like this.

She hurried towards the gate, Gabriel following behind her like a shadow. Miles tried to grab him to insist he shouldn't let Charlee pressure him, that they'd drop him off at home, but he slipped out of reach.

Miles whirled to Charlee instead. Her face was the picture of innocence. "What are you doing?"

"What?"

"You know what. No way you're doing this out of the goodness of your heart when you've been trying to keep me away from him since day one."

"I don't know what to tell you. I've got a weak spot for pathetic-looking strays." She shook her head at his expression. "You can't make him go home when he clearly doesn't want to."

"It's not cool of you to push us into this."

"Please, I'm doing you both a favor. He gets to spend the night with his big cuddly boyfriend instead of going home to his murder house, and you get to keep an eye on him and make sure he doesn't have a breakdown." She snagged her gunk-smeared shovel and started trekking after Gabriel and Emily. "I'm too tired to argue. Tonight was a shitshow. Let's just go home."

Miles would never admit it, but Charlee had been right—it was embarrassingly easy to sneak Gabriel into their house. Stealth wasn't even necessary, which was lucky considering how they stumbled over each other past the front door and up the stairs. The sound of his dad's thunderous snores through his parents' closed bedroom door could've masked the noise of an oncoming train. It was nothing like the horrific mental image he'd had weeks ago of Charlee helping Gabriel clamber through his bedroom window.

It helped that he'd entered a surreal place where he was too tired to really feel the anxiety ricocheting around inside him. Making sure his parents didn't catch him didn't seem nearly as important as crawling into bed as soon as humanly possible.

"I'll grab you some pajamas," he told Gabriel, leaving him in the hall with Charlee.

The thought of Gabriel wearing his clothes should've given Miles a heart attack, but he just grabbed the first T-shirt and pair of plaid pajama pants he could find in his dresser. A distant part of his brain marveled at the absence of panic. Lack of sleep might be the secret cure for anxiety.

He passed Gabriel the clothes and all but pushed him into the bathroom.

Charlee yawned. "See you in the morning."

"Wait." Miles caught her arm. "Where are you going?"

"To my room. You know, the place where I can change out of these disgusting clothes and zonk out."

"Charlee. You can't—I can't—" She couldn't leave him alone with Gabriel. The boy he looked at and, nine times out of ten, thought about wanting to kiss.

"You'll be fine. You're both exhausted and had an awful night—I doubt he's going to try and jump you just because you're sleeping in the same room."

Miles flushed. "What am I supposed to do?"

"Stop freaking out, to start. You're not exactly making him feel welcome. And comfort the poor guy. He nuked half a graveyard to save your life. I think that's earned him bedtime cuddles."

"*Charlee.*"

She snickered and disappeared through her bedroom door. Asshole.

Miles turned and found Gabriel hovering in the bathroom doorway, holding his folded clothes and pointedly avoiding eye contact. He'd clearly heard them.

Worse, he was wearing Miles's too-big pajamas, rolled at the sleeves and ankles, hanging off his slender frame. He looked unbearably cute.

"I can go home," Gabriel murmured. "I shouldn't have accepted your cousin's invitation in the first place and made you uncomfortable. I don't know what I was thinking."

His words punched Miles in the gut. Hard. Gabriel looked so small and vulnerable in his hallway and in his clothes. It made Miles want to bundle him up, get him safe and warm, and show him how it felt to be taken care of.

"No," Miles insisted, then again more vehemently. "*No.* You aren't making me uncomfortable. I mean, a little, but that's just because you're you and I—" He cut himself off before he said something really stupid. "Stay. I mean it. I want you to."

And suddenly he did. More than anything.

"C'mon." He caught Gabriel's hand and tugged him into his bedroom. "I'm seriously about to fall asleep right here."

Gabriel came easily, more willing than usual. Softened by exhaustion and, Miles hoped, the comfort of being here.

He closed the door behind them, giving the space a quick critical scan—he'd learned his lesson since the last time Gabriel unexpectedly came over and had been keeping his room tidy. Still, there was a mug of tea perched on his bedside table and a stack of clean laundry he hadn't gotten around to putting away yet on his desk chair.

His gaze landed and stuck on his bed.

"We can't sleep together," Miles blurted, then immediately wished for a swift and sudden death. "I mean, like, in the same bed. My bed's too small, and I wouldn't—I don't—I'd never suggest that anyway, that would be weird if we—"

"Miles," Gabriel interrupted, palpable fatigue weighing down his words. "Give me a blanket and a pillow, and I'll sleep on the floor."

He forgot his mortification. "What? No! You're the guest, take my bed."

"I appreciate the sentiment, but what happens if one of

your parents or sisters comes in? You take the bed and I'll sleep on the floor"—he gestured on the opposite side of the bed—"so I'm not immediately visible."

It was a fair point. That didn't mean it was right to make him curl up on the hardwood floor. Even with the shag rug, it would be far from comfortable.

"Fine. But give me a sec."

Miles went down the hall to Charlee's room. The lights were off and she was starfished across her bed.

"Whaaaaa…?" she slurred sleepily as he started pulling blankets off her bed.

"Go back to sleep."

"Kinda hard to do when you're stealing all my warmth," she grumbled, wrestling a knit blanket away from him.

"You're fine." Charlee was a certified nester, burrowing under a mountain of blankets before she got too hot and threw them all off in the middle of the night. "Gabriel needs them."

She spluttered in protest, but he was already out the door with half of her stash.

"I'm going to make you the world's comfiest floor bed," Miles told Gabriel, dropping Charlee's blankets in a heap.

"That's not necessary—"

"It'll only take a minute."

He folded and stacked all of them, adding a pillow from his bed. It seemed a little weird to give Gabriel his main pillow, so he chose the backup one that always ended up on the floor.

"Here." He yanked his main comforter free. "It gets chilly, and we don't run the heat very often."

Gabriel sat down on his makeshift mattress, looking

satisfied as Miles draped the comforter over him. "I run warm anyway."

It was a sleepy, off-hand comment, but it was such a strangely intimate thing to know about someone.

Miles padded across his room and switched the light off, plunging the room into darkness. He changed into his pajamas, skin prickling with the knowledge that Gabriel was only a few feet away, then crawled into the safety of his bed.

The quiet was stifling. Miles stared up at his ceiling, irrationally self-conscious about making a sound, but able to hear every breath Gabriel took, every rustle of his blanket as he got comfortable.

"Are you okay?" he asked, knowing he wasn't going to be able to sleep until he did.

"I feel better now." His sincere answer soothed Miles's jitters. "You were hurt tonight. I heard you scream."

"Yeah, but I'm okay." It felt like the truth, even with his body aching and a lingering throb in his core that he suspected was shame. He wanted to tell Gabriel what'd happened, but that would mean admitting how easily he'd given in to the magic, how weak he'd been in the face of pain.

The grimoire was supposed to tempt you, entice you. But with Miles, it had gone straight for the stick over the carrot. It had wanted to hurt him.

Gabriel didn't push, and Miles didn't mention the death they'd left behind in the cemetery. It was okay—they'd both be ready to talk eventually.

A car passed outside, a flare of light across his wall. Some poor person was up even later than them. "Why do you think Jocelyn didn't come?"

"Does it matter? It didn't work." Gabriel sighed. "It could've been me, the ritual, the magic… perhaps I was wrong about it being able to undo itself. All I know for certain is that we're not using the grimoire again."

"As soon as we find the curse, we can set it on fire together."

"Agreed." Blankets shifted with a low rasp as Gabriel adjusted. "It deserves to burn after it hurt you."

Hearing that probably shouldn't make Miles feel so pleased, but he blamed it on his sleepy brain.

He was just starting to drift off when Gabriel spoke again. "I owe you an apology."

"We all agreed to use the grimoire. We all thought it was worth a shot."

"I meant that I owe you an apology for the last few days."

Miles was suddenly wide awake. He didn't dare look over the edge of the bed. "Oh."

"I'm sorry for so many things, I'm not certain where to start," Gabriel confessed, and Miles's heart thumped. "For leaving like I did and being too afraid to tell you. For treating you poorly because of my own emotions. For having to see you nearly die tonight before I realized what an idiot I've been."

It was hard not to reassure him that it was okay, that he had nothing to apologize for. But the memory of fear during the days he was gone—then the anxiety and hurt once he'd returned acting like a stranger—still sat heavy in Miles's gut.

"I know you've been struggling," he said instead. "I'm sure you're not used to having someone breathing down your neck, and I'm not always great at taking a step back when someone needs space." He huffed into the darkness.

"I just… I wish you would let me in. It feels like you don't trust me."

"I do trust you. But I'm also angry with you."

Ridiculously, Miles perked up at that. It was progress. Insight. Anger, he could manage. Charlee had once said he was embarrassingly good at groveling.

"I'm mad at you," Gabriel continued, "for having no survival instinct. After I told you about my premonition, you should've walked away without looking back. Told me to stay away. Taken my offer to separate. I want to yell at you for being so frustratingly irresponsible with your life."

Honestly, that was fair. Miles had no defense—he had practically yelled at Gabriel for being so nonchalant about his own death all those weeks ago.

"I can see how that might piss you off."

"I appreciate your understanding." A current of amusement ran through Gabriel's voice, before it dipped back into somberness. "More than that, I'm angry with myself. How can I blame you for not leaving when I can't either? Even knowing it might save your life, I'm selfish enough that I let you convince me to stay. I've watched you *die* and I'm still too weak to walk away from you." Miles had guessed as much—partially from his conversation with Emily, partially from the emotions he'd sensed in Gabriel tonight—but he let Gabriel talk. It was important he got out what he needed to. "I feel so guilty when I look at you. All I want is to know that I can save you, so I don't have to hate myself for wanting to be with you."

"I don't have some magic answer," Miles finally said. "I had to choose to believe in a better future. That was the only way I could keep doing this without losing it."

Blankets rasped as Gabriel shifted. "I don't have your optimism," he admitted. "I'm trying to believe that I was given the premonition of your death so I can save you, but I'm afraid that nothing I do will matter."

"It matters." Miles blinked rapidly up at the ceiling. The fact that Gabriel cared mattered more than he realized. "You're showing up for me even though you're scared. You're not making me do this alone. Those things all matter."

Gabriel's head appeared after a few silent heartbeats. He crossed his arms on the edge of Miles's bed, resting his chin on them. "I'm tired of being angry and afraid," he murmured. A faint golden glow came in through Miles's parted curtains, barely illuminating his face. "And I'm tired of this distance between us. Tell me how I can fix it."

Something about his whispered words made Miles's face flush. "All I want is for you to be honest with me. It was the not talking, not knowing, that was driving me crazy."

Gabriel considered him for a moment. "I'll be blunt, then. I've been an ass, and I regret it. I regret the days I've wasted. I'm frightened of the future, but when I think about making the most of what little time I might have left, all I picture is spending it with you." He peered at Miles, his lashes casting long shadows across his cheekbones.

A dizzying rush of emotions went through Miles. Tonight had taken a turn he hadn't expected. He was glad he was lying down.

He rolled over to face Gabriel more fully. "I—can you be a bit more specific? I mean—we haven't talked about us. Or our relationship, since we… you know. In the cemetery."

"We kissed, Miles. The word isn't going to bite you."

Miles flushed down to his toes. "I know that. I'm allowed

to be a bit flustered after you smooched my face off, then didn't mention it again."

Gabriel made a small, distressed noise caught between a snicker and a groan. "You did not just use the word 'smooched' unironically."

"It's not funny." Miles couldn't bite back his grin.

"Oh, I'm aware."

God, Miles was making a fool of himself. If Gabriel could be blunt, so could he. "What I'm asking," he explained, swallowing around his dry tongue, "is what you mean exactly? Because that all sounds kinda romantic, but I don't want to make any assumptions." The words were coming out too fast, tripping him up. "Did you mean it like that? Like, do you want to be… boyfriends? Dating?"

There. He'd said it.

The corner of Gabriel's mouth quirked up. "What makes you think I know anything about dating?"

It was such a Gabriel answer, Miles had to laugh. "I guess we're both a bit new to this, huh?"

"I suppose then, it only makes sense for us to undertake this learning experience together." His gray eyes gleamed with humor. Relief stole Miles's breath.

He reached over to flick Gabriel's shoulder for messing with him, but Gabriel caught his hand and tugged him closer to the edge. Startled, Miles caught himself before they bumped foreheads.

"What—"

Gabriel closed the inches between them and kissed the question right out of him.

His mouth pressed against Miles's firmly. Certain. A dizzying shiver spread across Miles, the fine hairs on his arms standing to attention. He didn't hesitate to kiss him back, sinking into the soft warmth of his lips. There was a salty bite to it from his earlier tears. Miles's heart flipped—this was a stolen moment of light to banish away the darkness. To forget all the pain, all the mistakes, all the uncertainties, and just feel.

Too soon, Gabriel pulled away. "I would like very much to date you," he breathed, the words brushed against Miles's lips. "Though, if you'd like to say no and make me suffer as retaliation for treating you poorly, I'll accept my fate. I won't kiss you again."

"Are you trying to bribe me into taking mercy on you with *kisses*?" Delight fizzed in Miles's stomach. "You're shameless."

"I was simply making your options clear."

As if there was any universe, any alternate timeline that existed where Miles would consider saying no.

"Hmmm." He pretended to consider, just to be an ass. "I might need to sleep on it and—" He laughed when Gabriel scowled at him. "I'm kidding. You know there's no question for me. I've been embarrassingly obvious about that."

"Mortifyingly," Gabriel confirmed, straight-faced.

Miles flopped back down and threw his arm over his face. "You're evil incarnate and I must be a masochist. Stop talking and go to sleep before I change my mind."

A snort escaped Gabriel, but his weight vanished from the edge of Miles's bed. When he peeked down a moment later, he found Gabriel tucked into his blanket pile, eyes closed and the faintest smile on his face.

13

It was an unexpected but delightful discovery that even prim and proper Gabriel Hawthorne splayed out in his sleep, one foot peeking from the blankets, an arm curled tightly around his pillow as if it'd tried to escape in the night. Miles had half expected him to sleep stiff as a board on his back and rise like Dracula from his makeshift mattress when he woke.

Miles's alarm wasn't set to go off for a few minutes still, so he sleepily watched Gabriel. Not in a creeper way—a foggy-brained, appreciative way, pausing to admire something he wouldn't see again anytime soon. Gabriel's hair fell messily across his forehead, his lips were parted in sleep, and the usual crease between his dark eyebrows was absent.

The wind shifted outside, rain pelting against his window. It was still too early for the sun to rise, but Miles could make out the vague shape of the tree outside his window.

He wanted to stay here forever, live in this moment for the rest of his life.

His bedroom door creaked open, sending his heart racing, but it was only Charlee in a pair of ratty sweatpants and a green hoodie with flecks of white paint down the front. He shushed her as she tiptoed exaggeratedly to sit on the edge of his bed.

She patted around the blankets. "Is Gabriel hiding in here?"

"Shhh! He's on the floor."

Charlee leaned over to peek. "Aww, look at him. Sleeping like a baby. You two must've had a good night."

Miles swatted at her. "Knock it off."

"Does that mean you didn't make out all night?"

"Oh my God." He should've known his peaceful little bubble would be popped by Charlee. "Go away, I'm not talking to you."

Just for that, he wasn't going to tell her yet.

"That's not how you treat the person giving your boyfriend a free ride home." She was teasing, but the word *boyfriend* sent an electric thrill through Miles. "We need to get going soon if we want to make it back before your parents get up."

He didn't want to take away even a moment of sleep from Gabriel. "I'll wake him when I get back." Miles threw back his blanket and immediately regretted it when the chill rushed in.

"Need to go brush your teeth before you wake him up with a kiss? Good call, nothing kills the romance like morning breath."

Miles was going to strangle her.

He slid from bed, whimpering when his feet met the freezing floorboards and padded to the bathroom. When he was done, he paused in the hallway—his parents' bedroom door was open.

They always slept with it closed.

Sure enough, when he crept close enough to peek inside,

the bed was empty, blankets rumpled and thrown back.

What the hell?

Downstairs, the kitchen light was bleeding gold into the gloom of the living room. Both of his parents were up, his mom digging through her purse while his dad pulled milk from the fridge.

His mom rarely got up this early, his dad never. And Miles knew he'd been on a job last night—he'd left right after dinner and wasn't back by the time they'd snuck out.

Were they up because of him? Waiting for him because they knew?

Adam spotted him. "Hey, you're up early. Everything okay? We didn't wake you, did we?"

"Uh, no. I couldn't sleep, and thought I'd make tea." Miles slid cautiously into the room. Not an ambush, then. He was in the clear as long as Gabriel didn't come stumbling down. "You guys have early plans?"

They were both dressed, his mom wearing a thick plaid coat. His dad had on his faded, mud-crusted work boots.

"We got a call that couldn't wait," Sarah explained, getting up on her tiptoes to reach two travel mugs in the top cupboard. "One of the maintenance workers at the cemetery found something weird."

Miles nearly choked. "Woah. Did they say what?"

"Only that it was strange enough they were calling the police right after us." The coffee maker chirped and Adam filled the mugs, talking over his shoulder. "It might be nothing, you know how superstitious some people are."

That was a bold criticism from the single most superstitious person in Thistle. He'd broken a mirror once and spent days doing every cleansing ritual he could find to "shake off the bad luck." If he saw a ladder, he didn't simply go around it, he crossed to the other side of the street.

Miles hid his face under the guise of pulling tea out of the cupboard. He was freaking out over nothing. They hadn't left anything behind last night that would connect them to the scene. There was no way his parents would know it was him.

Sarah took her purple mug from the counter, checking that the lid was screwed on tight. "We need to head out. Will you get your sisters up before you leave for school? And I got an email from your teacher about the after-school assignments this week." She paused, and Miles braced himself. But for the first time in days, she looked him in the face, blue eyes searching. When she went on, her voice sounded normal. Warmer than before. "Text me when you're done, and I'll come pick you up."

Guilt squirmed up Miles's throat. He'd ignored the olive branch at dinner the other night, but here she was, trying again. Making the decision to trust him. Attempting to fix things, while Miles was lying straight to her face.

"I will."

He had to lie. It was the only way. But part of him feared he was breaking something that couldn't be fixed. That his parents would never trust him again, or would decide he wasn't worth forgiving when the truth came out.

Adam gave Sarah's shoulder a squeeze before steering her out of the kitchen. The front door closed and a moment later, the sound of their car starting rumbled from the driveway.

Abandoning his tea, Miles sprinted back upstairs. "My parents just left to investigate the cemetery," he announced, flinging his bedroom door open. "We might be screwed."

Thankfully, Gabriel was already awake and sitting cross-legged at the foot of Miles's bed, bleary-eyed and messy-haired. He and Charlee were only a few feet apart and unbelievably, neither had killed the other yet.

Last night came rushing back, and Miles's face went up in flames. "Uh, good morning."

Gabriel mumbled something unintelligible around his yawn, covering his mouth in an attempt to hide it. It was hard to tell in the dim light, but Miles thought the bridge of his nose was pink.

The bridge of his *boyfriend's* nose.

Miles had to bite his lip so he didn't grin like an idiot and embarrass himself. Charlee was already squinting at him suspiciously.

"What did your parents say?" she prompted. "Should we be worried?"

"Probably. They said they're going to check it out, and if they find anything—"

"Won't they assume it was a prank or graverobbers, like you said?" Miles's shirt was so big on Gabriel, it slouched off one of his shoulders, showing a curve of pale skin.

Miles made himself look away. "Yeah, in a perfect world. But the circle of death we left behind is a bit weirder than digging up dead bodies. They're going to realize it was magic and look into it."

"We didn't leave anything behind." Gabriel shrugged. God, if Miles had even a fraction of his confidence, he'd be unstoppable. "They won't be able to find out what caused it or who's responsible."

He didn't know that for sure. Miles's parents could have a spell they didn't know about that revealed culprits. Or, what if one of them had left footprints behind? Or dropped something out of their pocket? Or—

"You're freaking yourself out," Charlee told him. "Even if they did find out, they're already pissed at you. It's not like your mom can get *more* mad."

That might be the naivest thing she'd ever said.

"Why am I the only one worried here? You guys could at least have a little solidarity panic attack."

"Hypothetically, if your parents did discover our involvement, we wouldn't leave you to fend for yourself. Even if it meant revealing our secrets." Gabriel studied Miles, brows furrowed like he was working a math problem out. "We'll be extra cautious from now on. We already agreed we won't use the grimoire again, so even if your parents suspect dark magic, we won't give them any further evidence."

Miles appreciated the reassurance. That was all he wanted.

Charlee snorted. "I'll worry when there's a reason to. Until your parents kick down your door and demand to know why you summoned zombies in the middle of the night, I'm not nervous."

And wasn't that a horrific mental image?

"What I'm more concerned about," she continued, "is getting Gabriel home at a decent time. We should've left five minutes ago."

"Yeah, yeah, we're going." Miles would've preferred some time to check in with Gabriel, but there was no dodging Charlee. He bent down to grab Gabriel's things, handing them over. Gabriel slipped on his shoes, tying the laces in perfectly neat bows. He didn't offer to change out of Miles's pajamas, bunching the long sleeves at his elbows.

Charlee snorted. "Aren't you just the cutest, coziest little thing?"

"I'm not little, your cousin is a giant. Blame your family's faulty genetics." He shrugged his coat on, looking ridiculous wearing that, red plaid flannel pants, and shiny dress shoes. Miles could only imagine how Edmund would react if he caught him sneaking in.

"I might die if I don't shower soon," Gabriel groused while Miles shoved on his own boots. "I feel disgusting."

"That wasn't even too bad. When I dig up a grave, you wouldn't believe the places I find dirt the next day."

"That's nothing," Charlee interjected. "One time, I climbed into a casket, and didn't realize how juicy the body was until I got embalming fluid all over my shoes."

Gabriel sidestepped the hallway table. "How did you know it was embalming fluid?"

"The smell," Miles and Charlee said in unison. There was no mistaking that scent, like the world's most potent pickle that had spent a decade in a musty basement.

Gabriel's mouth twisted in disgust.

"Trust me," Miles went on, going first down the stairs, "dead-person juice has a totally different smell. It's kinda like if a—" He stopped on the bottom step so abruptly, Gabriel bumped into him.

Aunt Robin stared in surprise from where she was settled on the couch, steaming mug and piece of toast on the coffee table in front of her.

Shit.

Miles had completely forgotten that she was up and about. From the sudden intake of air behind him, so had Charlee.

A loaded beat of silence passed. Miles's life flashed before his eyes. "Uh, good morning," he choked out.

Sneaking a boy out of the house first thing in the morning wasn't a great look, but if she didn't recognize Gabriel, this was potentially still salvageable.

"Is it?" Aunt Robin asked lightly, and Miles knew they were screwed. "A Hawthorne in our home would typically imply the opposite."

Miles winced. "This isn't what it looks like," he insisted—then realized it was in fact, exactly what it looked like.

Behind him, the stair creaked as Gabriel shifted forward to press against his back. Miles didn't know if he'd lost his balance or he was trying to be reassuring, but he appreciated it either way.

"Would you like to explain, or should I start guessing?" His aunt's airy tone hadn't changed. He didn't quite know what to make of it.

Resigned, he came down the rest of the stairs, Gabriel and Charlee following. Gabriel joined him by the coffee table, but Charlee kept going, passing through the living room and vanishing into the kitchen without so much as a look at her mom.

Probably a good call.

Gabriel cleared his throat and stepped forward to offer his hand. "I'm Gabriel Hawthorne. It's nice to meet you."

"You don't have to lie on my behalf." Aunt Robin's bluntness was softened by a tinge of amusement, but she took his hand. "I'm Robin Stephens, Miles's aunt." She didn't mention Charlee.

"Gabriel needed a place to stay last night," Miles explained. They'd been caught in the act. All he could do was be honest and hope for mercy. "My mom—well, I'm sure you heard, but she lost it when she found out we were hanging out, so I figured it would be best if she… didn't know he was here." Miles rubbed the back of his neck.

His aunt nodded sagely. "Felicity is a raw spot for her, a wound that never got to heal. She probably doesn't appreciate you poking it."

Miles was tempted to question her further, but they were already treading dangerous waters.

Gabriel had no such reservations. "Do you know what happened between them?"

"I do. But it's not my story to tell."

What little Miles knew—the photo of his dad with Felicity when they were younger, and what his mom had said when she'd confronted him about Gabriel—didn't reveal much, so he hadn't bothered to clue Gabriel in. Mostly because he was scared they'd have to discuss the possibility their parents had dated as teens. Ew.

"Whatever happened between them, she can't get past her issues enough to listen to me."

Aunt Robin's expression shifted into sympathy. "Your mom might not be able to see past her own bias now, but give her time. In the meantime, I'll hear you out."

Miles exchanged an uncertain look with Gabriel. If anyone was going to understand their fight against the future, it would be her. Being honest was the only chance they had of convincing her to keep Gabriel's presence a secret. The only way to make her understand why Miles couldn't walk away, no matter what his mom thought.

"We're trying to break a curse on Gabriel's family. And the reason we met and decided to work together…" Miles hesitated, but Gabriel tilted his head in encouragement. "We're trying to stop a death premonition."

Aunt Robin recoiled against the cushions as if he'd physically struck her. "You can't. I told you before—"

"I know. But we have to try."

She pressed a trembling hand to her breast, clutching the ring hanging from her neck. "I suppose it's not in your nature to give up without trying. But how did you see it? You're not a seer."

"Gabriel is," Miles shared, because it was easier than opening that whole can of worms. He didn't even fully understand himself how Jocelyn was forcing the visions on him.

She turned sorrowful eyes on Gabriel. "I'm so sorry. A death premonition is a terrible burden to bear. Our gift... I wouldn't wish it on anyone."

"If I can save a life," Gabriel responded, "it will be worth it."

Her gaze turned pitying, like she already knew the outcome, how futile their quest was. "Who?"

"It doesn't matter," Miles answered swiftly. That was the last thing they needed to get into. "What matters is that we don't have time for my mom to get on board. Please, don't tell her Gabriel was here. Or wait until after we finish this. Lives could literally be at stake."

The only reason he was getting away with sneaking out at night was because Sarah had no idea he was crazy enough to do it.

His aunt considered for a long second. "I won't tell her." Relief punched the air out of Miles's lungs. "But promise you'll come to me if you need help. If not with the premonition, then with the curse. That kind of magic can be tricky."

"We don't know much about it, except that it's tied to the Hawthornes' gifts. We still need to find the right spell in the grimoire."

"Grimoire?" Her gaze sharpened. "What grimoire?"

Mentioning the sentient book of evil probably hadn't been the best move when he was trying to keep her worry to a minimum.

"It belonged to my ancestor," Gabriel chimed in. "That's all we know about it."

"Those books are incredibly dangerous. You two haven't used it, have you?"

Miles avoided Gabriel's gaze. "No, of course not. We're only looking through it to find the curse, that's all."

His aunt bit her lip. "I still don't like it. Even reading one… You shouldn't be interacting with it at all, especially not alone. Let me look through it and find what you need, or at the very least, supervise."

"We don't have it with us." Technically not a lie; it was in his backpack upstairs. "We have to leave it at Gabriel's house so his mom doesn't notice it's missing. But we're being careful, I promise."

Gabriel shot him a perplexed look. Miles loved his aunt, appreciated that she cared enough to offer this, but she'd only just managed to pull herself out of her grief to try and get her life back to normal. He'd fight tooth and nail before he let that wretched grimoire anywhere near her.

Robin frowned. "I'm sure you are, but… you don't let a child play with a gun, then tell yourself you're not to blame when they shoot themself."

Cheerful.

"Nothing's going to happen to us," he reassured her. "I promise. And the second we get what we need from the grimoire, we're ditching it."

She clearly wasn't happy. "I'm trusting you to be smart about this, and to come to me if anything happens. Okay?"

"Okay. Thank you, Aunt Robin."

He gave her a hug, taking in the scent of incense from her hair as she returned the gentle squeeze. It was comforting to know someone else had their back.

"We seriously need to get going," Charlee called from the kitchen, annoyance honing the edge of her words. The timing was too perfect for her not to have been eavesdropping.

"She's right, Gabriel needs to get home before school." Miles ushered him towards the kitchen.

But Gabriel hesitated, giving Robin a solemn look. "I have no intention of allowing Miles to get hurt," he told her, unknowingly mirroring Miles's words to Edmund after they'd gotten back from the old Hawthorne house. "By the grimoire, or anything else. You don't need to worry about him."

Warmth tingled at the tips of Miles's fingers.

She studied him over her mug. "It was nice to meet you, Gabriel. You've given me a lot to think about. Perhaps a Warren and a Hawthorne working together isn't as impossible as I'd thought."

14

Gabriel slid into his desk a few minutes before the bell rang. His hair was fluffed in a way that Miles was starting to recognize as half-dried from a recent shower, and he was wearing a sweater vest Miles hadn't seen before, deep blue and charcoal argyle.

"I can't believe you made it," Miles teased. "I figured I'd have to call later and make sure you hadn't drowned."

When they'd dropped him off at the Hawthorne gate this morning, he'd warned Miles he'd be taking a three-hour minimum shower to feel "any semblance of clean again."

"You can thank Edmund. I'm quite sure he broke every single speed limit on the way here."

Miles made a mental note to never let Edmund and Charlee get in a car together.

"Here." Gabriel pulled a bundle of dark fabric from his bag and passed it over. "Since you were so irked last night."

Miles made the mistake of peeling back the scarf, and caught sight of a plain wooden hilt. It was the kill-anything knife.

"You can't bring this to school," he hissed, jamming it into his backpack. "If someone sees it, I'll be expelled."

This was the second surprise knife Gabriel had whipped

out in the last twenty-four hours. Miles hoped this wasn't becoming a pattern.

The lack of concern on Gabriel's face was a little insulting. "Then don't let anyone see. I assumed you'd prefer to have it with you."

Well, yeah. But what if he pulled out his binder and it fell on the floor? Or worse, what if he poked himself with it? Would it kill him?

Okay, now he understood why Gabriel wasn't eager to carry the thing around.

"I don't know why I have to be the pack mule," he muttered, adjusting the knife so it was nestled beside the heart-jar.

"Should I start by pointing out that you're closer to the size of a mule, or that you're the one who insists on carrying a pack everywhere?"

Nice to know being Gabriel's boyfriend didn't mean Miles was spared from his snark.

From the way he was looking at Miles, teasing him like before, he didn't regret their late-night decision. But he could take it back, blame it on stress or sleep deprivation, and Miles wouldn't blame him.

The corner of Gabriel's mouth ticked up. "Should I be concerned you're already trying to find an out?"

Miles kicked halfheartedly at Gabriel's seat, knocking his own knee on the underside of his desk. Mind-reading your new boyfriend was just unfair.

The shrill bell rang, a few stragglers settling into their seats as Ms. Padilla called the class to attention. "Since so many of you have asked: no, homecoming week doesn't mean the test on Friday is canceled. In fact"—she grabbed a stack of papers from her desk and strolled to the front row—"I have your study guides right here."

Everyone groaned in unison.

"I'm sure you'll all survive." She handed out the sheets as she made her way down the row. "If you've been keeping up with the assigned reading, it should be easy."

Miles leaned across the aisle as she drifted around the room. "By the way," he told Gabriel, "I knew you were lying when you said you didn't care about Spirit Week. I think it's cool you decided to join in."

His eyes narrowed. "What are you talking about?"

Miles did a slow, deliberate scan of the room—most of the class were dressed head to toe in various shades of blue, from jeans and T-shirts to increasingly absurd hats and sunglasses, one guy even wrapped in a turquoise feather boa—before settling back on Gabriel's sweater vest.

Gabriel glowered down in disgust. The color was dark enough to almost be mistaken for black, but it didn't matter. He fit right in.

"It's color day, and juniors got blue." Miles didn't bother hiding his delight. "Such school spirit, Thistle High must be winning you—"

"You know this wasn't intentional. It isn't funny."

It was hilarious.

"If you have any questions about the study guide," Ms. Padilla stated as she headed down the row next to Miles's. "I'll have the answers up Thursday—"

The stack of papers exploded out of her hands and into the air. She shrieked. Several people jumped, whirling around.

Miles's necklace gave a pulse of heat. Gabriel reached into

his pocket, pulling out the chain of charms Miles had gifted him. His gaze cut through the room. Miles ducked down, unzipping his backpack to check that the containment box was still properly sealed, the grimoire locked away. It was, but something was up.

"The air conditioning must've switched on," Ms. Padilla stammered, flustered but trying to hide it as her papers swept lazily through the air to land on the floor. "I'll have to call maintenance."

Miles thought it was an explanation for the phantom gust of wind—but a moment later, he felt a cold breeze. Other students started rubbing their bare arms, glancing around in confusion.

The lights flickered, triggering a chorus of screams. At the front of the room, a ghostly figure appeared by the whiteboard.

Gabriel's hand shot across the aisle to thwack Miles.

"I know, I see her."

They were the only ones who could, judging by the lack of terrified yelps and hysteria.

The ghost was an older woman, in her sixties if Miles had to guess, her bobbed golden-blonde hair streaked with gray and wrinkles at the corners of her mouth. Her clothes were outdated, a matching jacket and flared skirt in a cheerful buttery shade and a floral scarf draped over her shoulders. Like all spirits, she was smudged and blurred at the edges.

She was staring right at Miles, wide-eyed, like he was the one who'd popped into existence in the middle of her government class.

"What do we do?" Gabriel prompted in a hushed voice.

The ghost vanished, only to reappear a moment later

outside the classroom, peering in through the window. She must want them to follow her, which meant she was lucid and probably not immediately malicious. Both wins in Miles's book.

"See what she wants, I guess. Call backup if she tries to kill us." He could only imagine the rumors if his parents burst into the school and started fighting off an invisible assailant.

Miles lifted his hand, catching a visibly shivering Ms. Padilla's attention where she was stacking her mess of papers into her desk. "I need to use the bathroom."

"Take the pass." She gestured at a plastic stegosaurus with their class number on its side hanging on the wall. Miles hadn't yet worked up the courage to ask her what exactly dinosaurs had to do with government.

Gabriel jumped to his feet and announced, "I also have to use the restroom."

She blinked at him. "Can it wait until he gets back?"

"No," he said, so straight-faced, you had no choice but to believe him. Miles stifled a snicker.

"Fine. Go together, but be quick."

Miles snatched up the stegosaurus and hurried out of the room, Gabriel hot on his heels.

The ghost was waiting for them in the hall.

"Is this smart?" Gabriel murmured.

"Probably not." But she hadn't tried to murder them in front of their classmates, so she clearly wanted to talk. She could be a teacher who'd died here at the school. There was a ghost janitor who liked to haunt the library upstairs, straightening books and humming rock music under his breath.

Her attention didn't move from Miles's face.

"Do you need help?"

171

"I'm sorry for disrupting your class, but your home was too well protected for me to enter."

Not what Miles had expected her to say. "Who are you?"

Her mouth twitched into a strangely familiar smile. *"You don't recognize your own family?"*

Family? What—

"Rosalie," Gabriel guessed, before Miles's brain could connect the dots. "You're Rosalie Warren."

"And you must be a Hawthorne. I can see Jocelyn, here"—she lifted her hand and grazed the shape of his chin, then his cheekbone—*"and here."*

Miles was wildly underdressed to meet a dead relative for the first time. "Oh, uhm… it's nice to meet you?" What was he supposed to say? *Sorry you died before I met you in person, hope I haven't been making you roll in your grave?*

"It's nice to meet you too. I wasn't sure I'd ever get to see family again." Her expression took on a wistful tinge. *"I barely have enough energy to be here right now after drifting for so long."*

Which begged the question…

"What *are* you doing here? No offense."

It was a massive professional oversight that his parents didn't know there was a ghost in the family.

"Miles's family are buried in the Thistle Cemetery. Were you one of the… reanimated?" Gabriel's chin dipped with guilt.

Oh, God. There was no way, right? Those bodies had been empty vessels. They hadn't summoned spirits.

Unless Rosalie's body being reanimated had pissed her off so much that she'd hauled herself back from the afterlife to kick their asses?

"No. But your attempt to summon Jocelyn last night sent

ripples through the afterlife. I sensed your call to her and knew she wouldn't be able to respond, so I came instead."

"How do you know that?" The sound of a door closing down the hall made Miles's heart skip, but the footsteps headed in the opposite direction. "Wait, someone's going to see us and wonder why we're talking to thin air. C'mon."

They went to the end of the hall where a staircase stretched to the second floor, a private alcove behind it. Miles had eaten lunch here once or twice when the cafeteria got too overwhelming.

"What do you know about Jocelyn?" he pressed, once they were safely out of view. "Do you know why the summoning ritual didn't work?"

"*Because the spell you used is the same magic that's holding her prisoner. It can't, or won't, work against itself.*"

Miles's suspicions had been correct in that regard, but he didn't say so. He understood why Gabriel had to try.

"Prisoner?" Gabriel repeated edgily.

Grief flooded Rosalie's eyes. "*That's why I'm still here. When Jocelyn went missing, I never gave up hope. I searched everywhere for her, snuck onto the Hawthorne property, tried every spell I could find… I thought about her until the day I died. I couldn't bring myself to move on without her.*" Unshed tears glistened, diamonds beneath the glare of the school lights. "*I've been here waiting for her, waiting to cross over with her. She was my soulmate.*"

"Oh." Miles wasn't sure what else to say. The undisguised adoration in her voice made his cheeks burn. "I'm sorry."

He thought back to the framed Warren family tree on his parents' office wall. He couldn't recall if Rosalie had ever married.

Gabriel found words first. "Do you know what happened to her?"

"*My brother, Harry, and I had our suspicions, but nothing we could prove. I tried—*" Her voice quivered. "*I tried so hard to get the truth, to find her, but it didn't matter.*"

"It was Florence," Gabriel explained. "She sacrificed Jocelyn in a ritual for more powerful gifts."

The window behind Rosalie started to rattle in its frame. Frost twisted up the panes of glass as the temperature dropped, goosebumps breaking out across Miles's body.

"*I knew it,*" she said fiercely, "*but I couldn't prove it. Jocelyn told me about the grimoire she found, about Florence's strange behavior, and when she blamed Harry with all those disgusting lies—*" She cut off with a muffled gasp, fist pressed against her mouth. "*I knew she'd done something terrible, but I couldn't do anything about it.*"

Miles lifted his hand before remembering he couldn't touch her. "I'm sorry. You were right, though I doubt that makes you feel better."

"Perhaps this will," Gabriel offered in a low voice. "We banished her ghost like she was nothing. We told her she'd lost, that Jocelyn helped bring about her demise, and then we showed her how little her power meant."

Rosalie's tortured expression smoothed out, settling like a disturbed lake once again going calm. She had the same brown eyes as Miles's dad, he noticed. The same as his.

"*Did it hurt her?*" she asked Gabriel. "*When you banished her?*"

"Yes."

"*Good.*"

"He's making it sound way more badass than it was."

Miles felt the need to point this out. "But now we're trying to break the curse she put on her family line. We didn't know if Jocelyn's spirit was stuck here because of unfinished business or magic."

Rosalie cocked her head. "*I thought you knew. Jocelyn's spirit isn't stuck here.*"

Miles and Gabriel exchanged a confused look. "What do you mean? You just said she's being held prisoner. That you're waiting for her to cross over."

"*I wasn't talking about her spirit. Jocelyn isn't dead.*"

Miles's brain took a moment to process that, unsure if he'd heard her correctly.

"Of course she's dead," Gabriel proclaimed.

"*She's not.*" Rosalie's tone left no room for argument. "*The two of us are bound together. I can feel her. I can feel that it's the same magic holding her captive as the spell you used last night. And I can feel that she's not dead. I would sense it if she was.*"

That was a lot to unpack. "You can sense her? Like, her exact location? If you know where she is, we could—"

"*Not like that. It's just a feeling in here.*" Rosalie lifted a hand to her chest. "*The flickering flame of her life, the warmth it still gives off. It's weak, but she's not dead.*"

He didn't want to disrespect Rosalie, but that didn't make any sense. Not only would Jocelyn have to be well over a hundred years old, but Miles had seen her in his premonitions, talked to her in his dream. She hadn't aged at all since she'd gone missing.

Plus, the way she'd been sending him visions had to be some kind of ghostly power. Unless…

She was still a Hawthorne. If she really was still alive,

would she have been cursed with unnatural gifts like the rest of her family?

Miles suddenly wasn't sure of anything.

"Dead or alive, she needs our help," he settled on, and Gabriel nodded. "But if you're right, why hasn't she died? There must be a reason if the grimoire's magic is involved."

"*I don't know. If I did, maybe I could've freed her years ago.*"

Voices echoed down the hall, reminding Miles of where they were. They'd already been gone too long.

"We have to get back," he told her reluctantly. He still had so many questions. "How can we reach you when we need to talk again?"

"*If you call, I'll come,*" she said simply.

15

"I'm not doing this," Gabriel announced, already backing towards the door. "This is worse than what you described. Much worse."

Miles had to agree. Even the deepest depths of his nightmares couldn't come close to this reality.

The homecoming committee had spread across the entire gym, massive banners laid flat to decorate—there were actual glitter pens, God help them—and shapes being cut out of cardboard. A group was wrangling what looked like giant balls of white fluff, another untangling the biggest knot of string lights in existence. On the opposite side of the gym, bolts of tulle, stacks of paint cans, and bags of sequins leaned against the wall.

"Why..." Gabriel trailed off, then tried again. "Why is it so... *shiny*?"

Between the glitter pens, silver sequins, metallic paint, bedazzled fabric, and shimmery streamers, they were trapped in the world's most nauseating disco ball. The gym looked like it had been possessed by an unholy sparkle demon.

When he'd heard the homecoming theme was Under the Stars, Miles had pictured something elegant. Understated. Less... blinding.

"Should we make a run for it before it's too late?"

But they'd already been spotted. A tall girl with deep brown skin and platinum-blonde braids strode over, clipboard in hand. Her school sweatshirt was smeared and spotted with fresh green paint.

"Are you here to help out?" she asked, pen poised over the clipboard.

"Yes."

"No."

Her eyebrows flew up and Miles hurried to explain. "I am, Mr. Keller should've signed me up. But he's just here to give me a ride home."

He gave his name and she checked a list. "Cool, thanks for volunteering. Feel free to jump in anywhere, it's all hands on deck." Her gaze shifted to Gabriel. "You sure you don't wanna help out? We need people on the clouds"—she pointed at the group wrestling white fluff—"if painting's not your thing."

Gabriel visibly shuddered. "I've never been more certain of anything in my life."

The girl frowned.

"He's got a project he has to work on," Miles hurried to say. "Big chunk of his grade, you know?"

"Uh huh." She clearly wasn't buying it but got distracted by waving across the gym. "I'm Alexis, by the way. Come find me if you need anything."

The bleachers were fully retracted to make more space, so they went to the far end where it wasn't as busy. Gabriel settled on the scuffed gym floor with a long-suffering sigh.

"We only have to be here for a few minutes. Fifteen, max," Miles reminded him. They'd agreed that was the best way to do it: Miles would show up long enough to be seen helping out, so Mr. Keller didn't tell his mom he was a no-show, then he and Gabriel could slip away to spend the rest of the time reading the grimoire.

It felt wrong bringing it to school, carrying it around in his bag like radioactive waste that put everyone in his vicinity at risk. If there was any other way, he'd take it in a heartbeat.

"I'm sure the time will fly by," Gabriel said dryly.

"Fifteen minutes won't kill you. Why don't you help me decorate these ugly banners?"

Gabriel slipped a battered paperback from his bag. "Your optimism truly knows no bounds. Or perhaps delusion is finally setting in."

"You could've just said no." Miles laughed. "Fine, read your depressing book. I'm going to go find something to paint."

He left him to his reading and went looking for a spot to jump in. There were a few familiar faces, but no one he knew well enough to join. The thought of butting in where he wasn't needed or wanted made the back of his neck burn.

"Miles!" Emily waved him over to where she was sitting cross-legged, cutting big stars out of cardboard. She was dressed head to toe in red like the other sophomores, with a scarlet skirt, a sweater embroidered with roses, hair pulled back in a big shiny scrunchie, and red laces on her sneakers. "I didn't know you were helping out the homecoming committee."

"Not by choice." Miles joined her, unreasonably relieved. "It's an extra credit thing for English. But Gabriel and I are slipping out to read the grimoire in a few minutes."

"Is he up for that, after last night?"

"He says he is." Miles took the stack of carboard, sharpie, and cut-out star to trace that Emily offered him. "I think he needs a win after… everything. But it turns out the botched summoning spell might not be our fault."

He leaned in and lowered his voice, explaining about Rosalie's visit.

Emily frowned. "Is it possible Jocelyn's still alive?"

"I'm not sure. I don't think we'll know until we find her." One of the gym doors was cracked open to vent out the hot glue and paint fumes, and Miles could see the downpour of rain beating against the pavement. "I hate to say it, but after last night, she's going to have to wait. We agreed we're not using the grimoire again."

"What if you need a spell from it to undo the curse?"

There was no good answer to that. Miles didn't know anything about breaking curses like this, if you used dark magic to get rid of dark magic, or if the solution was simpler. Please, let it be simpler.

"How are you feeling after last night?" he asked, changing the subject.

Her expression darkened. "Fine."

Yeah, because that was convincing.

"Is everything okay? I know things got pretty scary, and the grimoire—"

"It's not that," she interrupted. "It's just… my mom is being extra herself. It's silly, I have way bigger things to worry about, but she still manages to get under my skin."

Miles felt like a jerk, so focused on his problems that he'd forgotten Emily had her own. "Is she still trying to marry you off?"

"Yep." Emily stabbed a piece of cardboard with her scissors. "She's decided I need to focus more on my gifts and building a reputation among the families to make me more… desirable or whatever. She wants me to give up soccer."

"What did you say?"

"That I'd think about it. It's normally not worth fighting with her, but this is different. She wants me to make this psychic stuff my entire life. I'm two seconds away from calling my grandparents and begging them to get her to go back to Colombia. Fake an emergency, fabricate some big lie, I don't even care, my morals are out the window. I just need her gone before she sucks every bit of joy from my life."

"What if you say no?"

"I don't think she's planning on giving me a choice."

Miles could relate to everything she was saying—except for that. At the end of the day, no matter how mad he was at his mom, he didn't believe either of his parents would force him to continue the family business if he told them he didn't want to. The problem was telling them. The inevitable disappointment, the confusion, the implication that the life they'd built wasn't enough for him. Finding the strength to put his own dreams over helping people and knowing everyone would think he was selfish for it.

"Fight her on it. At some point, you'll have to tell her you're not going to be forced into a relationship. This can be your boundary-setting test run."

"Would you?" Emily challenged with a sideways glance. Not unkindly, just knowingly.

A week ago, Miles would've said that was fair. "I did. When my mom found out about Gabriel. I mean, she didn't listen to me, but I felt better knowing I'd tried for once." He traced a sloppy star. "Charlee thinks Gabriel's bad attitude rubbed off on me."

"I didn't realize how close you two were."

"Me and Charlee?"

"Gabriel." She wasn't looking at him, popping open a tube of gold paint. "You really care about each other."

There was nothing explicit about the comment, but it was clear from what she *wasn't* saying, exactly what was being said.

The noise of the gym was suddenly thunderous in his ears. "We aren't—I mean, I'm not—"

"We aren't talking about it," Emily stated firmly. "Not until you want to. Or never, that's cool too. I only brought it up so you know I'm here if you ever do want to. That's all." She laughed a little sheepishly. "Sorry, that sounded way less lame in my head."

"No, it's… nice. Thank you." Miles reached inside and poked at where his embarrassment burned the hottest, surprised to find it was already fading away. Emily knowing seemed… right.

"I feel a little bad dragging you into this mess," he told her, "but I'm glad you're here. Not just because you're the smartest person I know, but I think it's good for Gabriel. He could use more exposure to someone like you." Miles only had so much warmth to give to combat a lifetime spent in the cold.

"And you too. Don't make it sound like you're not making a difference," she admonished. "I've seen how he loosens up around you. Softens a little."

Miles flushed. "I want him to know what it's like to have people around him who care. Who want him here, you know?"

"I get it. Just don't put too much pressure on yourself."

"He doesn't make me feel like I have to. He makes me want to."

Gabriel had seen Miles defeated, frustrated, hurt, and he still cared about him. He accepted all parts of Miles with no conditions or expectations, no judgment.

Emily gave him a wide, lovely grin. "I'm going to win him over. Not even Gabriel Hawthorne can resist my charm."

Maybe she hadn't seen it, but after last night, she'd already won him over.

It wasn't her style to be bothered by anyone else's opinion, but Miles still hoped she got a chance to see the rare moments when Gabriel's mask came off. That there was more to him than his cold front.

"We should probably get going." Miles handed her supplies back, climbing to his feet and feeling the lingering ache in his muscles from last night. "Lots of evil spells to comb through."

Gabriel spotted him coming, snapping his book closed. "Please tell me it's time to go. If I have to listen to another minute of inane arguing over yellow or gold as a base color"—he gestured to a wooden monstrosity being painted, two shooting stars crossing over each other to form an arch tall enough to walk under—"I'm going to lose the will to live."

He was starting to sound as dramatic as Edmund.

"Yeah, c'mon, let's get outta here."

Gabriel packed his bag, then hesitated. "I had a thought… we should go to the football game."

Miles wasn't even moving and he nearly tripped over his own feet. "What?"

"The football game this Friday. We should go together."

He could've suggested joining the talent show and Miles would've been less shocked. "I know I joked about embracing the school spirit, but you're starting to worry me."

Gabriel rolled his eyes. "I'm aware that it's a ridiculous event, but I'm being serious. Emily mentioned they have popcorn. And"—he shifted, staring at Miles's shoulder as the tips of his ears went scarlet—"I thought perhaps it could be our first date."

First date. Miles's gut gave a distracting swoop.

"Unless people who are already dating don't go on dates," Gabriel continued, eyebrows furrowed. "Do the dates come first, to lead to the decision to date? What is the protocol?"

"I have no idea and honestly, I don't care. Nothing about our relationship has been conventional. Why start now?" Miles wanted to take Gabriel's hand, but they were surrounded by people. "I'd really like to go with you. And get you some popcorn."

"Then it's decided," Gabriel confirmed briskly, like he didn't want to give Miles the opportunity to take it back. He headed towards the gym exit, Miles chasing after him. "I'm surprised you didn't laugh at me."

Miles got the door for him, the handle clanging. "Why would I laugh at you?"

"It's foolish, wanting to spend an evening watching teenagers throw balls at each other when we have significantly more important things to spend our time doing."

Gabriel thought he'd be laughed at, but he'd still been brave enough to ask. "Speak for yourself. Spending time with you is important to me, no matter what we're doing."

He hadn't been to a football game, so he wasn't sure

what to expect, but any time with Gabriel was well worth braving icy bleachers and screaming crowds.

Gabriel met his gaze, eyes curious. "Even such frivolous, asinine, normal teenage experiences?"

Miles smiled at him, wide enough to make his cheeks protest. "Especially those."

16

They went up to the library. Without Blanche to drive them somewhere more secluded, it was their best option. The lights were on, but no one was there after hours—Miles walked through all the shelves to double-check. Even the librarian was gone, the checkout desk empty, the door behind it closed.

The only soul still hanging about was Thistle High's ghost janitor. Miles could hear him humming a Journey song in the fantasy section. Some ghosts had a purpose keeping them here and weren't ready to leave; as long as they hadn't started to descend into madness, there was no problem giving them time. This guy was harmless, mostly shelving books that'd been left scattered about and straightening chairs.

Miles was pretty sure the grimoire couldn't influence a ghost. But he'd keep a lookout, just in case.

Claiming a table in the back corner, Miles tugged the containment box from his bag and popped it open. The grimoire's dark aura washed over him, carrying a memory of pain that made him flinch. The taste of blood flooded his mouth.

He didn't bother asking Gabriel if he was sure he was up for this—neither of them would touch the grimoire again if they didn't have to.

"Be careful," he murmured, passing it over.

Gabriel flipped through the pages, brushing the coarse paper. "Its magic feels... farther away. More reserved than usual."

"It wore itself out last night trying to kill us, and needs a nap." It was a joke, but Miles's humor faded. "Or it's... full."

The possibility was chilling, but at least Gabriel was getting some relief. Miles was trying his best to trust his promise that he'd be cautious, put the grimoire away if needed, but he still worried. Especially after last night.

"We're nearly halfway through already." Gabriel laid the open book across the table. The leathery cover squeaked against the polished tabletop. Even a brief glance at the narrow, jagged writing made Miles's vision swim, a headache instantly thumping behind the bridge of his nose.

"There's still plenty left. Don't worry, it'll be in there."

Gabriel shrugged, as if he didn't care. The lie was so obvious, Miles wasn't sure why he bothered.

Over by the shelves, Miles caught a flash of overalls and a bushy beard. He turned away swiftly—the last time the ghost janitor realized Miles could see him, he'd talked his ear off about kids vandalizing books and how good rock music died in the early 2000s.

He dug out his math textbook and tried to focus on equations while Gabriel read. The library was hushed aside from the pattering of rain against a window and Gabriel's occasional mutter to himself as he turned the page.

It didn't take long to realize homework was a lost cause. The numbers were swimming across the page, jumbling into more nonsense than usual. And there was a spot where a single silky lock of Gabriel's dark hair was curling behind his ear, a stark contrast against his pale skin. As Miles stared, mesmerized by the gentle swoop, goosebumps sprang up across the exposed skin of Gabriel's neck where his crisp white collar had pulled away.

"Miles."

He started, totally caught. "Sorry, I wasn't—"

"No, Miles, look at this." Gabriel angled the grimoire towards him.

The Gift of Power

To bind your bloodline and divine magic together to unlock gifts aplenty
For those who wish to know their true power

Offerings:
- A sacrifice of life

Only one offering is required, but it is the most meaningful. Only life can fuel such magic, only the greatest of sacrifices can bring such power. Sacrifice must be of magic-touched blood and unwilling. Tools needed to complete the ritual and binding are provided upon invocation of magic.

Preparation:
- To invoke the magic, write the intended sacrifice's name on parchment and burn to ashes. Mix ashes with blood of summoner until wet. Use the mixture to sign family name below.

Best performed during the night of a new moon to embrace limitless possibilities and beginnings.

Sacrifice must be performed on the same night or preparation ritual must be repeated.

Once completed, the power will enter, binding together with blood and body and soul.

That was the end of the page. Written below in a smudged, dark ink was *Hawthorne*. Not ink—Florence's blood.

Miles turned to the next page but found himself staring down at a hex to bring misfortune upon enemies.

That wasn't right.

"Where's the rest?" he demanded. The paragraph on how to undo it. How to unbind the bloodline. There had to be a part for take-backs.

"It was torn out," Gabriel said grimly, running his fingertip down the center where a jagged edge of ripped paper was visible. "Someone didn't want us to find it."

"That's impossible. When we found this thing, it hadn't been touched in forever."

That didn't change the fact that the rest—if there was more to it—was gone.

"This was all a pointless waste of time." Gabriel's jaw was so tense, it was a miracle he could grind the words out. "The curse can't be broken."

Miles put his head in his hands, trying to think. This couldn't be it. There had to be something they could use. They didn't have anything else.

"Maybe..." He stopped, drawing a blank. "That might not be it. What if there's another—"

"Stop. It's over."

"But if the page was stolen so we wouldn't find it, that must mean there's a way to undo the curse."

"You said it yourself. No one's touched the grimoire in years or knew we'd be trying to undo the curse. It's most likely another spell that's been torn out."

No, Miles refused to believe that. It couldn't be a coincidence.

"We might not be the only ones who've tried to undo it. Someone else could've found the grimoire, ripped out the page—"

"Even if they did, they clearly failed and now the page is gone." Gabriel stood with a squeal of his chair, snatching the grimoire. His nails dug into the cover. "This thing is useless. We can't break the curse."

He whirled around and stomped away, disappearing down an aisle.

Miles let out a long breath, shoulders slumping. He'd give Gabriel a minute to compose himself before chasing after him. He hadn't stormed off towards the library exit and he wouldn't leave while he still had the grimoire.

What a mess.

Fear mounted in Miles's chest that Gabriel was right, but he pushed against it. He needed a clear head to think, to—

"Excuse me." Gabriel's tense voice shattered the silence of the library. "What are you—"

There was a loud thud, a strange choking noise, and what sounded like books hitting the ground. The hair on Miles's neck prickled.

He sprinted after Gabriel, weaving through the tight aisles. When he emerged at the end of the history section, he found the librarian—a middle-aged man in a tie-dye shirt and orange crocs who insisted students call him Joe instead of Mr. Boone—pinning Gabriel against a bookcase, fallen books littered at their feet. His arm was pressed against Gabriel's throat, free hand yanking the grimoire Gabriel was still holding.

"Hey!" Panic roared through Miles. He didn't think before shoving Joe as hard as he could, focused only on getting him off Gabriel. The librarian hit the ground.

Gabriel was frozen flat against the shelf, eyes wide and lips parted.

"Are you okay?" Miles ran his hands over Gabriel's shoulders, shaken by the sudden unexpected violence. "Did he hurt you?"

"I—" Gabriel swallowed, pale fingers lifting to his throat. "I didn't say anything to him. I don't know why he attacked me."

Miles spun back to where Joe was hauling himself from the floor, one of his orange crocs left behind. "What the hell was that? What's your problem?"

He didn't look at Miles, didn't acknowledge that he'd spoken. Gaze locked on the grimoire in Gabriel's hands, his lips peeled back to bare his teeth.

He lunged. Miles managed to shoulder check him and send him crashing into the bookcase instead of Gabriel. Joe wasn't as tall as Miles, but he was built surprisingly sturdy for a high school librarian. Getting hit by him, even a glancing blow to the shoulder, rattled Miles's teeth.

Books cascading around him, Joe shoved himself back with an angry noise, his attention snapping back to the grimoire. The look on his face was hauntingly familiar—Miles had seen the same razor-sharp desperation in Gabriel when they'd first found the book in the old Hawthorne place and it wormed its way into his mind.

Miles's fear had come true: an innocent bystander had been enthralled by the grimoire's evil magic. He lifted his mental shield, recoiling from the swirling maelstrom of darkness enveloping Joe.

That explained why it hadn't been bothering Gabriel—it was too busy setting its sights on someone else.

Gabriel stumbled back from the force of Joe's stare as Miles planted himself between them in the narrow aisle. "Listen to me," Miles implored, lifting his hands to try and capture Joe's attention. "Something's messing with your head right now, okay? This isn't—"

Joe collided into him with the force of a truck—missing a shoe didn't slow him down at all. They hit the ground in a heap, Miles getting jabbed in the spine by several books. He didn't even get a chance to suck in a breath before Joe was crawling towards Gabriel. Having zero experience in a fight, Miles did the only thing he could think of and wrapped himself around Joe to hold him back.

He had to look absolutely ridiculous—both legs pretzeled around their librarian, his head shoved dangerously close to an armpit, his hands clenched around fistfuls of faded tie-dye like his life depended on it.

Well, Gabriel's life.

"The grimoire," he grunted, straining to maintain his hold. Either carrying books was more of a workout than anyone knew, or this guy was juiced up on grimoire magic.

Gabriel sprang forward and thumped Joe over the head with the heavy book. He didn't hold back either, the force of the hit vibrating through to Miles.

"No," Miles wheezed. The blow didn't slow Joe down. He struggled, clawing at the threadbare carpet to drag himself towards Gabriel. "The grimoire is controlling him. Put it in the box."

"Oh."

Gabriel darted away. Joe twisted, flailing around in Miles's grip to try and follow. Miles narrowly avoided getting an elbow to the jaw. He only needed to hold on for one more—

Joe went limp. Rolling away with a groan, Miles flopped against the floor, arms and legs trembling. He ached like he'd just tried to wrestle a buffalo on steroids.

Panting, Gabriel reappeared, the closed containment box in his hands. His shoulders slumped in relief as Miles got to his feet. "Are you—"

"Ow!" Blinking in bewilderment, Joe sat up and clutched at the shoulder he'd landed on when Miles shoved him. There was a tear at the collar of his shirt. "What happened?"

"I think you got hit by a book," Miles lied breathlessly. "You were unconscious when we came over."

"I…" His gaze darted from the books on the floor to the broken shelf he'd pinned Gabriel against. His bushy eyebrows furrowed. "I was in my office…"

The door behind the checkout counter was ajar—that explained where Joe had come from. He must've been working after hours, and the grimoire's energy had crept over. Miles should've known better; he'd sensed it reaching through the floor of his bedroom in search of a victim the first night he'd brought it home.

"Here, let me help you up." Miles gingerly pulled Joe to his feet. "You might have a concussion."

He wondered what the grimoire had told him to make him so desperate to steal it. When he mentally reached out to check that Joe wasn't hurt, he found only a low thrum of pain beneath his confusion and unease.

Joe declined when Miles offered to see if the nurse was still here, stiffly putting his croc back on and tugging at the rip in his shirt. Every time he looked at Gabriel, his forehead crease got deeper. He didn't protest when they went to leave, muttering about cleaning up.

Miles snagged the waist of Gabriel's sweater vest, tugging him away. "Let's grab our stuff and go, before we accidentally summon another murderous hippie." Talk about new fear unlocked.

It was pouring as they went out the front entrance, the sky an angry charcoal, so they sat on the empty covered stairs instead of their usual table on the grass. The cold of the concrete immediately seeped through Miles's jeans, making him shiver.

Gabriel set the containment box a step below them, flexing his fingers. He didn't say anything, but leaned in until their arms pressed together, grounding Miles against the jittery adrenaline aftershocks.

They listened to the thunderous rain against the pavement and the cawing of crows in the nearby trees. Tension uncoiled from between Miles's shoulder blades. He rarely got to be this close to Gabriel and simply enjoy his nearness, to breathe in his clean laundry and crisp winter air smell and feel his warmth where they touched. He would give anything to stay like this for a little longer.

Gabriel exhaled. "What did I do to give you the impression that sacrifice is necessary for my company?"

Heat crawled up Miles's face. "Leave me alone. I just saved you from a very scary librarian, I get a free pass on embarrassing thoughts for the next ten minutes."

"I'll give you fifteen because it was such an impressive rescue."

Miles worked an elbow between them enough to nudge him in the ribs. Jerk. "I'll have you know, that move is called the Human Octopus and it's reserved for the direst of situations. You should feel lucky you got to see it in person."

"It's a sight I'll never forget, that's for certain."

"You're not funny." Miles turned his face back to his knees, but he knew Gabriel could hear his smile.

They were cracking jokes, but if Miles hadn't been there, hadn't heard the attack, hadn't been fast enough…

"You can't watch me every moment." Wet leaves fell through the air to stick against the stairs, decorating the stone with shades of autumn. "Though, if you insist on performing such daring rescues, I might consider hiring you as a full-time bodyguard."

Miles's laugh got stuck in his throat. He'd almost lost Gabriel twice in the last twenty-four hours.

"Foolish of you to think you could get rid of me so easily." Gabriel plucked at Miles's jacket sleeve, refusing to let him wallow. "I can't die until I get the football popcorn you promised."

"Are you trying to cheer me up? I appreciate the effort, but maybe leave out the death reminder in the future."

"I happen to know you like my morbid sense of humor."

Before Miles could answer, Gabriel's phone vibrated against him where they were pressed together. He glanced at the screen, typed quickly, then slipped it away. "Edmund is almost here."

Time just kept moving, no matter how desperately Miles wished it would stop.

He raked a hand through his tangled hair. "We should talk about the curse."

"Not right now. I need space to think." It might've stung, if Gabriel's voice wasn't uncharacteristically soft, almost a plea.

"Okay." It was an easy thing to give him. He eased Gabriel's hand out of where he'd tucked it into his pocket, running his thumb along the groove of his knuckles. "I'm here whenever you're ready."

Exhaling slowly, Gabriel lowered his head to rest against Miles's shoulder, making Miles's heart clench. "I know you are."

17

Gabriel didn't talk about the curse until lunch the next day.

Miles gave him the space he'd asked for, but it was difficult. He struggled not knowing what Gabriel was thinking, what hole he was sinking into. He'd experienced Gabriel's conflicting emotions firsthand and could now picture the negative ones preying on his defeat.

"We should discuss our next steps," Gabriel said as a greeting when Miles slipped into the chair beside him. The cafeteria was extra loud, everyone dressed up for Throwback Thursday and the excitement for homecoming was palpable as it drew closer.

Not for the first time, Miles wished he knew what it would be like for the biggest worry in his life to be what he would wear to homecoming. What exactly a boutonniere was. How to dance without stepping on anyone's toes.

"We've hit a dead end with the curse and the premonitions." There was a stiffness to Gabriel's voice, as if he'd rehearsed this. "Without any leads to follow or proactive steps to take, I think we should reevaluate what we're doing."

He must've been up all night spiraling, assuming the worst.

"I'm all for reevaluating, but you might be jumping the gun," Miles said. "The curse told us everything we need."

Miles had spent all night with Charlee, texting Emily and trying to find anything that would send them in a new direction. Emily had finally had a breakthrough, giving Miles his first surge of hope in days.

He fished a notebook from his bag and plopped it triumphantly onto the table. He'd ended up having to write out the whole ritual by hand last night after trying to take pictures to send to Emily, only for the page to show up blank in every single one. More frustrating magical bullshit.

"Emily and Charlee helped me work on this last night." He flipped to the scribbled page, covered in words circled, underlined, and crossed out. "And we realized that the original ritual might actually tell us how to undo the curse."

Gabriel leaned in as Miles traced the top line, where he'd circled "bind" in red pen. On the other side of the cafeteria, there was a commotion and a bunch of cheering as a group brought out the ballot boxes to vote for homecoming queen and king. They both ignored it.

"The spell says it's binding your family and the magic together." Miles's finger slid down to where he'd underlined another part. "And that Jocelyn's life is what fuels the magic. So this isn't just a spell, it's a bargain. Give and take. Jocelyn's energy, or life or whatever, in exchange for the magic in your family. That explains why Jocelyn is still here, and why Rosalie can still sense her—the magic must be keeping her alive. It's like a parasite, and Jocelyn is the host. The longer it can keep the host alive, the longer it can feed. It's only here because she is."

What Rosalie said had slid the final piece into place. It

didn't make any sense for Jocelyn to still be alive and held captive—unless she had a use.

Gabriel drummed his fingers against his thigh. "So, if we freed Jocelyn…"

"Then it should undo the bargain," Miles finished for him. "That's how deals work—if you don't keep up your side, neither will the other. No taking if you're not giving, right? The magic won't be bound to your family anymore."

Skimming the written-out ritual again, Gabriel frowned. "How do we know the magic would leave? It's already been bound, the sacrifice made. This doesn't say anything about keeping the sacrifice alive."

"It's probably on the missing page. There's no reason for Jocelyn to be alive otherwise. It must need a continuous source of life to feed from, or it would've just killed her immediately. Nothing else makes sense."

Gabriel watched the line of students filter up to the ballot boxes on a table near the cafeteria entrance. "It's only a hypothesis. We don't know any of this for sure."

"We've made bigger leaps based on less," Miles pointed out. "But yeah, you're right. Which is why I think we should ask Jocelyn herself."

"That's a fair idea in theory, but we already tried summoning her with the most powerful spell we could find."

"Exactly. We tried *summoning* her. I only want to talk to her. Get her to tell us where she is or how to free her."

"She hasn't historically been forthcoming with her information. What makes you think this time would be any different?"

That same question had kept Miles up all night. "The reason she wouldn't tell me anything before is because she didn't want to send me down the wrong path. But we know what we need to do, we're already on the path that's leading straight to her freedom. It would be crazy for her not to help us now."

She'd been trapped in some dank tomb for the last hundred years, being used as a food source for dark magic—there was no way she wouldn't give them a hand with this final step. Not if she had any sense of self-preservation.

Gabriel didn't look convinced, twisting a button on his cuff. "Even if we could get her to tell us where she is or how to free her, how do you propose we speak with her in the first place?"

"Rosalie. She has a connection to Jocelyn. What if there's a way we can use that connection to reach out to her?"

"That seems like a rather large reach," Gabriel remarked dubiously. "Have you heard of this being done before?"

"Well… no. That just means we'll be the first." Miles was making it sound easier than it would be, based on their track record, but he needed that dull, hollow look of Gabriel's to fade. "Listen. I get it. This has been… let's just be honest, a shit road for us so far." Gabriel had probably spent the whole night talking himself into a hopeless pit of despair and didn't want to get his hopes up, pull himself out only to tumble back in. "We've almost died more times than I want to count, we've messed up even more, and pretty much every time I think we're about to make progress, we get screwed over. I don't blame you for wanting to call it quits. I'm tired, I'm still sore from the cemetery, and I hate that the grimoire didn't give us more." He put his hopefully-not-sweaty hand on Gabriel's where it was resting on his leg beneath the table. "But please, don't give up yet. Not when my gut knows we're so close."

"Well, if your gut says so…" Gabriel grumbled, lacking any real thorniness. He stared down at their hands. "I don't want to give up. I'm just… exhausted from all of this. And I'm afraid."

His moments of painful candor always made Miles ache to hug him tight. "Me too," he admitted. "I don't know what we're going to do if this doesn't work."

Gabriel flipped his hand around to squeeze Miles's back. "Then I guess we'd better hope it does."

It suddenly seemed like a great idea to kiss him, right there in the middle of the cafeteria.

Clearing his throat, Miles glanced around. "Uh, hey, Rosalie. It's me… Miles. You said you'd come if I called so… consider this me calling. We might have a plan to help Jocelyn, but we need your help."

He scanned the cafeteria for any sign of her, for a ghostly wind or sudden chill, but nothing happened. A guy tripped over a chair and stumbled, but from the jeers and hoots of his friends, it was just normal clumsiness, not a ghostly attack.

"Well," Miles said, after a minute, "she didn't say she'd come quickly. And we're here all day."

"What do we do if she doesn't come back?"

"She will."

She had to.

Miles was starting to consider leaving the family business and giving up his life as a psychic to wage a one-man war against hot glue guns and all their manufacturers.

"*Ouch!*" he hissed for the sixth time, stuffing his singed

fingers into his mouth. It did absolutely nothing to help with the pain and made everything taste like burnt plastic.

"I told you a dozen burns ago to put that thing away," Gabriel snarked without glancing up from his book. It was nice to see him reading something other than the grimoire, though Miles doubted that *The Complete Tales and Poems of Edgar Allan Poe* was a much lighter read. He should lend Gabriel one of Charlee's sappy romance books.

"Your scathing commentary isn't helping." Miles took his finger from his mouth and examined the red blister, wincing. "It was this or glitter pens. What was I supposed to do?"

When they'd entered the gym after school, Miles had immediately been put to work. A harried-looking Alexis had marched him over to a black background leaning against the bleachers and given him a hot glue gun, a screwdriver, a reference sketch of the painted stars glued down, and an ominous, "Don't mess it up."

Miles was dreading the moment she came back and saw the mess he'd made. In his defense, the last time he'd crafted like this, he'd been making paper plate turkeys in third grade.

"We shouldn't have bothered coming here at all," Gabriel said.

"I heard you the first ten times." Miles picked in vain at the wispy strands of glue all over his shirt. "I'm not going to leave just for Rosalie to show up the second we're not together. We owe her as much time as we can give. And I told Mr. Keller I'd be here."

Refusing to disappoint his teacher somehow felt like it would make up for what he'd done to Joe the librarian yesterday. The least he could do was suffer a few burns to clear his conscience.

Gabriel lowered his book, flashing the story he was reading—"The Fall of the House of Usher"—and gave Miles a look of disbelief. "The only way you can help that monstrosity at this point is to put it out of its misery."

A laugh escaped Miles before he could catch it. "C'mon, don't tell me you don't want to go to homecoming just to pose in front of this beauty." He'd stuck a few stars on lopsided, and the black backdrop was littered with stray drips and strings of glue, but it wasn't hideous. "Think of the picture potential."

"I'd rather stand in front of the nearest speeding car."

With a *whoosh*, a huge banner laid out in the middle of the gym billowed up, glitter and sequins flying. Several people shrieked, others running to close the gym door. The scoreboards started rapidly flashing numbers and times.

A hazy white shape flickered in and out of existence by the door to the boys' locker room.

"Rosalie's here."

Grabbing an alert Emily as they crossed the gym, they slipped inside the open locker room door. It was freezing, Miles's breath coming out in white puffs and the mirrors glazed in a thin layer of frost. He stepped over gym bags and —*gross*, a pair of plaid boxers tossed on the floor—the smell of body spray, dirty socks, and disinfectant flooding his nose.

Rosalie appeared, barely visible under the bright lights. She took in their shivers and cloudy exhales, frowning. *"Would you believe me if I said I can't control the chill?"*

"It's okay," Miles told her, zipping his jacket up to his chin. Gabriel crossed his arms, his black sweater vest not covering nearly enough to keep him warm. "This is Emily, by the way. She's helping with all of this too."

Emily gave a little wave.

"I had an idea I wanted to run by you..." he continued. "You feel Jocelyn's energy. Soul. Whatever it is. Do you think there's a way you could use that connection to reach out to her?"

Rosalie's expression grew wistful. *"I've tried so many times, but never with any success. I'm searching in the dark without direction. I believe the connection would have to go both ways for us to find each other again."*

Like how Miles had only been able to feel Gabriel after he'd opened the doorway between them.

"Damn it."

"What about Miles?" Emily asked. Frost was starting to form on the wall behind her, jagged vines creeping across the grimy blue tile.

He blinked. "What about me?"

"Well, Jocelyn's been giving you those visions, reaching out to you. There's obviously a connection there. Could you follow it back to her?"

"How do these visions work?" Rosalie questioned him.

Teeth chattering, Emily went over to crank on the showers with a squeak, steam immediately billowing from the stalls. She groaned in relief, the damp heat making her chestnut hair curl. Good thing one of them was using their brain, or they would've frozen to death in here.

"I have no idea," Miles told Rosalie. "Initially, she was just sending me premonitions of Gabriel's death. Once, she managed to come and talk to me in a dream, and then later, she appeared during my math class. When I tried to reach out to her on my own, something blocked us from talking."

Rosalie considered his words as the warmth from the showers started melting the ice frosted over the mirrors and faucets, dripping onto the floor. *"Your connection to her might be enough. Together, perhaps we can push through the block."*

"Gabriel's her blood. That might matter more than our... mental bond."

Gabriel shook his head and untucked his hands from his armpits. "If that mattered, she would've reached out to me."

But she'd chosen Miles as her noble knight, Gabriel's protector.

He met Rosalie's eyes. "I suppose there's no reason not to try."

"Wait." Gabriel slid Miles a disapproving look that he had no idea what he'd done to earn. "It's not that simple. We don't know how Jocelyn's getting these visions to Miles, but they hurt him."

"It's not a big deal. Nasty headaches, sometimes a nosebleed..."

"And the seizure?" Gabriel asked flatly.

Emily gasped. "You didn't tell me you had a seizure."

"Charlee said it *looked* like one." Miles appreciated the concern, he really did, but it wasn't up for debate. "I'm sure it's fine, one more time can't hurt."

"Miles—"

"At the cemetery, I trusted you even when I didn't like it," Miles told Gabriel gently. "Let me try. I'll be okay."

He could feel Gabriel fuming, chewing over his words and wanting to spit them back. "I *don't* like it," he finally muttered, "but if you insist, at least lie down so you don't fall and crack your skull open."

"I'm pretty sure the bacteria on this floor are more dangerous than a busted head."

Gabriel just pointed at the bench in front of the nearest row of lockers.

It was a small price to pay for his cooperation, so Miles lay down across the metal bench, trying to find the least awkward position possible. His feet ended up dangling over the edge, hands folded on his middle.

Emily appeared over him, a folded white towel in her hand. "Here." She gestured for him to lift his head.

He studied it suspiciously. "Where did you get that?" No way was he using a footballer's butt towel.

She grinned, flashing dimples. "Don't worry, I grabbed it from the clean shelf."

He let her tuck it under him, giving Gabriel a sheepish look that turned to one of disbelief as he sat down on the grimy floor beside Miles. Of his own free will.

"You're making me nervous, watching me like that."

Gabriel shifted closer, crossing his legs. The bottom of his pants shifted up, revealing argyle socks that matched his sweater vest. Why was that so cute? "Be careful. I'm going to be annoyed if I have to go into your head and pull you out of psychic limbo."

"That's not even a thing. But it's sweet you're worried about me," Miles teased, then flushed when he remembered Emily standing there. "Oh, here." He lifted his head enough to slip his charm necklace off, handing it to Gabriel. He didn't want to make things harder. "Okay," he told Rosalie, looking up at where she was floating over him. "Time to talk to Jocelyn again."

18

Being back in the tomb, even in the safety of his mind, made Miles shiver.

Gray stone. The smell of must and damp earth. Light flickering as if from a flame. A sigil of a tree on the far wall.

There was a body on the stone floor. Gabriel. Gray eyes lifeless. A trickle of blood down the side of his face. A red pool under his head. A blood-smeared chunk of rock beside him. His pale hand outstretched, fingers reaching towards Miles.

Behind him was a lifted platform, a woman laid out on it. She turned her head and looked at him with eyes that blazed like twin suns, dark with determination and rage. Her face was tear-streaked, her hands curled into claws against the stone.

He tried to conjure the memory perfectly, down to every last painstaking detail. Even the ones that hurt.

Another presence joined him. Rosalie's energy was surprisingly comforting for a spirit, like the gentle heat of sunshine warming him through his jacket, with a herby, rosemary scent. She smelled like summer days in his mom's kitchen.

"Can you see Jocelyn?" He wasn't sure if she could hear his thoughts, so he whispered them out loud, feeling more than a little silly.

"*Yes.*" Rosalie's voice was thick with emotion. He couldn't see her, since she wasn't part of the memory, but her voice was clear in his head. "*What is this place?*"

"Where Gabriel's going to die. Or me. We tried to figure out where it was, but we hit a dead end."

"*I've never been here. It's not somewhere I know.*"

"Yeah, that would've been too easy."

Rosalie's energy shifted closer to Gabriel's body and her sorrow enveloped Miles, a twin to his own.

He couldn't look at the body directly, the curl of pale fingers and the blood-slick shine on the floor making his stomach roll.

"*Poor child,*" Rosalie murmured. "*Such a terrible, un-imaginable cost for something so inconsequential.*"

"I don't get it either, hating your gift so much that you'd murder to change it."

"*Florence never understood the privilege of being a healer. The day my gift made itself known to me and I realized I could heal people's pain, I thanked the universe with my whole heart.*"

Jocelyn had mentioned many times in her journal that Rosalie and Florence shared the gift of healing, that she hoped they could connect over it. Having met Florence and experienced her charm firsthand, Miles could see why that hadn't worked out.

"You never wished you had a different gift?"

"*I'd be lying if I said never, and we'd both know it.*"

Miles had been there more than once. It was normal. Killing because you were bitter about it, not so much.

"Can you sense the connection between me and Jocelyn? I don't know if it's been completely cut off."

"*It's still here. Only a thin, fragile thread, but enough to follow.*"

Before Miles could ask how exactly they were going to do that, his gut gave a swooping lurch, like he'd woken up from a dream of falling. The room revolved around him, colors smudging together in a nauseating blur.

When everything steadied, the room had shifted. Miles locked his shaking knees and took slow, measured breaths so he wouldn't puke. With each exhale, the tomb sharpened, details focusing.

The space was bigger now than in his visions, rough pillars positioned throughout and broken chunks of rocky debris littered across the floor. It was a strange mix of natural and man-made, the walls and floor uneven stone, as if the room had been chiseled into the side of a mountain, but the Hawthorne crest carved into the wall was precisely done, its lines clean.

It felt so real, so starkly different from his memory, that for a moment, he had the ridiculous thought that Rosalie had teleported them. But he could feel the cold metal bench beneath him; he was still in the locker room.

Whatever this was, it was more than a memory. He knew if he reached out and touched the wall, he'd feel the rough texture against his fingers; if he opened his mouth and spoke, the words would echo around the space.

Apprehension grew as he scanned the room again and realized there wasn't a door.

"Rosalie?" Miles couldn't see her anywhere, couldn't feel her energy. She was gone.

It was just him and Jocelyn. Even Gabriel's body had vanished, thank God.

Jocelyn looked the same as always, laid flat across the lifted stone platform, still as a corpse. Her ebony hair was

CAMILLA RAINES

knotted around her shoulders, white nightgown down to her ankles. The only thing out of place were the blood-red flowers sprawling across the wall behind her, a fierce splash of color. Poppies, their petals lush and velvety, a bitter, almost burnt smoky smell radiating from them. At first, Miles thought they'd been attached to the wall in a baffling decor choice, but as he drew nearer, he could see the stems were growing out of the stone.

He made himself turn back to Jocelyn. Now that he was looking for it, she didn't seem like a typical ghost. She wasn't hazy or translucent, which really should've been a glaring flaw in his assumption from the get-go. If the magic of the curse really was keeping her alive, it hadn't let her age past the day she'd been sacrificed. She was like Snow White, preserved eternally on the cusp of death.

"Miles Warren." Jocelyn's voice made him jump, her eyes opening. "I was expecting you."

"Oh. I guess you know Rosalie's here too, then. Well, was here. I'm not sure where she went."

Grief creased Jocelyn's face, so visceral that Miles's heart twinged. "She won't be back. It's not my time to see her again."

"I'm sorry," he said, as a tear streaked down her alabaster face to vanish into her hair. He'd give her a moment if he could, but with Rosalie gone, he had no idea how long he had before he was yanked out. "You probably know this too, but I'm here because Gabriel and I found the spell Florence used. We know everything now: how the magic's keeping you trapped here, that you're bound to it, and that freeing you will end the curse."

She didn't seem thrilled by the news. "Then why have you sought me out?"

"Uh, because we need you to tell us where you are so we can come get you? No offense, but we're kinda ready to be done."

"I have already told you. I cannot give you answers to guide your journey."

"But…" They'd figured it out. Solved the mystery of the Hawthorne curse. "This could all be over tonight. I don't think you understand, we have zero clue where you are and no leads. We're not going to find you if you don't help us."

"My answer remains the same."

Miles pressed his knuckles to his face, hard enough that black spots exploded across his vision. "Then why even bother with the visions and warnings in the first place? I've jumped through every single hoop, done everything you asked—I found Gabriel, I kept the grimoire safe, I'm trying to save his life. All I want is your help on this one thing." His words ricocheted around the room, too loud, too aggravated. A petal fell from one of the poppies, swooping gently down to rest on the back of Jocelyn's white hand like a bloody kiss.

"I know you're angry," she said. She studied the petal, twisting her wrist slightly so it drifted to the floor. "I don't blame you. Contacting you was always part of this path, but assisting you here isn't. I cannot risk sending you to an unknown end."

"That's bullshit. I'd rather take the risk of an unknown future than one that for sure ends in death. Why are you so determined to let fate call all the shots when we can change it?"

"What do you think it is that I'm trying to do?" she demanded, the first hint of spikiness in her voice. "I have called upon you to help me change this tragic future and prevent Gabriel Hawthorne's death."

"So you say, but you conveniently can't tell me anything useful." Anger burned hot as a coal in his throat. "You know what I think? You're playing a bigger game here, toying with us. You probably don't give a shit about Gabriel. This is all some sick, twisted, convoluted plan to help yourself, or see his family cursed forever after what your sister did to you."

Her expression shifted into something darker. "I would never lie about this."

"But you can omit the truth however you want, right? Like the premonitions Gabriel's having of my death… let me guess, you just forgot to mention that part?" An ugly, wet laugh escaped Miles. "What did you call me before? A noble knight? More like your sacrificial lamb."

He didn't realize how betrayed he'd felt until he voiced it out loud and saw her flinch. She'd known, and she hadn't warned him.

It wasn't fair. What a naive, childish thing to think, but it just wasn't fair.

Jocelyn's eyes fluttered closed. Miles hoped it was from shame. "I'm sorry. The future has so many paths. Ones where you save Gabriel. Ones where he dies. Ones where you save me. Ones where you die."

"You should've told me."

She sighed, the noise swallowed up by the hollow tomb. "I knew my own demise was coming, wrote the details of my visions down to try and decipher the clues so I could stop it. It did not matter. It did not help. All it did was make me more afraid. I wanted to spare you that."

Well, excuse him if he wasn't grateful she hadn't bothered to warn him of his potential death.

"Help me stop the killer, then." He didn't care that he was begging. He'd get down on his knees if it made a difference. "Neither of us has to die. Tell me who it is. Is it Felicity? Is Gabriel's mom going to do it?"

It was the first time he'd voiced his suspicions to anyone. He hated how rotten they tasted, how heavily they sat in the air. He wanted so badly to be wrong.

She didn't answer. He'd known she wouldn't.

"I want this to be over," he admitted, his outrage fading with the words, snuffed out beneath a surge of exhaustion. He wanted to sink to the floor and sit in the darkness for a while, let everything fade away. "I'm so sick and tired of helplessly spinning in circles when it doesn't change anything."

There. He'd said it. The thing he couldn't tell Gabriel or Charlee or anyone else because he had to keep them going, keep their spirits up, remind them that the future could be changed when the horrible truth was that nothing they'd done mattered. Death was still waiting for them in that tomb, and they were still barreling straight towards it.

He was starting to lose faith.

Jocelyn's hand twitched against the stone as if she wanted to reach for him. "I understand. I have been trapped down here for what feels like an eternity, gradually devoured by insatiable magic as it corrupts my bloodline. This is the first chance I have been given to change my fate and so much could go wrong. There are so many pieces in play that must move correctly. I have witnessed every revelation and confusion you've had, each path you've dismissed. The most

213

minuscule of changes have huge consequences. I have seen what happens if I help you here now, and believe me when I say you would not thank me for it."

Her words were a terrible reminder of just how easily this could all fall apart. How blind Miles was, being puppeted around by forces he couldn't break free of.

"So despise me if you must," Jocelyn continued, voice softening, "but know that when I deny you information and tell you to stay on the path, it is because I have seen the consequences. Despite your passion and fury, I cannot risk squandering this opportunity. Too much is at stake."

Miles sat down, too tired to stand any longer. He'd forgotten for a moment that she wasn't the villain, that his frustration and suffering were a pinprick compared to hers.

She'd bet her one shot at freedom on him. An anxious, overwhelmed, sleep-deprived teenager who couldn't keep his emotions in check.

"I'm sorry I yelled at you." He hugged his knees. It was strange—he couldn't feel the chill of the room, but his body knew it was there. "It wasn't fair of me. I'm just... I can't believe all of this is because of a stupid book. That one of us might die because of it."

"It is the foulest, most irresistible kind of temptation," Jocelyn agreed solemnly. "It offers you the answer to your deepest regrets and insecurities, your worst fears. That kind of magic should not be underestimated. It is a wolf, leashed or not, and it will strike out on its own to hunt if it is not fed."

"Like it did with Florence, you mean. Giving her a way to become powerful, to get rid of a part of herself she hated."

"Desperation has a way of pushing good people to the

darkest of places and deeds. Once, before my parents became obsessed with wealth and status, before it turned them cold and cruel towards their own children, Florence was my sister. She taught me to make flower crowns and snuck out every morning for weeks to feed the motherless kittens taking shelter under our porch."

A pang of sympathy went through Miles, and he cursed himself for being such a limp noodle. Florence had tried to kill him, damn it. Kittens didn't change that. "Desperation doesn't excuse murder," he made himself say.

"Of course not. I do not excuse my sister, but I do feel compassion for her. And I believe that if not for the grimoire, she never would've made such a terrible choice. It turned her against her own family so easily, simply by whispering into her ear."

Speaking of Florence—

"I should probably tell you, Gabriel and I banished her. She's… moved on."

That was nicer than "hopefully she's rotting in the deepest darkest depths of hell."

A complicated mix of emotions passed over Jocelyn's face. "I hope she managed to find peace in the afterlife."

Or not. If anyone deserved a little unrest, it was Florence.

She gave him a knowing smile, as if she'd heard his thoughts. It wouldn't be the first time a Hawthorne had surprised him with that extra skill.

Around them, the walls started to warp and smear, melting upward towards the ceiling. It was beyond unsettling. Whatever Rosalie had done to get him here was wearing off.

"Our time is almost at an end," Jocelyn confirmed. "You

won't be able to visit me again. The next time we meet will be the last."

Cool. Not ominous at all.

"I guess I'll see you then." This had been a massive waste of time, as much as he understood where Jocelyn was coming from. "I'll tell Rosalie…" He trailed off, not sure how to finish.

"Tell her the days she visited and found me sitting in the red chair by the sitting room window, I was daydreaming of time with her. Traveling away from our families, away from Thistle, just the two of us." Jocelyn's gaze drifted, going wistful and distant. "My family made our home my prison, even after death. The only thing I ever wanted was to leave—as long as she was with me. Tell her that I would've been honored to grow old and gray with her, on some silly adventure across the world."

Miles's throat was tight. "I will."

"Thank you," she murmured, and she was gone.

The locker room came back in a sear of blinding light and throbbing pain. Miles rolled onto his side, coughing around the taste of hot metal that burned in his throat. Blood splattered across the tiled floor and a pair of scuffed sneakers.

"Woah!" Emily skipped back, dodging the crimson spray. "That's blood. Guys, that's blood!"

"I have eyes," Gabriel snapped. He caught Miles's shoulder, rolling him back before he toppled off the bench. His fingers dug in, an anchor point. "Breathe, Miles. Listen to me."

He tried, lurching upright and wheezing to clear his throat. "Fine," he managed, bloody spit dripping from his mouth

216

onto his jeans. That had to be an attractive look. "Blood… down… wrong pipe."

"I'm fairly certain you're not supposed to have blood down any of your pipes," Gabriel said grimly. He grabbed the towel Miles's head had been resting on and handed it to him.

Miles stared at it blankly, his brain a fog of pain. The universe had clearly decided to take it as a personal challenge when he'd insisted one more time couldn't hurt.

"For your…" Gabriel took it back, lifting it to Miles's nose and pressing down. He eased off when Miles hissed. "Your nose is bleeding."

"Gushing," Emily corrected. Her voice was light, but the quiver at the end gave her away. "Like a full-on fountain."

At least he knew where all the blood had come from.

"Disgusting," he croaked.

"I've seen way worse on the field," Emily reassured him. "One time, this girl took a soccer ball straight to the face and her nose, like, exploded in this geyser—"

Gabriel silenced her with a cutting look. "Are you hurt?" he demanded.

He hurt, but he wasn't *hurt*. "I'm okay." His head was pounding, his body shivery, feverish, but it wasn't any worse than the previous times. Maybe he had Rosalie to thank for that. Speaking of which. "Have you seen Rosalie? She disappeared when I got to Jocelyn."

"She blipped back in for a moment," Emily answered. "She had to use all of her energy to push through the barrier around Jocelyn and get you to her. I think it drained her because she poofed right after that."

That was fine. Miles didn't have any good news for her anyway.

Gabriel pulled the towel away. The blood must've stopped because he didn't immediately shove it back. "You spoke with Jocelyn, then?"

"Yeah, but she wouldn't help." The visit wasn't remotely worth the rotten migraine crushing his brain.

"She didn't tell you anything? Did you explain to her—"

"I told her everything, but it didn't matter. She doesn't want to take any chances messing up the future." Miles didn't bother trying to hide his dismay. "Can we talk about it after I get some water?" He needed to rinse the taste of blood out of his mouth before he puked.

Gabriel and Emily each took an arm, helping him stumble to his feet. The room spun for an alarming second, but they didn't let him fall as he lurched to the nearest water fountain.

Normally, he'd die before using a public water fountain, especially the one in the boys' locker room, but desperate times and all that. It did a good job of washing out the blood. Only a hint lingered on his tongue and at the back of his teeth.

"Here." Gabriel conjured up a clean towel, wetting it and wiping Miles's cheek. From the way he scrubbed—giving Miles flashbacks to his mom attacking his dirty face with a washcloth as a kid—it had to be crusted with blood.

"Pretty sure scraping my skin off isn't going to help with the bleeding," he mumbled around the fabric.

Gabriel's touch gentled. "I wish you weren't covered in blood in the first place. Let's agree right now—no more bringing on visions."

"Hey." Miles caught his wrist, fingers over his thumping

pulse. He dipped his head to catch Gabriel's gray eyes. "I'm okay. Really."

His face was paler than usual. "Don't ask me to watch you do that again."

"I won't," Miles promised. "I couldn't even if I wanted to—according to Jocelyn, our painful little meetings have come to an end."

"She truly has no intention of helping us."

That pulled Miles back to himself. He couldn't show how hopeless, how lost he felt. If he gave up, Gabriel would too. "We don't need her. We always figure things out. This isn't any different."

"Yeah," Emily chimed in. "If the rule is no help from Jocelyn, we'll find her another way. What does it matter, as long as we win in the end?"

It mattered because Miles was sick and tired of being yanked around, beaten up, and forced to watch other people get hurt for this quest. He made himself remember the promises he'd made.

"Emily's right." The scarlet dots of his blood on the floor reminded him of the poppies around Jocelyn, and the scent of bitter smoke filled his nose. "All that matters is how this ends. I don't plan on us losing."

19

Charlee thumped Miles on the back of his already sore head. "I can't believe you brought on another vision. I swear, you have no self-preservation."

He'd caught her up on all she'd missed when she picked him up after school. She hadn't been pleased. And that was without telling her about Jocelyn confirming his potential death.

He flicked sudsy water at her from the sink, most of it landing on the kitchen floor. "I'm prioritizing. Sorry, but with murder looming on the horizon, saving myself from a migraine and a bloody nose doesn't come close."

That only made her grumpier. "How about from now on, when Gabriel's the voice of reason trying to stop you, take that as a sign you're about to do something seriously stupid and don't?"

Miles scrubbed another bottle and passed it to her to rinse, letting her stew in her feels. He'd been stressed since Aunt Robin caught him and Gabriel, waiting for her to change her mind and rat them out. Plus, neither of his parents had mentioned their investigation at the cemetery, and Miles was too chicken to ask. Keeping his hands busy was a good distraction so he'd offered to clean and refill his mom's empty ritual bottles that had piled up on the counter. He'd gotten a surprised smile, a mug of Earl Grey, and hopefully, some brownie points.

"Jocelyn better hope I'm not there when you find her," Charlee muttered, rubbing viciously at a stray herb plastered to the bottle. "I'm about to kick her ass for being such a stubborn, infuriating waste of time."

Miles wished he were mature enough to say he wasn't upset, but apparently, you could be pissed at someone while still understanding why they were doing something. His brain didn't like the conflicting emotions.

"I feel bad for her, trapped down there for a century. Half-alive, half-dead."

"That complicates our job too. How would you even release her once you found her?"

He'd asked himself that same question. "I have no idea. We might have to wing it once we get there. Bring supplies to release her spirit and free her physically if she's being kept captive."

It wasn't a great plan, but it was all he had.

"Since the first premonition, I've had at least some direction." He passed Charlee the last bottle and unplugged the sink. Water and soap swirled down the drain, gurgling. "Now everything's a mess. I don't know where to go from here."

It hurt to admit that the needle of Miles's compass was wavering. He felt cracked open after confessing to Jocelyn, leaking ugly truths left and right.

"Your direction hasn't changed," Charlee retorted, turning the faucet off with a dismissive smack. She dried her hands on her jeans. "You're just frustrated, and Jocelyn only made things worse."

She wasn't wrong.

Hands no longer submerged underwater, Miles checked his phone. He had a text waiting for him from Gabriel.

> Any further side effects from your vision?
> Your cousin hasn't called me in a panic,
> so I assume all is well.

Miles wasn't above admitting that Gabriel checking in gave him butterflies.

> All good over here... the only diagnosis
> from doctor charlee is that I'm an idiot

Charlee peeked at his screen as she shuffled by. "Is that Gabriel?"

"Yeah." The butterflies shriveled up and died. "I didn't tell him, but I asked Jocelyn if Felicity's the murderer."

A bottle clattered across the table as it slipped from Charlee's fingers. "And? What did she say?"

"Nothing, of course." Miles slipped into the chair across from her. All the refill ingredients were laid out on the table, a herby, musky smell mingling with lemon dish soap. "But Jocelyn made a point to talk about how easily the grimoire can turn you against family. It seemed like a *hint-hint* moment."

Charlee worried at her bottom lip, twirling a dried twig of rosemary. "You know I'm the farthest thing from Team Felicity, but killing your own kid is hardcore. Do you really think she's capable of that?"

He didn't know, and that scared him. "Jocelyn said the grimoire preys on your worst fears. I'd be willing to bet hers is losing her powers, and through that, her money. If she finds out Gabriel is trying to break the curse, he could end up as collateral."

They'd discussed this exact possibility before. Miles despised how real it felt now.

Charlee's harsh exhale blew errant rose petals across the table. "I guess I can't argue with that. Blood didn't matter to Florence. And look at my own mom—me being her kid doesn't mean shit to her."

"That's different." Trauma and shame halting a relationship wasn't even close to committing murder for your own gain. Charlee was still hurting from Robin's cold shoulder the other morning. "All I'm saying is, it's not beyond the realm of possibility. How am I supposed to tell Gabriel she's my top suspect?"

Amy and Jenna paraded into the kitchen, grabbing a jug of apple juice from the fridge. They were chatting about a movie they'd watched the night before, ignoring Miles and Charlee.

Charlee leaned in and lowered her voice. "Gabriel knows his mom. It can't be that much of a surprise to hear."

"She's still his mom." Miles didn't quite know how to explain. "There's this… wistfulness when he talks about her, like part of him is hoping she might come around. That she might start caring about him." Charlee had turned to rage to cope with her mom's coldness; Gabriel went with detachment. Another of his carefully crafted masks. "I don't think I can tell him."

"Keeping secrets never goes well," Charlee warned.

"I'm trying to protect him." He could hear how that sounded, like every toxic half of a relationship trying to justify their questionable actions.

Charlee made a face.

"Fine, you're right. I'll talk to him."

Amy skirted around the table to give the two of them a suspicious look. "What're you guys talking about?"

"Mind your own business," Charlee snipped. She corked a bottle of lavender and set it aside.

Amy scowled and grabbed Jenna's arm, almost spilling her glass of juice. "You know what, we have something to say. We've been feeling seriously out of the loop and underappreciated." Her chin jutted out in a pout. "We know you're talking about Ger—Gabriel. We deserve to hear what's going on after we saved his life."

Miles ran a hand down his face, feeling a thousand years old. "You didn't save his life, and Emily was the one who—"

"Maybe we should ask Mom," Amy interrupted snidely. "Get her opinion."

That little brat.

"Don't act like you're going to blackmail me."

"I wouldn't have to if you told us what's going on."

"We just want to know if Gabriel's in trouble," Jenna murmured meekly, tugging at a loose string hanging from her ratty sweatshirt. "Amy's getting ready to do her first job, and Aunt Robin's been teaching me about spells and charms. We could help."

It was hard to say no to Jenna when that tentative confidence was shining in her eyes for the first time Miles could remember.

Charlee's tone was noticeably gentler when she said, "How about we promise we'll tell you if we need help. But until then, you two have to keep quiet. Because if you tell your mom or anyone else, it's not Miles who'll get in trouble, it's Gabriel. And he'll never come over here again. Is that what you want?"

They shook their blonde heads in unison.

"I didn't think so." Charlee rattled a bag of shriveled juniper berries and muttered to Miles, "I guess it runs in the family."

"What?"

"Weakness for a pretty face and a bad attitude."

Miles kicked her under the table.

His phone buzzed loudly, and Charlee snickered. "He knows we're talking about him."

"That's not funny."

> I've been reading over the notes you sent me.
> I think I've found something helpful.

Before leaving school, Miles had scribbled down what he could remember of his conversation with Jocelyn, minus the Felicity part, for Gabriel and Emily to look over.

> When Jocelyn passed along her message
> for Rosalie, she said that her home was her
> prison, even in death. If she's being literal,
> it's a fair conclusion to draw that her tomb
> is on my family's property.

Miles had to read it twice before what Gabriel was saying clicked. It matched with what he'd read in Jocelyn's journal—her parents doing everything to keep her in the house, too embarrassed by their poverty to venture into Thistle and face the judgment of the townsfolk. Too focused on their image and reputation to risk it by letting their children run free. She'd been trapped, suffocating within its walls.

> We already checked the old house…
> you thinking there's another
> hidden room we missed?

Miles's mom came into the kitchen. He shoved his phone into his pocket, nearly knocking over a jar of graveyard dirt in his haste. She must've chalked it up to his usual clumsiness because all she said was, "I'm making a batch of rosemary oil if you'll set me aside a few clean bottles."

"Sure thing." Charlee started tapping off measuring spoons and twisting on caps. "Hey, I saw Thistle Cemetery was on the news for grave desecration or something… did you and Uncle Adam look into it?"

Miles was going to have a heart attack. His mom was digging through the cupboard, so he gave Charlee a warning look.

"We tried." Sarah sighed, piling bundles of dried rosemary next to the sink. "The cops beat us there and had the whole place locked down. And the cemetery refuses to let us investigate. You know how they feel about us… if we're not charlatans, we're using black magic. They don't want us there. We can't push the issue, no matter what we suspect."

"Maybe it was just some gross prank," Charlee suggested, knotting a bundle of crow feathers.

"Maybe. But the pictures online are strange." Sarah pursed her lips. "I want you two to be careful and keep an eye out for anything else strange going on. If this is something supernatural, hopefully the next occurrence will be somewhere we can investigate."

Thank God they'd agreed to not use the grimoire again.

"We'll be on high alert," Charlee told her, and Miles murmured agreement. One of them must've cashed in some good karma because they'd just dodged a serious bullet.

Once his mom was safely occupied stripping leaves from the stems, Miles slipped his phone back out to read Gabriel's message.

> No. We need to find where the other
> end of the tunnel comes out.

The tunnel. Goosebumps sprang up across Miles's body.

> Is that a good idea? What if another one of
> those things is down there? I thought it was
> an escape tunnel and just leads out on the
> property

He was aware he sounded like the world's biggest chicken, but if he was going to be dragged back down there, he wanted to make sure it was worth it. Even if they found the other entrance and managed to get back down there, they'd eventually reach the place where it had collapsed— and that meant another place to be cornered by a demon dog with no escape.

> I said that it might be.
> Where else could Jocelyn's tomb be?

Anywhere else, preferably.

"Gabriel wants to go back into the monster tunnel," he whispered to Charlee, his words covered by the rush of the faucet. "He thinks Jocelyn's tomb is hiding down in that creepy, smelly, dirty—" A thought struck him, stopping him mid-sentence.

"Dirty…?" Charlee prompted.

"C'mon." He tugged her from the table. "I need to check something."

They went up to his bedroom, where Jocelyn's journal was tucked away in his desk drawer. He hadn't touched it since Blanche's accident.

"I thought you already read that thing," Charlee commented as he filed through the thin pages.

"Shhh."

Charlee waited, radiating impatience as she crossed her arms. He'd forgotten how difficult Jocelyn's tiny handwriting was to read, but he eventually found the page he was looking for.

"Jocelyn wrote down the details of her own death premonitions to try and save herself." Miles rotated the journal towards Charlee, pointing at one of the final entries. "Look— *dreams of slick stone, the smell of dirt, a crushing weight.* When I first read it, I thought this was her foreseeing her body being buried. But that never happened. She was taken to the tomb."

Charlee's freckled nose wrinkled in confusion. "So? Stone and dirt, it sounds like a tomb to me."

"I was just there, there's no dirt. It's all stone. But the tunnel has a dirt path. The whole place smelled like wet earth. If Florence took her down there, or knocked her out and dragged her through…"

228

"Dirt doesn't exactly narrow it down. Maybe she attacked Jocelyn outside because she didn't want to make a mess in her house."

"Then created an invisible tomb to lock her body in?" That was the key here. Gabriel was right, there was nowhere else for it to be. "There are no other buildings on the property. The tomb must be under it."

He should've known. It was never going to be through a cozy hidden passage in the Hawthorne mansion, with plenty of light and an easy escape route. No, instead they had to go back to the murder hole from Miles's nightmares.

Charlee patted his shoulder. "Let's just hope nothing tries to eat you this time."

> I think you're right... jocelyn's
> journal hints at the tunnels too

Gabriel must've been waiting for his text because he responded immediately.

> We need to go down there.
> My mother is gone until tonight.
> This could be our best opportunity for days.

Shit. "Gabriel wants to go now. Any ideas how to get past my mom?"

Charlee shrugged. "Tell her I'm running some errands and want you to come with. She'll either buy it or she won't. If not, we'll have to sneak out tonight."

Miles was going to die if he went one more night without more than a few hours of sleep. He glanced at the time—it was still early enough that they could get back before dinner and keep his mom's suspicions to a minimum.

Gotta get past my mom... I'll keep you updated

"Let's give it a shot." Charlee turned to leave, but he caught her arm. He'd been putting off telling her, but if she was driving him to Gabriel's, he couldn't procrastinate any longer. "Hang on, I need to tell you something first... Gabriel and I are dating. Like, for real. Officially. He's my boyfriend."

It gave him a giddy, head-spinning thrill to say it out loud.

He'd expected an eye roll or a sarcastic comment, but Charlee grinned. "I knew it. You were way too gooey-eyed and giggly after he slept over."

"I was not!"

"You totally were." She gave him a hug, stepping on his toes. "I'm glad he got his brain working again. Idiot shouldn't have made you wait so long." When she pulled away, she nudged him playfully. "So, is it everything you dreamed of and more? You two sneaking off to make out in the janitor's closet?"

If spontaneous combustion was possible through mortification, Miles would've burned to a crisp by now. "I thought it would feel different, but he's still just... Gabriel. It's easy because nothing's really changed."

Charlee arched a brow. "Nothing?"

"I mean, there's a bit more... touching." Charlee snorted and Miles pinched her. "Shut up. We're taking it slow, just letting it be natural. And, in case you haven't noticed, we haven't had much time for romance between getting attacked and digging through the grimoire."

"Letting the passion build up, huh? See who snaps first?"

"Oh my God, this isn't one of your books." Miles ran a hand down his face, wishing he could disappear. "Can we please stop talking about this and go lie to my mom?"

Charlee's expression sobered. "Are you going to tell her?"

He'd been trying not to think about it. The excuse he'd always made to give himself time to come out was that he'd do it when he had a boyfriend. Now that time had come, and he hated his past self for making that decision.

"I don't know."

"There's no rush." They linked arms and she tugged him into the hallway. "Do you see how much I love you—I didn't make one comment about your terrible taste or how you could do a lot better than stink-face sweater vest boy."

"I'm very proud of you."

They returned to the kitchen, Miles's mom chopping the mountain of rosemary. A green, herbaceous smell filled the room.

Charlee leaned casually against the fridge. "I was going to run a few errands, stop by the craft store and the library... you mind if Miles tags along?"

Sarah paused, setting her knife down and studying them. There was no way this was going to work; she'd see right through their flimsy lie.

"That's fine," she finally said. "Just be home by seven—I'm making chicken and dumplings for dinner."

Either Miles had sudden good luck, this was some kind of sneaky trap, or his mom was giving him the benefit of the doubt and choosing to trust him.

"Easy peasy," Charlee chirped, then turned to Miles. "I'll go grab my keys."

As she ran upstairs, Miles went to get his coat, but Sarah

stopped him. "Wait a minute. I wanted to talk to you about something." She hesitated, and his insides gave a violent, nervous twist. She blew out a breath. "I... I haven't been a very good listener lately, have I? I'm sorry."

Miles didn't say anything. He hadn't been prepared for an apology. Part of him wanted to tell her it was okay and brush it off, but they'd both know it was a lie.

His lack of an answer didn't seem to bother her.

"I should've said that days ago, but I..." She swiped her hair out of her face. The remorse in her voice made him want to grind his teeth. "I'm ready to listen, if you have anything to tell me."

She suspected something was going on. She had to.

If Miles opened his mouth right now, there was a solid chance he'd puke. He wanted to feel triumphant that she'd apologized and admitted she'd messed up, but it was smothered beneath a wave of apprehension. Here she was, handing him the opportunity to come clean on a silver platter, to finally rid himself of the weight of his lies.

And he couldn't take it. He wanted to believe so badly that it would go differently this time. That they could sit down at the table, and she'd listen to the whole story before saying a word.

But it wasn't worth the risk.

Miles made himself turn away from her. "I don't."

She was wearing her charms, but he swore he could feel her hurt. The sting his words inflicted. He struggled not to flinch.

"Okay." She scraped the cutting board as she turned back to the stove. "Have a nice time with Charlee."

Miles fled the kitchen without a word, hating himself with every step.

20

"I can't believe you're making me do this."

Miles knocked on the front door of the Hawthorne mansion—this was his first time back since he'd found out Gabriel had vanished—and gave Charlee an incredulous look. "*You* insisted on coming in. You threatened to run me over if I left you behind."

She glared up at the ivy-covered building as if daring it to mess with her. "Felicity's our top suspect. I can't let you venture into her murder mansion without backup." Her gaze flitted to Miles. "Are you going to tell him?"

"Yeah."

The door swung open with a low creak to reveal a perplexed Gabriel. "I didn't realize you were bringing your cousin."

"Do you not understand that other people can hear you, or do you just not care?" Charlee slipped past Gabriel, bumping his shoulder.

"She's here to help," Miles told him apologetically, following her.

It was quiet inside, a solemn, heavy silence you'd usually only find in churches or graveyards. Miles double-checked that all his shields were firmly in place.

Charlee stopped dead in the middle of the foyer, wet white sneakers squeaking on the marble. Her gaze jumped around the room, from the gold-accented table holding a painted vase of white roses, to the massive gleaming staircase curving up to the second floor. When she saw the chandelier hanging overhead, a tangle of black iron vines forming a sphere and dripping with teardrop-shaped gems, she scowled so thunderously that Gabriel shifted uneasily.

"You're kidding, right?"

"What would I be kidding about?"

"Seriously? Look around. You don't think this is a bit much?"

"Hey," Miles interjected. "He didn't judge our house." If she thought this was over the top, she should see the ballroom. The chandelier there was twice the size.

"Yeah, because ours is normal." She shivered and rubbed at her arms, dragging her striped sweater sleeves down. "I don't like being here. It feels gross."

Gabriel looked offended. "I assure you, we have several maids who—"

"Not that kind of gross," Miles hurried to explain. "Bad aura gross." He turned back to Charlee. "You get used to it." That wasn't completely true, but the itchy sticky feeling did fade into the background.

She didn't look convinced.

Gabriel cleared his throat. "Should we begin our search? I thought we should start with the house before venturing out on the property—having an entrance here would make more sense for convenience, though I don't know how Bram or I wouldn't have stumbled upon it. Either way, a double check of the ground floor and basement won't hurt."

Anxiety squirmed behind Miles's ribs. "Actually, can we wait a second? I have something to talk to you about first."

Taking her cue to give them space, Charlee walked away to examine the dark landscape paintings in a nearby hallway.

"What's wrong?" Gabriel asked, his shoulders creeping up beneath his white button-up. Miles could make out the shadowed curve of his collarbone through the thin fabric.

"I'm not really sure how to say this, so I'm going to rip the Band-Aid off and spit it out, okay? I've been going over all our clues from Jocelyn about your death and I think your mom might be the killer."

Gabriel's expression didn't change, frozen in an unreadable mask. He didn't say anything, the beat of silence stretching too long.

"I know that's a first-class dick thing to say, and I'm sorry," Miles continued in one jumbled exhale. "I'm sure you don't want to even consider it, because it... well, it's super sucky, but she fits. Now I'm here, and she's gone, and I know we're supposed to be tunnel hunting, but this might be our only chance to snoop. Charlee and I talked about it on the drive over—if you take us to your mom's room, she can do her thing, see what she picks up."

In an ideal world, he'd have the proof to back up his suspicions before revealing them, but to get that proof, he needed Gabriel in the loop. There was no way around it.

"You want your psychometrist cousin to go through my mother's private things," Gabriel said haltingly, "to find out if she's going to kill me? Because you think that she's not only the murderer, but that she's been planning my death to the extent that Charlee will be able to sense it?"

Miles wanted to slink away and hide. "I didn't say that last part. It's a long shot, I have no idea if Charlee would even pick up anything, but I think it would be stupid not to check. What if we could find out for sure?"

They were too close to the tomb, to Jocelyn and her premonition. Miles needed to know who to protect Gabriel from. He'd gotten so wrapped up in freeing Jocelyn and breaking the curse, he'd almost forgotten that the most important thing was saving Gabriel's life. It didn't matter when they got down into that tomb, or learned how to undo the curse, if Gabriel was still going to die there.

He'd been failing in his quest without even realizing.

"Fine," Gabriel stated abruptly. His expression hadn't changed, hiding any hint of how he was feeling. He whirled around and strode over to the staircase. "I'll take you to her room."

Miles felt like scum on the bottom of a shoe. Maybe it'd been selfish of him to put this weight on Gabriel simply because he was too weak to keep a secret.

Charlee appeared beside him. "He didn't take it well?"

"What'd you expect?"

First, he'd rejected his mom's attempt to make peace earlier, and now he was hurting Gabriel. If he was making the right choices, why did they feel so terrible?

They trailed up the stairs after Gabriel, footsteps echoing through the cavernous foyer. At the top, Edmund was lounging in the same stuffed chair as the first time Miles had met him, scrolling through his phone. Miles wondered if he needed specialized touchscreen gloves.

"Good evening," he greeted Miles cheerfully, not remotely surprised to see him. "I'd ask what sort of mischief the two of you have planned, but Gabriel's already warned me to keep my questions to myself."

"Uh, sorry. And thanks for not ratting us out."

"Don't worry about it. Just make sure you're gone before Mother dearest gets home tonight. She's been in a real mood lately. I'm not sure you'd escape a confrontation alive."

He was joking, but a chill still ran down Miles's spine.

Charlee stepped forward to peer around the landing. Edmund perked up, his green eyes alight with curiosity. "Gabriel, you didn't tell me you made another friend."

It was impossible to tell if Charlee or Gabriel scoffed the loudest. "This is my cousin, Charlee," he explained. She gave Edmund a dismissive once over and a stiff nod. "She's... helping out for the day."

"She gets to be in on the adventure, but I don't? I'm hurt." He threw her a charming smile. "I don't suppose you want to clue me in?"

Charlee didn't even blink. "Don't waste your time. One Hawthorne is already more than I can tolerate."

He barked a laugh and settled back in his chair. "Fair enough. You know where to find me if you change your mind."

Charlee didn't give him a backward glance as Gabriel led them to the left. Miles hadn't been to this part of the house yet, but it was nearly identical to the hallway outside Gabriel's bedroom.

"My mother's office is there"—Gabriel gestured to a closed door with a tilt of his chin, then to the door at the end of the hall—"and her bedroom is there."

The choice was clearly up to them. Charlee shrugged. "Bedroom first?"

As expected, Felicity's room was immaculate to the point of cold, unwelcoming in its lack of comfort or personality. Her bed was neatly made, the indigo comforter's edges crisp enough to slice, two pillows positioned perfectly against a black velvet headboard. Her bedside table held a sleek silver lamp, a folded pair of glasses, and one of those disc phone chargers. At the end of the bed was a cushioned bench, a plush knit throw folded pristinely on it. Twin charcoal armchairs were positioned on either side of a narrow black table, a single empty teacup resting on a marble coaster. In the corner of the room, to Miles's surprise, a cello leaned against the wall. It wasn't covered in a sheen of dust or draped in cobwebs, but he could sense it hadn't been touched for a while. It looked like a prop, a piece to help fill out the room.

The space was missing more than a soul—there was no sign of Gabriel's dad anywhere. The second bedside table was empty aside from a matching lamp, there was only one coaster on the table, and when Charlee cracked open a door to reveal a walk-in closet, there was no sign of men's clothing.

Gabriel stood with his hands shoved in his pockets as Charlee poked around.

"I can wait in the hall with you," Miles offered.

He shook his head, stubborn even when he was fuming.

"Hey." Miles shuffled closer. "I really am sorry. This… doesn't feel right, but I don't know what else to do." He raked a hand through his hair, wishing he had better words. "I don't want you to be pissed with me, but I get it. I just… I don't want to go into the tunnel with us not talking this through. What can I do to fix this?"

It was selfish, horribly selfish, but if anything went wrong and Miles's last interaction with Gabriel had been hurting him, he couldn't handle it. The thought made his chest feel like it was splintering apart.

A muscle in Gabriel's jaw ticked. "I'm not angry with you. I know my mother, and I understand why you suspect her. It would be... illogical not to."

Miles wanted to be relieved, but Gabriel's face still looked like *that*. Still, it meant the world that Gabriel was talking to him. "Then are you upset because it might be her?" He realized how stupid the question was as soon as it was out of his mouth. "I mean, it might not be *murder* murder. Accidents happen all the time—"

"I'm upset," Gabriel interjected, "because I can't think of a single reason why you're wrong. Why my own mother couldn't possibly be the one to kill me." His shoulders strained against his shirt as he forced his fists deeper into his pockets. "I don't have any defense for her, not even a flowery notion of familial bonds. I want to say you're wrong, that she would never, but I can't. Not if I'm being honest with myself."

It was a painful reminder that Miles would never truly understand what Gabriel was going through. His fight with his own mom seemed so childish and trivial in comparison.

"I don't know what to say to make this better," Miles admitted. He reached over and brushed his fingertips along the sliver of Gabriel's skin where his sleeve had ridden up, half to soothe, half to apologize. "But Charlee could just as likely find something to change our minds and convince us your mom's not involved. For what it's worth, I really hope that's the case." Even if that put them back at ground zero with no suspects. He'd take anything over Gabriel having to know his own mother would sacrifice his life for power.

Charlee came out of the attached bathroom. "Nothing exciting in there but a mostly empty bottle of Ambien." At Miles's questioning look, she explained, "It's a sleeping pill. Mom was taking them for a while after the accident."

He hoped Felicity was losing sleep over what a rotten person she was.

Charlee planted her hands on her hips. "This is the room of a psychopath. Who lives in a space this sterile?"

Miles caught a flash of black and white tiled floor and a massive clawfoot tub before she closed the door. "Nothing's... speaking to you?"

She gestured around wildly. "Like what? This is basically the world's fanciest jail cell."

Stalking around the room one more time, she gave a resigned huff and reached down to brush her fingertip along the delicate handle of the teacup. Her gaze glazed and went distant before she pulled away, head cocked in confusion.

"What is it?"

Ignoring Miles, she moved to the bedside table and rested her fingers against the glasses for a moment. Then the silky pillows on the bed.

"It's weird," she finally shared. "I can feel echoes of things, emotions and thoughts, but they're blurry. Kinda foggy, like there's this—"

"Dark cloud?" Miles finished for her.

She nodded, twisting a red curl around her finger.

"You can't sense anything?"

"I didn't say that. The echoes are there, I'll just have to work harder to get to them."

She sank to her knees back at the table, wrapping her hands around the painted porcelain cup. A minute ticked by, her freckled face scrunched in concentration.

"Felicity drank this before she left this morning, but she'd already been awake for hours. She's worried she's running out of time. There's a specific stress associated with your brother."

"Bram?" Gabriel's voice spiked with alarm.

"The other one, from the hall. He's all twisted up in her thoughts, feeding into her anxieties."

"They are arguing more than usual. As Edmund said, she's been... in a mood."

Should they warn Edmund to take it easy? The last thing they needed was another Hawthorne life in their hands.

Charlee released the teacup and stood. "That's all I've got. She finished her tea and went to her office, but something had her seriously pissed. I'll see if I can pick the emotional thread back up in there."

Based on the few times Miles had had the misfortune of meeting Felicity, her being pissed wasn't an anomaly.

They crossed the hall to her office. Like her bedroom, it was limited to dark, muted shades and borderline barren. A wide desk and leather office chair squatted in the middle of the room with dual sleek monitors, one wall lined with neat bookshelves, a marble fireplace on another. It didn't look recently used.

The space was nothing like his parents' office—no framed family photos haphazardly placed, no sun-bleached curtains over the windows, no dusty knickknacks on the shelves. There wasn't even a jar of mismatched pens on her desk.

There was a notepad, names and times crossed out with

vicious slashes of black ink. Gabriel leaned over to study it.

"I recognize these names. They're clients of my mother's."

"Why would she be canceling all her appointments?"

"I have no idea. With Halloween approaching, she's always more busy than usual, perhaps she overbooked."

Or if she was having trouble sleeping, maybe she didn't trust herself to hold séances. The safety of her clients didn't seem like something she would prioritize, but miracles occasionally happened.

Charlee sank into the chair with a grimace and squeak of leather, trailing her fingers down the arms. Her eyelashes fluttered.

"She's thinking about visiting her grandmother today. She needs… advice. Help. But she's nervous."

"My great-grandmother Marjorie," Gabriel confirmed.

It was hard to imagine what she could help with, spending her days watching the rain in that fancy retirement home. Unless Felicity needed help slipping a possessed object to an unsuspecting innocent.

"Can you see what for? What has her so freaked?"

"It's hard to pick up direct answers, I mostly get emotions and impressions. I'll dig a little deeper."

She sank her fingers into the leather armrests, the chair creaking. Miles sent a plea to the universe that the answer was anything but advice on how to kill one of her kids.

"I'm getting a name in the front of her mind. Uncle Barnaby. Her fear is connected with his killing."

It took Miles a moment to recall why that name was familiar.

"Isn't that the guy your grandma mentioned?" he asked Gabriel.

"Yes, my great-uncle. He died in an accident."

"No." Charlee shook her head, curls bouncing. "Your mom is definitely thinking about how he was killed. That it was… a punishment."

Gabriel recoiled. "Punishment for what? Are you saying he was murdered?"

"All I know is what I said."

"Try again." Miles held himself back from grabbing things from the nearest shelves to shove at her. If Gabriel's great-uncle had been killed as a punishment, it could give them an idea of Gabriel's fate. Marjorie herself had said that Gabriel reminded her of Barnaby, that he too had questioned his gifts, and it had cost him his life. Was history about to repeat itself?

Charlee caressed the top of the desk, trailing over the keyboard and mouse, but shook her head. "Nothing about you," she told Gabriel.

He scoffed. "I'm not even worth a fleeting thought to her. What a surprise."

"That's not what she's saying," Miles assured him.

"Don't take it personally. There's too much emotional mess here. It's radiating from this desk and blocking everything else out." Charlee's head tilted like she could hear a voice. "Something's hiding…"

Her hand dipped down to the bottom drawer, sliding it open. A line of manilla folders filled the space, but she reached behind them and pulled out a wooden box the size of a small book.

"Here." She passed it to Gabriel. "Whatever's in there, your mom sat here and had a big juicy breakdown over it."

He didn't hesitate to crack open the lid. Nestled on

emerald-green lining sat a heavy old-fashioned iron key.

Miles asked the obvious question. "What does it open?"

"I've never seen it before." Gabriel picked it up, pale fingers stark against the dark metal. "This house doesn't use keys like this anymore. My mother had everything updated years ago."

"Could it be for the old house?" A bit pointless when that place didn't even have a front door anymore.

"Perhaps." Gabriel offered the key to Charlee.

She took it, sucking in a breath. "Ew, yeah, loads of nasty energy on this thing. Your mom wasn't happy the last time she used it, that's for sure. I'm seeing... wine bottles against a brick wall. And the number sixty-three."

"I don't know about sixty-three," Gabriel said, "but the rest sounds like our wine cellar. There aren't any doors down there, though."

Charlee shrugged. "Don't shoot the messenger, that's all I've got."

"We are looking for a secret underground tunnel entrance," Miles pointed out. "And now we've got a mysterious key. Doesn't feel like a coincidence."

If Charlee had saved them hours of searching, Miles was going to buy her an entire gift basket of candy.

Gabriel slipped the key into his pocket. "I suppose there's no harm in checking it out."

21

Gabriel led them downstairs towards the ballroom, taking a hard right into an open kitchen. Unlike Miles's, there wasn't a battered table crammed in the corner—there must be a cavernous dining room around here somewhere—but a massive island with four metal stools squatted in the center. He'd never seen so much counter space in his life, gray-streaked marble-top cabinets painted a shade of blue so dark they were almost black, gobbling up the light. It was immaculate, the appliances all gleaming stainless steel, no knickknacks or plants on the windowsills, pots and pans hanging neatly on the wall over the stove.

It looked like a stage kitchen.

"Fancy," Charlee deadpanned.

Bram popped his head out from behind the island, eyes bright with curiosity. "Hello," he greeted Miles. "I didn't know you were coming over today."

"What are you doing on the floor?" Gabriel helped him to his feet, brushing down his burgundy sweater.

"Balthazar saw a spider." The black cat appeared with a twitch of his long tail, weaving around Bram's legs. "We were trying to find it so we could take it outside."

Miles shuddered, scanning the floor.

245

"Hey, kid." Charlee gave him a wave. "I'm Charlee, Miles's cousin."

Just as he had with Miles, he stuck out his hand. "I'm Bramwell Hawthorne. You can call me Bram if you'd like."

Charlee shook it. "Nice to meet you. Cool cat."

Bram beamed at her, and Miles could practically see her melt. Apparently her one-Hawthorne-only rule didn't apply to cute little brothers.

"We're going down into the wine cellar to look for a hidden door," Gabriel told Bram. "Have you seen one?"

"No. But that's where I found Balthazar, maybe he came through it."

Miles shot Gabriel a questioning look.

"The wretched beast appeared without warning one day." Gabriel ignored Bram's indignant protest. "It must've snuck in and found its way down there."

A weird cat for a weird house. How fitting.

"Or he came through a secret door." Miles winked at Bram.

"Balthazar and I can help you look," he offered. "He's good at fitting into small spaces, and he always checks the dark corners for me."

The cat's chest puffed up, like he understood he was being praised.

"I suppose you two can tag along," Gabriel relented. "More help won't hurt."

There was a plain door on the other side of the kitchen, the knob turning easily beneath Gabriel's touch. Wooden steps descended into darkness, making Miles shiver.

"What's the chance we're going to get trapped in this creepy basement and the one lightbulb is going to mysteriously go out?"

Gabriel smirked. "Zero." He reached over to click a switch, light after light turning on to illuminate every step down and the room waiting at the bottom.

Charlee stifled a laugh.

"How was I supposed to know the one place in your haunted mansion that doesn't have spooky vibes is the basement?"

"It's a wine cellar," Gabriel corrected, descending the stairs.

"You don't have to be scared," Bram told Miles evenly. "Balthazar wouldn't let us go anywhere dangerous."

"Good to know the cat has my back," Miles muttered.

The wine cellar ended up being exactly that—shelves stacked from floor to ceiling with bottles, massive barrels lining one bricked wall. The room was cooler than upstairs, and Miles watched himself shiver in one of the many mirrors mounted over a polished wooden bar. As Gabriel had said, there was no door.

"Any ideas about sixty-three?" Miles inquired hopefully.

"The sixty-third brick is a secret lever that moves one of these walls?" Charlee suggested. "Or the sixty-third bottle?"

"That seems a bit farfetched," Gabriel scoffed.

Miles snorted. "Are you forgetting about the other secret doorway we found? Face it, your family has a flair for the dramatic."

Gabriel looked ready to protest—but he sighed in defeat. "Perhaps it's a bottle with a year ending in sixty-three on it."

They tried every possible combination they could think of, to no avail. The biggest issue was that to count, they needed a starting spot, and no one could agree on which was most likely. The shelf farthest to the left, or the first one upon entering the cellar. The brick wall straight ahead from the stairs, or the one beside the bar.

Tired of prodding at bricks, tugging on bottles, and looking for hidden hinges, Bram and Balthazar eventually retreated to the kitchen for snacks.

"I'm starting to suspect this might be pointless," Gabriel grumbled, watching Charlee slide wine bottles in and out of their cubbies one by one. She'd painstakingly worked her way through two whole rows already, swearing into the empty air.

"You know, we've been ignoring a very likely possibility…" Miles hauled himself up from where he was peeking under a shelf with an old-man groan. He couldn't remember what it felt like to not ache all over. "What if I'm wrong? The tunnel entrance at the old house might be the only one, and Florence collapsed it behind her to trap Jocelyn there forever. We might be looking for something that doesn't exist."

Gabriel swiped a hand across his forehead. "Then I suppose we'll need to acquire shovels."

The only thing that sounded worse than crawling around the cold wine cellar searching for hidden switches was digging out a collapsed tunnel in the dark.

"There has to be a door." Charlee yanked another bottle free of its slot. "Why else would Felicity have the key and—"

Something knocked, wood groaned, and with a low rasp, the wine rack and all the bricks behind it swung out in one piece, revealing a sturdy wooden door set into a concrete wall.

The bottle Charlee was holding slipped from her hands and shattered against the floor. Glass exploded, a wave of wine washing over the toes of Miles's shoes. "Shit! Sorry."

Gabriel didn't give the mess a second glance. "How did you do that?"

"I have no idea."

Miles swung the shelf inward to study the racks, the spot where the now-broken bottle had come from. "Sixty-three," he muttered. "Six bottles over, three rows down."

Charlee threw her hands in the air. "Of fucking course."

The key slotted easily into the lock, a dull *click* echoing through the room. Before Gabriel could reach for the knob, the door swung open with a creak that made all the hair stand to attention on the back of Miles's neck.

There was no switch, no industrial-strength lights to illuminate their way this time. Darkness seemed to seep from the doorway, too thick to peer through, a rich, earthy smell rising from whatever lay beyond.

Miles could guess what: dirt, rocks, a low ceiling waiting to collapse right on top of their stupid heads, and probably another shadow monster that wanted to eat him. Hell, why not two this time?

"Is this the part where we argue over who stays behind?" Gabriel asked dryly.

Miles bit his lip. Either Gabriel had heard his thoughts, or they were on the same page. "I guess that depends on how open you are to being convinced."

"Not even remotely. You're welcome to give whatever drawn-out and painfully noble speech you've constructed, but fair warning—it's not going to work. And I've come to terms with the fact that nothing I say will convince you either."

Miles was still tempted to try and conjure up the magical words that would work. To lock Gabriel up until this was all over. Play dirty and clue Edmund in so he'd help.

But his promise—in the cemetery, and when he'd hunted

Gabriel down at Sage and Starlight—was that they were in this together. No matter how tough things got.

"This is touching, but we don't have all day," Charlee butted in. "Are we doing this or not?"

"We are," Miles stated. "But we stick together. And if we find Jocelyn's tomb, no one goes in alone or does anything stupid. Okay?"

All they could do at this point was hope that knowing what was coming would give them an edge. If they ran into Felicity, Miles was throwing Gabriel over his shoulder and hauling ass out of there.

He stepped through the doorway.

A crimson glow flared to life around him, light racing up the walls. Miles yelped, whirling to see a symbol flash above the doorway.

"Don't!" The barked word halted Gabriel mid-step, inches from the threshold.

"What is it?" Charlee demanded. A tremor ran down her body like she wanted to charge in after him.

Miles got his phone flashlight out, standing on his tiptoes to study the jagged symbol carved into the dark stone. It looked like an eye pierced by an arrow, with four swirls to the east, west, south, and north. Atop the point of the arrow was a crescent moon curved around what looked like a backward S.

He'd seen a similar one in his own house. A warding sigil.

On either side of the doorway hung two identical bundles—sticks with spiky yellow flowers and a red center, and long stems topped with clusters of small white buds. Witch hazel and anise, two of the most powerful protection herbs. Tucked into their twine wrappings were chunks of amethyst and smoky quartz.

"There's a serious ward here," Miles told Gabriel and Charlee. He reached towards them and his hand hit an invisible wall, cool and firm against his skin. He strained, but it didn't budge, the sigil pulsing red.

Gabriel watched, his eyes narrowed. "How do wards work?"

"It's a protective measure, like a barricade. We have a few around the house to help keep out spirits. I've never seen one that works on physical things before."

"What does that mean?"

Miles tried to keep his voice light. "It means I'd better hope this tunnel leads to an exit because I'm stuck on this side. It won't let me through."

A low curse exploded out of Charlee.

"Can't you simply break the ward?" Gabriel questioned. "Or undo it?"

"No. Only the person who casts it can break it. That's one of the reasons they're so effective." He studied the sigil again. "You'd think whoever cast it would've put it on the inside, to keep people from going into the tunnel. But this one—"

"Is designed to keep anything from coming out," Charlee finished.

Miles glanced over his shoulder at the endless dark and shivered.

"What if there's no exit?" Trust Gabriel to ask the question no one else wanted to.

"Then we'll have to hope your mom can undo the ward, because I'd rather take my chances with her than starve to death underground." He took a fortifying breath—nowhere else to go but onwards. "Wish me luck, I guess. See you on the other side."

"Don't be an idiot." Gabriel crossed the threshold in one swift move to stand nose to nose with Miles, haloed by the flare of red light. "I'm not letting you go alone."

Miles wanted to shake him for being so stupid. Or kiss him. He hadn't made up his mind yet.

"No," he told Charlee sharply, before she could take more than a step. "Seriously, don't. Think it through—we need someone here to bring Felicity if we can't get out. Go find Bram and wait with him."

Her hands clenched at her sides. "I don't like this."

"I know." He didn't either. "I'll text you when we find a way out, okay?"

When, not *if*. For his own sanity.

"Be careful. If anything goes wrong, come back here and we'll knock down this whole wall. The ward can only be so big."

He choked out a laugh. Knowing Charlee, she'd rip it apart with her bare hands, one chunk at a time.

"See you soon," he promised.

"Watch his back, Hawthorne," she called after Gabriel.

Miles expected a snarky comment, but Gabriel nodded. "I always do."

Their footsteps were muffled by the packed dirt as they followed the tunnel. Miles pulled out two flashlights—he'd added them to his backpack after last time, nestled between the jar-heart and death-knife—the beams reaching farther than their phones. Being able to see if anything was coming at them was a blessing and a curse for Miles's nerves. If the shadow monster dwelling down here decided to attack them, he'd rather it just killed him quickly before he had time to scream at the sight of it.

"It doesn't bode well that my mother knows about this place." Gabriel broke the silence. "I suppose that's another point towards her being the killer."

Having the key to the tunnel that almost certainly led to Jocelyn's tomb didn't prove Felicity was guilty, but it didn't look good.

"At least she's not home today," Miles offered weakly.

"She didn't say where she was going. She could be in Jocelyn's tomb waiting for us."

Wasn't that a comforting thought?

"I won't kill her," Gabriel said quietly.

A dip in the ground sent Miles stumbling. "What?"

"That's what the knife is for, right? That's why you've been carrying it around. So when the killer comes, I can defend myself."

Miles's backpack suddenly felt ten times heavier. "I don't know. I've been trying not to think about it, to be honest." He'd questioned so many times since leaving Nadia's shop if taking it had been the right move. "There has to be a path where no one dies. If we break the curse or destroy the book, she might break free of the grimoire's influence."

Gabriel kicked a loose rock, sending it skittering ahead of them. It was impossible to make out his expression in the gloom. "You probably think I'm stupid for not wanting her gone after everything she's done. Or will do."

"I don't think that at all. Your relationship is... complicated, but she's still your mom." Gabriel was a person who cared, who gave second chances and held out hope, no matter how hard he tried to pretend otherwise. That was one of the things Miles admired about him. He'd never want him to change, not even for this.

"I must be a masochist." Gabriel shivered in his thin button-up—the temperature had been steadily dropping as they ventured deeper. "I know that no matter how much I give her, I'll never get anything in return. Not approval, not affection. Some days I wish she hated me, simply so I knew she felt *something*."

Miles gripped his flashlight between his teeth and shrugged out of his jacket, draping it over Gabriel's shoulders. "Here." The chill numbed his nose, but his body was so flushed from unease that it wasn't sinking in. His sweater was thick enough he wasn't going to freeze to death. "You're not a masochist. I think everyone wants their parents' approval, no matter how illogical it is."

"It can't be healthy," Gabriel griped, slipping his arms into the sleeves.

"It's not." Miles zipped the coat for him. It was comically oversized, huge in the shoulders and hanging over his hands, and Miles liked seeing him in it too much. "Look at me—I know my parents love me and I still work myself into a mess every day trying to please them. If you're a masochist, what does that make me?"

He adjusted the collar where it had got caught, knuckles brushing against the warm skin of Gabriel's throat. He heard Gabriel's breath catch, and his mouth went dry.

"A good person who cares too much," Gabriel replied, peering up at him.

The tips of Miles's fingers tingled, heat crawling under his skin. He had officially entered the danger zone of distracted. Would it be totally crazy to kiss Gabriel right now?

Amusement curled the corner of Gabriel's mouth up. "You're not allowed to kiss me in this disgusting tunnel."

An intoxicating mix of embarrassment and delight lit up in Miles. "Does that mean I can when I get us out of here?" He took a step closer, the toes of their shoes bumping. "You really have to stop bribing me with kisses, that doesn't feel like a healthy relationship dynamic."

"Why would I, when it's so effective?" Gabriel's teeth glinted in the dim light as he smirked. "It's a mutually beneficial arrangement."

Miles laughed. "You're awful. But you're not wrong." He caught Gabriel's hand and tugged him down the tunnel, flashlight held aloft. "Let's find the exit before I start digging at the walls."

They trekked forward until they hit a fork in the tunnel. Miles shone his light down each one as far as it would go, but they were both identical—more dark dirt and stone walls. The air down here was stale and heavy, trying to choke Miles with each breath.

"Left or right?"

"Left," Gabriel picked without hesitation.

Miles wasn't one of those "right is always right" people, but when the left path immediately started sloping downwards, he wondered if he should be. His legs burned, and all he could think was that if they encountered a monster and needed to run away, this massive hill was going to seriously slow them down.

The walls grew slick and wet as dripping water echoed through the tunnel. Anxiety gathered in the pit of Miles's stomach, heavy in his steps, sweat prickling on the back of his neck. It was getting harder to breathe, the stone pressing in from every direction.

Gabriel's flashlight beam shifted over, blinding him. "Are you alright?"

"Not really." Miles attempted a weak grin, failing spectacularly based on the concern furrowing Gabriel's brow. "It's cool."

"Do you want to stop for a minute?"

A wheeze whistled out of him. "God, no. Let's keep moving. Please."

If they stopped, reality would sink in with a full-blown panic attack hot on its heels.

Gabriel's flashlight went back to the path, but Miles could feel his attention on him. The only thing worse than freaking out was freaking out in front of your perpetually cool boyfriend. He focused on counting his steps as they walked, skirting around filthy puddles and slick mud.

"I just thought of something," Miles told him, attempting to distract himself. "We're not going to die down here. You know how I know that? Because we haven't suffered through Shakespeare's incomprehensible writing yet."

That managed to pull a laugh from Gabriel. "Finally, we can agree on at least one thing about classic literature."

"Not a fan?"

"Of convoluted, melodramatic plots?" Gabriel's nose wrinkled. "Certainly not."

Miles was pretty sure that was nearly every book he'd been forced to read in English, but he restrained himself from pointing it out.

The ground leveled out, making a lazy curve. "We

must've walked across a huge portion of the estate by now," Gabriel observed. "If this tunnel connects to the other, we should come to the collapse soon."

Which meant, unless they'd taken a wrong turn, the tomb had to be close. If it was here at all.

Miles's beam caught on a bright splash of color. Panic sent his heart racing—until he realized what he was looking at.

A blood-red poppy.

Gabriel approached it, reaching out to touch a silky petal. "How is it growing down here?"

"I have no idea. But hey, we must be going the right way—these are the same flowers I saw in Jocelyn's tomb."

"These exact ones?" Gabriel's eyebrows met. The tunnel ahead was littered with more, a crimson trail leading the way. "You didn't tell me they were poppies."

"I didn't realize the type was important. I was more focused on the fact they were growing out of solid stone."

Gabriel glanced around, flashlight lingering on a trickle of water traveling down grooves in the wall. "In the spring," he told Miles, "red poppies grow along the shore of the lake. No one planted them, and my mother's tried to remove them, but they come back every year."

"The lake…" The ceiling pressed in closer as Miles tilted his head back. "Are you saying that's where we are?"

"Underneath it, yes." He sounded remarkably calm for someone realizing a bajillion gallons of water were hanging above him.

"Okay, cool. No big deal, that's not terrifying at—" A thought occurred to Miles. "Wait. When Jocelyn warned me the future hadn't changed, I saw her coming out of a lake. This lake." He wanted to smack his head in frustration.

"I'm so stupid. She was trying to tell me where she was. I should've put it together."

If Jocelyn wanted all her half hints and cryptic messages decoded, she really should've found someone smarter.

"How could you have known? Even if you'd suspected, we wouldn't have realized there was a tunnel underneath. We would've dredged the lake for nothing."

True, but it'd still been right there in front of his face.

The poppies led them to an abrupt turn. Beyond it, two things emerged from the darkness. Down the tunnel, far enough that his flashlight beam could barely reach, was the collapse. And to the left, a massive tree was carved into the stone wall.

"It looks like my family crest. But not quite."

Gabriel was right—the trunk and roots and the pointed star were identical to the Hawthorne crest. But the branches were different, straight and sparse instead of twisted. There was a thick line on either side of the tree, going all the way down to the floor and meeting at the top in a curved arch.

"I think it's a door." Miles stepped back as far as he could, shoulders meeting damp stone on the opposite side of the tunnel. It was definitely door-shaped. "But there's no handle."

He pushed at it, straining until his feet slid in the moist dirt and he almost fell. "Damn it." Digging his nails into the crack didn't work, and kicking it only made his toes throb. "What do we do? This has to be the way into the tomb. Jocelyn's right there."

"Let me try," Gabriel offered. "Perhaps it's spelled to respond to the touch of a Hawthorne."

They swapped spots, Miles holding the light while Gabriel tackled the door. When he laid his palms flat on it, the stone thrummed briefly, but nothing happened.

"It could be another ward. And only your mom can open it."

If that was the case, they weren't going to be getting in anytime soon. They'd have to keep her under twenty-four-hour surveillance, follow her down here, and slip inside behind her without her noticing.

Yeah, as if. They'd have better luck with pickaxes, going in on this wall Seven Dwarves style.

"It could be a puzzle." Gabriel traced the lines of the tree. Some of the branches were darker, but that could be from discoloration or water. "If it is, I have no idea how to solve it."

"Me either."

They'd hit another dead end—literally this time—but neither of them wanted to say it.

"Let's focus on finding a way out of here," Miles proposed. "We can always come back once we figure out how to get inside."

Warring emotions rose in him—he was undeniably relieved for an excuse to put it off a bit longer, but he'd also been so ready for this to end. He didn't know if the universe was rewarding him with more time with Gabriel, or punishing him by dragging out their agonizing quest even longer.

Either way, moping about it wasn't going to change the fact they weren't getting through that door. And Miles was beyond ready to get out of this claustrophobic hellhole.

"You're right." Gabriel sounded equally conflicted, lingering at the door. "It must not be our time yet."

22

"It feels wrong to leave," Miles muttered as he and Gabriel hiked back the way they'd come, starting the climb up the slope.

"I know. But I doubt standing there all day would've made a difference. Perhaps there's a clue, or directions in my mother's office. Or in the grimoire. I don't recall seeing a locking spell, but there's still a large chunk I haven't read."

Going back to the grimoire was the last thing Miles wanted to do. "I'll reach out to Nadia first, see if they know anything."

Gabriel gave a noncommittal hum.

At the top of the agonizing hill—Miles would've been self-conscious about his brink-of-death gasping if Gabriel didn't sound equally out of breath—they made it back to the fork, heading down the other path this time. One led to the Hawthorne wine cellar, one to Jocelyn's tomb, so this third path had to come out elsewhere. Miles was betting on a secret opening in a tree, right on the outskirts of the woods surrounding the mansion. If he'd learned one thing about the Hawthorne family, it was to never underestimate their love for hidden doors.

Moving away from the lake now, the path turned dry again, littered with pebbles and cobwebs hanging from the ceiling. It didn't look like anyone had come this way in a long time.

The reason why became apparent a minute later—the tunnel came to an abrupt end. Not another collapse, this path simply… stopped. Like it'd been half-formed when the diggers decided it wasn't worth their time.

There was no way out.

They were truly trapped down here.

The tunnel tilted and Miles's butt hit the ground. It should've been jarring but he barely registered it, struggling to suck oxygen into his shrinking lungs. His entire body locked up, paralyzed by the panic clawing its way up his ribs.

He was going to die down here. Choking on musty air he couldn't breathe.

He needed to get out.

Freezing fingers landed on the back of Miles's neck with a shock, Gabriel crouched in the dirt with him. If he was talking, Miles couldn't hear the words over the white noise in his brain. Couldn't hear over the wheezing gasps he could feel sawing out of his throat, or the beat of his heart, going so fast it threatened to swallow him up.

Spots exploded across his vision. He was going to faint.

Gabriel's grasp tightened, tugging Miles's head up to meet his eyes, cast in deep shadows from the flashlights discarded at their feet. "Listen to me," he demanded, like he could hear the screaming mess in Miles's head. "You're having a panic attack. You need to take a deep breath."

Miles tried, he really did. But the air refused to go in, to release the fist constricted impossibly tight around his chest. He sank his nails into the earth, body shuddering like it was on the verge of collapse.

He wasn't in control.

"Look." Gabriel refused to let Miles's head drop, holding him captive with his unrelenting grip and steady gaze. "Watch me. Match mine." He took a slow, exaggerated inhale, then another. "Do it."

It hurt, but Miles did as he commanded. Made himself count exhales and inhales, focused on Gabriel's nods of approval and the press of his fingers. Did it until his brain and body realized he wasn't suffocating, that the oxygen was good, and his limbs unlocked from their trembling terror.

"I'm okay," he managed to rasp out. It tasted like a lie on his tongue, sour panic and salty tears.

"You are," Gabriel said firmly.

"I'm sorry." He wiped his tear-streaked face on his sweater sleeve in a gross kid move. He was so mortified, he didn't even know what to say, what to do. Dying down here didn't sound so bad now. "My brain, it doesn't—"

"You have nothing to apologize for," Gabriel interrupted. "Or to act all embarrassed about, so stop it."

Another sniffle escaped Miles. "You're scary when you get all bossy."

"Good. Listen to me or suffer the consequences." Gabriel reached for the zipper of his coat. "Here, you're shivering."

Miles stopped him. "It's the adrenaline, I'm fine. Keep it." The jitters and sweat would take a while to fade.

He stood and offered his hand. "Can you stand?"

"Up for debate." Miles steadied his shaking legs enough to be pulled upright. His knees, however, seemed to have vacated his body, so he wobbled dangerously.

Gabriel helped prop him up against the wall with an insistent, "Don't move," before scooping his flashlight up and stalking to the end of the tunnel.

"What are you doing?"

"Finding us a way out."

Even Gabriel couldn't conjure an exit through sheer stubbornness. "I think the solid stone wall has us beat."

"It doesn't make any sense." He spun in a slow circle. "Why would you build a tunnel that doesn't go anywhere?"

"Maybe it was never finished." It made sense, considering how short this tunnel was compared to the others.

Gabriel frowned, swinging his light to the floor, then the ceiling and stopped. "Or it ends here for a reason."

Miles looked up. Almost directly above them, the rough stone ceiling smoothed out into a flat plane. In the center, a square had been cut into it.

"What is that?"

"I'm not sure, but it must be a way out."

Jello legs forgotten, Miles reached up, but his fingertips were at least a foot or two shy of touching.

So unbearably close to freedom.

"C'mere." He got down on one knee, gesturing to his bent leg. "Stand on me, see if you can reach."

Gabriel didn't move. "I don't want to hurt you."

"Would you rather go back to the wine cellar and wait for your mom?"

He immediately stepped onto Miles's thigh, clutching at his shoulder to steady himself. Miles tried to brace him and not topple over at the same time.

"I can barely reach it with the flashlight." Gabriel's voice was strained. "I need to be up higher."

Miles considered his options—he could get down on his hands and knees and let Gabriel stand on his back, but he didn't think he could take any more embarrassment today. Shoulders it was, then.

He helped Gabriel down, then crouched as low as he could go, bracing his hands against the ground. "Get on my shoulders."

Gabriel stared in disbelief. "I'm not a toddler."

"Just… get on my shoulders so we can get out of here," Miles told him impatiently. "Then we'll never mention it again, okay?"

"I can't—how do I—" Gabriel hands settled awkwardly on Miles's shoulders, then his head.

"Swing one leg up, then hop and get the other. I'll grab you so you don't fall."

"You know I'm not exactly athletic."

"I hate to break it to you, but this isn't a feat of athleticism." Miles had done it a million times as a kid, and carried Amy and Jenna around this way even more.

"You want me to… put my legs around your head."

Miles's cheeks burned. "Don't say it like that. You're just getting on my shoulders, it's no big deal."

At least, it hadn't felt like one before.

Gabriel muttered under his breath but finally swung his first leg over Miles's shoulder. Miles was now second-guessing the sanity of his decision. Was this really less embarrassing than letting Gabriel stand on his back?

He took hold of Gabriel's knee, holding him steady. "Use my head to stabilize yourself and get your other leg up here."

It took two tries and a lot of cursing, but they managed. Gabriel had a death grip on Miles's hair, making his eyes water.

"Okay, I'm going to stand. I'll go slow so I don't smash your head into the ceiling."

"That would be preferable."

Miles cautiously moved into a less severe hunched crouch, his legs shaking from the strain. He embraced the burn, focusing on it instead of the fact Gabriel Hawthorne's legs were currently draped over him.

"Left," Gabriel directed him. "Left. Forward a step. Okay, I'm directly under it."

Miles stood, feeling Gabriel stretch upwards and a low sound, the grind of stone on stone. A glorious rush of cool air ruffled Miles's hair. He had to blink away sudden relieved tears.

"I've got it," Gabriel grunted. "Push me up."

Easier said than done. Miles got the back of his head kneed, a sting like an entire handful of his hair being ripped out, and his spine tromped on before Gabriel's weight disappeared as he wiggled through the hole.

"Oh."

"Good oh or bad oh?"

"I'm in the mausoleum. We moved one of the marble tiles."

"Great." Miles couldn't have cared less where this came out, as long as it wasn't another tunnel. "Is there something up there you can use to get me out?" Even if he could jump and reach the edge, and that was a huge if, he wasn't delusional enough to think he could lift himself with his unimpressive upper body strength. Let's just say he'd never broken any pull-up records during PE tests.

"I don't see anything." Noises moved away and clanged. "The door's not locked," Gabriel called. His face reappeared in the hole a moment later, squinting in Miles's flashlight.

"I'm going to find something. If I have to go to the house, it might be longer, but I'll be right back."

Miles's throat was tight. "Yeah, okay."

Gabriel met his eyes. "I'll be right back."

"I know."

Gabriel wasn't leaving him here. He was coming back. Miles repeated it over and over as he waited. The exit was right there, he wasn't trapped, he wasn't getting left behind. All he had to do was breathe and wait. In and out, and wait.

After an eternity, there was another clang overhead.

"Gabriel?" Miles's voice was shrill. "Is that you?"

"Yes." He sounded winded. "We brought you a stool from the kitchen."

"*We?*"

Charlee's freckled face and mass of fiery curls appeared. "Watch out, we're dropping it down."

Miles caught it, scared it would break in the fall and he'd be trapped even longer. He climbed on it, gripping the edge of the hole as Gabriel and Charlee each took one of his arms to yank him up. For a scary moment, his feet kicked at the empty air, the tunnel refusing to let him go; then he was sliding up onto cold marble.

If he'd had any energy left, he would've wept into the dusty floor. "I never want to go down there again."

Charlee wrapped her arm around his shoulders, Gabriel still gripping his wrist and mercifully not reminding him they'd have to go back eventually.

"Hey, we're out of the tunnels," he joked weakly, rolling over to face Gabriel. "How about that kiss?"

Charlee made a noise of disgust and pushed away from him. "In front of me? Really?"

But Gabriel laughed under his breath. He had a smear of dirt across his chin. "I seem to recall the deal was if *you* got us out. I'm the one who found the exit."

"You're heartless." But Miles was grinning, their banter helping calm his racing heart. "Don't act like the panic attack wasn't super attractive."

"The part where you nearly fainted at my feet was especially charming." Swiftly, he leaned in and pressed a kiss to Miles's cheek. It was a fleeting brush of warmth, and left Miles stunned. "Take your consolation prize and stop complaining."

A blaring, dramatic retch came from Charlee and echoed around the mausoleum. "We're literally surrounded by dead people, and you two are the nastiest thing in here."

Neither of them had the energy to give her a dirty look.

They took their time getting up—Miles ached like he'd aged a hundred years. When Gabriel kneeled to push the marble tile back, he groaned out loud like his weary bones were protesting.

The marble walls of the mausoleum were illuminated by the weak light coming through the stained-glass window as the sun inched below the horizon, casting a rainbow across the vaults. It was the most color Miles had encountered on the Hawthorne property, and only the dead could appreciate it.

It must've rained while they were underground because the grass was soaked, immediately wetting Miles's boots and the hem of his jeans. He scanned the stormy clouds and begged them to hold out long enough for them to get back indoors.

Gabriel closed the double doors behind them with a muffled *boom*.

23

Miles's parents were waiting for him when he got home. He was expecting it—he'd have to be stupid not to. Not only had he and Charlee missed dinner and several calls, but they didn't even have a believable excuse ready. Miles had just sent them a vague "I'm alive, be home soon" text and started praying to any higher power willing to take pity on him.

"Come in here, please," his dad called, leaning out of the office doorway. His expression was unreadable.

As Miles crept towards the office and saw his mom sitting at her desk too, he knew he was screwed. Charlee tried to follow him in, her squared shoulders and scowl suggesting she was ready for battle, but Adam stopped her with a touch on the shoulder. "Go on upstairs," he urged gently. "We'll come talk to you later."

A pang of guilt went through Miles—Charlee had no problem being his accomplice, but he'd never wanted to drag her down with him.

Her chin jutted up. She could refuse if she wanted. Adam wasn't her dad, and she was an adult. But after a tense moment, she nodded and strode away, shooting Miles an apologetic glance.

The office was messier than usual—always a sign that his dad was picking up extra jobs—with tall stacks of books and papers on the dining table and supplies spilling out of his desk drawers. It smelled like coffee, ink, and herbs.

Adam pulled out a seat for Miles from the table, then scooted his desk chair over to sit with Sarah. Two against one. Never great odds.

His mom didn't say anything. His dad sighed, running a hand down his face with a rasp of callused skin on stubble. "We know you were at the Hawthorne manor."

Miles's stomach bottomed out. After what his mom had said in the kitchen, he'd assumed she suspected he was still seeing Gabriel. It was pointless to deny it now; he could see in their faces that they *knew*.

"How?" he managed to croak out.

"We had a hunch… then we checked your phone location to be sure."

Ah. It probably would've been smart to turn that off. His whole family location was shared on their phones in case a job went bad. Miles had enabled the feature forever ago and promptly forgot all about it.

He'd never been cut out for all this sneaking around and lying. It was always destined to end with him making a stupid, amateur mistake.

The jig was up. Miles had no idea what came next. The grounding of a lifetime? Locks on his bedroom door and windows? Twenty-four-seven surveillance?

His mom leaned forward, her desk chair squeaking, and Miles braced himself. "I realized I wasn't fair earlier," she said softly. Too softly. Were his parents doing a good-cop, bad-cop routine? "I expected you to be honest with me when I haven't done the same. As your parent, it's my job to lead by example."

Adam put his hand on Sarah's knee. "And I can forget to be a dad. In this line of work, the hours, the things I deal with… it takes over. I haven't been here for you as much as I should be, and I'm sorry."

This was so much worse than if they were just angry.

"No, it's not—" Miles tried.

"We should've talked to you weeks ago," his dad interrupted. "Before we took you to the Hawthorne party. Or when you asked for answers. We were… selfish. Our history with the Hawthornes, with Felicity, is something that neither of us like to revisit."

Unexpected indignation rose in Miles's throat. He'd been suffering, second-guessing himself and worrying that he'd never be able to repair what he'd broken, wondering if they'd ever forgive him. All because it hadn't occurred to them to put aside their discomfort.

Sarah must've sensed it. "We want to tell you the truth. And we want to understand what's going on between you and that boy."

"His name is Gabriel," Miles bit out. "And I already tried to explain, but you punished me for it."

Regret shone in her blue eyes. "You don't owe us—me—a second chance, but we're asking for one."

He wanted to be furious, stubborn, to make her understand how it stung to have her pleas ignored, to not feel worthy of an explanation. They'd hidden so much from him, treated him like a traitor to their family.

More than that, Miles wanted to tell them everything—unload it all, get a warm hug, hear them say they were proud of him for doing what was right.

It was so much easier living in other people's emotions than trying to untangle his own.

He stared at the framed family tree, tracing the branching lines and willing the hurt to fade. "What happened with Felicity?"

He needed to know her story, find out if she was truly capable of hurting her own son.

His parents exchanged a lingering look. Adam spoke up first. "We were friends when we were younger, after we met at one of the Hawthorne parties. Neither of us wanted to be there, and we ended up stealing chocolate cake from the kitchen and getting my skateboard out of the car so I could teach her how to ride it in the driveway." His smile was small, but tender with the memory. "She was... different back then. Shy, and a bit socially awkward, but whip-smart and curious. We were friends for months."

This was the first Miles had ever heard of Felicity where she sounded human. It was like holding two pieces from completely different puzzles in your hand and trying to find a way to make them fit together. The magic had altered her so completely.

"Then I met your mom," his dad continued, taking her hand. Miles had heard the story before—Adam tagged along on an emergency haunting call with Grandpa Henry and met her there. Apparently, he'd heroically saved her from a falling wardrobe. "We didn't start dating until later, but we became fast friends, so I introduced her to Felicity. They were..."

"Inseparable," Sarah finished in a whisper. Her throat bobbed as she swallowed. "The day we met, I found my best friend. Your dad had Robin growing up, but I was an only child. All I ever wanted was a sister. Felicity… I thought she was that, for a while."

She'd never spoken about Felicity without hatred in her voice. Hearing the pain, the regret, was worse.

"Felicity's home life wasn't easy, anyone could see that. But something changed. We met one night, and she showed up with a suitcase, begging me to run away with her." Her voice caught, snagged in a trap of memories. "She was scared. She said I didn't understand the pressure her parents were putting on her, the expectations. That she couldn't do it and she had to get out of Thistle, leave her family."

It wasn't hard to see where this story went. "You said no."

"I couldn't up and leave everything like that. I was graduating in a few months. All my family was here. And she wanted to cut out all the psychic stuff, which meant Adam."

"We'd started dating a few weeks before," his dad added, tugging at his cuffs to straighten his faded flannel. "We didn't realize how upset she was about it. We'd made her feel unimportant and left out."

Sarah's arms settled around her middle, holding herself upright. Teetering on a precipice Miles couldn't see. "She wouldn't explain anything to me. I told her she was being irrational, that her fight with her parents would blow over. I said no, but that Adam and I would meet her the next day and help her figure everything out. I was going to talk to my parents about letting her stay with us for a while."

Miles could picture it all too well. If Gabriel had asked him to run away, to uproot his whole life and leave everything behind, his answer probably would've been the same.

"We were supposed to meet her the next day, but she never showed." There was an undercurrent of sorrow in his dad's voice. "Weeks went by before we saw her again. She never answered any of our calls or met us in our usual spots. When we did see her…"

"She wasn't the girl we knew. The coldness in her eyes, the way she spoke to me and the things she said…" Sarah shook her head. There was a distant noise from the hallway; Miles wondered if Charlee was listening in. "When she stopped seeing us, I knew she was angry, thinking I'd picked Adam over her. She threw away our whole friendship without another word. She cut us out like we meant nothing to her."

Since meeting Marjorie and feeling the difference in the darkness around her compared to Gabriel and Edmund, Miles had wondered if there was a point where something changed. A certain amount of time that had to pass before the magic fully settled, or a specific trigger. Felicity's story all but confirmed that theory.

That had to mean it wasn't too late for Gabriel or his brothers. The corruption would leave once the curse was broken—as long as it hadn't changed him yet.

Miles's relief was snuffed out by a horrible realization: his parents didn't know about the grimoire or the curse. They had no idea that Felicity had been transformed against her will.

It still hurt; Miles could hear it in his mom's voice. The lack of closure was a heavy burden she'd been carrying all these years.

Would it heal them to know their friend hadn't willingly turned on them, or hurt them worse to know what she'd gone through? What they might've been able to save her from?

The rain started outside, tentative plinks that turned into thunder against the street outside. Sarah's gaze drifted to the window as the wind blew a gust to batter the glass. Demanding to be let inside.

"Our family passed down warnings about the Hawthornes," his dad admitted. "We just thought Felicity was different. And we were wrong."

Miles's entire body went cold. Was this his future with Gabriel if they failed? To look into his eyes one day and see an unrecognizable person? For Gabriel to have everything that made him *him* erased?

The clock on the wall ticked ominously over his head.

"You weren't wrong," Miles declared. He'd made his decision. His parents deserved to know the truth. "There's something evil, a curse on the Hawthornes, and it infects them with a darkness. It changes them."

He explained everything that he could. His premonition and running into Gabriel at the Hawthorne party. Jocelyn reaching out through the visions to save Gabriel, putting the pieces together about the grimoire and the curse, unraveling their families' history. And if he made it sound like they'd averted Gabriel's death by banishing Florence, conveniently forgetting to mention that he might be on the chopping block now, it was only so he didn't get locked away for safekeeping, called an idiot for actively pursuing a killer, or give his parents a heart attack.

"We're trying to break the spell that Florence cast," he finished tiredly. "And save Gabriel's family."

Sarah, who'd gotten progressively paler and more visibly distressed as the story went on, sniffled. She had a white-knuckled grip on Adam's hand. "She was trying to leave. She knew it was coming and she begged me for help. I should've listened to her."

"You didn't know," Adam soothed, wrapping an arm around her shoulders and kissing the top of her head. "Neither of us did."

Miles felt like he was intruding on a private moment, but he needed to finish. "What happened to Felicity... I'm not going to let it happen to Gabriel. Or his brothers. I promised him."

"He's lucky to have you in his corner." Adam leaned forward and clasped Miles on the shoulder, giving a firm squeeze. "He couldn't ask for anyone better."

His mom crossed the room to pull Miles into a hug, not much taller than him even when he was sitting. He could feel her quiver against him. It was too tight, her hair itching his nose, but he couldn't pull away.

She didn't have to speak.

"You and Felicity. Jocelyn and Rosalie. Me and Gabriel..." he said once they'd pulled away, everyone in the room acting like they weren't wiping tears away. "Our families keep finding ways to each other. What if the universe keeps bringing us together for a reason?"

"To break their curse?" Adam offered.

No. It was more than that, more than playing a role in someone else's story. "Rosalie never moved past losing Jocelyn. You couldn't help Felicity. And now, Gabriel is facing a lifetime of having dark magic inside him if I don't change the future. Maybe our family is doomed to be continuously given chances to save someone we care about and failing." Miles struggled to speak around the sudden lump in his throat. "Maybe this is about breaking our curse too."

Sarah blinked a few times. Her fingers combed through his hair, slipping down to cup his cheek. "I think you're right."

24

"Invite Gabriel over for dinner tonight," Miles's mom instructed, turning down the radio as they rolled up to the stop sign at the end of their street.

Miles nearly choked. "What?"

When she'd offered to drive him to school this morning, he knew she wanted to talk about last night. He thought he'd been prepared for any turn the conversation might take, but apparently not.

"Your dad and I spoke last night and agreed it's important that we meet him. We took tonight off for a family dinner." She flipped on her blinker, waiting for a woman in magenta earmuffs to cross the road with a golden retriever, its tail wagging happily. "Does he like lasagna?"

"I—I don't know." That was so far from important right now. "Mom, this is kinda last second, I don't think he—"

She slid him an amused look. "If you two can find time to sneak around every day, you can make time for one dinner."

Damn it.

"We actually already have plans for tonight. We're going to the football game."

The brakes squeaked as she hit them a touch too hard. "Since when have you started going to football games?"

Miles tried to banish the heat crawling up his neck. "It's not a big deal."

"Well, the game won't start until six or seven, so we'll just have dinner a little earlier than usual. And Gabriel's obviously free, so it shouldn't be a problem for him."

Double damn it.

A group of kids scurried through the crosswalk, backpacks and pom-pom hats bobbing. Miles chewed over his words, trying to find a way to say them as nicely as possible.

"I don't think it's fair," he said slowly, picking at a snag on his jeans, "to invite him over so he can be gawked at like a freak. I know last night was a lot, and I'm sure you have questions for him, but it's not... that's not..."

He couldn't tell her that part of him hoped the first time he'd have Gabriel over for dinner, it would be as his boyfriend, not a Hawthorne. Sweet and awkward and potentially mortifying. Not the interrogation he was already picturing.

He was tired of letting this curse steal things from him.

His mom's expression fell. "That isn't what this is. We can tell he's important to you and I..." She blew out a breath, drumming her fingers against the steering wheel. "I've been so worried about you being lonely, and feeling guilty because our lifestyle isn't exactly conducive to easy friendships. He's the first friend you've made in years, Miles. That means a lot. That's why we want to meet him."

Miles appreciated what she was trying to do. She had something to prove to him, and to herself. But the thought of sitting through a painful meal with Gabriel and his family with multiple elephants in the room that none of them would acknowledge sounded like literal hell.

He wouldn't even know how to tell Gabriel that he was expected at his house tonight for a Warren family dinner.

Scoffing, Miles could handle. For once, he'd prefer it. Give him disbelief, even a snarky comment or two. The more terrifying possibility was if Gabriel wanted to come.

If you'd asked him a week ago, Miles would've said there was no way. But this was the new Gabriel, the Gabriel who'd been forced to rethink his priorities and somehow landed on dating Miles and having ridiculous normal teenage experiences with him.

And what was more awfully cliché than the dreaded first dinner with your boyfriend's family?

They pulled into the school drop-off line, the entrance looming. On the sidewalk, a kid dropped a basketball and had to sprint down the hill after it, kicking up wet leaves in his wake.

Miles snatched his backpack from the floor, all but lunging for the door handle. "I'll see if he's free," he settled on. "But no promises. Thanks for the ride."

His mom let him escape, pulling away as he hefted his bag over his shoulder and trudged over to the courtyard.

Emily and Gabriel were sitting together and amazingly Gabriel didn't look like he wanted to bludgeon himself with the nearest heavy object. Either Miles was imagining things, or there was a glimmer of amusement in both of their eyes.

"Am I interrupting?" Miles teased, sliding into the seat beside Gabriel.

His expression smoothed out in a flash. "You're late. I was worried I was going to be stuck hearing about football until my brain leaked out of my ears."

Emily grinned, hands cupped around a stickered red

thermos. "Don't let him fool you, he was enraptured the whole time. If I didn't know any better, I'd think he was considering joining the cheerleading squad for the homecoming game tonight."

Gabriel's chin lifted haughtily. "As if they'd be so lucky."

A burst of laughter exploded out of Miles, and Gabriel flushed pink.

Emily crowed with delight. "He does make jokes! I knew it."

A few people from the packed table beside theirs glanced over curiously, wondering what the ruckus was. The attention didn't bother Emily as she tossed her long braid and knocked shoulders with Gabriel, still chortling.

When her mirth faded, she turned to Miles. "Hey, real talk, though—Gabriel told me about last night. Bummer you couldn't crack the door open. Did you get ahold of Nadia yet to see if they have any ideas?"

That was unexpectedly forthcoming of Gabriel. "Yeah, we texted a bit this morning." Miles tucked his chin into the sheepskin collar of his jacket, searching for warmth as a frigid gust of wind whipped across the courtyard, sending scarves flapping and flipping textbook pages. When he'd first put his coat on this morning, it'd still smelled like Gabriel, but his crisp scent had faded now. "I was going to wait, but Charlee said they're always up early to open the shop."

"Hmmm." Emily took a long sip from her steaming thermos, the bitter smell of coffee drifting across the table. "Interesting that Charlee knows their sleep schedule so... intimately."

She sank so much implication into that final word that Miles blushed.

"How is that remotely interesting? I became well acquainted with their schedule when I stayed there." Gabriel's mouth pinched. "The practicality of an hour-long lunch break when you're running a business still eludes me."

Miles took pity on him. "It's interesting because it means they've been chatting consistently enough that Charlee knows their schedule. And Charlee doesn't chat with anyone."

He saw the moment it clicked. Gabriel tilted his head, considering. "Nadia did say my company made them realize how painfully lonely they were. I assumed it was merely an unimaginative insult."

That pulled a giggle from Emily. "What did Nadia say?" she asked Miles, leaning across the damp table eagerly. "Did they mention Charlee?"

"Uh... no. We were pretty focused on the door." He pulled out his phone and passed it over.

> i can do some digging and hit the books
> but its impossible to know what im looking for
> without seeing it in person
> stone door with a tree doesnt narrow it down
> much

> What about a way to just unlock it?

> theres a thousand rituals for that
> locking spell
> protection spell
> ward
> ancient blood ritual
> a boring hidden keyhole

I get the point... so what do we do?

i can be there tomorrow
ill close the shop for the day
get me to the door and ill see what i can do

Miles hadn't responded yet, wanting to run the plan by everyone else. Between tomorrow being Saturday and the fact his parents were in the know now, it shouldn't be a problem to get Nadia over there and down to the tunnels.

"I'm in," Emily proclaimed. "We meet up, go to the tunnels, kick the tomb door down, and free Jocelyn."

Yeah, Miles was sure it would be that easy.

Gabriel looked similarly doubtful, but shrugged. "No harm in trying now that we know the way and have an exit. If my mother is home, we'll go through the mausoleum."

Miles texted Nadia back, getting an immediate reply.

Sounds good, thank you... here's my address

perfect
tell your cousin i cant wait to see her

He showed Emily that last part and she snickered as the bell rang overhead and the courtyard exploded into a flurry of movement. The Friday of the homecoming football game was always Spirit Day, so there was green and white everywhere, from jerseys and face paint to tulle skirts and striped socks.

"Are you alright?" Gabriel questioned as they gathered their things, Emily already snatched away by a group of her friends heading to first period. "You have a strange look on your face."

If Miles had to guess, it was the "needing to tell your secret boyfriend he was invited to family dinner" face. But that meant diving into the conversation he'd had with his parents last night, including what he'd learned about Felicity. Not exactly a casual conversation you could squeeze in during the two-minute stroll to History.

"All good." He wasn't chickening out; it was a strategic delay for Gabriel's benefit. Really.

He had all day to tell him.

By the time lunch rolled around, Miles still hadn't told Gabriel about the dinner invitation. In his defense, classes had been crazy busy, full of Friday pop quizzes and project presentations—he'd barely been able to get in a few words.

"Hey." Miles found Gabriel at their usual lunch table, touching his elbow gently. "Do you mind getting out of here? I had something I wanted to tell you."

The lunchroom was extra crowded and loud with Spirit Day festivities. The cheering as people went to cast their homecoming court votes literally shook the floor as Miles and Gabriel slipped into a hallway.

"What is the purpose of the homecoming king and queen?" Gabriel inquired as Miles led the way. "Should I expect thrones?"

"I don't actually know. I think it's just like… a popularity contest. The richest, prettiest people in each grade get a chance to flaunt it even more than usual for one night."

His nose wrinkled. "That seems rather outdated."

"You'd be surprised how many people use tradition as an excuse to keep outdated ideals around." The cheering rose to painfully shrill heights, even this far away.

"There's nothing surprising about that. Bigotry is as resilient as a cockroach."

But sadly, it couldn't be squashed as easily.

They went to the alcove where they'd spoken to Rosalie, sitting against the wall in the empty space beneath the stairs. It was quieter here, and part of the track was visible out the window, blurred by the haze of rain.

Normally, Miles would've gone to the library, but he had a suspicion Joe wouldn't be thrilled to see them.

"Last time you had something to tell me, it was that you think my mother wants to murder me," Gabriel commented wryly. "Should I brace myself?"

"For once, I have good news. Kinda." He wanted to temper Gabriel's expectations. "I told my parents about… well, all of this. Last night. They found out I was at your place yesterday, and everything just came out. It was a lot."

That might've been the world's biggest oversimplification.

"And?" Gabriel prompted, when Miles paused. "If you're trying to drag out the suspense, consider me on the edge of my seat."

"I was getting there." Miles knocked their knees together. "I should make you wait just for being an ass. But, since I have a reputation to uphold as the reasonable, benevolent one, I won't."

Gabriel's eyebrow arched. "And here I was thinking your reputation was as the local antisocial giant with a questionable wardrobe." He plucked at one of the fraying strings hanging from a hole in Miles's jeans. "My mistake."

Swatting his hand away, Miles bit back a laugh and dug through his backpack until he found his lunch. He shoved a baby orange into Gabriel's hand.

"What am I supposed to do with this?"

"Eat it. You can't keep insulting me if your mouth is full, and I'd like to finish my story sometime today."

He'd been joking, but Gabriel took it with a quirk of his lips. "Please, continue."

"As I was saying, we talked and it went… surprisingly well." Outside, a miserable-looking group started jogging around the track. He couldn't see her, but Miles knew Mrs. Ballenski, the PE teacher, had to be lurking nearby with her stopwatch. "I told them the truth and they didn't lose it. I think they're trying to be supportive."

Removing the orange peel in one long strip with deft fingers, Gabriel frowned. "Supportive of your potentially suicidal quest? I was under the impression that my mother was the questionable parent here."

"Okay, I might've left that part out."

"You just said you told them the truth."

"*Most* of the truth, whatever. Omitting certain details to spare them from worrying is a necessary evil."

Gabriel opened his mouth and Miles gave the orange a pointed look. Gabriel rolled his eyes but ate a segment, flicking his wrist for Miles to keep going. The fresh, citrus scent made his mouth water.

"The point is, we have one less thing to worry about now. My parents are officially in the know—mostly—and they're on our side."

"You must be relieved. You've been struggling with keeping this from them since the day we met."

Relieved wasn't a strong enough word. Miles could finally breathe again. "I didn't need their approval to know I was doing the right thing, but it feels good to finally have it."

"They should've supported you this whole time," Gabriel sniffed, but Miles thought it was more a reflexive defense of him than actual ire towards his parents. It was sweet.

"They're trying to be here for me now." Miles chewed his lip. "And they finally told me what happened with your mom."

He recounted the story, trying to remember every detail. Gabriel listened intently, half of his orange forgotten beside him.

"You act like you're a lost cause, but I don't think that's true. As long as your"—Miles waved his hand around Gabriel—"dark cloud is still hanging around, I think you're good. Which is a wild thing to say."

Gabriel frowned. "We don't know for sure that once the change happens, it can't be undone. My mother could... revert back to her own self."

"I mean, yeah, it's possible. Change isn't necessarily permanent." But Miles had an awful sinking feeling when he thought back to Marjorie, how completely it had encased her. How unmovable it seemed.

"The person they described... there's not even a hint of her in my mother." The words were low, Gabriel's gaze fixed on the window. Down the hall, a locker clanged. "She was so different, I can't picture it. A smile on her face or affection in her voice."

It had to hurt to hear what you'd always wished for had existed before you came along. That in another life, Felicity could've been a good mom, and Gabriel raised in a home that knew joy.

He was probably wondering if she'd ever been given a chance to love him.

Miles took his hand, giving him silence, but letting him know he wasn't alone.

"She tried to escape," Gabriel murmured. "And it didn't matter."

"I know." That was the biggest tragedy of Felicity Hawthorne. Not that she'd been changed by this curse, but that she'd tried to run. She'd believed she could leave it behind.

"I couldn't imagine facing this alone."

Miles heard the words he didn't say: *thank you*.

There wasn't a clock in this part of the hallway, but when Miles saw the poor runners on the track start to head off towards the gym, he knew the bell would ring soon. He was out of time.

"There was one other thing." Miles rubbed the back of his neck. "My mom invited you to dinner at our place tonight."

Gabriel blinked. "Excuse me?"

Distant cheering sounded from the cafeteria, as if the whole school was celebrating the end of Miles's procrastination.

"Yeah, like I said, they're trying to be supportive. They want to meet you, and thought dinner was the right call. I told my mom we're going to the game, but she just moved the time."

"Dinner," Gabriel echoed in disbelief.

"Lasagna, specifically. But don't worry, you don't have to come," Miles reassured him. "I'll tell her you're busy, and I can meet you at the game after—"

"I'll come."

There it was. "It's really no big deal," Miles insisted quickly. "Don't worry about it."

"I'm not worried. If it goes badly, at least I won't be accused of being too cowardly to show up." Gabriel shrugged, fiddling with a button on his cuff. Footsteps thudded over their heads as someone hurried down the stairs. "It's not like they can hate me more than they already do."

"Hey, no, that's not—"

"You don't have to lie to me."

And to think, Miles had assumed only moments ago that the mood couldn't possibly get any lower.

"Listen, my mom feels bad that she's been unfair to you. She wants to get to know you because you're important to me. That's already earning you major brownie points."

Surprise flared in Gabriel's gray eyes. "Did you tell her that we're dating?"

Miles knew his cheeks were turning red. "No. And not because I'm like, embarrassed of you or worried because you're a Hawthorne or anything." He stumbled over the words in his rush to get them out. "I swear it's not that. I'm just... I haven't told my parents I'm gay yet."

He wasn't sure why it sounded like an admission of weakness.

And he wished that being with Gabriel was the push he needed to do it, that it could give him the bravery to tell them despite his fears. He didn't want Gabriel to feel like a dirty secret. It wasn't fair to him.

"No. You can't do it for me," Gabriel stated firmly, reading his mind. "I don't care about any of that. When you tell them, it needs to be because you're ready. Do it for yourself."

Miles wasn't sure why that made his lower lip wobble. "And what if I'm never ready?"

"Then that's your business. Your parents can think I'm an insufferably clingy friend for all I care." He smirked. "But you'll tell them eventually. And not simply because you're a terrible, guilt-ridden liar. You're also braver than you give yourself credit for."

Miles wasn't brave enough to lean over and kiss him where someone might see, which was a shame. He settled for clearing his tight throat and briefly pressing his lips to Gabriel's knuckles. His face had to be disturbingly tomato-colored by now, but Gabriel didn't tease him.

"I won't come to dinner if you don't want me to." His gaze was tender. They were still stumbling their way through what dating entailed, but the look on his face told Miles that he wasn't at all opposed to hand kisses. "Your family is willing to give me a chance. No one's done that before. But your opinion is the only one I care about."

He meant it. But he didn't know Miles's parents. And suddenly, Miles wanted him to. It felt unbearably important that he sat with people who listened to him when he spoke, treated him with kindness, and—if Miles knew his mom—made him eat too much lasagna.

He'd face his anxieties a thousand times over before telling Gabriel he wasn't welcome in his home.

"I want you to."

25

The kitchen smelled of baking bread, garlicky tomato sauce, and anxious anticipation. The latter was Miles's contribution to the evening's ambiance.

He reorganized the napkins and silverware on the table three times before Charlee came over and smacked his hand.

"Stop fidgeting. You're stressing me out."

"I'm not—" No, he was. Denying it was a waste of air. "Let me panic in peace."

"It'll be fine." Behind them, the oven hinges squeaked as his dad peeked inside. The lasagna was already out, foil-wrapped and resting on the counter. Gabriel was supposed to arrive any minute. "And if it's a disaster, Gabriel won't care."

"Are you sure about that?" Miles was only half-serious. Worries, some irrational and others frighteningly possible, whirled through his head. That he'd throw up or pass out at the table. That his sisters were going to act like love-struck little freaks and embarrass him. That his parents would ask a bunch of questions and put Gabriel on the spot. Or worse, they'd see Miles's feelings written obviously on his face, and Gabriel would have to experience the full messy drama of an on-the-spot coming out.

"Do you think they're… going to be able to tell?"

"Tell what?"

"You know, about me and Gabriel." He made a vague gesture.

"I guess it depends if they're using their eyes or not."

He dug his elbow into her ribs. "Seriously, what do I do? Not look at him all dinner?"

"Yeah, because that won't be uncomfortable at all. I'll just pinch you every time you start to stare longingly."

"You're not funny."

"And you're freaking yourself out because your brain is mean and likes to torture you." Charlee leaned in for a moment, warm and smelling sugary sweet. "It'll be fine. Who knows, it might even go well."

"You don't really believe that."

She shrugged. "We're off to a good start—my mom isn't here."

Aunt Robin had opted to spend the night in her room instead of joining them. She was doing better, but entertaining company was still too much for her right now, especially such an exciting guest. Miles was secretly relieved to have one less person gawking at poor Gabriel while he tried to eat.

"What if they don't like him?"

"Who cares?"

He didn't, not really. But everything would be so much easier if they did. Surely wanting that didn't make him a bad person.

"Why isn't he here yet?" Amy whined, coming up behind Miles. She'd made their mom do her hair earlier, pinned half-up with glittery star clips that matched her pink shirt. "You didn't scare him away, did you?"

"Amy!" their mom chided, setting a massive bowl of salad down in the middle of the table. "Don't be rude. You need to support Miles now that he's making friends."

He was really starting to wish she'd stop saying it like that, with a level of awe reserved for miracles.

"A friend he kept secret because you and Dad hate him so much," Amy muttered.

"They don't hate him," Jenna pointed out as she plopped into her usual chair. Thank God she was at least pretending to be casual, in her regular paint-splattered jeans and purple hoodie. She looked like the stagehand while her twin was the star of the show. "They hate his family."

"Don't say that." His mom glanced over her shoulder like she was expecting Gabriel to materialize in the middle of the kitchen. "We don't hate him or his family, we—you know what, it doesn't matter. Just don't say that, okay?"

Before Amy could respond with something undoubtedly bratty, there was a brisk knock at the door.

"He's here," she squealed, clutching Jenna.

Gabriel wasn't even in the house yet and they were already making Miles cringe out of his skin. It was going to be an excruciating dinner.

"I'll get it." He hurried from the kitchen before anyone could beat him to the front door.

His hand trembled as he opened it. "Uh, hey." It was already dark out, the street behind him cast in shadows, the porch light bathing Gabriel in a yellow glow. "Sorry in advance for—are those flowers?"

A ridiculous question—they very clearly were. A whole bouquet of golden sunflowers clasped in Gabriel's hand. Were they... for Miles?

Pink dusted the bridge of Gabriel's nose, bleeding color down into his cheeks. "They're for your mother. It was Bram's idea. He insisted it was bad manners to show up without something."

Of course they weren't for Miles, what a stupid thought. Charlee was right—his brain was a jerk.

"They're really nice," Miles reassured him, then stepped aside so he could come in. "My mom loves sunflowers, good call."

"They're in season." Gabriel shifted the bouquet to his other hand, clearly nervous, which made Miles feel better.

He'd put on his nicest sweater and a pair of dark jeans so Gabriel wouldn't look or feel so blatantly out of place among Miles's casually dressed family. It was the right call—Gabriel was wearing a forest-green wool knit vest over a white button-up and his usual slacks. They almost matched.

"There's still time to run if you've changed your mind."

Gabriel raised his eyebrows. "My mother is home tonight and in a terrible mood. You're going to need to try harder than that if you want to get rid of me."

"In that case"—Miles gestured him towards the kitchen—"sorry for my sisters, and good luck."

His parents were trying to play it chill, his dad turned to the stove and his mom straightening the salad dressing she'd set on the table. It just meant Miles had to clear his throat awkwardly to get their attention.

"Uh, Mom, Dad, this is Gabriel." He gestured to him with a jerky jazz hand wave and immediately regretted it. "Gabriel, these are my parents."

"Are those for me?" Amy demanded before anyone else could speak, staring at the flowers hopefully.

Gabriel blinked. "Oh, I—"

"Knock it off," Miles told her, as if he hadn't almost asked the same thing two seconds ago. "They're obviously for Mom."

Taking his cue, Gabriel stepped forward and presented them to a surprised Sarah. "Thank you for inviting me to dinner and into your lovely home, Mrs. Warren," he said formally. Miles would bet he'd practiced it on the way over, which was agonizingly adorable. "It's a pleasure to finally meet you."

It seemed they'd all collectively agreed to pretend their previous encounter at Jane Bryant's birthday party had never happened.

"Oh, thank you. And Sarah and Adam is fine, we're not much for formalities in this house." She was flustered, looking around for a place to put the flowers. "We're happy to have you over. Miles…" She faltered for a moment, clearly intending to say something generic, like that Miles had told them a lot about him. "He wasn't sure if you'd be able to make it."

"I'm glad I could."

Adam appeared with a vase. "Hope you brought your appetite," he told Gabriel, shaking his hand with an easy smile. "I made enough lasagna to feed an army."

Ugh, he couldn't sound like more of a dad if he tried.

"Yeah," Charlee told Gabriel with a smirk. "If you don't eat at least three pieces, you'll never be invited back. We take dinner seriously around here."

"Ignore her, she's joking," Miles said when Gabriel frowned uncertainly.

Miles's dad set the vase of sunflowers on the counter, then

checked the oven. "The bread just needs another minute, then we're good to go. Charlee, will you grab plates?"

She pushed away from where she'd been leaning against the wall. "C'mon, Hawthorne, we're on plate duty."

He obediently followed her across the kitchen, peering into the cabinet when she opened it.

Miles's mom nudged him. "He's… nice."

There was nothing wrong with the way she said it, but Miles still prickled. "He is."

The bread came out, Adam taking it to the table as everyone dished up lasagna. Their table was too small for all the food on family dinner nights, so they always served the main course from the stove. Gabriel didn't seem bothered, dutifully sliding a saucy slice onto his plate.

Miles steered him to the far end of the table, hoping he'd feel less cramped and less scrutinized. When Amy saw that Gabriel was sitting beside Jenna, her lower lip jutted out.

"Hello," Gabriel greeted Jenna as he sat down. He peered at the book sticking out of her hoodie pocket. "Are you reading anything interesting?"

She went scarlet and took a gulp of her juice. "It's about what happens to our bodies when we die. The author is a mortician, so she's an expert."

"That sounds fascinating."

"It is. The chapter I'm on right now is all about flesh-eating insects."

"Jenna has an interest in the more scientific aspects of death," Miles's dad told Gabriel proudly as he sat. "She devours every book she can get her hands on about it."

Ducking her head, Jenna shoveled a steaming bite into her mouth.

"My family library has a whole section of medical and science books," Gabriel told her, cutting his lasagna into neat pieces with his knife and fork. "You're welcome to borrow any that interest you. My younger brother is an avid reader as well, though he usually stays in the fiction section."

"Really? That would be awesome. I've already read through most that Thistle Library has, and I never know where to start online. There're too many choices."

"Have you looked up the FBI body farm? It might interest you."

Jenna's expression brightened. "What's that?"

"Did Miles tell you we helped when you were missing?" Amy interrupted. She leaned forward, nearly dragging her hair through her dinner. "I'm pretty much the reason we found you. I bet he took all the credit, didn't he?"

Miles and Charlee exchanged an eye roll.

Miles's mom looked lost. "Have you all met each other already?"

Gabriel glanced at Miles, clearly unsure if he'd misstepped. He'd mentioned to his dad that Amy and Jenna were helping out; he just hadn't given the details.

"He came over for a few minutes after the car accident, waiting for his brother to pick him up."

"It was a brief interaction," Gabriel reassured them. Miles wished he didn't think he needed to.

"More importantly, did Amy say you were *missing*?" Miles's dad questioned, slathering up a piece of bread with butter.

"That wasn't the case, it was a misunderstanding. I was visiting a friend and unable to get ahold of anyone for a few days."

"Hey, Dad," Miles jumped in. "How did that poltergeist job go the other day? I forgot to ask."

Adam took pity on him, launching into a description of the poltergeist haunting a restaurant over in Bellingham and how close it'd come to locking him inside the walk-in refrigerator. He was a good storyteller, adequately dramatic and overplaying the danger, and Gabriel seemed interested, questioning around bites.

"Jenna and I are going to start helping with jobs soon," Amy shared with Gabriel. "If you ever need a partner."

Charlee snorted into her bite of salad.

"He doesn't do that kind of thing," Miles told her.

"I've taken a more recent interest in it," Gabriel amended. He shifted and pressed their knees together under the table. "Your brother has told me a lot about what your family does. It's very admirable."

"We try our best." Sarah smiled contentedly at Adam. "I'm sure it's nowhere near as interesting as..." She faltered, and Miles knew she'd been about to mention Felicity. He'd made her promise there'd be none of that while Gabriel was over. "What other families in the area do," she finished.

"I don't expect you to censor yourselves in your own home. My mother is a rather unavoidable topic." Gabriel's eyes gleamed with amusement. "Though she has plenty of other wicked qualities, saying her name won't summon her like a demon."

Miles choked into his glass of water.

"I was actually hoping you might tell me more about her," he continued. "From when you knew her before."

Under the table, Miles nudged his foot against Gabriel's. He glanced over and gave a reassuring nod.

"It was years ago," Miles's dad started after a moment of hesitation. "I think we must've been around…" He trailed off.

"Fifteen," Sarah filled in. "Remember, we had to sneak her out of the house for my birthday party? The one where you got knocked into the pool?"

Miles's dad chuckled. "I'd forgotten about that." He took Sarah's hand, turning back to Gabriel. "Your mom was hilarious. I've never met anyone who could come up with a comeback as quickly as her. She was a terrible skateboarder, but she insisted on learning no matter how many times she scraped herself up, and she showed me how to drive a stick-shift on one of her dad's old classic cars."

"Until you almost wrecked it," Sarah pointed out.

"*Almost* being the operative word." He gave an exaggerated wink.

"She didn't even get mad," Sarah told Gabriel. "She just switched seats, cranked up the music, and backed right out of the ditch onto the road like she'd done it a million times. The next day, she showed up with a toy car for him and told him if he cared about the safety of the public, it was the only car he'd ever put his hands on again."

Both Miles's parents laughed.

Gabriel set his fork down gingerly. A complicated series of emotions crossed his face. "I can't even picture her like that," he admitted. "You're talking about a stranger."

Miles wanted to reach over and comfort him. He hoped Gabriel got to meet the real Felicity when they broke the curse. He and his brothers deserved a second chance with her, to know the woman she'd once been.

His mom's mirth faded. "Most curses have a loophole, no

matter how tricky the magic. If there's a way to bring her back, we'll find it."

"That's kind of you to say." He didn't sound like he was holding out hope.

"Hey, Amy," Charlee jumped in. Miles supposed she could relate to having a complicated relationship with your mom. "Why don't you tell everyone about the school musical you want to try out for."

Amy happily did exactly that, filling the silence with relentless chatter and unrestrained glee at being the center of attention. She only paused for a breather when everyone's plates were clean and Miles's mom brought dessert to the table, a cheesecake she'd been finishing when Miles got home.

His dad jumped on the opportunity to interrogate Gabriel about his classes and how he liked being in public school.

"It's very loud," Gabriel responded primly, making everyone laugh.

"He's getting culture shock from Spirit Week," Miles clued the table in. "Seeing Thistle High at its finest."

Gabriel cracked a smile. "The school certainly has more… character than I expected. Though there are aspects I don't agree with—required physical education classes, for one, and impractical electives—my experience overall has been pleasant."

"Only because you bullied your counselor into giving you a pass for workshop."

"I prefer to think I simply educated her on the ways my time would be better spent."

Miles laughed—he still didn't know how Gabriel had

managed to do it. The counselor was a notoriously stubborn, stoic woman who didn't take no for an answer. It must've been an immovable object meeting an unstoppable force.

"Are you planning to stay there until graduation?" Sarah asked.

Gabriel hesitated. Miles didn't know the answer, they hadn't talked about it. "I'm hoping to," he replied, and it sounded like the truth. "Especially if I'm fortunate enough to have most of my classes with Miles next year too."

Feeling his mom watching him, Miles took a long drink of water and hoped she didn't notice his red cheeks.

It was halfway through his slice of cheesecake, listening to Gabriel explain exactly why he'd refused to go to his workshop class, that it hit Miles: things were going well. Around the table, there were real smiles and chuckles, his parents nodding enthusiastically at Gabriel, his sisters watching him with silly adoring expressions, and Charlee shaking her head in good-humored disbelief. Against all odds, Gabriel looked like he fit here, at the cluttered dining room table of Miles's kitchen, eating strawberry cheesecake off a chipped plate while muffled music played gently from his dad's record player in the other room. Warm and safe and comfortable.

Miles loved his family fiercely in that moment, so much that his heart ached, for making Gabriel belong here with them.

Safely hidden under the table, he looped their pinkies together, beaming at Gabriel when he gave him a curious glance.

When the cheesecake was gone and everyone else filed into the living room, Miles took the plates to the sink with his mom. It filled with hot, soapy water as the record scratched then turned off, Miles's dad swapping to Led Zeppelin per Gabriel's tentative request.

"He's not what I expected." Sarah took the top plate from the stack and scrubbed it down.

Miles rinsed it, settling it on the drying rack. "Yeah. Me either."

"It's hard to imagine Felicity capable of raising a good kid, but she managed."

"Three of them," he corrected. "They're all good."

She hummed thoughtfully, scraping at a stubborn bit of pasta sauce. "I like the way you are around each other. You need friends in your life who get you, and I can tell he does. You two are a good pair."

He knew she didn't mean anything by it, but a swell of emotion rose in Miles's throat. Everything felt so right in this moment, he wanted to freeze-frame and capture it forever.

"I like him," Miles said softly, rinsing a bowl and watching the water swirl down the drain as snippets of Gabriel's voice floated from the other room.

"I do too."

"Mom…" The words were there, suddenly in reach when they'd been impossibly far away before. His heart wasn't even racing, his fears subdued by the gentle kitchen light, the rushing water on his hands, and the love radiating from his mom beside him. Maybe this was what he hadn't realized he'd been waiting for. For it to feel natural and easy. Right. "Gabriel and I… the thing is, I like boys. And I *like* him. We're more than friends."

After everything, it wasn't even hard to say. The words practically fell out of him, eager to finally be free.

She went still beside him as she processed his words. He could pinpoint the moment it clicked and she understood.

Without a word, she dropped the plate she'd been holding into the sink with a plopping splash and turned to gather him into a hug. Her hands were wet, soaking into the back of his sweater, and the top of her head nearly knocked his chin.

It was the best hug he'd ever had.

"I love you," she declared fiercely. "Don't you dare think this changes a thing, okay? Not even for a second."

"Okay," he managed to get out, his voice more than a little choked up.

She didn't let go of him for a long time.

When they pulled away, he wasn't the only one fighting back tears. "If you cry, I'm gonna cry," he told her wetly.

She sniffled. "They're good tears. Every mom wants her kids to live a happy, honest life as their true selves and I'm just… I'm so proud of you. Thank you for telling me."

The way she was smiling up at him made his heart swell to the point of bursting. Miles couldn't remember the last time he'd felt so light.

"You and Emily…" A crease formed between his mom's eyebrows. "I mean, she isn't…"

"I'm gay," Miles clarified, realizing he hadn't been specific. Every time he said it, it got easier to get the words out. "Boys only, so no. We're just friends."

She covered her mouth, horrified. "Oh my God, I'm the worst. I'm the worst mom in the whole world."

"You're not the worst." Miles couldn't help but laugh. "Only a teeny tiny bit. But I know you were trying to help."

"I'm sorry. And I love you so much."

"It's okay. And I love you too."

She hugged him again, like she couldn't help herself. They probably looked like a couple of weirdos, crying and grinning and embracing over a sink full of dirty dishes.

There had to be a million things going through her mind. She hadn't even mentioned Gabriel, but part of her had to be panicking that he was dating a cursed Hawthorne boy. But she was holding herself together for him.

"Mom." A minute had passed and she still hadn't let him go. "This is nice, but Gabriel and I have to go soon or we'll be late for the football game."

She did a weird, wiggling squirm, like a snake had dropped down the back of her shirt. "Is it a date?" He realized he was witnessing a disturbing display of excitement. "Miles Warren, are you going on your first date tonight?"

"No," he insisted, too loudly, and flushed. "I mean… yeah. But it's not a big deal."

Muttering to herself, she went and dug around in her purse on the counter, fishing out a twenty. "Buy yourselves a treat," she commanded, making Miles take it despite his protests. "And be home at a decent time."

"On job nights, I don't get home until three in the morning," he pointed out.

"Be home before sunrise," she amended, swooping in to kiss him on the cheek. "Have a great time. And run Robin her dinner before you leave."

He grabbed the covered plate from the counter, skirting around the edge of the living room where Gabriel was on the couch with Charlee, talking about the ghost hunting show bingo she was putting together for the new season.

Aunt Robin's door was closed, so he knocked. "Come in," she called.

The curtains were drawn, the only light coming from the stained-glass lamp on her desk where she was sitting, writing in a journal. In a silky cream shirt with her hair up, silver earrings gleaming, you'd think she was the one who'd dressed up for dinner. When Miles got close enough, he could see the weary downturn to her mouth, but she looked better than she had in a long time.

"Hey." Miles had to resist flipping the light switch on—the weak lamplight barely illuminated the room, the corners cloaked in deep darkness. "I brought you dinner."

"Thank you." She slid a ribbon into the pages of her journal and closed it, taking the plate when he offered it. "How did your parents take meeting Gabriel?"

She'd remembered his name. "Not too bad," he told her, passing the fork he'd bundled in a napkin. "Thanks again for not telling them. I know they found out anyway, but..."

"Things worked out the way there were supposed to."

In a way, they kinda had.

"I'm sure Mom's going to invite him to the next one too. You should join us. We missed you tonight."

She gave one of her smiles that he could never quite pin down. "I doubt it."

Her grief was an awful, uncomfortable thing. It would be pointless to deny it, but it could never make her unwanted. Miles would gladly weather the pain if it meant sharing a meal with her. "I wouldn't say it if I didn't mean it."

She turned away under the pretense of tucking her journal in a drawer. "You don't speak for everyone."

It was clear she meant Charlee. He was always careful

not to say anything, it wasn't his business, but she'd brought it up first. "I know for a fact that everyone would've been happy to see you tonight. Even if they aren't good at showing it. Little steps can make a big difference."

"Sitting down for a dinner won't fix things," Robin murmured. "Not with so much unspoken."

"Then speak it." That was the biggest obstacle between Charlee and her mom. She wanted to yell and demand apologies, but she was too stubborn. And Robin needed to make amends, acknowledge that she'd let her grief destroy her relationship with her daughter. "I think we build up conversations we're scared to have into these big, scary monsters in our head, until we forget the most important thing—we're talking to someone who cares about us."

Even if she and Charlee ended up screaming at each other, saying ugly things, it had to be better than this limbo they were trapped in.

Aunt Robin didn't say anything, so Miles gave her hand a quick squeeze. "All I'm saying is, you might be pleasantly surprised. I'll see you later, okay? Have a good night."

26

"Who made the unfortunate choice of a toad as your mascot?" Gabriel asked as they weaved through the crowd clustered outside the bleachers, everything a blur of green and white.

"I think Thistle High has always been the Toads." Miles dodged a kid with a ketchup-slathered hotdog, getting his toes trampled for his trouble. "Whoever founded the school must've wanted us to stand out among all the tigers and eagles."

"You certainly do that." Gabriel grimaced at a person dressed in one of those disturbing green morph suits. "Do I dare ask why everyone is wearing frog-themed outfits? Has the public education system failed you all to the point that no one knows frogs and toads are entirely different species?"

Miles cracked up, grabbing Gabriel's elbow to guide him up the bleacher stairs. "Are you bothered by the lack of warts? People like frogs, so frog merch is easier to find. They're objectively cuter."

The bleachers were packed, unoccupied spots saved by sweaters and blankets. Miles didn't see any open ones for him and Gabriel to squeeze into, unless they wanted to seriously invade someone's personal space.

"Miles! Gabriel!" Emily's holler cut through the crowd as she stood on her bleacher to wave them down. "I saved you seats!"

"You okay with that?" Miles could tell Gabriel liked Emily despite his protests, but sitting beside someone so chatty for hours could easily shift into overwhelming him.

Dinner had gone well—Miles hadn't thought to warn his mom that Gabriel didn't really do casual touching, so he'd been subjected to one of her hugs on their way out the door, and a flurry of future invites—but it had been a lot to take in. Miles was used to it, and even he'd started to feel overstimulated halfway through.

But Gabriel started up the stairs. "I need an explanation of what's happening on the field."

Miles didn't know the first thing about what made seats good or not, but theirs seemed decent—halfway up on the second tier of bleachers and smack dab in the middle of a row. Emily was sitting with a few vaguely familiar girls, all decked out in Thistle High's colors. She was similarly dressed, her soccer jersey layered over a dark sweatshirt, a clearly handmade green and white tutu over her jeans. Her hair was in twin braids, glittery green ribbon woven between the dark strands, and tied off with little fuzzy frog heads. Gold glitter covered her eyelids and she had a green, bug-eyed frog painted on one cheek.

"Miles and Gabriel are here," she announced to her friends, beaming in excitement.

Miles's heart did a funny flip. It was the first time he'd heard their names said together so easily, so naturally, like they were a pair.

"You barely made it!" she told them as they joined her. "The game's about to start. But you missed the marching band. And I can't believe you guys didn't dress up."

Gabriel sat down, giving her and her friends a scrutinizing scan. "What's the point of the costumes?"

"Has this week taught you nothing about school spirit?" Miles teased.

"Yeah, it's basically the main reason anyone comes to these." Emily fluffed her tutu with a grin. "Well, that and it's the perfect place to hang out with your crush outside of class. It's cold so you can huddle together or share a blanket, and it's loud so you have to lean in close to talk. What more could you ask for?"

She all but wiggled her eyebrows.

Gabriel didn't so much as blink. "Comfortable seats and eighty percent less people would be preferable. And Miles promised me popcorn."

"Try and hide it all you want," Emily singsonged, "but I know you're a romantic at heart."

Miles and Gabriel both intently looked anywhere but at each other.

"Do football games always put you in such a good mood?" Miles asked her, hastily changing the subject.

"I get to hang out with friends, scream my heart out, and not be around my mom for a few hours. What else could I ask for?"

Yikes. Her mom must still be getting on her about dropping soccer, then.

"I've heard that your mother's trying to marry you off," Gabriel commented.

If Miles thought Emily wouldn't notice, he'd step on

Gabriel's toes. They needed to have a serious conversation about tact.

She waved his words off. "No surprise there, she's not exactly discreet. Except now, she's decided it needs to be my entire life. Every time I see her, she brings up soccer and how it's a waste of my time and does nothing to make me more desirable as a wife." She yanked on one of her braids. "I can't escape it."

Judging by the way Gabriel was scrutinizing her, he could relate to being crushed beneath the expectations of a pushy mom. "If this... sport is important to you, it's worth fighting about."

He probably detested anything that involved running simply on principle, but it was so unexpectedly supportive of him that Miles gave him a sneaky thumbs up. Gabriel wrinkled his nose, but Emily's face bloomed into a smile.

A loud horn blared, making Miles jump. The cheerleaders were doing all kinds of leaping and kicking, shaking their green and white pom-poms frantically. The marching band came to life, their music drowned out by the screams and whoops as the football team ran onto the field. Gabriel looked alarmed as Emily grabbed his arm and pulled him to his feet, trying to get him to join in with the stomping and cheering. He clapped tentatively, gazing around the stadium in disbelief.

"We can leave anytime," Miles all but yelled, "if it gets too much."

Gabriel nodded.

The game began—Emily patiently explaining that it started with a kickoff, the Toads playing defense since they were the ones kicking, while the other team, the Spudders, was on offense—and the crowds settled down around them to watch.

"I bet you feel bad making fun of the Toads now." Miles pointed across the field to the Spudders' lumpy mascot. "It could've been so much worse."

Gabriel's nose scrunched. "Is that an angry potato?"

"I think it's trying to look intimidating. Or having an existential crisis."

Another group squeezed in at the end of their bench, everyone cramming together to make room until Miles was pressed against Gabriel from knee to shoulder. They were so close, he could feel Gabriel breathing.

"This okay?" Heat crawled up his neck. "We can ask Emily's friends to scoot down, or move somewhere less crowded."

Gabriel didn't look bothered. "It's fine. Now I don't have to worry about getting cold."

Miles blinked. On Gabriel's other side, Emily grinned.

She kept them informed as the game progressed, answering Gabriel's questions and beaming like a proud mom when he started calling out what was happening on the field. There was genuine interest in the way he leaned forward to watch, his gaze following the ball.

The Toads made a touchdown—not a goal, as Emily had to remind them more than once—and the stands exploded into screams. Emily stomped and hollered, throwing her arm around Gabriel and shaking him. He went stiff as a statue, but when she released him to swing her striped scarf around in the air like a lasso, he leaned into Miles's shoulder and let out a huffing laugh against Miles's neck. There was a smear of neon green on his cheek, Emily's frog smudged from where she'd smushed their faces together.

Miles had to bite his lip. "You've got—I think Emily frogged you."

Gabriel went hilariously cross-eyed for a second trying to see. "Do I even want to know?"

Rubbing his thumb over the paint, Miles tried to wipe it off, but mostly smeared it around more. Gabriel looked like he'd been smooched on the cheek by an overly friendly leprechaun.

"I made it worse," he admitted.

Gabriel's face reddened beneath Miles's fingers. "It's fine, you can leave it."

"That was six points." Emily leaned in, radiating excitement. "That means we're winning!"

Miles honestly couldn't care less about who was winning or losing or what was happening on the field at all. He just wanted to sit here all night.

The Toads scored two more touchdowns, and the Spudders got one—which caused the crowd around them to erupt into enthusiastic booing—before the halftime buzzer went off. Miles didn't want to leave, irrationally worried they'd make room while he was gone so he didn't have an excuse to squish up to Gabriel, but he'd promised popcorn.

"I'm running to the concession stand. You good staying here?"

Emily slung her arm around Gabriel's shoulder. "Don't worry, I'll take care of him."

"I don't appreciate being made to feel like a child in need of babysitting," Gabriel grumbled, but he didn't duck away.

"If you behave, I'll bring you back a goodie." Miles patted him on the head like he would one of his little sisters, snickering when Gabriel swatted at his hand with a thunderous scowl.

Everyone was taking advantage of halftime to stretch their legs, grab a snack, and use the bathroom. The student-run concession stand was packed, and Miles had to wiggle through a dense crowd to find the end of the line.

"Can I get a popcorn?" After an eternity of waiting, a frazzled girl took his order at the register. Thistle High merch was spread across the front counter, one thing in particular catching his attention. "And one of those, please," he added, pointing with a grin.

Gabriel was going to kill him.

He made it back to his seat right before halftime ended, the marching band and cheerleaders filing off the field as the horn blared. Emily was chatting animatedly to Gabriel, gesturing at the field.

"Your popcorn has been acquired," he told Gabriel, presenting the bag to him with a dramatic flourish.

Gabriel popped a few pieces into his mouth with a crunch and nestled back up against Miles's side. "I hope you're going to eat at least half of this."

"Emily can help." Miles ate a handful, licking salty butter from his fingertips. "You never told me you were such a big fan of popcorn."

"It's Bram's favorite, he always makes it for our movie nights. I suppose it's grown on me."

Everyone cheered as the teams ran back onto the field. Miles waited until they were done to say, "I got you something else too."

He held up his choice from the merch, a sparkly green headband with googly frog eyeballs on long springy stalks that bobbed and dipped with the slightest movement.

Gabriel took one look at it and declared, "Over my dead body."

"C'mon, it's your first game and the Toads are winning. Don't you think you should show a little support for your team?"

"Excuse you, I'm wearing green." Gabriel gestured to his sweater vest. "You're the one lacking in the school spirit department. You need it more."

"I have all the school spirit I need in my heart," Miles proclaimed loftily. "And this isn't about me. This is about you getting the full high school football game experience and embracing your toady love."

Gabriel's face scrunched in disgust. "Never say that again."

He wasn't going down without a fight. That was okay. Miles had the ultimate weapon.

"Emily!" He reached past Gabriel, ignoring his sputtering protests, and tugged on her scarf to get her attention. "Look at what I got Gabriel."

Her whole face lit up. "Oh my God, that's so stupid cute. Put it on!"

"I don't think—"

It was too late. Emily snatched it from Miles, spreading the headband wide and perching it on Gabriel's head. Emerald glitter shed into his dark hair, the ridiculous eyes bobbing around on their springs.

Miles cackled into his jacket while Emily cooed. "I'm so glad you guys are here," she said, giddy. "This is seriously the best night ever. Let's bring Charlee to the next one, okay?"

"For sure," Miles promised, despite knowing he'd have to drag her kicking and screaming.

Emily turned away, gesturing to her friends and pointing at Gabriel's headband with a joyful squeal. Two of them got up to go buy one, poking the bouncing eyeballs as they scooted past.

"I'm going to kill you," Gabriel muttered, shifting so Emily wouldn't see his murderous glare. "The second she's distracted, I'm taking this thing off and throwing it as far as I can."

"Even you aren't cold enough to crush her happiness like that."

"As if I care," he scoffed. But he watched Emily for a moment and left the headband on.

The night went on, getting colder until Miles could see his breath in the air and his fingers started to get numb. Emily's friends pulled out blankets and passed them around, a plaid fleece one ending up down by Miles.

"Oh, that's okay," he protested, not wanting to take someone's blanket.

"Don't be silly, there's plenty for everyone." Emily unfolded it and draped it over him and Gabriel, tucking the ends around them to create a cocoon of warmth. "No one wants to freeze their butt off."

Miles gave Gabriel a sheepish look. They were practically wrapped up in a burrito together. Emily looked immensely satisfied with herself.

"Want me to grab my own?"

"No." Gabriel shifted, moving under the blanket, his cold hand finding Miles's. He intertwined their fingers and rested them together on Miles's leg. "This is perfect."

⁓

The Toads ended up pulling off an unexpected win. Emily celebrated the entire walk to the car where she hollered goodnight. The moment she was out of sight, Gabriel ripped the frog headband off. He still had the smear of green on his cheek, stray flecks of glitter caught in it that gleamed when he turned his head.

Miles pulled onto the road leading out of Thistle to take Gabriel home. If he drove a little slower than usual, that was his business. He wasn't ready for the night to be over yet.

"I appreciate you coming with me," Gabriel said once the flood of headlights leaving the school had faded in the rearview.

"Thanks for inviting me. Did you have fun? Get the night off you wanted?"

"I did." His tone wasn't particularly happy, and as the streetlights flashed by, they illuminated his conflicted expression.

Concern squirmed in Miles's core. "What's wrong?"

"Nothing's wrong." Gabriel ran his thumb over the headband, sparkles raining onto Charlee's seat. "I'm not quite sure how to put it into words. Being there tonight made me feel… as if I saw an alternate life. My life, if things had gone differently."

"You mean, if the curse hadn't happened?"

"Or if I wasn't a Hawthorne at all."

Miles understood. He carried the burden of his own name constantly, the expectations of being a Warren heavy on his shoulders. He could never kid himself into thinking his life would be normal.

"I think about that a lot," he admitted, making a slow turn. For a moment, he was back in Blanche, driving home in the dark after a job, and calm washed over him. "What my future could be if I was like everyone else."

"What do you picture?"

Miles had never shared this part of himself with anyone else before, but he trusted Gabriel to be gentle with his silly dreams. "Leaving Thistle. Going to art school in Seattle. Making friends and staying out late watching movies or walking around the city, trying new places to eat. Having my own place, small but cozy, with like, the perfect spot at the window to draw and a couch big enough that I could stretch out all the way on it." He gave a self-conscious shrug. He didn't want his entire life and all his memories confined to one small Washington town. "Literally the most boring stuff ever. I guess I'm not a very exciting person."

"It sounds perfect," Gabriel murmured.

"I haven't thought about it as much lately." Miles had a surge of bravery, not caring how much the words revealed. "It's hard to dream about leaving when you have something that makes you want to stay."

They'd left the streetlights, the other cars, and the town behind. "I didn't bother pondering the future much before now. What was there to look forward to?" Gabriel's fingers knotted together in his lap. "I never wanted to die, but it was sometimes difficult to remember what exactly I was staying alive for."

Miles hated to hear him say it as much as when he'd said he felt like a ghost in his own life. Intangible. He wished he could rip the feeling out of Gabriel's head and toss it into the rushing darkness outside the car. Leave it on the side of the road to rot.

"It's rather ironic, isn't it?" Gabriel continued. "Now that I'm looking forward to the future for the first time, it might be snatched away from me. Perhaps there's a lesson to be learned there."

"The lesson is that the universe has a sick and twisted sense of humor." Outside, the clouds shifted, revealing the milky moon. "Tell me what you're looking forward to now. What you're going to do once we break the curse and everything gets back to normal. Well, normal for us."

Gabriel pondered. "I'm not sure. I'd like to do more of this."

"Football games?"

"Spending time with you," Gabriel responded bluntly. "Going on dates."

"Oh." Miles had to refocus on the road before he drove them off the side by accident. Death by charming distraction, what a way to go. "How about… we go to the movies next time? So we don't have to freeze our butts off outside. Or, if you want to be cold, we can go get ice cream."

"I enjoy ice cream. Mint chocolate chip, if they have it."

Mint chocolate chip fit Gabriel perfectly. "Ice cream it is. There's a place right in town that has the best waffle cones. You can smell them a whole block away."

A small smile curled in the corner of Gabriel's mouth, the one that Miles sometimes selfishly thought was only for him. "What about homecoming? Would that qualify as a date?"

The car swerved for a second before Miles righted it.

"*Homecoming?* Are you—did you want to go? Are you asking me to go? You said you'd rather stand in front of a speeding truck."

"I said that about taking pictures in front of that horrific backdrop, not going with you. One of those things is much more agreeable than the other."

He had to be trying to make Miles blush. "What if that's my stipulation for going? A minimum of three cheesy pictures together in front of the backdrop I put my blood, sweat, and tears into making."

"Then I suppose I'd have to agree. But only three, and I never want to see them."

It'd been a joke, but Miles still wanted to lean across the middle console and kiss him. No one had ever wanted him before, or been willing to do even silly little things to have him.

The Hawthorne gate loomed ahead, and Miles pulled off the road to park beside it.

"I want to go with you." He shifted in his seat to face Gabriel fully.

Gabriel could read him too easily. "But?"

"But… going with someone usually means things. Slow dancing together. Taking couples' photos. Sneaking off to make out in the hallway." He ignored Gabriel's arched eyebrow. "I'm not out, and while I'd love this to be my heartfelt teen drama movie moment where I stand in front of my classmates and tell them I don't care about what they think…" The thought made anxiety claw at his chest. "I don't think I can."

No disappointment flashed across Gabriel's face, not a hint of frustration. "I have no expectation that you would, and I would never want you to compromise your comfort or privacy for my sake. All I'd like is to be there with you, however you'd like. We could conveniently show up at the same time."

"Even if we just awkwardly lurk near the punch table the entire night?"

"I can't think of anything I'd rather do," Gabriel said solemnly.

It astounded Miles that he'd once looked at Gabriel and thought he was cold and uncaring. Heartless.

"You wouldn't mind? If people knew you and I were… together?"

"Because you're a boy? No. I imagine most people have more pressing reasons to dislike me." Gabriel flicked his wrist dismissively. "Strangers making assumptions about me is nothing new, I'm sure my sexuality has come up before. And they're welcome to speculate as much as they'd like. I'm still figuring it out myself."

"Oh." Miles was surprised, only because Gabriel seemed to know himself so well. "Well, you like me, I suppose that's a start. But labels don't matter."

"I do like you," Gabriel agreed, so easily that Miles's breath caught. "This is… new for me. At the risk of sounding terribly cliché, I've never felt like this about anyone before, never got to know anyone well enough outside of my family to consider attraction or affection."

If Miles could get away with a T-shirt that read "Gabriel Hawthorne's First Crush," he'd wear it every day. It would be a badge of honor, sharing the precious thing he'd been entrusted with.

"It's the debilitating anxiety." He pitched his voice into

exaggerated seriousness. "Most people don't realize this, but it's irresistible. You never stood a chance, I'm sorry."

Gabriel smirked. "That must be it." His seat creaked as he leaned closer, eyes searching Miles's face.

Miles moved slowly, hoping he was reading this right, but leaving Gabriel plenty of time to pull back, turn away, stop him, but he tilted his head up to meet him eagerly. They kissed, tender and aching with the promise of the future they'd talked about. Sealing a pledge to each other that they'd survive and make it there together.

He wasn't nervous. There wasn't anything to be nervous about when Gabriel pulled him closer by the collar of his coat, other hand curled over his shoulder and thumb notched into the bare skin of his collarbone. When Miles shivered and stroked the dark curl of hair behind Gabriel's ear and the silky skin where his pulse pounded. When Gabriel melted against him, letting out a quiet noise that made his own stomach freefall.

Miles felt simultaneously boneless and steadier than he'd been in forever.

When they separated, Gabriel didn't let him go far, nudging his nose against Miles's. "You never said if you'd go with me tomorrow," he remarked, the words fluttering against Miles's jaw.

"You know my answer's yes. Of course it is."

Miles was gifted with a smile so stunning, it lit up the entire car. It overwhelmed him for a moment, made his head spin that he could cause such an expression. That he had made Gabriel smile so beautifully.

"It's a date."

27

Bzzzzzzt. Bzzzzzzt.

Miles woke with a groan, patting around his bed for his vibrating phone. He'd been up late after dropping Gabriel off, then telling Charlee about the game and coming out to his mom. There had been an embarrassingly tearful few minutes, leaving him to crawl into bed all sniffly and puffy-eyed past one in the morning.

Something hit the floor with a clatter, where it proceeded to buzz louder. Great.

Stretching sleep-stiff muscles, he slung his arm lazily off the bed, groping around until he managed to find his phone. It was still pitch-black outside so the light made him squint, blinking at the notifications. It was six in the morning.

Gabriel—4 missed calls.

Fuck.

Miles lurched up, pressing the callback button with trembling fingers.

Gabriel answered on the second ring. "Miles."

It was all he said, only his name, but the second Miles heard it, he knew something was terribly wrong.

"What happened?" He threw back his blankets, already

scanning his room for the nearest pair of jeans. "Where are you?"

"I'm at home. I—I'm sorry if I woke you. I didn't know what else to do."

Fear trailed icy fingers down Miles's spine. Gabriel sounded shattered.

"No, it's okay. Tell me what's going on." He found his jeans and started tugging them on.

"It's Edmund. He's—I think he's dying."

The room spun. Miles had to sit down, his jeans halfway up one thigh. For a dizzying moment, he couldn't recall when he'd last seen Edmund. It must've been when he took Charlee to the Hawthorne house, right? But that was only two days ago. He'd been fine. Completely fine.

"Is he hurt?" Miles made himself speak evenly. He needed to stay calm. "Do you need me to come and take him to the hospital?"

"Our family doctor was here already." A small, helpless sound escaped Gabriel that made Miles want to scream. "Can you come over? Please. I wouldn't ask—"

"I'm getting dressed right now." Miles steadied himself through sheer force of will and stood, tugging his jeans on the rest of the way. He didn't bother changing out of his wrinkled sleep shirt; his jacket was slung over the back of his desk chair. "I'll get Charlee's keys and head right over, okay? I'll be as fast as I can."

"Alright."

Miles stepped into his shoes without bothering to tie the laces and raced to Charlee's room. He couldn't stop and process, because if he did, he'd waste time panicking. Gabriel needed him now.

There was no way Charlee was awake, so he didn't bother knocking before he slipped into her room. It was bathed in a pinkish glow from her salt rock lamp and the fairy lights strung around her window. The mass of blankets on her bed rose and fell with her breath.

Her purse had been tossed haphazardly on her desk, contents spilling out. Miles dug through quietly, but there was no sign of her keys. They weren't in the mess on the desk either, so he dropped to check in case they'd fallen on the floor.

"What the hell are you doing?" Charlee's groggy voice demanded.

Miles jumped, cracking his head on the underside of her desk.

"Jesus." He backed out, skull aching. "Sorry, I was trying not to wake you up. I need your car keys."

She yawned and squinted at her clock. "It's not even six."

"I know, it's an emergency. Where are they?"

The sleep cleared from her eyes. "What kind of an emergency?"

"Gabriel called, something happened to his brother. He thinks he's dying."

Charlee's lips parted. "Bram?"

"No, his older brother, Edmund." Miles spotted her keys half-hanging off her bedside table and snatched them up.

"Hey." She crawled out of bed and pulled them from his grasp. "Give me two minutes. I'll drive."

He didn't argue.

Miles knew death well, had seen it in just about every form, at every stage. He lived among it, dealt with the dead on a daily basis. It didn't faze him much anymore to crack open a casket and stare down at a body, to expel lingering souls. It had become familiar and monotonous. Easy to wash himself clean of at the end of the night with a hot shower.

But this was Edmund. Someone he knew. Someone he'd just spoken with. Nothing about him dying was that mundane.

Charlee got dressed and led the way downstairs. They passed the open door to Miles's parents' room, a quick peek revealing his dad passed out, leg hanging off the bed and snores rattling the bed frame. His mom's side of the bed was empty; she must already be awake.

Sure enough, they found her down in the living room, nursing a mug of what smelled like fresh coffee. The TV was on, playing a cooking show.

"What're you doing up?" she asked when she spotted them.

"Charlee and I have to go to Gabriel's." Miles needed her to understand that this wasn't the time for an interrogation, not when Gabriel was waiting for him. "His brother's hurt, and he needs help."

She set her drink on the coffee table with a *clack*. "Is he okay? What kind of help?"

"I don't know yet, he just asked me to come."

He could see the questions pushing forward—and the moment she forcibly made herself sink back into the couch. "Keep me updated," she told him firmly. "Call if you need anything."

Miles stopped to give her a hug on the way to the front door.

With Charlee driving and the roads mostly empty, they made it to the Hawthorne estate in record time.

Miles pointedly didn't check the speedometer—the *oh shit* moment he had every time they took a tight corner told him all he needed to know.

The big iron gate was open, so Charlee drove right up to the front door. She was twitchy about it, glancing over her shoulder as she parked.

"How do we know Felicity's not here?"

"We don't." Miles couldn't care less. "You can go wait outside the gate if you're worried."

"I'll figure it out." She leaned over to open his door, pushing him out.

Gabriel was waiting at the front door, a pale-faced shadow tucked against the encompassing gloom of the house.

"Hey." Miles didn't know what to say. He looked smaller than Miles had ever seen him before, swallowed up by an oversized black sweater, eyes sunken and dull. "Are you okay?"

Gabriel nodded, paused, then shook his head. "I…" He swallowed, throat clicking. Hesitantly, he leaned into Miles until his head rested on his shoulder. A painful ache bloomed in Miles's chest like a thorny flower. "I don't know what to do."

Miles bit back the reassurances and false promises that rose to his lips. "I'm here," he said instead, the only truth he had to give. He wrapped his arms around Gabriel, wanting to curl around him until he felt safe. "For whatever you need, okay?"

"I don't know what happened." Gabriel spoke into his jacket. "The doctor didn't do anything, and Mother won't answer any of my questions."

"Edmund's still here?"

"In his room. I'll show you."

The Hawthorne house was always empty, always eerily hushed, but it sat differently today. Heavy. Stifling. As they made their way up the stairs, their footsteps seemed to have less of an echo, the sconces dimmer.

Edmund's bedroom was only two doors down from Gabriel's. Miles hadn't realized they were so close. Maybe Bram's was the room between them.

His room was like Gabriel's in layout—a four-poster bed, massive wooden wardrobe, and desk with a leather chair, but in surprisingly warm shades of burgundy and burnt orange. Two floor-to-ceiling bookshelves were packed to the brim with records, a sleek turntable sitting between them. There was a polished piano by the window, bench slightly askew. Miles hadn't realized Edmund played, or had such a love for music.

Edmund was in bed. Miles might've thought he was sleeping if not for the wires connecting him to the out-of-place machine beside him. It was mostly screen, wiggling lines on the left side that Miles assumed were pulse monitors, and numbers on the right. He had no idea what any of them meant, but nothing was flashing wildly or beeping for their attention. Edmund's chest rose and fell steadily, and Miles couldn't see any visible injuries.

Someone had removed his gloves, the skin of his hands too pale, too thin against his burgundy sheets, and shocking in their normality.

"He won't wake up," Gabriel explained. "I didn't know until this morning, but Mother called Doctor Freeman last night. While I was gone."

"Your mom didn't say what happened? Did she just find him like this?"

"She's been closed up in her office on the phone all morning. All she told me was to leave him be, that there's no point in taking him to the hospital because they can't help him."

"And the doctor just agreed?"

Gabriel's expression darkened. "Doctor Freeman does whatever my mother tells him. He showed up with all this equipment before even looking at Edmund."

That couldn't be ethical. Edmund should be in the hospital if he'd dropped into a coma without warning.

"Does Edmund have any sort of medical issues that could've caused this?"

"No." Gabriel twisted the hem of his sweater. "I think my mother did something. You heard what Charlee sensed in her room—she was upset with him. It's the only reason she'd be keeping him here like this. Her finding him last night doesn't make any sense—she said she found him in his bed. But she never comes into our rooms. I was gone for days, and she never noticed."

Felicity certainly didn't seem like the type of mom who'd come check out of concern if one of her sons missed dinner.

The way Edmund was lying there, so stiff and unmoving, made Miles's skin crawl. His eyes were sunken in their sockets, his skin sallow and his jaw sharper, as if he'd lost weight in the night.

"Did you try looking into his mind?"

"Right before you came. There's nothing but darkness, without any hallways or doors for me to go through."

Miles desperately tried to conjure up an answer, but came up empty.

He raked a hand through his hair. "Okay, let's say your

mom is responsible... she's obviously trying to help him, or she wouldn't have called the doctor. If she's keeping him here, she must know something we don't." He studied Edmund, looking for a clue. "What if this has to do with the curse? A... side effect, or bad reaction?"

Before Gabriel could respond, the door creaked open and Bram peered in. The poor kid looked exhausted. "Are you here to help Edmund?" he asked Miles.

"I'm trying. Do you know what happened to him?"

Bram came in, Balthazar slipping through the crack behind him. "No. I heard him going downstairs late last night. He goes to the library when he can't sleep." He picked up his cat and placed him on Edmund's bed. Balthazar sniffed delicately at the pulse monitor on Edmund's finger before sinking down beside him. "I'm going to leave Balthazar here. He'll protect him and let me know if he gets worse."

Gabriel put his hand on Bram's shoulder.

"Smart plan," Miles told him. "You're good at looking out for your brothers."

"Not all the time."

On the bed, Balthazar suddenly puffed up, black fur standing on end, and let out a low growl. His yellow eyes were fixed on the door, pupils shrunk to razor-thin slits.

"Mother's coming," Bram and Gabriel said in unison.

Shit. If she caught Miles here, there'd be hell to pay. He really should've asked Gabriel at some point if this place had a dungeon, and how one might hypothetically escape if locked inside.

"I'll just explain to her why I'm here." Miles squared his shoulders, thankful for his height for once—he needed every advantage he could get over Felicity. "I'll be honest, and if she—"

"As admirable as your bravery is…" Gabriel crossed the room and opened the wardrobe. "Get in."

It was a tight fit, but Miles crouched down and shuffled back until his shoulder blades met wood, and Gabriel managed to close the door. He could make out a sliver of the room through the narrow crack, part of Edmund's bed and the table beside it.

Felicity's clacking heels announced her arrival. "What are you two doing in here?"

"Making sure our brother isn't dead," Gabriel snapped back. "Since you can't be bothered."

From the shocked noise Bram made, Gabriel had never spoken to his mom like that before.

"I told you to leave him alone." Felicity's voice was tight. "I'm taking care of it."

"You haven't given me any reason to believe that's true."

A beat of silence passed.

"Bramwell, leave." Felicity's words cracked like a whip.

"But I—"

"*Now.*"

Reluctant footsteps went to the door, smaller ones following behind as Balthazar trailed after him.

Felicity sighed as the door closed. "I expect more from you, Gabriel. You're usually the level-headed one, but lately, you've been following in Edmund's footsteps. You see why that's a problem, don't you?"

Gabriel didn't respond. Miles wished he could see his face, but he didn't dare move.

Heels clicked and Felicity came into view beside

Edmund's bed. She leaned in to straighten his blankets, the hem of her long black coat sweeping the floor. "Your brother made a poor choice, as he constantly insists on doing, and now I'm cleaning up his mess."

"Tell me what you did to him," Gabriel demanded, matching her coldness.

She gave him a withering look. "Are we throwing around baseless accusations now? I thought you knew better than to let your emotions get the best of you."

"Tell me what you did to him," Gabriel repeated with more force.

"I haven't done anything to him. Tuck away whatever villainous little fantasies you've created about me and do as I say: stay out of this room and stop wasting my time. You don't know anything about what's happening here."

"Then tell me."

She threw back her head and laughed. "Your entitlement is astounding."

Gabriel's voice quivered with fury. "And your arrogance is laughably transparent. Your control is slipping. We can all see it. I'm not afraid of you, and I refuse to leave Edmund here to die simply because you say so. The moment you leave this house, I'm taking him to the nearest hospital."

Felicity's expression cracked, ugliness peeking through. "Then your brother's death will be on your hands."

"Is that a threat?"

"No, Gabriel, it's a fact. You may not approve of my methods, but I'm the only thing keeping him alive. This is your final warning—cease your meddling or understand it will have consequences. We live in a world where rash actions are punished. Your brother is a prime example of that. Perhaps you can learn from his mistake."

"How can you not care that your son is dying?"

Felicity moved out of sight. Miles leaned forward, ears straining.

"Don't you ever presume to tell me how I'm feeling," she warned, so deadly quiet he almost didn't catch it. "Now leave. If I catch you in here again, you're going to find yourself locked in your room."

Gabriel's anger was so palpable, Miles could feel it blistering the air. Without a word, he strode out, slamming the door behind him.

Thighs screaming from crouching so long, Miles turned into the collar of his jacket, irrationally afraid Felicity would be able to hear his breathing in the new silence.

She stepped back into view, staring down at Edmund. "You stupid boy," she murmured, brushing his hair back from his forehead.

A moment later, she left too.

28

There was nothing Miles could do for Edmund, so he ended up leaving the Hawthorne estate not long after Gabriel came to fetch him from the wardrobe. He invited Gabriel to come back to his place, but he refused to leave either of his brothers. Miles offered to stay, but Gabriel insisted there was no point, that he needed time to think.

It felt wrong to leave him when Felicity's words had so visibly shaken him, when they hadn't done anything to help Edmund, but what else could Miles do?

Charlee drove him home, forced him into bed where he somehow managed to fall back asleep for a few fitful hours, then shoved him into the scalding shower when he woke up anxious and disoriented. Desperate to keep busy, he reorganized his desk, helped his sisters put up new posters in their bedroom—they were going through an intense K-pop phase —and pestered his mom until she let him clean the supply shelves in the office. In an amazing display of self-control, she didn't ask him a single question about last night, and limited herself to a brief, "Is there anything we can do to help?" when he told her Gabriel's brother had fallen into a coma.

He checked his phone obsessively for updates from Gabriel. There weren't any.

"Give me something to do," he told Charlee, wandering into her room. She was curled up in her thrifted purple chair, reading one of her cutesy rom-coms.

"Relax."

He plopped onto her bed. "Something realistic."

She sighed and lowered her book. "The realistic thing is realizing nothing I tell you to do is going to stop you from wallowing."

He kicked at her halfheartedly, too far away to make contact. "Don't be a jerk, Edmund might be dying. And we weren't—"

"Weren't what?" she prompted.

"Weren't supposed to be dealing with this." Miles knew exactly how it made him sound, but it was unfair. His biggest worry today was supposed to be figuring out how to tell his dad he was gay before his mom slipped up. Planning what he was going to wear to homecoming. Begging Charlee to let him borrow her car again. Things that now seemed so… unimportant. Edmund was dying and Miles couldn't do anything but keep his hands moving and his mind searching for a solution he didn't have. "Last night was so nice. I guess I wasn't ready to come back to reality yet."

Charlee gave him a knowing, sympathetic look. "That's the curse of playing pretend. At some point, you're going to face a rude awakening."

"We weren't playing pretend." Miles picked at a hangnail, a bead of blood welling up. He loathed the implication that anything about his time with Gabriel might've been fake.

"I didn't mean it like that." Her apologetic tone only made him feel worse. "I'm sorry you two didn't get a bit longer. And about Edmund. If he's half as stubborn as Gabriel, he'll pull through."

"Yeah." Miles wanted to believe it, but he couldn't shake the sight of Edmund in that bed, how close he'd looked to death. He crossed his arms, digging his fingers into his sweater until he could feel his ribs. "I feel helpless."

Ironic that he'd been working to stop death this whole time, and now that he was faced with someone actually dying, he was frozen.

"You're not helpless," Charlee said fiercely. "There's always something we can do. We just need to figure out what."

A door thudded downstairs. "Miles!" his mom called. "You have a visitor."

A visitor? Gabriel wouldn't come over without texting first, and who else—

Nadia. Shit.

"Okay, don't kill me."

Charlee set her book aside menacingly. "Who is it?"

"I meant to tell you, I really did, it just slipped my mind." Miles inched towards the door. "In my defense, it's been a wild twenty-four hours."

"Who. Is. It?"

"Nadia. They're here to help with the tunnel. They said they needed to see it in person and—"

She shrieked and flew off her chair to shove Miles out of her room, slamming the door behind him.

"What was that?" Miles's mom questioned when he came downstairs, peering up at the ceiling in concern.

"Charlee. Don't ask."

Nadia was helping themself to a mug of tea in the kitchen, dunking the bag enthusiastically. They looked hilariously out of place in their black leather pants, shredded blue sweater held together by rows of safety pins, and spiked combat boots against the backdrop of pottery dishware and crazy plants in colorfully painted pots.

They greeted Miles with a jaunty wave. "Hey, sick place. Your mom let me in, hope that's okay."

"Totally. Sorry, there's been... a lot happening, or I would've checked in this morning."

They leaned against the counter and crossed their ankles. "What's going on?"

Miles caught them up, including all the grisly details. They listened, sipping their tea pensively and fidgeting with their necklace.

"Fuck," they muttered when he'd finished.

Yeah, that about summed it up.

Tipping their head back, they gulped down the rest of their tea and set the empty mug in the sink. "Alright, so the tunnel is off the table today. I've got a trunk full of books on all kinds of magical shit. Maybe there'll be an answer to Edmund's mystery ailment."

"Worth a shot." Miles was so relieved to have a task, he could cry.

He helped load up books from the trunk of Nadia's car—a cherry-red Mini, its bumper plastered in stickers—and led them upstairs. His mom watched curiously from the office, but didn't pry.

"Any chance Charlee's planning on joining us?" Nadia probed as they climbed.

"Let's find out." He stopped outside her door and shifted his stack of books to one arm so he could knock. "Charlee? Nadia's here if you wanna help us—"

Her door flew open. "Of course I'll help," she said, as if she hadn't shoved Miles out of her room a few minutes before. She'd put her hair up in a ponytail and changed into a green shirt that made her eyes extra bright.

Her room was clean too, Miles noted as he filed in. From the way the closet doors were bulging, he could guess where everything had gone.

"This is cute." Nadia spun in a slow circle to take it all in. They touched an embroidered luna moth hanging on the wall. "Did you make this? It's sick."

"Yeah, it was easy," Charlee lied. The bloodstains on the back from where she'd stabbed herself with the needle a dozen times said otherwise.

Nadia claimed the purple chair, unzipping the bag hanging from their shoulder. "Before I forget, I brought you something. I heard you like sweet treats, and my grandma Dima makes the best ghraybeh in the world."

They handed Charlee a Ziploc filled with small pale cookies dusted in powdered sugar. Atop each one was a single pistachio. She dug one out immediately, taking a bite with a groan of appreciation. Miles could practically see the cartoon hearts floating over her head.

Nadia gave him a conspiratorial wink.

They dug into the books—Charlee joining Miles on the bed, flipping pages between cookie bites—but he glanced up more than once to find them staring at each other instead of reading. Whatever exactly this thing going on between them was, Miles really didn't like sitting in the middle of it.

His phone buzzed, making him jump out of his skin, but it was only Emily.

> Any chance my tall muscular bestie wants to
> come help set up homecoming? A bunch of
> people dipped and Alexis is scaring me
> You can make sure its nice and pretty for Gabriel

"Gabriel?" Charlee asked.

"Emily. She's getting the gym ready for homecoming and wants help." He hesitated—he wasn't going to the dance and really couldn't care less about the decorations, but he was starting to feel like a third wheel. "I should stay, this is more important."

"We've got this." Nadia tossed their book to the side and grabbed another from the stack. "We'll let you know if we find anything."

Charlee nodded enthusiastically.

"What if Gabriel calls?"

"Then you tell them something came up and you peace out."

It must be so nice to live without social anxiety.

"Fine." Miles rolled off the bed and stretched—he wasn't making much progress anyway. He'd been staring at one page for the last fifteen minutes straight. "But seriously, tell me the moment you find something."

"We will," Charlee promised. "Keys are on the counter downstairs. And put gas in my car while you're out."

"I'm broke."

"I guess you'd better start walking, then."

"You're ruthless," he grumbled. "I'll see what I can scrape together." He might have a few bucks tucked away in his change jar.

Charlee popped another cookie in her mouth. "That's what I thought."

After stopping to put a grand total of four dollars' worth of gas in Charlee's car, Miles made it to the school gym to find Emily waiting for him with desperation in her eyes. She deflated when he explained that his homecoming plans for the night were canceled, pulled him into a rib-creaking hug, then promised to keep him so busy that he wouldn't have a spare minute to worry.

She wasn't exaggerating—the dance was scheduled to start in a few hours, and it didn't look even half set up. Alexis looked so happy to see him, he expected her to burst into tears. Instead, she went on a five-minute rant about no-shows and lack of integrity, then freaked out about wasting five minutes before putting him to work hanging clouds, stars, and streamers from the ceiling. According to her, it made sense to give him the jobs that required the ladder since he "didn't need to climb up as high as everyone else."

His arms ached and sweat gathered on the small of his back, but it was still easier work than digging up a half-frozen grave at midnight. After everything was hung up, he moved onto inflating endless balloons with Emily, securing the starry backdrop he'd helped make, and pinning and draping long sheets of golden curtains. There was a moment of chaos when the lights wouldn't work and Alexis nearly snapped her clipboard, but someone managed to flip the right switch.

The gym went dark, blue and purple lights illuminating the ceiling and reflecting off every bit of glitter and tinsel, golden lights twinkling in the clouds and on the backdrop pieces. Hanging stars swayed and spun, bundles of balloons bobbing where they were tied to table centerpieces. Even the monstrous glitter tulle-wrapped arch took on a dreamier feel beneath the moody lighting.

Miles had to admit, it looked pretty good. Tacky as hell, but in a way that managed to be almost charming.

Everyone clapped and cheered as chaperones and early students started filtering in through the doors. Miles hadn't even noticed the time flying by so quickly.

"Thank you all for the help," Alexis yelled to the team as they started hauling supplies away. "Let's have a magical night under the stars."

Miles bit back a groan at the cheesy line.

"Nothing from Gabriel yet?" Emily checked.

He double-checked his phone despite knowing the answer. "Nope. At what point should I start worrying?"

"We both know you're past that." She handed him a heavy box of leftover lights from a table. "Text him when we're done. He's not going to be bothered by a check-in."

What if he hadn't texted Miles yet because he was waiting for him to reach out with good news first? Counting on him to come up with a solution?

It was impossible to shake the awful feeling that he'd failed him.

"I have to run home and get dressed." Emily hesitated, biting her lip. "Are you sure you don't want me to cancel? I can come help you guys research, or we can bring Gabriel dinner, make sure he's doing okay?"

It was such a selfless offer. "No, have fun at the dance. Drink the spiked punch for me," he teased. Someone might as well have a good time tonight.

He helped clean up all the supplies, organizing them in

the storage room until the music in the gym kicked in and more people started showing up. One guy grabbed him to help carry a massive bowl of punch out to the refreshments table, then trays of miniature desserts from the cafeteria fridges. He tried and failed to not feel like a waiter, following the wall and staying out of the way of the partygoers.

Once he was the only volunteer left, he threw on his jacket and made his way out into the parking lot—lingering in the hallway was too pathetic even for him. A group of giggling girls stumbled past in a swirl of pastel and sweet perfume, two guys in suits following close behind. Brake lights painted the damp pavement scarlet as a car pulled up and stopped, letting out a squealing group who ran for the front doors.

Miles was the only one walking away.

He settled against the hood of Charlee's car, the warmth of the engine long faded, and checked his phone. Still nothing. Homecoming had hit full swing from the sounds of the thumping music and shrieking laughter. Every time the front door swung open, the swirling lights illuminated the sidewalk for a brief moment.

Part of Miles wondered if Edmund was his and Gabriel's punishment for yesterday. It was a brutal reminder of where they belonged: a healthy distance away from normalcy. A warning that it could never be real.

"Charlee said you were here." Gabriel appeared, as if summoned by his wistful thoughts. His white shirt glowed like a ghost in the gloom of the parking lot. "I thought I might've missed you."

Miles sprang off the car. "What're you doing here? Did something happen? Is everything okay?"

"Nothing happened. I'm here for the dance."

"You…" Miles gaped at him. "Don't you think you should be at home? Homecoming isn't—"

"I've been home all day," he interjected sharply. "I'm tired of it. I told you I'd be here, so here I am."

"That was before." Miles's shoes scraped against the pavement as he shifted closer. "I didn't expect you to come. You shouldn't have."

Gabriel's mouth flattened into a thin slash. A car turned behind him, headlights dusting his midnight hair in gold. "You don't want me here."

This was all wrong, jagged and dangerous between them. Miles was wobbling on a tightrope with each word. "That's not what I'm saying. I don't think you should feel like you have to be here at a stupid school dance with everything else that's going on."

"What else would you like me to do, then? I can't help Edmund, I can't help Bram, and I can't sit in that house another minute thinking about how useless I am."

Miles reached for his hand, but Gabriel shifted away, shoving his fists in his pockets. A little sting of hurt had to be tucked away before Miles could speak again. "You're not useless," he said softly. "That's not—"

"I'm going to the dance," Gabriel stated curtly, cutting him off. "Join me or don't, it's your decision."

He strode away before Miles could answer, shoulders braced against the cold wind. At the entrance, he didn't stop to see if Miles was following before going in.

The sound of the door closing behind him echoed across the parking lot.

29

Miles followed Gabriel into the dance, his shields buckling beneath the weight of so many people and such heightened emotions.

The music felt louder than before, thumping through him, making his bones quake. It was more crowded too, the air growing sticky and hot in the short time he'd been outside. He scanned the dance floor, which was predictably twenty percent rhythmless jumping, eighty percent blatant grinding. The chaperones weren't even bothering to try and break it up.

Gabriel had wandered around the edge of the dance floor, attention fixed on the twinkling clouds and shimmering stars hanging overhead. "The fruits of your labor. It looks better than I expected," he commented. "Though that might be because all the lights are off."

Miles couldn't force himself to laugh. The fake nonchalance in Gabriel's voice made his skin itch, too close to when Gabriel had his mask up. He was upset and hurting, blaming himself for not being able to help Edmund, or for not warning him about their mother. Detachment was the only shield he had.

Miles had been in a similar place once, when Charlee's

dad had died and sharing her pain was all he could offer her. He'd clung to the hope that if he waited long enough with her, she'd start to get better. It chewed him up and picked his bones clean.

"Listen," he tried, "why don't we go where we can actually talk?"

"Don't you understand that I don't want to talk about it? About any of it?" Gabriel wouldn't meet Miles's gaze. "All I wanted to do was come to this dance with you and forget for a while."

"Acting like everything's okay isn't going to change it. It's just going to hurt worse when you can't pretend anymore."

Gabriel flinched.

"But if that's really what you want right now, what you need, let's go grab punch and a table. I'll stay as long as you want."

The music changed to a slow song, the dance floor shifting on cue as everyone grabbed a partner to sway with. Laughter echoed across the gym. Gabriel's eyes went glassy, shiny like the stars hanging above them.

"No," he murmured. Miles had to lean in to hear. "You're right. I shouldn't have come here. I don't know what I was thinking."

He was thinking that he'd suffocate if he didn't get out of that house. That he'd scream if he had to look at Edmund in that bed any longer. That he could escape it all for a little while in loud music and flashing lights.

"It's okay," Miles reassured him. He couldn't imagine the hell Gabriel had gone through today. "None of this is your fault."

Gabriel laughed like Miles had said something funny,

the sound swallowed up by the music. He laughed like Miles had never seen before—big, punched-out sounds that shook his whole body.

Then his expression crumpled. Miles didn't realize what was happening until he saw the tears. Until Gabriel covered his face, shoulders heaving. "I need to get out of here," he choked out.

The path to the entrance was too far away, too crowded with dancers, so Miles took his arm and led him out the side door and into the hall where he'd hauled supplies to the storage room earlier. The white lights were harsh compared to the dimly lit dance, but it was empty.

Gabriel slumped against the row of blue lockers, gasping and crying, trembling hard enough that he should've fallen apart right then and there. Miles didn't know what to do, so he kept his grip on his arm, holding him upright.

"It *is* my fault," Gabriel confessed wetly, the words pulled straight from a painful, guttural place in his chest. "I knew about my mother, about the curse, about the dark magic, and I didn't tell him. I didn't warn him. Edmund's going to die because of me."

Not caring if anyone walked out and saw, Miles wrapped his arms around Gabriel and held him tight. If Gabriel was to blame, then so was Miles. This burden wasn't his to carry alone.

"We thought we were keeping him safe," Miles told him, biting back his own tears. "We didn't know."

They were empty, meaningless words, but they were all he had. If he thought he'd been helpless earlier, it was nothing compared to now, or to the feelings eating Gabriel from the inside out.

Gabriel was trying to pull himself together with deep hiccupping gulps of air, but the tears won out for another minute, long enough that the shoulder of Miles's jacket grew damp.

"Tell me what you need," Miles murmured. "How I can help."

Gabriel pulled away with a low sniffle, face splotchy and red, his eyes bloodshot. "Will you take me home? I shouldn't have left Bram there without me."

"Of course."

He didn't move. "Tell me Edmund's going to be okay. Tell me we can fix this."

"If there's a way, we'll find it." Miles couldn't bring himself to lie to Gabriel, even when he was pleading for it. "We're not going to give up and leave him to die, okay?"

He'd go up to Felicity and demand answers, threaten to spill her nasty family secrets. He'd open the grimoire and look for a spell himself, risks be damned. He'd do anything. Whatever it took.

The hallway bulbs flickered overhead. The gym door they'd come through clanged loudly.

Gabriel wiped his cheeks and straightened. "What was that?"

Miles tried the handle. "It's locked."

Around his neck, his charms grew hot enough to burn.

The lights died at the end of the hall, plunging it into darkness. Unnatural darkness, the kind that hurt Miles's eyes and made the nape of his neck tingle. Something was looking at him, he could feel it.

A rattling groan came from the shadows.

Miles took an involuntary step backward.

The next section went out, and the next, a yawning black rush coming at them like a hungry mouth. Metal clanged like a war drum, a racing heartbeat, the lockers rattling as they flew open.

Miles grabbed Gabriel's arm, yanking him down the hall. "Run!"

It was coming behind them, getting closer, shadows nipping at his periphery. A phantom wind whipped around them, like the darkness was inhaling a great breath to suck them in.

Miles hit the door at the end of the hall, bouncing off it. He shoved at the bar, but it wouldn't budge. They'd been locked in.

"No, no, no." It was a dead end, all other doors behind them already swallowed by the darkness. Another light went out, only one left between them and the void.

"What do we do?" Gabriel demanded.

Panic had its teeth at Miles's throat. He backed up and charged the door with all his strength, smashing into it with his shoulder. Pain exploded, shooting down his entire arm, but the exit flew open.

He pushed Gabriel through, the night air cold enough to ache when he hissed through his teeth. The courtyard grass was slick, Miles almost falling twice as he bolted behind Gabriel to the parking lot.

"C'mon, Charlee's car is over here." Miles locked his jaw against the throbbing pain, digging the keys out of his pocket. He could see the silver Honda from here.

Gabriel's fingers bit into his wrist. "Look."

Behind them, the door they'd come through was hanging open on busted hinges. Darkness swirled inside, creeping over the threshold to prod at the pavement. As they watched, the security lights mounted above the door exploded, black tentacles extending along the shadowed grass.

"What is that?" Gabriel breathed.

"I don't know. And I really don't want to find out."

They made it to Charlee's car, Miles lowering into the driver's seat with a groan. Pain so intense he was woozy with it pulsed down his arm to his numb fingers. He couldn't move it enough to get the keys to the ignition, resorting to his left hand.

"You're hurt." Gabriel reached for his shoulder, then seemed to think better of it.

"Yep." Dislocated shoulder, if he had to guess. His dad had gotten one a few years ago after a poltergeist tried to throw him through a wall. Miles bit his tongue and reversed. Across the courtyard, the darkness crept closer, avoiding the glow of the dance and snuffing out the lampposts illuminating the path. "We have bigger things to worry about right now."

Throwing the car into drive, he didn't swing it far enough and swiped the green truck parked beside them with a screech. Fuck. If he wasn't currently fleeing from shadows of death, he'd get out and leave them a note. A mental apology would have to do.

The headlights illuminated a writhing black mass for a brief second, all the shadows peeling away from the surface of the courtyard and forming together. It didn't have any discernable shape or face, but Miles could sense it turn to watch as they drove away.

He hit the gas, taking the right out of the parking lot

too fast and gasping in agony as they hit the curb. There was no one at the stoplight, so he ignored the red and blew through, Gabriel clutching his seatbelt.

The next turn jostled his shoulder. Black spots swam across his vision. "If I pass out, grab the wheel," he croaked at an ashen Gabriel. "Is it still following us?"

He twisted in his seat. "I don't know. I can't see anything."

Miles wasn't taking any chances. It looked like the shadows that had tried to take Gabriel in the tunnels, times a hundred. If it got ahold of them, things were going to get really ugly, really fast.

"We're going to my house." He raced through another red light, cars honking at him. "My parents will know what to do. Plus, it's warded. Nothing bad can get in."

In the rearview mirror, streetlights started blipping out on the stretch of road behind them.

"It's coming." The speedometer crept up as they raced through town. "Once I park, run for the house. Go straight inside, don't stop, okay?"

"Be right behind me so I don't have to."

They hit Miles's street, ignoring the stop signs and swerving around a biker taking his sweet time. The house came into view and Miles slammed the brakes, pulling alongside the curb in a squeal of tires and the reek of burning rubber. It jolted him against his seatbelt with a blinding flash of pain. He fumbled to open his door and puked onto the street.

"Go!" he rasped, pushing off Gabriel's concerned hands. Bile burned his throat and his nose. He was shaking so hard, he couldn't get his seatbelt undone.

Gabriel jumped out but scrambled around to Miles's

side like a suicidal idiot. Ignoring his protests and puke, he undid Miles's seatbelt, yanking him from the car.

At the end of the street, the lights vanished. Wind morphed from a low howl into a roar, brown leaves skittering down the road. Beside them, a horde of crows exploded from a tree with shrieking caws.

Taking Gabriel's hand, Miles sprinted to the gate, flinging it open with a squeak of rusty metal, and up to the front porch. The knob refused to turn under his sweaty palm. It was locked, the keys still in the ignition of Charlee's car.

"Open the door!" He pounded against the wood, praying someone was right there. "Hurry, open the door!"

The bulb over their heads exploded, raining glass onto them. Miles could hear an awful sound, the rasping scrape of a huge mass slithering across the pavement, heaving itself up the stairs behind them. Gabriel choked out a frightened noise.

The front door flew open, Charlee's alarmed expression the most welcoming thing Miles had ever seen. They scurried inside, slamming the door behind them as Miles locked it with a shaking hand.

"What the hell's going on?" Charlee demanded.

Footsteps pounded down the stairs and Miles's parents appeared. Adam held a bat. Sarah's purple robe was hanging half off as she stumbled across the living room towards them.

"What happened?" Her gaze darted across all three of them. "We heard screaming."

"We were chased from the school, this big—"

The front door blew open in an explosion of wood, shards

flying across the room. Several people screamed, and Miles yanked Gabriel back as all the lights were snuffed out.

Poised at the threshold was a pulsating wall of darkness, a vast, fathomless horror. Miles's entire body went cold, sweat freezing on his skin. His panting breath crystalized in the air. Shapes shifted within the darkness, impossible to make out, but he had that horrible sense once again of being watched.

"Back up!" Adam yelled from the other side of the living room.

Warm orange flared as the warding symbols carved into either side of the doorframe caught fire. They burned for a bright moment—then crumbled away to ash. Only a smudge remained.

The darkness didn't hesitate.

Tentacles lashed through the air, coiling around Gabriel's arms. He hit the floor, struggling as it reeled him across the wood, a powerless fish on a hook. His eyes caught Miles's, wide and terrified.

Miles lunged, grabbing him under the armpits and digging his heels into the rug. His shoulder screamed and his right arm gave out. "Help!" he yelped, scrabbling to find purchase as they were both pulled towards the void.

He was grabbed by the coat, more hands latching on to Gabriel. They heaved, Miles's dad hooking his leg around the office doorway, Charlee kicking at the nebulous shadows like she expected to hit something solid.

There was a *bang* in the other room and Miles's mom appeared, a flashlight in hand. Its blinding beam cut across the shape filling the doorway. An ear-ringing screech shattered the night. The smell of rotten garbage filled the air, the rope-like tentacles sizzling and recoiling as quickly as they'd invaded. The monster vanished as if sucked up into a giant vacuum.

Wheezing, Miles stumbled to his feet, dragging Gabriel up with him. Everyone whirled around, looking for any sign of the thing.

"Mom?" Amy's scared voice floated down the stairs. "What's going on?"

"Go back to your room and close the door," his mom commanded, scanning the porch with her flashlight held aloft like a sword. "Now!"

He could hear twin sets of footsteps scampering back down the hall, then the slam of a door.

"We shouldn't have brought it here." Gabriel clutched at Miles. "We need to lead it away."

"You're not going anywhere," Miles's dad stated firmly. He'd lost the bat. "What is that thing?"

"I don't know." Miles let go of Gabriel, reaching for his mom. They needed to find more flashlights, *now*. "It's tried to take Gabriel before. It feels the same as what came out of the grimoire, just… bigger."

Charlee peered around the living room. "Whatever it is, I think it's gone."

"C'mon." Adam put a hand on Gabriel's shoulder, steering him into the office as Miles moved to the kitchen. "We need to get you protected right—"

The office window exploded inward, blowing back the curtains and pelting Miles's dad with glass. Another shadowy tentacle, a thick black spike, lanced through the jagged hole. It shot straight towards where Gabriel stood in the middle of the room.

Miles moved, already knowing he wouldn't be fast enough, that he was too far away. It was going to take Gabriel as he watched.

Then Charlee was there in a blur of fiery red, shoving Gabriel out of the way.

The shadow punched straight through her like a spear. Charlee's back arched, a harrowing scream ripping out of her as she was lifted into the air.

Wind whipped around the office, Charlee caught in the center of a tornado. Books flew off shelves, bottles shattered, Gabriel's face frozen in horror as he watched from the floor where he'd landed. The shadows spun over her body before diving into her chest. With an explosive pop that reverberated through Miles's skull, they were gone.

Everything went still.

Charlee hit the floor with a dull thud, limbs crooked across a mound of glass and torn paper. Overhead, the lights flickered back on, illuminating the room in a cheerful glow.

Sobbing came from behind Miles. Someone touched his shoulder, saying words that didn't make any sense. He couldn't feel his legs, his hands, anything in his body except for his pounding pulse.

Charlee didn't move.

30

The beeping of Charlee's heartrate monitor reminded Miles of one of those bombs in the final act of an action movie, the hero racing to remember which wire to pull as the numbers counted down. Except Miles was no hero, and this bomb had no timer. It was impossible to know when the inevitable explosion would happen.

She looked dead, despite the monitor saying otherwise. Wilted against the bleached sheets, lips blue-tinged, sickly purple bruises around her sunken eyes. Miles could only breathe when he saw her chest rise and fall.

He felt trapped in some kind of endless nightmare loop. Charlee in the hospital bed. Edmund's colorless, hollowed face. Charlee's freckled skin crisscrossed with trailing wires. The wavy line of Edmund's pulse on a screen. Images flashed behind his eyes, repeating again and again. Ruining him again and again.

The door creaked open, and he jumped to his feet as his parents entered. Adam's expression was grave. Sarah immediately went over to take Charlee's hand.

"What did the doctors say?"

His dad rubbed the bridge of his nose. "About what you'd expect. They're freaked out, running tests without knowing what they're looking for. Your mom and I were talking about what we can do, but…"

But they'd never dealt with anything like this.

In the center of Charlee's torso where the darkness had pierced her was a ragged black mark. An uneven starburst imprinted onto her skin. Radiating from it, flashing in and out of visibility with each pump of her heart, a river of black lines pulsed under her skin.

She hadn't opened her eyes since she'd hit the office floor. Hadn't moved once.

"Is she going to die?" Miles managed to ask.

"The doctors are doing their best to keep her stable. We still have time."

There was an answer in the way he hadn't answered. Miles wanted to scream that their best wasn't enough, that Charlee deserved better.

"We have to do something." He refused to sit here and watch her fade away. It filled him with a strange calm, his anxiety gone for once.

His dad squeezed his uninjured shoulder. "Leave that to your mom and I. Why don't you go take care of Gabriel? He's still waiting in the hall."

He'd been sitting in one of those sickly yellow plastic chairs, staring blankly at the wall last time Miles checked. When asked, he'd refused to come into Charlee's room.

Miles had this irrational fear that if he wasn't watching Charlee breathe, she'd stop, but he couldn't leave Gabriel out there alone. "Come get me if anything changes, okay?"

It was late, the hallway empty aside from a few nurses in colorful scrubs flitting in and out of rooms and speaking in hushed voices. At the end of the long, sickly mint-green hall, the door to the waiting room was closed.

Gabriel barely glanced up as Miles collapsed into one of the chairs beside him. "How is your arm?"

"Fine." He'd been right about the shoulder dislocation. It stopped hurting so badly once the doctor dosed him with pain meds and worked it back into place, but now he was stuck in an annoying sling, with strict instructions on icing and stretching that he couldn't care less about. "But Charlee's not. No one knows what to do. They're talking about her like she's a lost cause."

Gabriel's hand quivered on the arm of his chair before he clenched it into a fist. "She shouldn't have pushed me out of the way like that."

"Yeah, well, you can lecture her once we save her life." Miles was too tired to navigate Gabriel's guilt. Too full of his own. A pair of nurses in squeaking sneakers walked by, flipping through a clipboard. He waited impatiently for them to pass. "We need to figure out how we're going to fix this."

"Miles—"

"I'm thinking we have two options: your mom, or the grimoire. I can't believe I'm going to say this, but I think the grimoire is the less risky option. We crack it open, see if we can find a spell or ritual—"

"*Miles.*"

"What?"

"There's a third, more logical option that we need to discuss." Gabriel wouldn't look at him. A phone rang on the desk at the end of the hall, the shrill noise reverberating off the shiny floors and paneled ceilings. "I go to my mother, or the tomb, and let things play out as they're supposed to.

Perhaps if we set things back on the right course, Edmund and Charlee will get better. Or I can barter with my mother—their safety in return for my cooperation."

The words worked through Miles's brain, struggling to make sense. "You… what? You're joking, right? How is that a logical option?"

"It gives Charlee and Edmund a better chance than turning to the grimoire. I may not know your cousin well, but I know she wouldn't want you risking yourself for her."

Gabriel was speaking so calmly, so resignedly. Panic rose in Miles's throat, and he painfully swallowed it down. "Then we'll go to your mom together, like I said. Confront her, threaten to expose your family if she doesn't help, whatever we have to do."

Before he even finished, Gabriel was shaking his head. "She'll never give in to us. You know that."

A short man passed them, a bouquet of cheerful, artificially colored daisies clutched in his hand. The sweat beading his forehead gleamed beneath the harsh fluorescent lights.

"We'll make her. I'll hold the grimoire over a fire, or call the other families and have them—"

"Miles." No one had ever said his name so gently. Miles hated that it was now, that it was because of this. "I've made up my mind. I think it's time we stop indulging a fantasy and accept fate."

Hot tears pricked at Miles's eyes. He couldn't handle this right now, not on top of everything else. "You're giving up because you're scared."

"Yes. In the last two days, we've lost two people we care about because of our actions. That should scare you too.

Who's going to be next? Bram? One of your sisters? Your parents?"

"Stop it. And stop talking about Charlee and Edmund like they're already dead."

"They will be if I don't do something. And you might die too." Gabriel let out a shuddering exhale. "My brother is dying because I kept the truth from him. Charlee is dying because she tried to save me from a problem I dragged to her doorstep. I can't bear to have another person's blood on my hands. Especially not yours."

He couldn't be serious. Didn't he hear himself?

"So, what, this is a noble self-sacrifice?" Miles barely recognized his own voice. A masked nurse wheeling by a diagnostics cart gave him a curious glance. "You've decided your life is worth less than ours? That's bullshit and you know it."

"I'm tired of fighting this. Of letting other people get hurt for me. Whatever came for me tonight, it's not going to stop. Our time is up. We need to stop being selfish."

His words rocked Miles. *Selfish*. Was that what this was? Was it selfish to want to change fate? To try and save someone he cared about?

No. He couldn't believe that. Not with Charlee barely clinging to life in the other room. Not with Gabriel so defeated that he was willing to roll over and die.

"Maybe it is selfish, but so is what you're doing. What about everyone you're going to hurt? Charlee, Emily, your brothers… you're going to do this to them after they've shown up for you every step of the way?"

"No, Miles. They've shown up for *you*. This quest became theirs the moment you cared about it, because they care about *you*. It's never really been about me."

"Don't say that when you know it's not true." Gabriel couldn't act like it wasn't real. Like he'd just gotten caught up in Miles's bubble, cared for by proxy.

An exhausted smile curled the corner of Gabriel's mouth. "Fine. Then that's yet another reason I need to do this. All of you put yourselves at risk to help me. It's past time I return the favor."

"That's bullshit too."

Gabriel didn't bother arguing. When he reached over and took Miles's hand, brushing warmth across his knuckles, Miles knew whatever he was going to say next would break him.

"I want you to know that even if this was all just borrowed time, being with you was the best thing that ever happened to me. Even if you couldn't change my fate, you changed my life."

No, no, *no*.

"I'm not going to let you do this," Miles choked out.

Horrible fondness filled Gabriel's eyes. "While I admire your stubbornness, you don't have a choice. You can't stop me."

Miles wanted to take that as a challenge, throw Gabriel over his shoulder and lock him up, toss him in the car and drive them both far away. He could stop him. He was bigger, stronger. Desperate. He could find a way.

But Gabriel's choices had been taken away from him his whole life. Miles couldn't bring himself to do that to him, even now.

Miles had to change his mind.

"I'll hate you if you do this," he declared, wet despair spilling from him. There was a box of tissues on the table beside him, sitting on a stack of ancient magazines, but he couldn't make himself reach for one. "I mean it, Gabriel. I'll regret the day I ever met you." He didn't know if the words tasted so rotten in his mouth because they were spiteful, nasty things, or because they might actually be true.

Gabriel's cool fingers found his cheek, catching a tear. "Knowing you hate me in my final moments," he said gently, "would be a small price to pay for knowing you'll live."

Misery crashed over Miles. He wanted to curl up and cry. It wasn't fair. He'd tried so hard to do the right thing, and in the end, it didn't matter at all.

Robin came through the door at the end of the hall, striding forward a few steps before suddenly whirling back the way she'd come. She repeated the movement again, wringing her hands while two nurses watched on in confusion.

Gabriel followed Miles's gaze, twisting in his seat. "Has she been in to see Charlee yet?"

"No." Miles was trying to not think about it because it made an ugly sensation churn inside him. "She's too scared."

His aunt had come flying into the office after Charlee was attacked, taken one look at her daughter, and stumbled away in horror. Miles's mom had chased after her and must've snapped her out of it, at least enough that she loaded the twins into her car and followed them to the hospital.

She hadn't made it past the waiting room yet.

"You should go make sure she's alright."

A nurse had a hand on Robin's shoulder, talking and gesturing down towards them.

He should, but they weren't done here. Not even close.

Robin shook her head, blonde hair flying, and backed

away. Miles could practically see the nervous breakdown looming over her.

"Go," Gabriel told him. "We can talk more later. I'm not going anywhere."

The unspoken *yet* hung in the air between them.

"Promise me."

"Where would I go?" Gabriel said wryly. "I don't have a car. It's not like I'm going to run all the way home. Besides"—he glanced up at Miles—"I still have things I need to say."

Goodbye, he meant.

Miles lurched to his feet, bile searing his throat. This wasn't how things were supposed to go. It couldn't be over, not like this.

He just needed time to think, to gather his thoughts and find a way to convince Gabriel not to go through with his suicidal plan. There had to be a way.

But Aunt Robin first. He could do that, get one thing right today.

"Hey." He reached his aunt and took her arm from the grateful nurse. "C'mon, let's talk out in the waiting room. Then we can see Charlee."

She let him lead her back out, where the receptionist gave them a sympathetic look over her purple glasses. Amy and Jenna were curled up asleep together on a sticky vinyl couch, their dad's jacket draped over them. No one else was in the waiting room aside from an older man with four empty coffee cups on the table beside him and a nervous leg jitter.

"Are you okay?"

Robin tugged at the collar of her oatmeal collared sweater, the neck stretched out and drooping. "I—I thought

I'd go check on her, but I froze. I keep seeing myself lowering her into her grave. I don't know if it's a premonition or my own mind trying to hurt me." Tears welled up in her bloodshot eyes. "I can't go through this again. I can't bury anyone else. I'll crawl into the grave with her."

Her hysteria barged past Miles's shields, grating against his nerves. His tongue was grainy and too big. It wasn't a good idea to talk to her like this, his emotions exposed and raw. "You have to go in there and tell her that. Give her a reason to come back to us."

"It won't matter. She already knows."

"Does she?" The words came out more piercing than Miles meant, a knife he hadn't realized he'd sharpened. "Because I'm positive she thinks you couldn't care less about her. And by refusing to go into that room, all you're doing is proving her right."

Aunt Robin recoiled, tears falling, but Miles couldn't bring himself to regret his words. It was far past time someone said them. He should have in her room the other night, instead of dancing around it.

"I don't know how to look at her without thinking about how horribly I failed her. Without wishing I'd been the one to die in that crash instead of Shaun." She pressed her palms to her face, voice cracking. "She's my daughter, and I let her dad die. Because of me, she lost the most important person in her life and that's all I can see when I look at her. And now I'm failing her again."

Miles had suspected, no matter how much Charlee insisted otherwise, but it didn't feel good to be right. Nothing about this felt good. Charlee deserved to know her mom loved her, and Aunt Robin deserved the chance to redeem herself.

"Losing Uncle Shaun was… the worst thing to happen to all of us," Miles told her. He had to move aside to let a stretcher go by, wheels squeaking. "I'll never be able to imagine what going through that was like for you. But Charlee is still alive. And she needs you with her right now."

A shuddering inhale wracked his aunt's body, her frail shoulders quaking. "What if I'm too late? What if she dies?"

"She's not going to die, okay? And when she pulls through this, she'll never forgive you if you're not there. You'll lose any chance you still had." He grabbed her elbow and waited for her to look at him, trying to harden his expression. "I need you to listen to me: put aside your own shit and show up for her, for once. You're her mom. You're supposed to be there when she needs you the most. Protect her. Do anything you can to save her."

She sniffled, wiping at her cheeks with a crumpled tissue she'd pulled from a pocket. Something must've resonated with her because she nodded, smoothing down the front of her sweater. "You're right," she croaked. "She needs me."

"She does."

Robin was barely holding it together, drawing from a well of inner strength he hadn't realized she had. Fear radiated from her, but with determination and a sense of purpose.

"I need to take the girls home first." Aunt Robin glanced over at Jenna and Amy, then at the clock mounted above the reception desk. "And pack a bag. Tell your dad I'll be back to stay the rest of the night with Charlee."

It didn't make up for the years of pain she'd dragged Charlee through, but it was a start. Hope bloomed to life in Miles, warring with despair from his conversation with Gabriel.

361

He hugged her, careful not to jostle his sling-arm. Her perfume tickled at his nose, familiar and comforting.

Getting through to his aunt should've made him more confident that he could change Gabriel's mind, but it only made him understand with thunderous certainty that he couldn't. Gabriel was doing what Miles had demanded of Robin—protecting them. Doing the only thing he could to save them.

If Miles was going to save him from himself, he'd have to do it first.

A plan formed in his mind. A dangerous, risky plan. He needed to go now, before Gabriel realized he was gone.

Leaving Aunt Robin to wake his drowsy sisters and Gabriel waiting in the hall, Miles slipped over to the elevators, calling Emily on the ride down.

"Yeah?" she answered groggily.

"Did I wake you up?"

"Kinda." She yawned. "I got back from homecoming not long ago; we made the stupid decision to go for late-night shakes after the dance got boring. It was a long night."

"Sorry, but I have a huge favor to ask you." The elevator doors opened to the dimly lit parking garage. "No pressure, but it's literally life or death."

"I'm getting out of bed right now," she said, sounding much more awake. "What's up?"

Charlee's car was right where his dad had parked it, crookedly taking up two spots, doors left unlocked in their rush. His parents' SUV was a no-go—all the windows shattered by the shadow monster—so they'd piled into Charlee's car. Its keys were currently still with his dad, but Miles only wanted his backpack.

"Is there any way you can come get me? I'm at the hospital and need a ride."

"The hospital? What happened?"

"I'll tell you when you get here, but I need you to hurry." He climbed into the backseat, digging out his bag from where he'd left it after the football game.

"Miles, I don't have a car or a license. I only got my learner's permit, like—" Emily cut off. "You know what, I'll figure it out and be there soon."

"You're the best."

Tucking his phone away, he unzipped his bag. The containment box was still there, nestled beside the heart-jar and scarf-wrapped knife. Regret nipped inside his chest—he should've had the knife on him, should've stabbed the mass of shadows the moment it appeared. Maybe he could've stopped all this from happening.

The metal of the containment box burned against his skin as he wiggled it free. Gabriel didn't think Felicity would care about the grimoire enough to barter for it, but if it had its barbs sunk into her as deep as Miles suspected, it would fight to save itself, influence her, control her if it needed to. If he offered her an exchange, threatened to destroy it if she refused, she'd have no choice but to accept. Once she'd helped him save Charlee and Edmund, and promised not to touch Gabriel, he'd destroy it anyway. No grimoire, no curse. It was his only shot.

Miles opened the box—and his stomach dropped.

The grimoire was gone.

31

When Miles got back to the waiting room, Aunt Robin had already left with his sisters, Nadia sitting in their place. They jumped to their feet when they saw him coming, hair twisted up into a messy bun, several safety pins hanging limply from their sweater.

"Miles! What happened? I went to see Edmund and when I got back to your house, it looked like a bomb went off. Gabriel texted that you were all at the hospital…" They noticed his sling. "Shit, are you hurt?"

"I'm fine. Did Edmund wake up?"

They shook their head. "I found a few things worth a shot, but they didn't work. I have no idea what's wrong with him—when Gabriel let me in, he said his brother had been getting worse through the day."

That only strengthened Miles's resolve to finish this.

Nadia peered around the near-empty waiting room— the guy collecting coffee cups had fallen asleep on his own shoulder—and asked, "Where's Charlee?"

Leading them back to the patient rooms, Miles explained what'd happened. When he got to Charlee's attack, they staggered, nearly tripping over their clunky boots.

"I should've been there," they muttered, face going

chalky. "Or I should've taken her with me, we—"

"Don't do that to yourself." The warning was as much for himself as for Nadia. Once you let those thoughts in, all they'd do was drag you under.

Outside Charlee's door, the chair Gabriel had been sitting in was empty.

Miles stopped dead. "Where's Gabriel?"

Nadia's forehead creased. "He left with a woman and those twin blondies. He was getting a ride home with them."

That didn't make any sense. He'd said he wouldn't leave yet. He'd looked Miles in the face and promised.

Had he somehow guessed that Miles was going after Felicity and decided to beat him to it? Could he have heard his thoughts all the way from the waiting room?

Fuck.

He was gone, and so was the grimoire. Something terrible was about to happen, Miles could feel it.

Gabriel couldn't have taken it, unless he'd seen Miles's bag in the back of Charlee's car, then slipped past him when he was talking to Robin to steal it. He tried to remember when he'd last seen it, if it had really been days ago after they'd found the curse.

"He's going to do something stupid," Miles told Nadia. He could only be a few minutes behind at most. "I'm sorry, I have to go stop him."

"Go." Nadia peered through the door window where Miles's parents were seated around Charlee's bed. "I'll watch her."

"Can you help her?"

"I don't know. The grimoire's magic is probably too powerful. But I've been known to get creative when times call for it." They mustered up a grim smile, their focus fixed on Charlee through the glass. "I'll text you if anything changes."

"Thank you."

Emily was waiting down at the curb in a black Audi Miles didn't recognize. He tossed his backpack in first before climbing in awkwardly with his sling. It smelled sweet inside, like expensive perfume and air freshener.

"Please tell me you didn't steal this."

"It's my mom's. She's going to kill me when she realizes I've taken it." Emily didn't sound too bothered. "Where to?"

"Gabriel's house." There was no way to sugarcoat the next part. "I'm pretty sure tonight's the night he's supposed to die, so we need to hurry."

She hit the gas and peeled out of the hospital.

He gave her directions to the Hawthorne estate, watching the speedometer creep up once they hit the main road. From her white-knuckled grip, her gaze flitting constantly to the rearview mirror, Emily wasn't comfortable, but she still got them there nearly as fast as Charlee.

The gate was open and waiting for them. The sight made Miles's nerves spike.

"Stay here," he told Emily as they pulled up the drive, parking at the base of the stone steps. Nothing looked unusual, twin lights on either side of the front door illuminating the porch. All the windows were dark, but that was to be expected at this time of night. "If anything happens, go back to the hospital. My parents are there."

She clicked her seatbelt. "Not gonna happen. Let's just say we argued, I won, and go get him."

Miles didn't have time to waste protesting. He swung

his bag onto his uninjured shoulder and followed her out of the car.

The front door was unlocked, opening easily with the slightest turn of the knob. Darkness shrouded the foyer, the only light coming from the porch, and that vanished too when Emily closed the door behind them.

"Woah," she breathed, scanning the room. "Poshy."

"You should see it when the lights are on."

Miles glanced at the stairs, then down the hall—he had a split-second decision to make. Bedroom or tunnels?

"Let's check upstairs," he decided. He couldn't imagine Gabriel going to the tomb without seeing his brothers one final time. And if he'd gone to find Felicity, there was a good chance she'd be up in her room or office.

It was deathly quiet as they crept up the stairs. "Is it always so creepy in here?" Emily whispered.

"Yeah."

He led her to Gabriel's bedroom, listening carefully outside the door before knocking, and when he didn't get an answer, cracking it open. It was empty.

"Where is everyone?"

Miles had a sinking feeling he knew.

Edmund was still in his bed. It hadn't been full a day, but he looked as if he'd been in a coma for years, his face sunken and skeletal, cheekbones jutting out sharp enough to cut. The blue of his veins glowed through his pale, paper-thin skin.

There was a sound from the bed. Emily jumped, startled.

If Edmund suddenly sat up, Miles was going to scream. "Hello?"

"Miles?" Bram's voice was tentative. His head popped out from under the bed, followed by Balthazar's.

"Hey." Miles helped pull him out, straightening his wrinkled shirt and checking him over for injuries. "Are you okay? What're you doing under there?"

"Hiding." Bram peered around, finding Emily by the door. "Who's that?"

"This is my friend, Emily. What do you mean, you were hiding? Hiding from what?"

"A monster," he said solemnly. His cat curled around his leg possessively, staring up at Miles with golden eyes.

Miles's heart leaped. "This monster, was it... made of shadows? Big and dark?"

"Did you see it too?" He backed up a step. "Is it still here?"

"No, no, it's not here anymore, it's okay. It didn't hurt you?"

"Balthazar and I hid really fast. I don't think it even saw us." Bram hefted Balthazar into his arms, cradling him close. He was like the cat version of that stuffed animal all kids had that they believed kept the boogeyman away. "Is Gabriel with you? He said he'd be home before I went to bed, but he never came."

"You haven't seen him?"

He realized how stupid the question was as it left his mouth. Gabriel would've never left Bram hiding like this, scared and alone.

He must've not been able to bring himself to see his brothers, listening to the same thing that made him leave the hospital without saying goodbye to Miles. Maybe he thought it would be easier this way.

"We need to hurry," he told Emily. "He's already gone down."

"Down where?" Bram questioned. "To that tunnel? But your cousin told me you two got stuck last time."

"We did, but it's okay, I'll go get Gabriel. Are you good staying here with Edmund?"

"I'm coming with you."

"You can't, sorry. It's too dangerous down there."

His jaw took on a stubborn set that Miles had seen a thousand times on Gabriel's face. "If it's dangerous, you'll need me and Balthazar to protect you. We're coming."

"Bram… I need you to stay here where it's safe."

"But what if the monster comes back?"

Damn it. He was being manipulated, but Bram had a point. Nowhere was safe for sure, but if he came with, at least Miles could keep an eye on him.

"Fine. But you and Balthazar have to stay behind us the whole way, and if I tell you to run, you listen. Okay?"

"Okay."

"Watch him," Miles murmured to Emily as they filed into the hall. "If things go badly…" At least two possible futures ended in blood. Bram couldn't see that. "Take him to that hatch I told you about. The stool's still there, you can get out that way."

She nodded and slipped off her protective charm bracelet, taking Miles's hand. Her fierce determination to protect this kid she'd just met washed over him—she'd do whatever it took to keep him safe.

They headed down to the wine cellar. In his rush, Miles had forgotten all about needing the key to the hidden door, but the tunnel was already open and waiting for them. A low wheeze came from the darkness, stirring the air.

"No turning back once we go in," Miles warned them.

He swung his backpack off, digging out one flashlight for Emily and keeping one for himself. He didn't have a third for Bram, but his hands were full of Balthazar anyway.

Miles considered the death-knife for a moment before unwrapping it and shoving it awkwardly through his belt loop. No part of him wanted to use it, and he prayed he wouldn't have to, but if the moment came, he couldn't afford to fumble around in his bag. Nadia had said it could kill anything—hopefully that was true if they ran into the shadow monster again.

His sling came off last, tossed to the floor—it'd only get in his way.

Emily crossed through the doorway first, the wards flaring around her to drench the tunnel in red. Miles went next, Bram following close behind with Balthazar clinging to his sweater, fur standing on end. Even the cat knew this was a bad place.

As they walked, Miles pointed his flashlight to the ground, hoping to find an indication that Gabriel had been here, but it was impossible to tell if the scrapes and footprints were recent. All he could do was take strange comfort in the fact that he knew he'd be there if Gabriel died. He still had time.

He was calmer than he'd expected with his goals so clear: stop Felicity, save Gabriel, free Jocelyn. Those were the only things that mattered. No more waiting, no more clues to decipher, no more mysteries to untangle.

"We go left here—" The words died on Miles's lips as they came upon the fork. Except it wasn't a fork anymore. Five identical passageways twisted away from them, leading in all different directions.

"I—I don't understand." Miles pointed his beam down each one, making sure it wasn't an optical illusion. "It wasn't like this the other day."

"What does that mean?" Emily asked. "How could it have changed?"

"It's trying to stop us from getting to the tomb."

That wheezing sound came again, in shorter bursts from all directions, like they were being cackled at. The shadows around them shifted, furling and unfurling.

Anger sparked in Miles's veins. "We'll try them all if we have to."

Except the first tunnel hit another fork. When Miles shone his light down the right branch, he could see three more tunnels. They backtracked and tried the next, but the same thing was waiting for them.

This place had morphed into a twisted maze. They had no chance of finding their way through.

"Damn it," Miles muttered, raking a hand through his hair. They'd have to pick one and start wandering. He'd seen enough horror movies to know they shouldn't split up, so dividing and conquering was out of the question.

Emily tugged at his backpack, startling him. "What're you doing?"

"That creepy jar Nadia gave you." She got the zipper open, fishing around inside. "It'll guide you when you're lost, right?"

Miles was a first-class idiot.

She yanked it free, passing it over to him. Her flashlight illuminated the fleshy organ inside, bits swirling in the cloudy water.

Bram leaned in to get a better look. "What is that?"

"Something gross that's hopefully going to save us." Miles waited, but nothing happened. He gave it a little shake, liquid sloshing, but still nothing.

Emily squinted at it. "How do you make it work?"

"I have no idea. Nadia didn't say." In retrospect, he should've asked. "Uh, hey, magical fox heart… we're kinda lost right now. Do you wanna do your thing and point us in the right direction?"

The heart bobbed, sinking slightly.

"Go down one of the tunnels and see if it tells you it's the right way," Emily suggested.

Miles did as she instructed. There was no reaction from the jar in the first two tunnels. He didn't know if that was a good or a bad sign.

"It's a dud," he declared, stepping into the center one. "Nadia did say—"

In the jar, the heart started to beat. Small, quick little movements, the flesh pulsing in and out. *Thump, thump, thump.*

"That's so nasty." He could feel the reverberation against the glass. "I guess this is the way."

The rasping laughter of the tunnels turned into a low, threatening hiss. It wasn't pleased at being thwarted. The air went eerily still, and Emily's charm bracelet emitted a faint glow.

Bram's voice broke through the silence. "Something is moving down there."

Beyond the reach of the flashlight beams, a shape writhed in the darkness, twisting and turning, folding in on itself. Shadows bled from the wall, feeding into the mass, helping it grow. Like the one that'd come for Gabriel, it had no distinct shape, no body or face.

Emily gave a squeak of distress as she stumbled. Bram grabbed Miles's sleeve like a lifeline.

They had nowhere to go. If they bolted down another tunnel, they'd either have to take the one-in-four chance of it leading to the mausoleum hatch or stop long enough for the jar to do its thing. And the exit behind them was warded shut.

"Back up," Miles commanded as the mass started coming down the tunnel, feelers venturing ahead to stroke along the stone walls. He dropped his flashlight, fumbling with the knife on his belt, his aching shoulder making his fingers sluggish and—

With an unearthly yowl, Balthazar launched himself out of Bram's arms. He hit the ground, fur puffed up, spitting and growling at the approaching shadows.

"No!" The cat would be swallowed up right in front of them. Miles rushed forward to scoop him up. Before he could take more than a step, an electric charge crackled through the air and Balthazar exploded.

Not *kaboom* like a bomb, but Miles didn't have any other word for it. One moment, he was staring at a black cat with a death wish; the next, his little body erupted with a whoosh. In its place was one of the hellhound guardian monsters that had tried to kill him and Gabriel their first time down here. He was even bigger than the first, pure black, built thick and corded with muscle. When he turned to look at them, Miles saw a spark in his sunken sockets. Ghostly silver mist seeped from between gleaming razor teeth.

Holy shit.

With a howl that froze Miles's blood to icy sludge, a sound that had haunted his nightmares, new-Balthazar threw himself at the shadow mass. They collided, and Balthazar chomped down with that powerful pit bull jaw.

A piercing shriek filled the tunnel. Miles ducked down, holding Bram against him and covering his ears. He watched as Balthazar slashed with obsidian claws and ripped chunks from the darkness, flinging them away where they dissolved and vanished. Tentacles thrashed and whipped, but if they were hurting him, the pain only spurred him on.

There was a clear winner in this fight, and the shadows knew it. Miles's ears popped from the shift in pressure as the mass vanished, sucked back into the depths of the tunnels. Balthazar panted, sides heaving and tongue lolling out of his demonic slash of a mouth.

Bram slipped free of Miles's hold, running forward. "No, Bram, wait—"

Balthazar did his transformation thing—inwards this time, like one of those massive tents that folded up to fit in a duffle bag—and he was a black cat again. He leaped into Bram's arms, kneading his claws into his sweater with a smug look.

Emily swayed, gaping at the cat in disbelief. "What—what—?"

"I told you he'd protect us," Bram told them, sounding disappointed that they hadn't taken him seriously. "He's really good at it."

That was an understatement.

"Uh, Bram, what—how—?" Miles didn't know where to start. All kids made themselves a protector, but it wasn't supposed to be *real*. Jenna had a teddy bear when she was younger that she said kept ghosts from hiding under her bed, but Miles would've noticed if it transformed into a vicious beast. "Where did Balthazar come from?"

"I told you before, I found him in the wine cellar. Next to where you opened the tunnel." Purring rumbled from Balthazar, his tail flicking playfully as Bram scratched his chin. "His other form was kind of scary, so I asked him to change."

"And he... listened to you?"

"Of course. He does whatever I say," Bram informed them matter-of-factly. "But we made a deal that I'll never make him do anything he doesn't want to, unless he's being bad. He likes being a cat best, so he only changes back when he needs to."

A guardian, the entry in the grimoire had said.

"That's... really cool," Emily got out. "Thanks for saving us, Balthazar. You kicked ass."

Bram beamed at her, Balthazar blinking lazily in his arms.

Miles wasn't going to complain about having an attack dog on their side, especially not one as powerful as Balthazar.

Letting the cat take point with a jaunty little swagger to his step, they followed the third tunnel down to the next fork. The heart started beating away in its jar, guiding them down the second path. Miles barely restrained the urge to giggle hysterically at how absurd this whole thing was.

Two more tunnels, two more turns, and they started making their way down a familiar slope. Anticipation tightened its chokehold as Miles spotted the first scarlet poppies.

When they reached the stone door, it was closed.

"No, come on!" Miles ran his hands over the tree, pushed

at the trunk. It should've been left open for them, like the tunnel entrance. Gabriel had just come through here. He was right there on the other side. "I don't know how it opens," he told Emily, hearing the dismay in his own voice.

Bram took the flashlight from Miles's hand without a word, studying the slab. "It looks like our family tree."

"Yeah, Gabriel thought the same thing, but your crest is more"—Miles gestured to the sparse branches—"full on the top."

"Not our crest, our family tree. The one hanging in the library."

Miles couldn't recall seeing one when he'd been in there, but he hadn't been looking.

"It's got the same branches," Bram continued. He traced up the trunk with his flashlight to where it split in two. "This would be Florence Hawthorne, my great-great-grandmother, and her sister." Only one of the branches broke off into more. "Then Great-Grandmother Marjorie with Great-Grandfather Eugene, and Great-Uncle Barnaby."

He listed more names, steadily following the limbs. Cordelia Hawthorne, Regina Hawthorne, Rupert Hawthorne. Aldrich, William, Felicity. Until—

"And this is Edmund, Gabriel, and me," Bram finished, pointing at the uppermost three branches. The beam of his flashlight caught on something glistening and dark.

Miles ran his finger along the middle groove. When he pulled away, the tip of his finger was smeared with fresh blood. He didn't need Bram to confirm whose branch it was.

Emily grimaced at the crimson smear, then reached her own hand up to feel the line to the left of Gabriel's. "Edmund's has it too. It's sticky, though."

"That's because it's been there longer." Pieces were clicking together in Miles's brain. "That's how you get in. Hawthorne blood on the right branch, like a lock and key." He followed the others. Felicity's branch was dark with old blood, then Regina, Marjorie, Florence. The only row that had more than one darkened like Edmund's and Gabriel's was Marjorie's.

"Who's this again?" he prompted Bram, gesturing to the branch beside Marjorie's.

He cocked his head, thinking. "That would be... Great-Uncle Barnaby. He died in an accident before I was born."

Barnaby and Edmund. Both hurt under mysterious circumstances, both with a sibling who'd entered the tomb as well. Both punished.

There was a pattern, the eldest child of each generation brought here, but Miles didn't know what for. But he knew how to get inside.

"I'm sorry to ask," he told Bram, "but we need your blood."

He offered his tiny finger without any hesitation. Emily swatted Miles out of the way, conjuring one of those mini thread and needle kits from her jacket pocket. Bram flinched when she poked him. She murmured an apology, Balthazar watching her menacingly until Bram assured him it was fine.

Miles had to lift him up so he could reach his branch, smearing the welling drop of blood along his groove.

The pointed star above the tree glowed red. Silent as a ghost, the door to the tomb slid open.

32

Candlelight flickered from deeper within the tomb, long wavering shadows cast along the floor and far wall. No one shouted, no footsteps raced towards them, so the door must've opened unnoticed, cloaked by the murky darkness. Miles could barely make out the ebb and flow of voices.

He was truly here. The moment he'd been dreading had come.

Gesturing for Emily and Bram to wait, he crept inside, far enough to peer around the stone pillar blocking his view of the room. He immediately found Gabriel—his white button-up was rumpled and creased, blood smeared from nose to chin. The sight was hauntingly familiar.

Behind Gabriel, laid out on the lifted platform, was Jocelyn. She was a phantom in her glowing white nightgown, glossy poppies sprouting from the wall around her. Several petals had fallen to rest on her breast like violent blotches of blood against the snowy fabric.

"—be so defiant." Felicity's frustrated voice floated over. "This could've gone so much easier if you'd simply done as you were told. This isn't how I wanted to spend my night."

"Which part, exactly?" Gabriel was too strained to land

the cool nonchalance he was aiming for. He wasn't tied up, but his posture radiated barely restrained tension. "The kidnapping or ritualistic sacrifice? I assumed this was an average Saturday night for you."

Kidnapping? Did that mean Gabriel hadn't come here of his own free will? That would explain why he looked like he'd been in a brawl.

Miles peered farther around the column, Felicity coming into view. She was standing beside a waist-high chunk of stone, the top littered with candles, beads of wax pearled along the sides and dripping onto the floor. Instead of one of her usual monochromatic pantsuits, she was wearing a calf-length gray dress with a subtle shimmer. She'd put in effort, getting dressed up for her son's murder. Miles resented her so much that his mouth tasted like ash.

"I don't know why you insist on acting like this is a joke," Felicity was saying. "If you stop and simply do as you're told, it will go a lot faster."

"You'd love that, wouldn't you?" Gabriel responded bitterly. "That's all you've ever cared about. Obedience to the point of brainwashing."

Felicity scoffed. From the shadows shrouding the edges of the room, another person stepped into view.

Aunt Robin, the grimoire open in her hands. And behind her, huddled against the wall, their hands tied with what looked like one of their aunt's silk scarves, were Amy and Jenna.

Shock sucker-punched Miles in the gut. Knocked every bit of air straight out of his body and turned his knees to jelly. He had to dig his nails into the stone of the pillar to keep from falling.

What was she doing here?

It didn't make any sense. There had to be a mistake. A misunderstanding.

Miles forced himself to turn away, to sneak back to the doorway.

"What's wrong?" Emily whispered. "Is Gabriel hurt?"

"He looks okay." Bram visibly relaxed at Miles's words. "But Amy and Jenna are here… with my aunt."

"Robin?" Emily's lips parted in shock. "What do you mean? Like, she brought them here? Is she working with Felicity?"

"I don't know." Miles's mouth was dry, the words a rasp. If she'd used his sisters as leverage, that would've gotten Gabriel here with a minimal fight—but pondering that possibility was too much right now. "All I know is, she's got the grimoire and Felicity doesn't seem bothered. Whatever's going on, we need to get my sisters out of here."

Emily nodded. "What's the plan?"

He explained where Jenna and Amy were, how Emily could sneak around to them if she kept to the shadows and hid behind pillars. Miles would create a distraction while she untied them and got them out.

Emily didn't like it, but when she couldn't think of anything better, she reluctantly agreed.

"What can Balthazar and I do?" Bram asked.

Miles shrugged off his backpack and placed it in front of the still-open door—hopefully, it would stop it if it tried to close. For all he knew, there was an equally confusing puzzle on this side, and they didn't have time to stop and solve it in the middle of hauling ass out.

"I need you two to wait here. Keep the door open for

us and watch our backs." Miles handed Bram the heart-jar. "When Emily gets my sisters, I need you to help her navigate out of here. Can you do that?"

Bram nodded solemnly. "We won't let anything happen to them. I promise."

Miles squeezed his shoulder gratefully.

"I hope you have an escape plan for you and Gabriel," Emily whispered so only he could hear. "I'm going to be pissed if I have to come back and save you two as well."

He didn't have a semblance of a plan beyond keeping everyone alive and trying to not get himself killed. The sight of Robin—and of Gabriel plucked straight out of his vision—had him so rattled that it was taking everything in him to step forward.

"Be careful," was all he said in return.

Together, they made their way back into the room, staying low and moving slowly. Miles waited until Emily had vanished into the darkness blanketing the edges of the tomb, before standing and walking out into the open.

Gabriel saw him first, the blood draining straight out of his face.

Miles attempted a reassuring nod, then cleared his throat to get Felicity's and Robin's attention. They whirled around at the noise. "Uh, hey. Am I interrupting?"

Felicity glared, lip curled in disgust, as if he were a bug who'd dared to crawl into her line of sight. "I should've known you'd show up."

It probably wasn't a great sign that she didn't look remotely worried.

Surprise, overtaken swiftly by guilt, flashed across Aunt Robin's face. It was such an undeniable expression, someone doing something they know is wrong and not expecting to get caught. All Miles's doubts collapsed, leaving a cavernous pit.

Behind her, his sisters clutched each other in terror. Amy mouthed his name, tears streaking down her face.

"I don't understand," Miles told his aunt hollowly.

Her fingers tightened around the grimoire. She refused to look at him.

"She's here for the ritual." Gabriel answered for her. "To bind herself to the magic, just as Florence did."

Robin didn't deny it. She didn't say anything.

"But… why?" Miles needed it to make sense. "You know how evil the grimoire is, you warned us yourself." Emily emerged from the shadows on silent feet beside his sisters. She put a finger to her lips as she started on Jenna's ties. "It won't just affect you. You'll curse our entire family—me, Charlee, the girls."

"I know you can't see it, but this is for all of you. Trust me, it needs to be done."

"You're talking about the same magic that's killing Charlee right this moment—"

"No, no, Charlee's fine!" she interrupted, gesturing wildly at Felicity. "She's all better. Felicity summoned the magic back and it worked. I called the hospital. Charlee's awake and healed. They said it's a miracle."

"Call it a gesture of good faith," Felicity remarked smoothly. "To solidify the newfound partnership between our families."

That was the biggest load of bullshit Miles had ever heard. A nasty, cruel trick.

"So, what? You went through the trouble of healing her

so she'll just wish she's dead when you curse her? It changes people, takes all their humanity and hollows them out until there's nothing left. It's evil, Aunt Robin. You know it is."

Jenna was untied, helping Emily free Amy. Another minute, and they'd be gone. Safe.

Robin yanked erratically at the collar of her sweater, ripping one of the seams. "You don't understand. It doesn't *have* to be evil. When it came to me two weeks ago, all it wanted was to show me how to bring Shaun back. And then I saw a vision of the future: him, alive and in my arms, Charlee smiling with us. Our family was whole again."

Two weeks ago. The night Miles had brought the grimoire home with him and sensed it reaching through his house before he'd gotten the containment box. It'd found his aunt that night, slithered under her skin and whispered its honeyed, poisonous words into her ear.

Gabriel caught his gaze, regret and remorse swirling in his eyes. They'd doomed Robin with such a stupid oversight.

"You were right, what you said in the hospital," his aunt continued frantically. "Charlee needs me. And I need to do whatever it takes to save her. The future is going to be mine to make as I want."

Miles wanted to cry. "It's not real, you know it's not. The grimoire's manipulating you, influencing you. It has been this whole time. What about the sacrifice? You're going to kill for this future?"

For the first time, uncertainty crossed her face. She turned, as if to glance over her shoulder before shame halted her.

Miles's sisters weren't there anymore, already scurrying away with Emily, but he understood. "Which one?" he demanded, blood thumping in his ears. "Or did you bring them both because you couldn't choose?"

Gabriel made an angry noise.

"I didn't know at first," Robin admitted. "I considered myself, so Charlee and her father could live a good life without me. A swap seemed fair. But then I had a vision." Her gaze went distant, staring at a point over his head. "Jenna's gift will manifest less than a month from now. She'll be a seer, the same as me. Her life will be filled with misery and despair. She'll never know peace. It's a terrible burden. I can free her from it."

"By killing her." Miles's voice quivered. "You're not even going to give her a chance."

"She won't be dead," she countered quickly, like the negligible difference between dead and whatever Jocelyn was mattered. "She'll be here, at peace, knowing she's saving her family, and free from a life of hopelessness."

Madness glimmered behind her eyes, a desperate, unhinged belief Miles knew he wouldn't be able to sway. Gabriel shook his head, seeing it too—the magic had gotten in too deep, pushed her too far for anyone to reach.

Robin wasn't herself anymore. His aunt would never consider harming her family.

"We need to get this moving," Felicity told Robin, bored and impatient. "The ritual still needs—"

A sound cut her off, a rock clattering across the floor. One of the girls must've tripped or bumped into loose rubble.

"Who's there?" Felicity's voice cracked, deadly as a whip. She spun around, scanning the gloom. A flurry of footsteps took off towards the door, a flash of blonde hair in the dancing candlelight.

Miles didn't stop to think. He lunged forward, hitting Felicity hard enough to knock her to the ground. His injured shoulder screamed in pain, but he caught himself on the altar, jacket sleeve brushing the candle flames. When he turned to his aunt, ready to take her down, Gabriel was already there, ripping the grimoire from her frozen hands.

"Burn it," he told Miles grimly, tossing him the book.

Framed by the altar candles was a small kitchen knife and a piece of worn paper with a torn edge—the missing page.

Miles grabbed it too, shoving it under the leather cover and holding the whole thing over the nearest candle. The fire sizzled and hissed as it licked hungrily up the book.

Good riddance. They should've torched this thing the second they found it.

His fingers stung from the heat, but the grimoire refused to catch, untouched by the flames. Miles pulled it back—there wasn't even a smudge of soot on it, the cover still cool to the touch.

Felicity laughed, picking herself off the ground. "Surely you didn't think such a powerful artifact could be destroyed so easily."

Miles snatched up the kitchen knife, driving it into the book with all his strength. The blade bent in on itself.

Holy shit.

"If you're quite finished with your games," Felicity sneered, "hand it over."

No way. He still had the grimoire. If he and Gabriel could make a run for it, get out of—

"Don't bother." Tendrils of shadows slithered across the floor, coiling at her feet like an obedient dog. "When they catch you, I can't promise they won't take a little taste."

Gabriel shook his head. They wouldn't make it out of here.

Wishing he could smash her in the face with it, Miles shoved the grimoire at Felicity and went to stand beside Gabriel, the tentacles perking up to track his movements in eerie unison.

She passed it to Robin. "It looks like you'll be using this one"—a dismissive nod at Miles—"now that your intended sacrifice has escaped. The better choice, if you ask me. He's been quite the inconvenience."

A mixture of relief and fear slid down Miles's spine. They weren't concerned with chasing down the twins, but only because he was on the chopping block instead.

His aunt bit her lip, the chapped skin splitting to release a dribble of blood. "It wasn't supposed to be him. Jenna was the doomed one, the one—"

"Yes, well, things don't always go according to plan. If you don't want to go through with the ritual now…"

Miles shifted closer to Gabriel as they argued. "What's the plan?"

"If you see a chance, run," he whispered. "No hesitation."

"You know I can't."

"Please, I—" Gabriel's voice cracked. "I need you to get out of here."

Before Miles could answer, Robin shuffled over. He searched for something familiar in her face, a hint of warmth, of the aunt who loved him. There was nothing. How long had he been staring into this mask without realizing?

"I'm sorry," she whispered, "but a sacrifice is required. And I know you'd rather it was you than Jenna. I have to believe this was meant to be your future all along."

Miles turned away. If she wanted forgiveness, understanding, he'd die before giving it to her.

With a sigh, she stepped away and opened the grimoire, flipping through the pages.

"And what about me?" Gabriel challenged. "I'm going to be another sacrifice? Jocelyn's replacement?"

Felicity looked genuinely surprised. "What gave you that ridiculous idea? We don't need a replacement. The magic can feed off of her indefinitely, as long as she's still alive. A merciful solution." She spoke as if Jocelyn wasn't mere feet away, glaring holes into her. "There are only two rules that must be followed: the magic must be rebound to her by a Hawthorne of the new generation, and the sacrifice must be of gifted blood. Traditionally, the firstborn would do it, but Edmund refused to go through with the ritual. An unfortunate pattern in our bloodline. The men have a tendency to be weak."

That explained the bloody branches of the tree, what the second siblings had been brought here for. Gabriel wasn't the sacrifice—he was doing the sacrificing.

"Your family murdered Barnaby because he refused to subject Jocelyn to more torture?" Miles couldn't hide his disgust.

"The magic killed him, and it will kill Edmund too if we don't complete the rebinding. Once the power is called forth, if the ritual isn't completed, it will turn on the summoner." She flicked her cold gaze over to Gabriel. "It's disobedient when it's hungry, as you and Bram saw when it came for you tonight. The only thing holding it back and stopping it from fully devouring Edmund's body and mind, is my promise to bring you here to complete the rebinding. But we need to be quick—I've already put this off longer than was safe because your fool of a brother insisted on disobeying me these last few years." Annoyance thinned her lips. "Jocelyn's bonds have been weakening, our gifts draining away."

The utter nonchalance in her voice made Miles's blood boil. "Gabriel isn't a killer like you."

"As your aunt explained, she's not dead." Felicity lifted her hand, palm up. Her lashes fluttered, lips moving silently, and a moment later, a stake appeared in her grasp. It was made of plain wood, engraved with swirling symbols. She twisted it so the silver tip caught the light. "Picture her as… a battery. All you need to do is plug yourself in, Gabriel, and you and your brothers will finally understand the true power of our family. Then we can all go back to normal, the way it's always been."

It was sick. Twisted. There wasn't a flicker of humanity or remorse in Felicity. Even the wooden stake in her hand oozed wickedness, thick and blunt, designed to hurt.

"What is there to go back to? We despise you, even Bram. You, our facade of a family, our prison of a home." Gabriel's bottom lip trembled. Miles wanted to reach over to take his hand, lend him strength. "Even Father left because he couldn't stand you. You've allowed yourself to become a monster and now there isn't a single person in your life who loves you."

Felicity didn't move, a muscle twitching in her face. For a moment, Miles thought Gabriel's words had broken through.

At her feet, the shadows coiled tighter, slipping up the bare skin of her ankles. Her expression hardened, cold and unforgiving. Untouchable. "Love is for the weak and sentimental. Power is what truly matters."

"You haven't always believed that." Miles braced himself so he didn't flinch when she whipped towards him. "My parents told me about when you were younger and friends. That you were funny and caring. A good person. My mom loved you like a sister."

Felicity tried to hide it, but he saw her fists clench. "Your mother lied."

"You begged her to leave with you so you didn't have to carry this curse. You didn't want this life, so much that you would've rather run away. And now you're forcing the same nightmare on your own children."

She bared her teeth, demonic in the candlelight. "I should have thanked your mother for abandoning me that night. She showed me the harsh truth of this world: the only ones you can rely on are family."

"Not me." Gabriel stared at his mom. "I won't do it."

"Oh, I think you will. Perhaps you simply need a little more persuasion."

With a gasp, her head jerked back, her entire body locking up. For a long second, she was frozen still, not even breathing. Then her free hand jumped into the air as if tugged by a string, fingers clawed. They flexed, drumming at nothing, faster and faster.

The ground to Miles's left split apart with a piercing snap that he felt in his bones. Rumbling like an angry beast, the tomb floor shifted, the crack widening into a toothless grin.

Once it was a few feet wide, it ground to a halt. Everything went still. Deep down in the hole, Miles could hear a distant whine, buzzing in his ears and growing closer. The charms around his neck burned white hot.

"I'll offer you an easy exchange," Felicity told Gabriel.

"The life of this Warren boy for your cooperation. Decide quickly."

Her wrist twisted violently towards the ceiling, and from the crevice, colorless gray hands emerged. Misshapen, humanoid bodies, hazy like ghosts and infused with smoky darkness, heaved themselves out onto the ground. Their mouths were screaming gashes, eyes hollow sockets as they writhed against the stone.

Miles had never seen anything like them. Ghosts or demons, lost souls or spirits, they didn't belong here.

Unnaturally quick, one scuttled forward on all fours and grabbed Miles's legs, yanking them out from underneath him. He fell back hard, elbows scraped and shoulder on fire.

"Miles!" Gabriel grabbed for him, but more of the demons crawled forward, pinning him down.

Biting back a scream, Miles thrashed, trying to escape the swarm of pawing hands. They clawed at his flesh, pressed bruises into his ribs, trying to burrow their way inside.

"Mother, stop it!" Gabriel cried.

"Agree to the ritual, and I will." Miles could hear the satisfaction in her voice. "Before it's too late."

With a rough tug, the hands started hauling Miles towards the fissure. He dug his nails into the floor, bit and kicked anything he could reach, but it didn't matter. They dragged him closer, inch by inch.

Robin watched from beside the altar, a hand over her mouth. She made no move to help him.

Gabriel was yelling. Miles couldn't make out the words over his own terrified wheezing and that low whine growing louder. These ghouls were going to drag him into the afterlife, straight into the bowels of hell.

His shoe reached the edge just as the hands went still and reluctantly pulled away. Wicked faces turned as one, awaiting Felicity's next command.

Blood slicked Miles's palms as he scrambled back. Part of him wanted to holler at Gabriel not to give in to Felicity, but he was so relieved, the words caught on the lump in his throat.

Except it wasn't Felicity they were all looking at. Emily stepped from behind her, sweat glistening on her forehead and shaking hands outstretched. "You're not the only medium here, bitch," she spat.

"Another friend of yours?" Felicity asked Gabriel wryly. "How cute."

Emily ignored her and pushed her palms forward, like she was straining against a stuck door. The demon ghosts started slinking back towards the crack.

With a mocking smirk, Felicity waved her hands, and they froze.

Emily huffed out a harsh breath, a bead of sweat rolling down her face. Felicity's smirk faded. The horde stumbled back another step, limbs twisting and jerking violently.

It looked like they were having a mental wrestling match for control. Miles didn't understand how Emily was even holding her own.

"Mother said our gifts were weakening," Gabriel muttered, helping Miles to his feet. "I don't know if Emily can win, but she should be able to hold her for a moment." His focus shifted to Robin and the grimoire. "We need the extra page, to see if there's a second part to the curse that can undo it."

Aunt Robin didn't put up a fight, letting him snatch

the grimoire away with barely a whimper of protest. She looked about to collapse in on herself and curl into the fetal position.

The loose page was still tucked into the cover, wrinkled, but legible.

In return for continued gifts of power through the bloodline, the sacrifice must be repeated by one member of each new generation. The same sacrifice can be used, so long as there is still life to fuel the magic. Gifts will not be given until the ritual is complete and the entry of power accepted.

Once the magic is invoked, the sacrifice must be completed, or the summoner will be taken as an offering.

If the pact between magic and blood fails, all gifts will be revoked. A price will be paid for breaking the bargain.

That was it. All things that Felicity had already told them.

"There's nothing," he told Gabriel, defeat heavy in his voice. "Pretty sure that's on purpose. If you want to break this deal, it sounds like it's going to come collect in an ugly way, so you're forced to keep going."

"No one forced my family to do anything," Gabriel uttered. "Each one of them came down here and made their choice."

"What if we take Bram and Edmund and leave Thistle, so no one can rebind Jocelyn? That could end it."

"Mother will never let us out of here, and even if she did, the shadows will come for us. They'll kill Edmund."

A piercing wail blasted through the tomb, the final

demon ghosts slithering back into their crevice. Emily was ashen, trembling so hard it looked like she was vibrating, but a wide grin broke across her face.

Felicity shrieked, strands of hair sticking to her glistening forehead and a harsh flush crawling up her neck. She sliced her arm through the air and the two sides of the crack collided, slamming closed in a poof of dust.

"I'm done indulging you," she snarled. Shapes rushed in the surrounding darkness and the shadow tentacles reemerged, wrapped tightly around Bram. They dragged him through the air, the tips of his shoes barely scraping the ground, and deposited him at Felicity's feet.

No. He was supposed to leave with Jenna and Amy.

From Emily's horrified look, she hadn't realized he'd snuck back in either.

Gabriel dropped the grimoire. "Bram!"

Balthazar hurdled over the altar with a yowl, transforming midair into his monstrous guardian form. But when Felicity wrapped her arm around Bram's shoulders, hand encircling his throat in a clear threat, he halted. Sinking back on his haunches, he growled deep in his chest.

Bram was on the verge of tears, bravely steadying his wobbling chin. The side of his sweater was torn, a ragged hole trailing wispy string.

"I tried being reasonable," Felicity snapped, smoothing her dark hair back with her free hand. "I really did. Here's the new deal. Gabriel—do as you're told and finish the sacrifice, or let the duty fall to your brother." The silver-tipped stake appeared in her hand once again and she gave Bram a meaningful shake.

"What kind of choice is that?" Gabriel demanded.

"One you have to make." Her eyes narrowed into dangerous slits. "Decide now, or I'll decide for you."

"I—" Gabriel turned to Miles. He would never let Bram take his place, be forced to do something so horrible. The magic would doom them all either way, but the sacrifice would break Bram's soul first. "Please, Mother. Don't make me do this."

Felicity released Bram and strode forward to cup Gabriel's chin, fingers digging into his flesh. "It's alright to be afraid," she murmured, the closest to tender Miles had ever heard. "That all goes away once you let the magic in. Let me show you." She pressed the stake into his palm, curling their fingers around it together.

Jocelyn gasped, piercing and desperate. In her chest, four identical stakes appeared, plunged deep into her body, pinning her to the altar.

Gabriel's would make five. Five generations of Hawthornes who'd agreed to her sacrifice, each one sealing their dark deal.

Felicity stepped back as Gabriel shifted the stake into his dominant hand, his face painted with lines of grief. He'd made his decision, and Miles couldn't fault him for it.

Miles couldn't breathe. The knife was hanging from his belt loop, hidden by his jacket, but he couldn't bring himself to reach for it. Couldn't imagine stabbing Felicity, feeling her warm blood on his hand, or doing the same to his aunt if she rushed to stop him.

He couldn't. Not even to save Gabriel from this.

Miles. A serene voice filled his mind. Time slowed as he met Jocelyn's blazing gaze. *I have one final vision for you. The gift of a choice for my noble knight.*

The room stayed, Miles's eyesight blurring, smudged in the background and around the edges. He had the sickening sensation that he'd taken a step out of his own body, his limbs not his own anymore.

Gabriel looked at him. His voice was quiet but clear. "I'm sorry." He smiled, a small, fond curl of his lips.

With a lunge, he got behind his mom, an arm around her to mirror the way she'd restrained Bram. The pointed tip of the stake rested against her jutting collarbone. Her nostrils flared with shock and rage, but she stayed carefully still.

"Get out of here," he begged Miles. "Take Bram and go. Please."

"You're making a mistake," Felicity hissed. "You'll doom all of us if you do this."

"Perhaps we deserve to be doomed." Gabriel dragged her back a step. "I think it's time we find out."

There was movement in the shadows behind him. Aunt Robin—forgotten and hiding in the darkness—rushed forward, wrenching his arm back. Felicity broke free, falling to the ground.

Gabriel wrestled with Robin as she clung to him and clawed at his shirt, madness blazing in her eyes before turning pure black.

They struggled for a split second, only a heartbeat, until Robin ripped the stake from Gabriel's grip and shoved him away in a surge of violence.

He went down hard, head cracking against the corner of Jocelyn's platform with a sickening crunch that sounded like thunder. The toll of Death's bell, ringing in Miles's ears.

Their time was finally up. That invisible countdown over their heads had struck zero.

Gabriel was dead when he hit the floor. Blood started to pool as his empty eyes stared up at Miles, his fingers stretched across the cold floor for him.

Everything stopped. Tears raced down Miles's cheeks, but he couldn't move to wipe them.

You already know the consequence of changing this future, Jocelyn's voice warned. *Should you choose that path, do not fear. Death is but a release to explore beyond this life, to venture to places unknown. Your story is not over yet, no matter which choice you make.*

It was the last thing she could give him. The most important thing. A future that was his to decide.

A fate that was his to make.

Gratitude washed over Miles, a sense of peace. He knew what to do, which path he needed to be on. All that was left to do was step onto it and change the future.

33

The world started up again, everyone back in their places like actors reset in a play.

Gabriel looked at him. His voice was quiet but clear. "I'm sorry." He smiled, a small, fond curl of his lips.

Miles returned it this time. Let his heart crack open and bleed across his face where Gabriel could see every silly, over-whelming emotion. He didn't have time for all the things he wanted to say, so a smile would have to do. "I'm sorry too."

Gabriel's eyebrows scrunched in that confused-concerned expression of his that Miles adored so much.

Before he could be stupidly heroic, Miles knocked the stake out of his hand as hard as he could. It went spinning through the air, landing in the darkness with a clatter. Felicity sprang after it like a dog on a chain.

Gabriel gaped down at his empty hand. "What—?"

"Trust me." Selfishly, Miles took one more second with Gabriel, brushing their fingers together in a fleeting flare of warmth. He was so beautiful. "Get Bram and Emily out of here, okay?"

Turning away was the hardest thing he'd ever done. But he made his legs move, racing after Felicity and the stake. If she didn't have it, she couldn't sacrifice anyone else.

Robin beat them both to it, staring down in confusion like she didn't understand how it'd gotten into her hand. The dark magic had given up on playing pretend, piloting her body around as it desired.

"Aunt Robin, listen to me, please." Miles held out his hand, shifting closer. "I know you're still in there. Just give it to me, okay?"

"Don't be stupid," Felicity scoffed. The strap of one of her heels had broken, flopping around limply, and her dress had a dirty smudge down the front. "Give it to me so we can finish this already."

Robin's attention darted back and forth, a frightened animal trying to decide which predator would strike first. Which path might provide safety.

Miles took another step. "It's not too late. You haven't hurt anyone yet." She'd only been *about* to let him get dragged into hell. "There's still time to fix this, to make everything right."

"Make things right by doing what you came here to do. Power is still yours for the taking."

"Don't listen to her—"

"He's a fool—"

"*Mom!*" A shout punctured through the chaos.

Charlee swayed in the doorway of the tomb, bone-white, but alive. Healed, just like Robin had said. Miles wanted to fall to his knees and sob.

How was she here?

She locked eyes with her mom. "Charlee," Robin breathed. Her grip on the stake went slack, the tip dipping towards the floor.

Felicity lunged, fast as a striking cobra, and snatched it

from her hand. Shoving Robin aside, she stepped in close enough that Miles could see the darkness swirling amongst the gray of her irises—the same stormy shade as Gabriel's— and stabbed him in the stomach.

Several people screamed, the sounds overlapping in a harsh cacophony.

It was funny. Miles had only a split second to think about dying before he'd committed to the idea, but it still didn't feel how he'd expected. He'd just been staked, like some lame vampire, a literal hunk of wood sticking out of him, and it didn't even hurt. All he could feel was an icy, numbing chill radiating from it. It was almost soothing.

The room tilted. Miles wound up on his side, blinking at grimy stone and Felicity's flopping shoe strap. Hands pushed at his no-longer-sore shoulder, rolling him onto his back. Gabriel's face came into view, which was unarguably a much better sight to die to.

"You idiot," Gabriel rasped. For a moment, Miles thought he had glitter streaked down his face like in the car last night, but they were only tears. "You absolute idiot. I told you to leave, I told you—"

Charlee threw herself onto the ground beside them, hands fluttering frantically over the stake lodged in Miles. "Oh my God, don't move, okay, don't move." Her hands went under his head, cradling him.

He wasn't planning on it. There wasn't any pain yet, but his hands and feet were starting to sting with pins and needles.

"How could you?" Charlee sobbed, the words mangled by rage as she threw them at her mom. "How could you do this?"

Aunt Robin flinched back, stumbling over her own feet. Her hand jumped to the ring around her neck, pulling the chain until it bit into her flesh.

"It's the magic," Gabriel told Charlee tightly. Miles was glad—he didn't have the breath for words, but she needed to know. Whatever happened, he didn't want Charlee to think her mom had done this intentionally. "She's being controlled by the grimoire. It promised your father back."

His words only made Charlee cry harder. Miles wanted to comfort her, but moving seemed impossible.

"Do the ritual, now," he heard Felicity bark. "You need your own stake, before he bleeds to death and becomes worthless to you."

"I can't—Charlee's here—" Robin stammered. She sounded like herself. "She's not supposed to be here."

Hot hands pressed against Miles's face like a shock. "Focus on me." Gabriel's frightened eyes hovered over him, silvery and wet. "Look at me."

He hadn't realized he wasn't. "Sorry," he mumbled.

"Don't—don't apologize." Gabriel leaned in and pressed his forehead to Miles's, and Miles felt his hiccupping inhale. "I'm not angry. Just keep your eyes open, alright?"

Gabriel's tears splashed down onto his face.

Footsteps echoed over the stone. Charlee let out a feral, animalistic noise. "Get away from him! I'll kill you if you touch him!" Her fingers curled into Miles's hair like talons, nails pricking his scalp.

"Gabriel, stop sniveling and get up," Felicity said cooly, not acknowledging that Charlee had spoken. "It's done. Take the stake to Jocelyn. Do your part before anyone else gets hurt."

"Don't close your eyes," Gabriel repeated, like he hadn't heard her. The words were barely a whisper against Miles's lips. "You're going to be fine. We'll get you out of here."

Miles wanted to believe him, but he knew it wasn't true. They'd never get that ice cream date. He'd never get the chance to kiss him again, on each knuckle, the delicate skin of his wrist, the curve of his shoulder, working his way meticulously through the million ways he wanted to. Never get to tell him that he had showed Miles the things important enough to fight for, and given him the courage for the first time in his life to do so.

Bram and Emily joined them, sinking to their knees. It was nice they were here. Miles wished he could see his parents too. He needed to tell them it wasn't Gabriel's fault, so they didn't go back to hating him.

"Amy and Jenna—" he tried.

"They're okay," Charlee reassured him. "They're with your parents outside, getting checked over. Just hold on, they'll be here any minute."

"It's okay," Miles tried to tell everyone. The words were slurred, bitter mush in his mouth. "This was supposed to happen."

Gabriel rattled against him.

Emily spoke too low for him to catch, linking hands with Bram and Charlee. Their arms formed a lopsided circle over him. It was sweet, like they were giving him one big hug goodbye. Ducking her head, Emily whispered to herself.

"Gabriel." Miles had forgotten Felicity was still here, her voice rapidly undoing the whole dying-in-peace sensation he'd been sinking into. "I'm not going to tell you again."

Her pale hand reached for the stake, still buried in Miles's stomach. Without releasing Emily and Bram, Charlee twisted and bit down on her arm. Felicity shrieked, falling back, fingers clamped over the bleeding wound.

His cousin grinned, her teeth stained red with blood. If Miles had the energy, he'd laugh.

"You little bitch!" Blood dripped onto the floor and gleamed like fat rubies. She drew her hand back as if to hit Charlee. "How dare you—"

A sudden gush of air whipped through the tomb, the candles sputtering. Electricity crackled, aching in Miles's teeth. In the middle of Bram, Emily, and Charlee's circle around him, Rosalie Warren appeared.

Emily stopped whispering, shoulders slumping.

Either Rosalie was unnaturally quick on the uptake, or she took a single look at Felicity and knew she was bad news, because before Miles could open his mouth to say hello, she waved her hand and sent Felicity flying into a nearby pillar.

It was about time someone handed her ass to her. Miles's money was on Rosalie, her face pure righteous wrath as she flew after her.

As much as he wanted to watch, seeing Rosalie reminded Miles that Jocelyn was still on her altar.

"Hey." Miles fumbled for Gabriel, clumsy with exhaustion. Black spots were starting to speckle the corners of his vision.

Gabriel squeezed his fingers. "I'm here. I'm not going anywhere."

"Jocelyn said… death is a release," Miles told him, guiding Gabriel's hand to the knife on his belt. "I need you to do it. I can't. Please."

He understood what Miles was asking. Sliding the blade

free of its hilt, he stood. Across the tomb, Felicity staggered to her feet, swearing at Rosalie.

Miles tugged Charlee's sleeve. "Help me sit," he croaked, tasting blood. The ceiling was starting to swirl, and it was making him sick. He didn't want the last thing he did to be puking all over his friends.

Charlee shifted him up enough that he could lean into her, his head resting on her shoulder. Her frizzy curls tickled his nose, smelling of sweet coconut and honey.

Together, they watched as Gabriel made his way to Jocelyn's platform. She gazed up at him with those blazing eyes. Her lips moved as she spoke to him, and her fingertips grazed his hand holding the knife.

He nodded, tears dripping down his pointed chin as he lifted it high.

"No!" Felicity screamed.

It was over quickly, the blade finding a home between the stakes in her breast. A stunning grin spread across Jocelyn's face, and she reached up to touch Gabriel's cheek. When she went limp, he caught her wrist, lowering her arm gently to lay at her side.

The knife that could kill anything, even those caught in limbo between life and death, had served its purpose well.

Without life to feed the magic, the bargain was broken.

The grimoire trembled and flew open on the ground, levitating into the air. It rotated slowly to reveal the page it was on—*The Gift of Power*. Written in blood at the bottom, the Hawthorne name turned to black sludge and slid off the page, dripping to the floor.

Like a drain sucking down dirty water, shadows started to swirl around the grimoire, pulled from every corner of the room. Faster and faster, a howling cyclone of darkness streamed into the pages.

Felicity cried out and fell to her knees, arms splayed wide, head bent back. For a moment, the magic that infected her was visible, covering her whole body in a hard, slick shell. It tore free of her skin and crawled forth from her open mouth as she choked. Black goo splattered across stone with each hacking cough before being pulled to join the whirlwind.

Gabriel clutched Bram, hiding his face against his shirt. The shadowy smog around them flickered; for the first time, Miles could see the strands wrapped around the brothers, tethering the nebulous darkness to them. They were thin, hardly thicker than string, their grip easily broken. The slightest tug from the wind and they snapped free, the dark cloud swept away into the current.

The grimoire hungrily took the shadows it had born, until every last scrap was called back and the book dropped to the floor with a heavy thud.

The tomb fell silent.

Scalding pain blazed through Miles, making him gasp. The stake had vanished.

"Shit." Charlee pressed her hands to his wound, trying to staunch the new gush of blood, making him cry out. He should've known he wasn't lucky enough to get out of this suffering-free. "Oh my God, help!"

Gabriel came running as Emily ripped off her jacket, wadding it up against his wound. Waves of spine-rattling agony radiated through Miles's body.

"Keep pressure on it," she commanded Gabriel. "I'm taking Bram up, we'll get help."

"Hurry," Charlee begged her.

As soon as they vanished from sight, Miles swiped weakly at Gabriel's arm. "Just let it go," he ground out. For some reason, his teeth were chattering. "You know it's too late."

"Shut up," Gabriel and Charlee snapped at the same time.

Miles grabbed Gabriel's hand. "I'm not getting out of here. Don't be stupid. Just go."

Gabriel was furious, eyes spitting sparks and jaw clenched tight. He snatched his hand away, putting it back on Emily's bloody coat. "You were the stupid one first," he hissed. "I should leave you behind just for that."

A mangled laugh managed to claw its way out of Miles, tasting of copper.

The room gave an ominous shudder. Miles thought it was his shivers, until Charlee and Gabriel both froze.

"We need to get him out of here *now*," Charlee told Gabriel. "We can carry him together."

They tried to lift him, but Miles was heavy and moving hurt so badly that he yelled. Another shake rumbled through the room, stronger this time. Dust rained from the ceiling. The pillar beside them groaned.

"That doesn't sound good," Miles croaked. If this place was coming down, they needed to leave. "Please. Go."

Charlee whimpered. She knew they were out of options.

Gabriel barely spared her a glance. "Go if you want, but I'm not leaving." He brushed hair out of Miles's face with gentle fingers, painfully sweet, even now. "I'm with you as far as this goes."

Damn him.

Miles willed his blood to pump a little faster. Bleeding out was better than being crushed to death, but his body needed to get it over with already so Gabriel had time to escape. He supposed he could always play dead.

Two hazy shapes flickered in the air—Rosalie and Jocelyn, holding hands. Ready to finally pass on together.

Gabriel bared his teeth at Jocelyn. "You knew this was going to happen."

"*I did*," she confirmed. "*As did he. The choice was always his to make alone.*"

"That's not fair, you knew he—"

"*You don't have time to waste if you want to leave here alive*," Rosalie interrupted. On cue, the tomb rumbled, the Hawthorne crest on the wall splitting down the middle. There was a distant sound, like ice cracking. Rosalie turned to Miles, gliding closer. "*Jocelyn told me that she gave you a final gift. I have one as well: the last of my energy to repay the sacrifice you made here.*"

Things were getting dim and hard to follow, so Miles just tried to smile as Rosalie leaned down and placed her hand on his chest. Her sunshine-warm presence sank into his skin and spread through his veins with a gentle heat. It washed away the lingering chill of the stake, the throbbing agony. Ghost painkillers were on another level.

"*Until we meet again*," Rosalie breathed. Her face looked younger now, radiant with happiness. She brushed a gentle kiss over his forehead and faded away, taking Jocelyn with her.

"That was nice of her," Miles said, "but can we get back to you two leaving?"

A strange expression flashed over Gabriel's face. He peeled the bloody jacket back. Where there'd been a gaping hole a moment ago, Miles's skin was smooth and unblemished.

"Holy shit!" He shot up, poking his abdomen. It wasn't an illusion—he really was back in one piece. There wasn't even any lingering pain. Rosalie had completely healed him.

Charlee collapsed against him, shuddering and sobbing. He held her, his gaze locked with Gabriel's. He couldn't think of anything to say.

"Let's do this later." A crumbling tomb wasn't the best place to have a meaningful conversation. Was it weird that he felt kind of embarrassed about the whole heroic sacrifice thing? Something to unpack later, he supposed.

Columns were starting to break, spiderwebs of cracks racing up the dusty stone. Small chunks splintered from the ceiling, shattering against the floor as they raced through. Halfway across the room, the open doorway beckoning them towards salvation, Charlee skidded to a halt.

Robin was sitting, staring at the wall. She'd taken off her necklace, the chain twisted around her fingers as tears streaked down her waxy skin.

A pang of guilt went through Miles—it was his fault she'd been exposed to the grimoire, his fault for not realizing the hole of grief in her chest would be an easy entrance for its magic to slither through.

He went over and put his hand on her shoulder. "Aunt Robin?" From the horror and grief on her face, the magic polluting her had returned to the grimoire with the rest.

"I don't know what happened," she whispered, not looking at him. "It was all so… clear in my head. This whole plan that was going to fix everything."

"I know." He understood now what Jocelyn had meant about the tragedy of Florence, how desperation and the grimoire's influence had blotted out her goodness. "C'mon, let's get you out of here."

She curled in on herself tighter. "I think I'll stay here, where I can't hurt anyone else."

Charlee marched over and hauled her mom up by her arm. "Don't you dare pull this shit on me," she growled. "You're not allowed to lie down and die after what you just did. You owe me."

Staring at her enraged daughter, Robin's face crumpled. "I wanted to bring him back for you. I thought, with your father here, he could fix it all."

Charlee's lip trembled. "We didn't break apart because Dad was gone. You did that. I needed you and you couldn't get past your own shit long enough to try." She barked out a wet laugh. "I would've given you any chance, if you'd just bothered to show up."

"I wanted to. I hated myself for every day that I couldn't bring myself to. And eventually, I knew you didn't need me."

"Don't you dare. My dad was gone—I always needed you."

Robin was weeping. "I'm sorry."

"Prove it." Charlee got in her face, pinning her with a steely glare. "Put me first, for once in your damn life. I'm telling you exactly what I need—for you to get out of here and make it all up to me, no matter how long it takes."

A beat of silence passed. Slowly, Robin nodded.

The ground shook threateningly, one of the pillars toppling over with an echoing *boom*, and Miles thought for a split second that this was it, their time was up. He grabbed Gabriel for support, struggling to keep on his feet as the room quaked.

Everything went still.

"Is it over?" Charlee whispered.

Movement caught Miles's eye. Narrow streams of water were racing down the walls, pooling on the stone floor.

Oh shit. He'd forgotten about the lake sitting over their head.

"Hurry," he commanded. Charlee went ashen as she spotted the water.

Rocks clattered behind Miles, and he whirled to see Gabriel going back the way they'd come.

"Wait!" Miles caught him by the elbow. "I don't think she made it."

The way the magic had torn through Felicity... how could anyone survive that?

"She has to be alive. I deserve answers."

"You do." He deserved more than that. Much more. But the universe rarely cared about such things. "But is it worth risking your life?"

The lake could come crashing down on their heads any second. Nothing would be able to save them then.

Gabriel's expression hardened. "It's not only me— Edmund and Bram deserve a chance to look her in the face and ask her why. She owes us that much."

Then they needed to be quick.

The altar had been crushed beneath a falling pillar, chunks of stone scattered about and the candles lost. Miles hadn't even realized the room had grown so dark without them.

They found Felicity there, muttering frantically to herself and digging through the rubble. "—start over. I can get it back. I just need to find it. It's here somewhere, it has to be. I can start over. I can get it back."

She was in bad shape—the magic purging from her body had nearly destroyed her. Her skin was raw and red, blood oozing from her ears and nose, streaked down the front of her dress. The way she was moving was wrong, jerking and stuttering like her limbs didn't want to cooperate. A broken toy burning off the last of its battery.

It had to hurt, but it didn't look like she'd even noticed.

"Mother." Gabriel approached cautiously, reaching for her. The water was lapping at their shoes now, carrying crimson petals. Miles kept one eye on the ceiling, praying it would hold just a little longer.

She twisted away without so much as a glance. "It's here somewhere, I know it is. It has to be. Once I find it, I can start over." Her gaze darted around, searching wildly.

"Mother, it's me." Once again, she recoiled from Gabriel's touch, mumbling the same words over and over. "We need to leave. The ceiling is going to cave in any moment."

"I have to find it, I have to get it back. Where is it?"

Gabriel had never looked more helpless. He was so small, his shoulders narrow beneath his bloodstained shirt, hands trembling at his sides.

He wouldn't look at Miles. They both knew, but neither of them wanted to say it.

Felicity Hawthorne was gone.

Miles suspected she'd died a long time ago, snuffed out by the grimoire's magic when she'd signed her soul away all those years before. All that was left of her was his parents' memories of a curious, clever girl who'd tried to escape her fate and failed.

The person standing in front of them was a shell,

desperately clinging to the only thing she'd known for a long time.

"It has to be here." Felicity reached between two stones, coming out with empty hands and a guttural moan. "Where is it? I need it."

The ceiling groaned a low warning. Water hissed as it sprayed from stone. Miles's socks were wet, and there was a terrible pit in his gut.

"Gabriel—"

"I know."

He tried again. The moment he took Felicity's wrist, she yanked free and slapped him across the face. It wasn't a solid blow, catching the edge of his jaw, but it sent him stumbling back. Miles managed to catch him.

Felicity's expression didn't change, empty gaze going right back to what was left of the altar. The water was rising, so she dropped to her knees, sweeping her arms through it. "I have to find it."

Gabriel shuddered against him. "Do you want me to try? I can carry her out—"

"No. She'll only hurt you." He touched the red mark spreading up his cheek. "There's nothing we can do."

It might've been Miles's imagination, but the cracks in the ceiling looked like they were starting to sag like they'd buckle any second. They needed to leave. Now.

Miles took Gabriel's hand in his, weaving their fingers together. He wanted to give him time, but they didn't have it. If he had to, he'd carry Gabriel out over his shoulder.

Gabriel squeezed, tight enough to ache, and gave his mother one final look. His face crumpled with grief. "Let's go. Before I can't."

They barely made it, tripping over debris hidden in the calf-high water and dodging pieces raining from above. Charlee waved frantically from the open doorway, yells lost to the roar of the spray and crumbling rock as it strained to hold back the weight of the lake.

Miles shoved Gabriel through, then hauled himself into the tunnel. There was no sign of Bram or Emily—he hoped they'd gotten out of here, to high ground where they'd be safe.

If the ceiling came down, the tunnels would fill with water in seconds. They'd drown.

"We need to close the door," he panted. He grabbed the slick edge, straining to shove it closed, but it wouldn't budge.

Gabriel shouldered him aside, hand hovering above the stone. He hesitated, scanning the room. There was no sign of Felicity.

He squeezed his eyes closed, tears gleaming on his lashes like morning dew, and slapped his palm down. The star above the tree flared scarlet, the door sliding closed with a laborious grinding noise.

The last glimpse Miles got of the tomb was the ceiling finally buckling and the monstrous waterfall that came crashing down.

EPILOGUE

The crimson poppies bloomed early around the Hawthorne estate's lake. No one could explain it—they were early summer flowers, but seemingly unfazed by the nightly frost and icy rain, they sprang up around the rubble and muck of where the tomb had collapsed anyway, blanketing the shore in a wave of glossy red right as the first chill of winter started to creep in.

Sitting in the Hawthorne séance room, Miles swore he could smell their bitter, smoky scent through the cracked windows when the wind blew hard enough.

"I'm ready," Emily announced. "Everyone hold hands."

Once everyone was connected around the table, Emily let out a deep breath. The stubby tealight candles flickered, and the thick velvet curtains swayed gently.

"We call to the spirit world, seeking out Blake, the... bus ghost. If you can hear me, please come forward. Blake, you came here once before to help—"

He appeared over the middle of the table with a friendly wave. "*What's up? I didn't think I'd hear from you guys.*" He saw Gabriel and broke out in a wide grin. "*Hey, you found your friend! I told you I saw him.*"

"Yeah, you were a huge help," Miles told him. "Thanks again."

He nudged Gabriel, who was looking a little shell-shocked. His gaze flitted from Blake's oversized polo and baggy jeans to his outrageously yellow frosted tips. "Yes, thank you. It was"—he spotted the puka shell necklace and nearly broke, his lips twitching—"very kind of you to assist them."

Blake waved him off. *"No problem, man. So what can I do for you guys? Lose another friend?"*

"Actually," Charlee said, "we're here to help you out this time. Unless you've changed your mind about the bus since we last saw you."

He squinted in confusion.

"We want to help you move on," Miles clarified. "If you're ready."

Blake's excitement was so intense, it rattled the paintings on the walls and swung open the doors of the curio cabinet behind Emily. *"You have no idea. Heaven, hell, I don't care, as long as it doesn't have purple seats and smell like feet funk."*

The ritual didn't take long, and Miles had the right supplies this time, so there was no need to raid the kitchen. Blake gifted them one last goofy grin before blipping out, leaving behind the scent of too-strong cologne.

Miles hoped wherever he went, he had access to all the early 2000s horror movies he wanted.

"That should give this room some much-needed good mojo," Emily noted, blowing out the candles and gathering her crystals. Her dangly star earrings bounced around as she packed. "And Blake a much-needed rest."

"You didn't tell me he was a member of the Backstreet Boys," Gabriel murmured to Miles.

He bit back a snicker. "I guess I forgot you were such a fan. Want me to summon him back so you can get an autograph?"

That earned him an elbow to the ribs.

They cleaned up, setting the séance room back to how it'd been, pushing the chairs in and straightening the crooked paintings. Gabriel lingered, meticulously adjusting items in his mom's curio cabinet—a silver pocket watch, pinned butterflies, and an engraved bell, all of which he'd explained were family heirlooms—with careful fingers.

"I can give you a ride," Charlee offered Emily as they all slipped out of the room to give Gabriel space. His eyes were sad as he fixed Felicity's collection. "I need to head out soon anyway."

"That'd be great, thanks. Mind dropping me off at school? I've got practice."

"Sure, I'll grab Nadia." They'd ventured down into the basement at Gabriel's insistence in search of items for their shop.

As Charlee walked away, Miles asked Emily, "Your mom finally made you pick between the psychic life and soccer, then?" She'd been coming and going, but it felt like they hadn't had a moment to stop and catch up. Things had been chaotic in the weeks since they'd crawled their way out of the tunnels, soaked and shivering, clinging to each other with everything they had left. Their worlds had changed over the course of a night.

"Nope." She zipped her pink puffer up with a cheeky smile. "I decided there's no reason I can't have both."

It was such a simple, obvious answer—Emily's light shone too bright to be fixed on only one thing—but Miles understood why it hadn't occurred to either of them. This life felt like it left no room for anything else. He'd never stopped to consider otherwise.

"I love soccer," she continued, "but being there for you guys that night in the tomb, holding my own, helping Rosalie and Jocelyn find peace… I want to be able to do that too."

"And your mom, she's okay with that?"

She shrugged, tossing her long hair over her shoulder. "She's going to have to be. I'm not going to let anyone tell me who to be or what I get to do. She thinks I can't find a balance and do both, so I'm just going to prove her wrong." Studying him knowingly, she gave his arm a quick squeeze. "Something to think about, yeah?"

Charlee and Nadia emerged from the hallway, a bulging bag over Nadia's shoulder. "Hey. Sounds like we're heading out. I snagged a few things down there I'm going to look into."

"I'll tell Gabriel. Whatever you took, I'm sure it'll do better in your shop than gathering dust in the basement."

They said their goodbyes, Miles promising Emily he'd be at her game next weekend, rain or shine, and pulling Charlee in for a lingering hug. "You sure you don't want me to come with you?"

She was going to visit her mom today.

After the tomb, Aunt Robin had a rough few days detoxing from the dark magic and recovering from the toll it had taken on her body, but her mind still needed healing. As soon as she could move, she'd rented a little cabin an hour away for the foreseeable future. Amy and Jenna had forgiven her—it was a hard first lesson on possession, but they understood that their aunt hadn't been in control. She just hadn't figured out how to forgive herself.

Miles's parents hadn't said it out loud, but he knew they were relieved she was taking space. Even after being reassured she'd been possessed, they were reluctant to let her be around the girls. It would take work to rebuild that trust.

Charlee hadn't been to see her yet, but they'd spoken on the phone a few times. She called it tentative progress at best, and insisted she wasn't getting her hopes up, but Miles thought it was going well. They were going to visit Uncle Shaun's grave together next weekend.

"Nah," Charlee mumbled into his collar. "Nadia's fully committed to being my buffer."

"I know," Nadia teased. "You're shocked that I'm both attractive and useful. What can I say? I'm the full package."

Charlee snorted, pulling away. "Plus, we've got an escape plan ready if we need one."

That made Nadia grin wickedly. "I'll give you a hint: sudden allergic reaction."

It was a shame Miles wouldn't be around to see that undoubtedly dramatic performance.

He walked them to the front door, a rush of exhaustion washing over him. He wasn't cut out for all this constant socializing—another day of it, and he was going to start wishing he was back at work digging up corpses.

When he turned around, Gabriel was sitting at the bottom of the stairs. Miles hadn't heard him slip out of the séance room.

"Hey." He went and joined him, soaking in the quiet. "Everything good?"

"Yes." Gabriel tugged him closer, until they were pressed against each other. His hand found the front of Miles's shirt, right where he'd been stabbed. There was no scar, but he'd memorized the spot. "Are you feeling alright?"

"Fine." He'd been in mint condition since Rosalie healed him, but it didn't stop Gabriel from worrying. "Tired. Glad this place is starting to empty out a bit, if I'm being honest."

"I can think of one guest in particular who overstayed their welcome," Gabriel muttered.

When the news that Felicity was gone started to spread, their father had come from Seattle. He was a thin, angular man with brown hair and a perpetual frown. Miles hadn't seen much of him—aside from a few withering glances and some judgmental sniffing. He'd made it clear he had zero interest in moving back to the Hawthorne estate or taking care of his children.

The only person who liked him less than Miles was his own dad, who seemed genuinely flabbergasted and distraught at the parental apathy he was witnessing.

Gabriel insisted it was for the best, that his father was a bastard and would only make their lives miserable again. And with Edmund now awake and over eighteen, he enthusiastically—if a little apprehensively—agreed to step into the role of guardian. After a long discussion with Bram, Edmund's first act as step-in-parent was to start the process of enrolling him in the local public school.

Their father had left early this morning without a backward glance, peeling out of the driveway in his stupid fancy Corvette that screamed midlife crisis. Asshole.

"He won't be missed." Miles yawned as Gabriel nestled against him, his head on Miles's shoulder. He could smell the eucalyptus shampoo Charlee had gotten Gabriel hooked on. "Think we could get away with skipping school tomorrow and just sleeping all day?"

"No. And it's my first day back. I promised Edmund I'd be on my best behavior."

"He'll let you put it off a little longer if you ask."

Everyone had told Gabriel he should take more time off before going back. School wasn't going anywhere, and now that the whole town knew Felicity Hawthorne had passed away under mysterious circumstances, the stares and whispers were going to be back in full force. But Gabriel insisted he was ready, that he wanted things to start going back to normal. To keep busy.

"Why would I do that when I'm so excited to go back?" he asked dryly. "How I've missed the crowded hallways, inane gossip, and pointless busywork."

Miles laughed. "Don't pretend like it doesn't have its moments. And I heard the class voted for *A Midsummer Night's Dream* first, so we're not starting *Romeo and Juliet* until next week."

Gabriel smiled into his shoulder.

Upstairs, footsteps pounded across the floor and kids squealed—his sisters and Bram were trying to teach his new cat how to play tag.

Balthazar had tragically vanished with the rest of the grimoire's magic. Bram had been inconsolable. So a few days ago, Miles and Gabriel had driven him to the nearest shelter to adopt a new cat. Bram had taken one look at Winifred—a tabby with one ear, a missing eye, and half a tail—and declared her as ferocious as Balthazar. She'd come home with him that afternoon.

The front door opened. Miles's parents and Edmund

filed in with a cardboard box in each of their arms. The sleeve of a black fur coat poked out of one, a rolled-up rug resting on another.

"Hey, boys." Sarah nudged the door closed. "How was the releasing ritual?"

"Easy peasy," Miles answered. "Need any help?"

"This is all of it." Adam put his box down gently, then stretched with an exaggerated groan. This week, his favorite jokes were all about his weary old-man bones and upcoming hip replacements.

After nearly dying, coming out to his dad had been nothing. The next day, Miles had found him in the ruined office and broken down, spouting a bunch of gibberish—*sorry I left the hospital without telling you, sorry I let the girls get kidnapped, sorry I raised zombies in the cemetery, sorry I didn't tell you I'm gay and dating Gabriel*—between snotty, hiccupping tears. Those last two had required further explanation once he'd calmed down, but his dad had listened intently, handed him a steady supply of tissues, and given him a spine-cracking hug once he was done.

"How'd it go?" Gabriel asked Edmund.

He set his box down by the stairs, wearing his exhaustion in the tense set of his mouth. "About what you'd expect. They'd already packed most of it up for us, so it didn't take long."

The morning after they escaped the tomb, news arrived that Marjorie had passed away peacefully in her sleep. Today was the first chance Edmund had to make it over to Oakes Hollow to collect her things. Miles's parents had jumped on the opportunity to help—Sarah was insisting on coming over practically every day to bring the Hawthorne boys food and assist Edmund with his newfound adult tasks. There was no way she would've let him go alone.

Edmund told Miles she didn't have to hover so much, but he wasn't doing a very good job of hiding how much he enjoyed being fretted over.

Miles gazed at what they'd brought back. It was so strange to see what was left behind when someone died compiled into so few boxes.

"This is for you." Edmund handed Gabriel a plain white envelope from his jacket pocket. Miles still did the occasional double take when he saw Edmund's bare hands. His and Gabriel's gifts had gone, only the most basic of their psychic skills remaining. Neither of them seemed bothered by it.

"What is it?"

"How would I know? It was on Marjorie's side table and your name's on it."

Sure enough, Gabriel's name was written on the front in dark, looping letters. He frowned, opening it hesitantly as Edmund wandered away. A single sheet of crisp white paper was tucked inside.

Gabriel,

Since your visit, I've spent a lot of time thinking about our family, reflecting on my own part within it. My mother, Florence, often told me that the most important thing I could do was put my family first in a world that would turn their backs on us, given the chance. In her eyes, the greatest of sins was to settle for mediocrity when we had the means to rise so far above.

I've found myself wondering what is mediocre about a life well lived, and braving uncertainties to build the future you desire. I've found myself wondering what power I might have found within myself had I been given the choice that you came to me to ask for.

Perhaps leaving the family manor has given me some distance and clarity. Or perhaps these are the common ponderings of an old woman who knows her end is near.

If you're given the chance to find out, take it. Do not fear the unknown, for I suspect that is where true adventure lies. Be braver than all the Hawthornes before you, as I know you are.

Your Great Grandmother,
Marjorie Hawthorne

Gabriel traced her signature, blinking rapidly.

"Are you okay?" Miles checked softly.

"Yes." He seemed surprised by his answer. "I'm… glad that she came back to herself in the end, at least a little. I only wish I'd had the chance to get to know the true her."

Miles suspected that had been on his mind a lot lately. Gabriel had been asking his parents for more stories of Felicity in her youth.

As he'd done already too many times in the past weeks— Miles figured he was allowed to overstep a little after what they'd been through—he lifted his mental shields to check

Gabriel's emotions. He'd initially been worried when he'd realized that with the dark cloud gone he could do this, but Gabriel had just shrugged and said it was only fair after he'd been able to read Miles's mind.

Content warmth washed over him, like sinking into a bubble bath with a soft, familiar song playing in the other room. Gabriel's happiness felt like comfort. It felt like home.

And tied up in it all was a golden thread that pulsed with a feeling Miles wasn't brave enough to put a name to yet, but knew was for him. He sensed it grow hot when Gabriel looked at him, thrum with joy when he laughed, glow like the sun when they held hands.

He turned just far enough to capture Gabriel's lips in a gentle kiss. The thread burned bright, a shooting star streaking across his mind as Gabriel pressed closer with a pleased noise.

It was a great kiss—Miles would make a joke about it being the death of him, if he hadn't just had a near-death experience and knew Gabriel would kick him for making light of it.

"Let's go for a drive," Miles said when he pulled away, wanting suddenly to get out of here. To have Gabriel to himself. "Anywhere you wanna go."

Gabriel hummed against him. "You promised you'd take me to that decrepit burger place you can't stop talking about."

"Done. Prepare to have your life changed by a bucket of greasy fries."

Miles lowered his shield back down, not worried about the undercurrent of sorrow he could taste, a salty burn in the back of his throat. It had been there since the night Felicity died and wouldn't leave anytime soon. She'd left behind a lot of questions and emotions, and her boys were all working through them in their own ways.

"Gabriel and I are going for lunch," he hollered into the depths of the house. "Be back later."

"Dinner at six," his mom called back. "Love you!"

They took Gabriel's car—Edmund had let him claim one of the many stockpiled in the garage. He'd picked the most practical one and only used it to let Miles chauffeur him around. Eventually, Miles was going to teach him to drive, but riding a bike would come first.

Spending time alone together had been keeping Miles sane these last few weeks. Slipping away to Gabriel's room, running errands just to get away from everyone, late nights at Miles's house to decompress with movies and pizza... Charlee had made a habit of butting in on that last one, swapping movies so she could "educate Gabriel on the healing power of rom-coms."

"I have a meeting with my guidance counselor after school tomorrow," Gabriel commented as they headed out of town. The restaurant was a bit of a drive, a small roadside diner on the way to several hiking destinations and beaches that served the most heavenly burger Miles had ever eaten.

"For missing so much school? I thought Edmund took care of that."

"He did. This is for something else." He hesitated, piquing Miles's interest. "I asked her to meet with me to discuss my potential options for college."

Surprise flared in Miles. He'd mentioned a few times that he was gathering information on local colleges, but Gabriel had never shown personal interest. "What brought this on?"

"Edmund. He's being his usual dramatic self, demanding I give him some idea of my plan for the next few years. Apparently, having a 'wild card' for a brother is going to push him over the edge." Amusement colored Gabriel's tone as he turned to watch a car with a paddleboard strapped to its roof pass them. "I've never had to consider what I want my future to look like before. It was always expected that I'd follow in my mother's footsteps."

This was good. Gabriel was long overdue a dream beyond survival.

"And you're thinking college?" Miles prompted. "Let me guess—English major?"

"It's certainly enticing, though I'll admit, I do enjoy the thought of exploring my options."

"Living life on the edge," Miles teased, turning onto a tree-lined road. Leaving the city behind, everything out here grew green and tall. A lake gleamed between the trunks, kayakers drifting through a swarm of unconcerned ducks. "Seriously though, I think that sounds great."

He deserved to explore what brought him joy, what he wanted to spend the rest of his life doing. The thought of getting to share that with him made Miles giddy.

"I haven't committed to anything yet. I feel... apprehensive about potentially leaving my brothers. Especially with Edmund taking on so much."

"You have options—online classes, somewhere close to Thistle, coming back for the weekends..." All things Miles had been considering for himself. "But Edmund and Bram would never be upset if you left. They'd know you'd always come back."

It was way too early to say it out loud, but Miles had

already adjusted his dream apartment in Seattle to a place big enough for two, just in case. Gabriel fit there well—his knit cashmere blanket folded on the couch, expensive French yogurts stacked in the fridge beside Miles's juice, half the closet filled with white button-ups and woolly sweater vests.

He hid his smile in the collar of his jacket.

"I'm not accustomed to having so many choices," Gabriel admitted. The sun came out from behind the clouds, turning the lake from a dreary gray to a deep blue that matched his sweater. "It's overwhelming. And I have so much to do already."

Miles reached across the center console to take Gabriel's hand. There were always going to be things to do. When the time was right, he needed to have tough conversations with his parents about his place in the family business. He needed to start shopping around for a new car within his meager budget. There was a text sitting in his drafts inviting Robin to family dinner, a bike to dig out of the shed for Gabriel, and a bingo sheet for the new season of *Specter Seekers* on his bedside table.

There were always going to be things to do, but they could wait. All that mattered right now was Gabriel's hand in his, the beautiful scenery outside the car window, and that there was no rush.

"We'll figure it out," he told Gabriel, knowing it was true. "We have plenty of time."

ACKNOWLEDGMENTS

Writing a second book is a notoriously difficult landmark in many writing journeys, and mine proved to be no exception. Looking back, I don't think I could've finished it without so many amazing people pushing me to meet my deadlines, letting me rant about plot holes of my own making, and reminding me that throwing my computer out the window wouldn't make my book write itself.

First and foremost, my eternal gratitude goes to Katie Dent. As my editor, your passion and insight help me grow into a better writer and make my stories the best they can be. As a person, the enthusiasm, support, and joy you share keep me writing with a full heart and a smile on my face.

Thank you to my agent, Kat Kerr, for your endless patience and unwavering belief in me. On days when I doubt myself most, I hear your voice cheering me on and reminding me of my accomplishments. I never would've made it this far without you.

To the whole team at Titan—especially Bahar, Katharine, Charlotte, Kate, Amy, Caitlin, and Nat, who did the gorgeous cover—thank you from the bottom of my heart for taking such wonderful care of my book and for always asking for pictures of my pets. Working with you all has been the loveliest experience.

The only reason I didn't fully become a hermit while on deadline with this book is because I have incredible friends who lure me out of the house with the promise of good company, a mug of tea, and swooning over *Pride and Prejudice*. Rebecca, thank you for keeping me steady through the uncertainty of imposter syndrome and publishing anxieties. Kelli, thank you for writing everything in such a sincere, charming, and true-to-yourself way that you constantly inspire me to do the same. Demory, thank you for never hesitating to celebrate a win with me, no matter how small, or to encourage me when I desperately need it. I'm so grateful for the friendship, laughter, and support the three of you bring into my life.

To Lindsay, who never stopped believing in me for a single step of this journey, and literally flew across the country to support me. I'll never stop feeling so lucky to have you in my corner. To Arianna, for always being just a message away, never saying no to a horror movie night, and talking me out of my self-doubt spirals. Our friendship is a constant light in my life.

And a huge shoutout to my writing group—Jill, Chel, Mike, Becca, Brittany, Jelly, Bella, Jacob, Andrea, and Emily. Thank you for putting up with my excessive love of Mothman, talking through silly plot ideas with me, and eating my baking experiments every week. I owe you guys more than I can say.

To Mom and Dad, for believing in me when I forget to believe in myself. It's only because you give me unwavering support and a loving space that I get to be my truest, happiest, weirdest self. I love you both.

Finally, thank you to every reader who picked up my first book, who messaged to say how much they enjoyed it and how evil I am for the cliffhanger ending, who left unbearably sweet reviews and shared gorgeous pictures, and who found themselves in my flawed, chaotic characters. My dreams were nothing compared to reality because of all of you.

ABOUT THE AUTHOR

Camilla Raines is the author of *The Hollow and the Haunted* duology. She was born and raised in a small town in northern Washington with lots of evergreen trees, seaside fog, and rainy days. Her writing career began in elementary school, where she spent years scribbling down stories for friends that were usually just knock-offs of whatever book she was devouring at the time. As a proud member of the LGBTQIA+ community and someone who openly struggles with chronic anxiety and depression, the most important things to her as a writer are representation, diversity, identity, and acceptance. Find her online @camillaraines.

For more fantastic fiction, author events,
exclusive excerpts, competitions, limited editions and more

VISIT OUR WEBSITE
titanbooks.com

LIKE US ON FACEBOOK
facebook.com/titanbooks

FOLLOW US ON TWITTER AND INSTAGRAM
@TitanBooks

EMAIL US
readerfeedback@titanemail.com